# BLACK CAMP 21

Bill Jones started his career as a print journalist, before establishing himself at Granada Television in Manchester as a documentary film-maker. During a television career spanning thirty years he produced multi-award-winning programmes for ITV, BBC, Channel 4, PBS, National Geographic, Discovery, Sky and numerous other international channels. His films have been presented by, among others, Billy Connolly, Martin Clunes, Sir Trevor McDonald and Joanna Lumley.

In 2011 he wrote his first book, *The Ghost Runner: The Tragedy of the Man They Couldn't Stop* (Mainstream), which won Best New Writer at the 2012 British Sports Book Awards and was runner-up in the William Hill Awards. His second book, *Alone: The Triumph and Tragedy of John Curry* (Bloomsbury), was published in 2014, winning the Outstanding Writing award at the British Sports Book Awards, and a second shortlisting for the William Hill Awards. Both books are currently in development as feature films.

Born in Bridlington, Bill now lives in Ampleforth, North Yorkshire. *Black Camp 21* is his first novel.

D1051531

# BLACK CAMP 21

## Bill Jones

First published in Great Britain in 2018 by Polygon,
an imprint of Birlinn Ltd.

Birlinn Ltd
West Newington House
10 Newington Road
Edinburgh
EH9 1QS

www.polygonbooks.co.uk

2

ISBN 978 1 84697 460 1
eBook ISBN 978 1 78885 062 9

*British Library Cataloguing-in-Publication Data*
A catalogue record for this book is available on request
from the British Library.

Typeset by 3btype.com

Printed and bound in Great Britain by Clays Ltd, Elcograf S.p.A.

After D-Day, in June 1944, almost every able-bodied Allied soldier was fighting overseas. Within a few weeks of the invasion, over 250,000 war-hardened German POWs had been sent back to camps in Britain.

The prisoners were well fed and their guards were often a mixture of reservists, volunteers and policemen. Few of the camps were ready – most were still under construction – and the flood of men moved quickly from chaos to crisis.

Around 70,000 of the Germans had been classified by their captors as 'black' prisoners. These were SS fanatics, usually very young, who had sworn to fight on until death. For them the war was far from over. It was only just beginning.

During the latter months of 1944, the most dangerous 'blacks' were transported north to the Highlands of Scotland, to a camp which still stands today on the edge of the village of Comrie, exactly as it was.

It became known as Black Camp 21, and the truly shocking events that climaxed there in December 1944 provided the inspiration for this story.

*For Kay — without whom, nothing.*

# Official Memorandum

*From:* *The Office of the Prison Governor*
*To:* *Various*

*I wish to report that today, in accordance with the verdict of the Military Court (12/7/1945), we have carried out the execution of five German prisoners. Commencing at 9 a.m. – at half-hourly intervals – the men were hanged at His Majesty's Prison of Pentonville by the state executioner, Mr Albert Pierrepoint. Each death was officially witnessed by myself, the prison chaplain and a qualified medical practitioner. In addition, there was a single (female) member of military intelligence in attendance. However, for obvious security reasons, I have omitted all names (including my own) from this memorandum.*

*There were only two incidents of note to report. Prisoner A – the first to be executed – was seen to spit in the chaplain's face, following which he was heard to shout his allegiance to Adolf Hitler before the necessary restraints could be applied. Prisoner E – the last to die – requested a very short private conversation with the solitary female witness before the court's judgement was executed. Given his extreme state of agitation, this permission was granted. Prisoners B, C and D went to their deaths in silence. Each of the condemned chose not to engage with the chaplain's formal blessing.*

*Following pronouncement of death, the five men – aged between 19 and 23 – were buried in an unmarked prison plot. As I understand it, there are no plans for the bodies to be returned to Germany.*

*Dated this 6th day of October 1945*

# 1

## 6 August 1944
## near Falaise, northern France

*03:15 hours*

There was no way to be sure, but tomorrow, thought Hartmann, it will be my birthday.

To keep himself amused, he tried to work it out, counting back to the last day when he'd known where he was. Things had changed so quickly.

Two months before, the men still celebrated their birthdays, necking stolen champagne from thick green bottles, sleeping off their hangovers under the stars.

Now, as he lay sleepless under his sludge-dripping tank, deep within another nameless wood, absolutely nothing was certain. Even if he was out by a few days, it didn't matter. Most of the people he'd partied with were already dead, and the ones who still breathed barely spoke.

Still, if it was his birthday – and if he had a wish – he knew what he wanted.

The rest of them could bitch about hunger, making themselves puke with plundered fruit, or tossing hand grenades at runaway chickens. Hunger he could abide. Russia had taught him that. If he could be guaranteed just one thing – even for a single minute – he'd happily forgo his potato ration, even his precious sliver of sausage.

Silence was the thing. Silence was what Hartmann craved most – next to certainty – and only the dead were guaranteed both.

War was noise; and the noises were universally terrible. Hidden

3

by the black canopy of oak above his shelter, shoals of enemy bombers droned in from the sea. Futile slices of tracer fire chased after them, followed by the occasional half-hearted squirt of a machine gun, while in every direction hot steel cooled and clanked like an invisible plague of robotic crickets.

Silhouetted by pools of paraffin light, he could make out tank crews repairing tracks and patching shattered sumps, and in the strange summer darkness every clunk and curse rang clear.

Nothing Hartmann did could shut it out. However tightly he buried his head in his arms, the sounds were still there. If his calculations were right – and if he slept – he would wake up a year older, but the noise would still be there. And by daylight it was always much worse.

The ear-shattering rumble of his Tiger; the screaming voices on his radio; the crashing trees and the horses galloping between crackling hedgerows; the rising whine of approaching fighter planes. The shells ripping through armour, followed by the pitiful sound of comrades burning.

For days – for ever, it seemed – they had been stumbling, leader-less, back towards Germany.

For the generals there was always some kind of escape. They could flee into the forest with their cyanide pills and their pistols. The rest of them were stuck with their garbled orders and their mantras.

Fight to the last man. That's what they'd always been told. Since they were kids, the same instruction: to the death.

Fight until the diesel runs out would have been smarter.

In the black void beneath his tank, Hartmann reached out a hand until he could feel its slick underbelly. Soon the fuel would be gone. Another two days; three at most.

He tried again to work out what the date might be, inching back closer in his mind to a day when he knew exactly what he'd been doing. Mid-May. Yes. He remembered it now. A good day. A happy day.

Everything had been certain then, when the spring roasted the pantiled rooftops, lighting up fields of apple blossom in a world he felt he owned, which he had risked his life to win.

4

It had been Koenig's turn for a birthday, and the two of them had hijacked an open-topped staff car, driving it out along deserted roads to the Normandy coast near Arromanches. Hartmann had taken the wheel, allowing his friend to grin and yodel at the village girls.

'You're twenty now. Behave yourself.'

But Koenig had just laughed and shouted louder. 'You're not going to stop the car anyway,' he yelled. 'What does it matter?'

Both had worn their laundered uniforms: grey caps with glossy black peaks and double-winged eagles; drab slate-coloured tunics enlivened by a double lightning bolt gleaming against their stiff black collars.

Above the speeding black Mercedes, a lone gull looked down on the two men.

Each of them could smell the sea and sensed from the knotty swept-back hedgerows that they were near. Since neither had ever seen it before, Hartmann's pulse drove him and them faster. All this was their land now, reawakening from its late frosts under their red flag; their swastika; their Führer.

Koenig, as always, had seemed absurdly high-spirited. Away from the front, his hair had thickened and the golden childhood mop Hartmann had always envied now riffled in a chill northerly wind.

'You're wearing the medal, Erich.'

Koenig threw his head back and roared. 'I'm a hero. I'm a hero.'

'Sure you're a hero. But can you swim?'

When the road ran out, they parked, looking out in wonder across the grey waters of the Channel.

Hartmann had been the first down on to the sand, ripping off his boots and wading deep into the surf. Behind him, Koenig had loitered in the dunes, collecting sticks for a fire.

To the east and west, a smooth plain of sand stretched unbroken to a distant point where it seemed to fracture along its own blue horizon.

Because the tide was low, line upon line of weed-matted wooden breakwaters had been exposed, marching in from the sea. When Hartmann saw them, he turned back.

'They look like men, Erich. They look like soldiers.'

But Koenig wasn't listening. Up on the cliff edge, a pile of bleached driftwood was already burning strongly in the dry wind. From the car boot, he'd pulled a blanket, a hamper, two full bottles of schnapps, and a gramophone.

'It's Charlie and his Orchestra,' he bellowed. 'Get your arse up here, Max, and let's dance.'

The sounds of a swing band drifted towards Hartmann in dreamy, disjointed phrases. Ahead of him, across a frigid expanse of sea, he could make out the English coastline. Surely they will never come, he thought.

Only a few hours earlier they'd driven behind a convoy of German sappers heading happily towards the coast, and up here, hidden within the marram grass, fresh concrete pillboxes were going up every day. Soon every grain of sand would be covered by a machine gun. From Kraków to Cherbourg, Hitler was building an impregnable fortress; a new frontier where nothing could ever die but the light.

Turning away from his thoughts, stirred by the icy water around his toes, Hartmann smiled. Above him on the ridge, silhouetted by orange flames, his friend was dancing alone.

Sometimes, it was true, Koenig scared him; most of the time, really, if he was honest. No one he'd ever known was possessed of such certainties, or such belief. And yet no one he knew was so joyously reckless either.

'I've always been too old,' he muttered into the breeze before stumbling up the cliff for his first waltz of the afternoon.

It hadn't taken much. Neither of them had tasted alcohol for months and the schnapps quickly unravelled them. To the hissing melody of illicit jazz, Hartmann swayed in his underpants while his salt-wet trousers steamed on a branch.

'May I have this dance?' Koenig whispered with a theatrical flourish. 'Or are you here with another man?'

Locked together for an hour, the pair had quick-stepped and tangoed. As the flames shrank to embers they slumped with their backs against a solitary tree and peered out over the deserted strand.

'Happy birthday, darling,' said Hartmann. There was a woozy slur in his voice.

'Why, thank you,' Koenig replied. 'It's been a wonderful evening.'

For a minute or two, neither could speak through the laughter. When they stopped, an awkward silence hung in the space between them.

Over two years lay between this and their last proper meeting. Away in the west, thick clouds were threatening, and as the breeze stiffened, red sparks peppered the gloom.

'You should move your trousers, Max. They'll burn,' Koenig whispered.

Slowly, Hartmann stood up and pulled them back on. It was growing cold and the booze was souring in their bellies. Since they'd arrived, Koenig had removed only his cap, placing it carefully beyond danger. Now, as the wind refreshed the flames, even the medal on his chest seemed to be burning, and when Hartmann bent down to touch it, it was warm.

'It's a close combat clasp.'

'Yes, I know.'

'The Führer presented it to me. In Berlin. The Führer himself.'

Hartmann rubbed the soft zinc between his fingers; a swastika over a crossed bayonet and stick grenade.

'He has very small hands. They're like an artist's.' Somewhere inland a guard dog was barking. Down below, the rushing tide had obliterated all but one footprint, and only a thin ribbon of beach held fast. 'His voice was very soft too, Max. Soft but not weak.'

Hartmann released the medal. Silence waited awkwardly between them.

'I'm sure he's a great man,' said Hartmann finally. 'You only have to look at what he's done for our country.'

With one powerful sweep of Koenig's leg, Hartmann was down and they were both rolling towards the sea. As they went, ribbons of barbed wire hidden in thick, flowering gorse sliced chunks out of their clothing. Face to bloodied face, throwing breathless punches at the water's black edge, neither man could gain an advantage.

'You're a German,' screamed Koenig. 'Show some fucking respect.'

'I'm sorry, Erich. I'm truly sorry.'

'We're in a war now. You can't be like this. If we kill more than they kill, we win.'

'You're right. You're right.' Hartmann had broken clear, and was panting heavily on the wet sand. 'I was just never quite as good at maths as you were.'

From the beginning, they'd always fought; so viciously, sometimes, no one else could remotely understand their friendship.

Hartmann had been born in Vienna, the only child of a woman who'd strolled out of his life when he was three. As a small boy, he'd been solitary. As a teenager, he'd been sullen and argumentative, but there'd been no war then and his German-born father – a professor in law, and devoted Nazi Party member – seemed untroubled by Max's adolescent unorthodoxy. Since the boy had no siblings, or mother, a little latitude was deemed necessary. And when it mattered most, his child had always been a model of convention. In early 1934, the two of them had packed their bags and moved to Munich where Max's father rose quickly through the party ranks.

To his relief, like every good Aryan child, Max had joined the Hitler Youth, wearing his black shorts and necktie without resistance. At the summer camps, he'd even been happy, thwacking the drum in a marching band with such zest that his instructors thought him destined for the Schutzstaffel.

'A son in the SS,' Professor Hartmann had told him. 'How I will sing on that day.'

On this, at least, father and son were united.

Hartmann had no issue with duty and – in the absence of anything better to do – proclaimed himself happy to die for Germany. Privately, however, the academic's son felt stifled by the dreary company of his fellow teenagers, and struggled with indoctrination. If Hitler needed him to kill Russians, Poles, Americans – the British even – that would be fine. Just so long as it all ended happily, and the company improved.

And then, at a torch-lit Youth Rally in Nuremberg, he'd met Erich Koenig.

Lying next to each other on the competition rifle range, they'd matched shot after shot. For an hour, they'd shredded helpless paper targets, and when the trophy was finally presented for top marksman – in front of the brown-shirted thousands – both boys had stepped up to share the honour.

To the ranks of braying onlookers, they had seemed an improbable pair.

Where Hartmann was tall and languid, Koenig was muscular and short. Where Hartmann's hair was sleek and black, his new friend's ran wild and blond, matching a personality incapable of concealment. If Koenig felt it, he said it. Hartmann, on the other hand, inhabited a face sentried by anxiety; a face with such high cheekbones that his eyes lurked in permanent shadow. A young man preoccupied, it seemed, by difficult questions; an affliction which his new acquaintance found baffling.

That night they'd got drunk together for the first time. After two beers and half a bottle of stolen schnapps, Koenig had passed out with his head on Hartmann's lap.

This is strange, Max had thought. The only things we share are our blue eyes and our uniforms. Erich is two years younger than me, and everything I am not. My father is an intellectual while Koenig's carves headstones. My mother has disappeared. Koenig's takes in other people's washing. He is driven. I am led. He is fanatical. I am resigned. He is terrifying and yet he has a weakness for laughter which marks him out, makes him interesting. Somewhere inside this drunken eleven-year-old, Max had felt certain, beat a heart worth looking for.

Ten years later, he was still looking.

Down at the shore's edge, on their knees, the pair had stopped fighting.

'I'm sorry,' said Hartmann. 'I should have known better. You're too easy to annoy.'

Koenig shrugged. Every fibre of his uniform was ruined. He felt sick and tired and had nothing left to say. Turning away from the sea, he picked his way through the crushed undergrowth back up towards the car. At the fire, he kicked the ashes back into life, threw on the last handful of wood, and stood glumly waiting for Hartmann to reappear. Far away to his left, the early evening sky was glowing, and the chug of a hidden fishing boat had been picked up by the wind.

'We should eat,' he said, when his companion loomed over the ragged edge of the cliff. 'You look like you've been in a war.'

Hartmann sagged back against the tree. 'We're not really friends, you and me. We're like those breakwaters. We just hold tight and cling on to each other and hope there's still something standing when the shit swirls away.'

'You always were a miserable bastard, Max.'

Neither man laughed, but the warmth was building again and each of them wanted to talk. It had been a long time and there were more secrets even than before.

'I thought you were going to die.' Koenig had broken the silence first. 'The last time I saw you there was a hole in your guts.'

Wearily, Hartmann's fingers circled the scar through his damp tunic.

He'd been lucky. He knew that. For years they'd fired guns at bull's-eyes. Then, in 1941, they'd started killing men. That spring, he and Koenig had been rushed into the 2nd SS Panzer Division – the so-called elite 'Das Reich' – and by midsummer they were poised in their armoured vehicles somewhere along Russia's immense western border. Just them and three million others, each one certain of victory over Bolshevism.

Through clouds of flying insects, they'd swept east, across vast plains, silencing every bleat of resistance. By mid-October, the first snows were falling, and as troop-carriers floundered in brown slurry, slaughtered Russians had been thrown on to the mud like planks. Too clearly, Hartmann remembered the ruined faces, but it was the sound – of the tanks crushing each corpse – which kept him from sleep.

'Did it hurt? Did you know what happened?'

'I knew it was a sniper.' He could still feel the flesh knotted thick around the old wound. 'I wasn't sorry to be going home.'

It was relief, not pain or guilt, which he'd felt the most. After botched front-line first aid, infection had torn through his body. For six days, he'd clung to life on a freezing, filthy train shipping the wounded back to the west.

In letters from Munich, his father had assured him that Communism was on its knees, but in his dreams Hartmann saw frozen tracks and frostbitten fingers and an endless quagmire highway paved with mutilated boys in uniforms.

'I was lucky, Erich. I'd seen enough.'

Boiling sap was dripping from the charred stump of a branch.

'You saw nothing,' said Koenig.

'I killed people. That was plenty for me.'

Koenig swallowed and spat into the flames. 'You killed soldiers, Max. Russian soldiers. You fought to the rules. After you'd gone there were no rules.'

Hartmann stared into the flames.

'They were animals out there. The partisans were nailing German soldiers to barn walls through their tongues. They were slinging them up with meat hooks through their cocks.'

'You saw these things?'

'Sometimes, yes. Sometimes we just heard. Rumours.'

'We were in their fucking country. What did you expect?'

'In the early days we shipped the prisoners back behind our lines. Then, after a while, we just started killing them.'

'You started killing them? You?'

Koenig had stood up, and was furiously stoking life back into the fire.

'Fuck, Koenig. Fuck.'

'No one seemed to care what we did. Or how we did it. Petrol, bullets, bayonets, fists. You were all right, Max. You were down the fucking Brienner Strasse drinking beer. Me, I was loving every second of it.'

'And the medal?' asked Hartmann quietly.

'They were Bolsheviks. Scum.' Koenig had slowed down. 'People did what they had to.'

Hartmann reached inside his tunic. They were damp, and a little crooked, but his Gauloises were still intact. From the edge of the fire pit he picked up a glowing twig, lit two cigarettes, and handed one across.

'French smokes.' Koenig smiled. 'One of the sweetest perks of our victory over the barbarians.'

In the thickening gloom, the wet paper sizzled and the blazing tips hovered like fireflies against the dark. From old habit, the two young men drew together, held the rich smoke deep, and released it in one long synchronised sigh. As their lungs emptied, Hartmann leaned across.

'Don't worry, Erich. I'm going to burn too, believe me.'

'I'm not worried. I never worry. We're all going to burn if we don't win. Let's go.'

While Koenig packed the car, Hartmann hoofed sand over the hot ash. It was a clear night, and the grey light of a full moon was flickering on the tide. To hide their dishevelled uniforms, both men had slung on their long army coats. With their caps on, they would pass muster. Recriminations were unlikely in any case. Since the war in the west had gone quiet, everyone had let themselves go a little. No one would look too closely, and people had lost the habit of asking questions.

'Heil Hitler,' barked Koenig with a questioning grin.

'Heil Hitler indeed,' retorted Hartmann. 'Your new best friend.'

Driving north to the coast, the roads had been forlorn. After nightfall, it was as if the entire country had been abandoned.

Above the hungry churn of the engine, they could hear nothing. Every farm building stood black in its field, and the trees seemed to draw back from the accusing sweep of their headlights. At the centre of a crossroads outside Creully, an immense boar stood and watched as they swerved by.

'He's directing the traffic,' mouthed Koenig.

But Hartmann couldn't hear and wasn't looking. In the dark, everything seemed so miraculously undamaged. In the dark, no one could see what they had done.

Shortly before midnight, they were back. Outside Koenig's billet, on the woody fringes of Villers-Bocage, Hartmann stopped the car and silenced its engine. Without speaking, Koenig opened his door, walked to the back and began clearing the boot.

Through the twin columns of the headlights, mayflies swirled like angry dust. At the end of a long gravel drive, they could just make out a gloomy farmhouse and beyond that the murky shapes of weaponry beneath grim drapes of mottled camouflage.

'This is me, then. I'm staying here.'

'I'm another hour away,' said Hartmann. 'No one will notice I took the car.' Somewhere behind them, a tawny owl was cooing; in rhythm, it seemed, with the cooling ping of the exhaust.

It would be good to be alone again. Koenig's fireside confessional had troubled him.

Everyone half knew things or half heard things, but back home his father's generation had their hands over their ears. What you didn't know couldn't hurt you. There were people in Germany, Hartmann had long ago concluded, who would prefer none of them to get back alive with their stories.

'Take care,' said Koenig, offering his hand. 'It could be a long time.'

'Oh, I don't know. Let's be optimistic. They might never come. In three months, we might be home cracking a bottle together for my birthday.' Hartmann eased out the clutch as Koenig stepped back.

'I've just realised, Max. You've never really told me what you've been doing these past few years.'

'You never asked.' The car was inching slowly into the darkness.

'Well? You've got two seconds.' In a moment, Hartmann would be gone.

'I got married, Erich. I think I have a child.'

# 2

# 6 August 1944

With a nervous shiver, Hartmann stirred. Sleep had taken him by surprise, but not for long. Never for long. Since that night, he'd seen, and heard, nothing of Koenig. Since early June, the shit-storm had broken their army into pieces, and now, in the hollow beneath his tank, he recoiled from the person he'd become. Grease-knotted hair lay in clumps across his scalp. Around his neck, where the lice had taken residence, a minefield of red scabs seeped into a sweat-black collar. At the end of each filthy finger, he could feel the sticky scum of battle; blood, and engine oil, and the dark brown dust he'd been tearing through for weeks.

Wriggling from the shelter of the tank, he could see colour and shape forming inside the black silhouettes of the night. Daylight was advancing fast. Figures were moving everywhere in a half-crouch, and the hiss of boiling tea had joined the chorus of morning sound. Soon there would be an order of some sort. Shortly afterwards – if the previous days were anything to go by – it would be counter-manded. Somewhere close by a radio operator was swearing furiously at his broken equipment. The Waffen SS, Hartmann thought. We're not so impressive now.

With his back against steel, he searched his ragged pockets for a smoke. That, at least, would be in good shape.

His father had carried the silver cigarette case in the trenches, carving his name and a date – 11 November 1918 – deep into the inside lid. Now it had gone to war again, providing an elegant sanctuary for the last few things in Hartmann's ownership that mattered. Dry matches, four Gauloises and a photograph.

As the match fizzed in his fingers, he drew the picture close to the flame. 'Alize. Alize Hartmann. Talk to me,' he whispered, before tucking the image carefully back inside the case.

As it always did now, the nicotine made him feel faint, and he closed his eyes to steady himself. There'd been too many days recently without food or sleep, and the scar of his old wound was stretched painfully tight across his shrunken belly.

Alize. How strange that it was his father who had reunited them.

Back in Vienna, they'd been accidental friends, no more. Once a month, Alize's father had visited the Hartmann home in Leopoldstadt to cut the professor's hair. And while the two men traded city gossip, Max would steer the barber's daughter towards a sunlit warren of attic rooms, where they contentedly read stories to each other, or quietly ransacked chests stuffed with his mother's old clothes.

They were a similar age, and she was blonde and pretty, but there'd been no letters – nothing had ever been said – and when the professor relocated in Germany the connection had been severed. Just occasionally, when Max saw a barber's pole, he'd unexpectedly found himself remembering her. Other than that, the girl had vanished entirely from his life.

'They've moved up to the north coast. Not sure where,' his father told him, after receiving a brief postcard from his old friend.

'What does he say?' Max had asked.

'He says to keep on top of the hairs in my ears.'

And then, just as suddenly, she was back.

She was now nineteen years old, ambitious, and had never left home alone before, nor expected to. But in the summer of 1942, as the bombing of Hamburg intensified, the city's brightest students were being ordered south from the Baltic shores to the few places in Germany the RAF hadn't yet blitzed. Improbably, Munich was still one of them, and to Alize Netzel, Professor Emil Hartmann represented two lifelines, being both a familiar name from her past and a chance to somehow complete her studies.

On a stifling July afternoon she'd boarded a train and inched fearfully towards the Bavarian mountains. That same evening, as the last snows glowed on the distant Alps, around four hundred bombers crossed the English Channel bound for the city where her parents lived. By the time Alize tumbled into Munich's crowded Central Station, she was an orphan.

Hartmann's father had known what to do. Since his wife's departure, and with Max away at the eastern front, he'd felt lost inside an enormous house on the northern edge of the city.

He already knew too much about loneliness. Vienna was his true home, not Munich. For years, most of his furniture had been abandoned beneath sheets in darkened rooms. Outside his work – and the party – he had nothing. Alize Netzel's tragedy would be his salvation; a small debt he could repay to the man who had once shaved his neck.

At the station, they'd embraced awkwardly. He'd carried her small bag back to his house, and when the news trickled south from Hamburg he made a promise to keep her safe. It was an arrangement that would suit them both. She was a diligent student with nowhere else to go. She could take the attic space, the house would rise from its slumber, and hopefully soon Max would be well enough to return home.

In fact, the professor's son had been well enough for months.

Throughout the previous winter, he'd hovered on the brink of death, weakened by the sniper's bullet which had blown a hole through his gut, and by the subsequent operation which removed an infected length of his intestine.

As the periods of delirium began to shorten, Hartmann had enjoyed thoughts of mutinous lucidity. To the fury of the nursing staff, he had taken to wearing his newly minted Iron Cross – a reward for he knew not what – pinned to his pyjama top. He was also overheard praising the valour and patriotism of the Russian army; remarks for which he was informally admonished by the surgeon who'd stitched him back together.

By the time he was strong enough to move, he had been back in

Germany for almost six months. In all that time, there'd been no word from Koenig, and precious little reliable information on the fate of his fellow soldiers out in the cold. In all probability, Koenig was frozen dead in a ditch along with the rest of them. No one said it too loud, but the winter had won and the 2nd Panzer Division had been wiped from the face of the earth. Or so the half-rumours claimed.

No bad thing perhaps, thought Hartmann, whose convalescence now proceeded in a military hostel hidden within an anonymous leafy suburb of Berlin.

Throughout it all, his father had stayed in touch. Every few days, a letter came from Munich, and in each one the professor seemed a little more desperate for Max to return. And then suddenly – during a glorious run of August sunshine – Emil's tone changed. *Do you remember Alize? I'm sure that you must*, wrote the professor. *The war has caused her a terrible loss, and she's staying in Munich now; here, with me in our house. You'd still like her, I think. She's a bright young thing and we're good for each other. I suppose neither of us really has anyone else! Come and see for yourself as soon as you're strong enough. You'll be amazed. I've even opened the curtains in the drawing room again . . . and I promise not to talk about politics.*

A few days later, wearing his SS uniform, Hartmann arrived back in Munich. Inside the railway station, huge swastika flags hung scarlet from every upper floor window. Around him exuberant crowds of passengers flowed out on to the sunlit concourse where a brass band played patriotic tunes watched by grinning, cross-legged schoolgirls.

It felt incongruous to him that the British had spared the city for so long. Berlin might be the brains, but Munich had always been the bloody heart of this blighted enterprise. As he strode homewards, every building seemed to be a Nazi shrine.

Hitler had ranted here, Hitler had raved there; in the Braunes Haus, the Sterneckerbräu, and the Hofbräuhaus. Pictures of the Führer glowered from walls and windows and yet the city itself seemed curiously oblivious of the filthy war Max had been fighting. True, the streets had been cleared of Jews, but – as yet – only a handful of bombs had fallen to break the spell, and the dogs still ate biscuits here, not corpses.

'You look magnificent,' his father had said, after a tense doorstep embrace. 'The war is going well then.' It hadn't really been a question.

'Depends whose side you're on, Father,' Hartmann had muttered, as the professor carefully decanted champagne into a slender flute.

'And whose side are you on, son?'

For a moment, over a toast, the two locked eyes. All around them, in the rambling rear garden, a warm breeze was lifting the scent off the lavender beds.

'To survival,' proclaimed Emil as the glasses chinked.

'Of the fittest,' replied Hartmann.

'And to the Führer,' said the professor, rising stiffly to his feet.

'And to the Führer,' whispered his son.

Later, when Emil's lodger returned – standing quietly at the back door – she was struck by how alike the two had become: the same thick crush of dark hair; the same shadowed intensity around their eyes. When they turned and stood, she saw it again in their lean, strong bodies, and when Max spoke she discerned the same kindness that had rescued her from despair.

'Come and join us, Alize,' he said, reaching out for her hand. 'Come and save us from an argument.'

'You remember me then?'

'Of course. They were happy days. And you haven't changed a bit.'

Later on, she could remember little of their first moments together. One glass of champagne had made her drowsy, the airless weather was draining, and the professor's son had seemed uncomfortable with small talk.

'Forgive me,' she had said eventually. 'I have an essay to write.'

Lying on her attic bed, Alize felt the day's heat building in her room. Through an open skylight she could still hear the men's muffled voices, rising up on the warm air; father and son. At times it sounded like shouting, but she wasn't sure, and in between there were long silences broken only by the sound of popping corks.

Working on her studies was out of the question. The professor's son had unsettled her. It wasn't just the whole Schutzstaffel thing. Men in the SS were supposed to have an aura, and like all her old school friends, Alize regarded the dark uniform as a potent lure. No, it was something else; something more intriguing. As a boy, he'd been brittle and awkward. Down there in the garden, he'd sounded wiser and more careworn than his own illustrious father. However perfectly his uniform had been tailored, he clearly wore it with unease. He had also become extraordinarily handsome.

All in all, Alize concluded, she would not be unhappy to see more of Unterscharführer Max Hartmann.

It was her good fortune that Hartmann felt exactly the same. Since his mother walked out, women had played so little part in his life he'd forgotten how to talk to them, and yet he couldn't shake the image of her lustrous brown hair, her sorrowful expression and the polka-dot dress that clung to her with such distinction. Nor did he particularly want to.

The following afternoon, he was waiting in the garden again; alone, and wearing a white shirt, navy flannels and his father's panama hat.

'The army hasn't changed me. I'm afraid soldiers are very dull.'

'I wouldn't know.' She smiled. 'But you don't look like a soldier today.'

Both of them sensed that time might be precious.

On that second night, they had talked until dawn. On the third night, they'd ridden a tram into the heart of the old city and linked arms to navigate the cobbles through medieval streets. On the fourth, they'd danced drunkenly in a basement club, sharing cigarettes and brandy, before lurching back through the blackened city to the professor's silent house. On the doorstep, they'd kissed deeply, and the following night Max had knocked softly on the attic door until it opened and Alize let him in.

Although for both of them the experience was new, necessity required rapid progress. At first, in the dark, they had proceeded only by the touch of trembling fingers. Then, under the muted glow of a paraffin lamp, they had examined each other's bodies with the rapt concentration of the uninitiated; making love frantically, inexpertly, while moths battered their wings against the scorching glass.

'I used to look forward to Saturday mornings in your house.'

The sheets were flung back. Hartmann's right arm lay across her breasts.

'I know what you're going to say,' he moaned. 'Please don't. It's too embarrassing.'

'You used to make me lie on my stomach on the floor to read a book . . .'

'Enough.' He had turned his head into the pillow.

'. . . then you'd sit beside me and slide up my skirt until my knickers were showing.'

'How could I forget? It was amazing. You wore silk.'

'Did I? Was it? Really? You were twelve. I nearly told my father. I didn't know what to do.'

'You do now . . .'

Later, as Hartmann stared silently at the girl's pale skin, Alize had bent down to kiss the raw welt of his scar.

'Will you tell me about it?' she asked.

'Not now,' he replied.

For two days, they scarcely left the attic. Not until they were certain Max's father had gone to work did they venture downstairs, wandering naked through sun-streaked rooms, stirring as if from a coma; looking for food but eating little and sleeping only when overrun by a languor neither could resist. For most of the time, they talked about their past lives. Not until the seventh night did the present contaminate their bubble.

'I'm afraid I've rather run out of excuses,' he'd said. 'They want me at barracks.'

When she turned to kiss him the next morning, there was a note on her pillow. *I think I may love you. I'll be back.*

It had felt empowering to pace back to the station through the Königsplatz in his Waffen SS uniform, and everywhere he looked, people had seemed genuinely happy. For those few unlikely days with Alize in Munich, he'd felt a faint stirring of enthusiasm for their war.

By the following evening, at a training camp west of Leipzig, that fragile optimism was floundering again in an organisation he scarcely recognised.

Russia had changed everything. Entire divisions had simply evaporated. Some people were saying that over a million had been killed and that two entire German armies were facing slow extinction in the streets of Stalingrad.

Koenig, he now knew, was not one of them. Somehow, his friend had made it back and dashed off a letter from his own secret training camp in Germany. *Can't say much and I can't see us meeting for some time either. But I'm well, Max — I've got a medal — and very much looking forward to kicking the British next. See you when we parade through London, perhaps!*

With a smile, Hartmann had folded away the note.

For everyone in the SS, old loyalties were being reassigned. After returning from Munich, Hartmann had been attached to the 1st SS Panzer Division, the so-called Leibstandarte, and from the clues in Erich's letter Koenig was now in the 12th SS Panzer Division; him and all the rest of Germany's death-or-glory teenagers. *I'm so very relieved you got out of there*, Hartmann wrote back that night. *Everything's all very top secret but I think you're right. I think we might be heading west. What happened? How many Russians did you kill? Tell me over a beer in Soho some time. Fingers crossed this letter will find you. Love Max.* There was no point in telling him about Alize. So far as he knew, Koenig had never had a girlfriend. He wouldn't understand. *PS I'm loving my toy tiger*, he wrote instead.

The censors would delete the postscript anyway.

Every day now was spent inside a new weapon which made him feel like a young god. In the thick woodland around Wallendorf, Hartmann's perennial misgivings were yet again in retreat.

The crews called it Königstiger — King Tiger. The top brass called it Panzerkampfwagen Tiger Ausf. B – Tiger Tank 2.

Whatever it was, Hartmann could calmly obliterate a target from almost two miles, while incoming shellfire skimmed off its steel skin. Ancient trees crumpled in its path like supplicants, and its brain-deafening power ignited his dormant belligerence. If they could ever eradicate its endless breakdowns, if the air raids ever stopped, and if the factories could build enough of them, then maybe Koenig's prediction would be vindicated. Maybe they would be rumbling towards Buckingham Palace in their tanks.

But then, as the summer receded, the Allied attacks stepped back up and the bombs began raining on Munich. *If you can get here for a few days then I really think you should*, wrote his father.

Over five months had passed without a word between Alize and Hartmann. The one time he'd started a letter, his words had stalled on the realisation that he barely knew her. *I know what you think of me*, the professor went on. *But I'm not asking for myself. It's Alize. She's still here and she's terrified. You must come. You have to come.*

It had not been easy to get back.

Hartmann's division – maybe the whole German army – was on standby for a move. No one was saying where. Quite probably, no one knew. This was Hitler's private war, Hartmann had decided, as his train creaked through Munich's outer ring of low-rise factories. For twelve hours he'd shivered alone in a compartment without light. Over the rooftops and the smouldering ruins he could make out the guard tower at the Dachau camp.

'For queers and commies,' his father had once told him. 'And Jehovah's Witnesses.' Beyond that, he had not asked.

This time, the old city was different. There was no music in the Hauptbahnhof; no stalls selling flowers on the streets. The giant swastikas still flapped, but it was a raw wind which shook them into crimson ripples and carved shapes in the drifting snow along the pavement. Against the wintry sky, the shelled-out remains of the cathedral looked like a hag's broken tooth. According to local folk-lore, it was the devil's spirit, not air, which swirled around its ruined cavity and tunnelled deep into the icy hearts of shopkeepers. This is a city of demons, he thought, turning his collar up against the cold.

Once again, he had chosen to walk, using the time to examine his feelings. Perhaps it had been unfair not to tell them he was coming, but there'd been no choice. Two days' leave was all he'd got. After that, he might never be back. And for all he knew, she'd forgotten about him already.

From the street, every window was black, and when he eased the front door open the hallway felt damp. Moving deeper into the house, he heard voices raised against the sound of music flowing from a radio. Quietly he tiptoed on, drawn by the melody and by the comforting smell of new-baked bread which streamed from the rear kitchen.

As he drew closer, he stopped. The door was half open. Sitting at the table, oblivious of Max's presence, his father sliced an imaginary conductor's baton through the air. With her back to him, Alize was pulling a tray from the oven. From across the room, he felt washed by the sudden surge of sweet-smelling heat.

And when she turned, he saw, and knew everything in a heartbeat.

# 3

## 6 August 1944

In his wood near Falaise, another match was scorching his fingers.

As the phosphorus spluttered, he pressed his lips to the photograph before gently folding his father's silver case and returning it to his pocket. Only half of his last cigarette remained. From its end hung a comma of ash which crumbled over his hand as he sucked hard and filled his chest. Clamping his teeth tight, he held the breath for as long as he could. Before the war, three minutes would have been easy, but hunger had made him weak.

As his lungs collapsed, water stung his eyes, and thin geysers of smoke began leaking out between his teeth. Soon enough, he would have to stir himself. One more drag and it would be gone.

All around him, he could hear the deep rumble of tanks firing up. Hidden by the trees, crews of men were slipping through their hatches and shutting themselves in. From where he sat with his back to the trunk of a fallen oak, he could see two officers stretching a map across the grass and, as he listened, the crackle of mild panic began to hop from radio to radio.

Two more minutes. One last drag.

Behind closed eyes, he remembered the bubbling coffee and the sibilant whisper of burning gas. He could see his father turning off the radio and striding out of the kitchen. Between her extended hands, Alize was holding three golden discs of flatbread on a tray. For the first time – that he'd seen – her hair was tied back and her anxious face appeared flushed from the heat. Silently, Hartmann had followed the girl's eyes down across her flour-dusted apron.

'You should have told me sooner.'

'I didn't know how to. I didn't know what you'd think.'

After that, they had embraced stiffly, each one encumbered by their ignorance of the other.

'Are you pleased?'

'Never more so.'

They'd been lovers for a week, and strangers ever since. Now she was carrying a child he might never see. Wiping tears from his face, he cupped her chin gently in his hand and kissed her.

There were no doubts in Hartmann's mind that the baby was his. Nor had his feelings for Alize been diminished by the shock. If anything, silhouetted in the kitchen's glow, she seemed more alluring and noble than she had in the summer; more desirable than she had when he was twelve.

In a war from which he felt hopelessly disconnected, Alize might just be his salvation.

'We have to make this right. Before I go back. Agreed?'

Alize had nodded silently.

Naturally, Max's father had pulled a few strings. In Munich, very little stood in the way of a good Nazi, and Professor Emil Hartmann had always been one of those. As January snow deepened outside on the deserted Marienplatz, his only son and Alize stood before a desk inside the city's immense town hall, and took their vows watched by rows of empty chairs. When they left, Hartmann carefully wrapped his full-length SS winter coat around his new wife's shoulders. Behind them, on the building's ice-crusted façade, the giant painted marionettes of the Rathaus glockenspiel were clanking into action.

'It's a love story,' said Hartmann, pulling Alize close. 'A local Bavarian duke marries his dream princess and organises a joust in honour of their love.'

'Does he always win?'

'Without fail. Every day for a hundred years.'

There'd been no honeymoon, no reception, and within a few

hours of the officiation, Hartmann was trudging back towards his unit in Leipzig.

All the previous night, shunning sleep for speculation, the pair had chased futile plans into the morning. Only two things seemed certain: that the child would be born in the spring and that its father would not be there.

'You can't stay in Munich,' Hartmann had argued. 'It's too dangerous now.'

'My mother had a sister in Cologne. If she's still alive, I could try there.'

'Do anything. Leave the country if you have to.'

They had not seen or heard from each other since.

Two days later, Hartmann's division had been sent back to the Eastern Front, a black horde of men and machines heading towards humiliation in Kharkov. On the day of his first wedding anniversary, Hartmann's tank was immobilised in a muddy swamp, going shell for shell with four Soviet T-34's. By the time he was recalled to Germany – miraculously intact – there'd been no news of Alize for fifteen months, and just one short note from his father which had travelled halfway around Europe before it found him. *I think maybe you were right after all. We are losing this war. Don't worry about Alize. She's well and has travelled to have the baby at her aunt's in Cologne. I do hope you get a chance to see it. I'm going back to Vienna until this wretched business is over. Take care. Heil Hitler.*

Hartmann looked at the date. March 1943. It had been sent over a year before. Somewhere in Germany, he had a wife and a child he knew nothing about.

Even if he'd known where to start, Hartmann was powerless to look for them. In the company he kept, sentimentality was a weakness and secret misgivings were dangerous. Among the SS fighters of the Leibstandarte, the collective belief in glorious victory remained absurdly high. Events in Russia had been down to bad weather, nothing more. No other explanation was permitted.

It wouldn't benefit Hartmann to reveal that his waking thoughts languished on the image of a baby boy – or girl – learning to walk in a city shattered by nitro-glycerine. And in any case, leave of any kind – compassionate or not – had ceased to be an option. Throughout April, the shattered remnants of the 1st SS Panzer Division had been recuperating in Belgium, swollen each day by hundreds of juvenile recruits, whose training often fell to Hartmann and whose callow patriotism filled him with ungovernable sadness.

'How old do you think I am?' he'd asked one pencil-thin volunteer on his first day

'Thirty-ish,' the boy had replied. 'Maybe more.'

'And why do you think we will win the war?'

'Because we are Germans. Because we are right.'

When the spring ripened, however, the warm breath of early summer lifted him, and the army began to move. Down every road, groaning columns of tanks and trucks crawled towards the French coast. It felt good to be warm and busy. It felt good to sleep in the open under the ancient constellations. As they progressed, the men travelled through a landscape which seemed indifferent to their presence. In the flat dark fields, people were still working, their backs bent to the stubborn lines of seedlings which rose towards skies untroubled by clouds.

By the middle of May, a huge contingent of SS and Wehrmacht divisions had assembled in the hedge-bound countryside south of Calais. Around the clock, the ground quaked with the movement of artillery, and in the dazzling daylight skies the air buzzed with friendly fighters.

Behind their wall of concrete, no one expected an invasion. After dark, the troops traded cigarettes for cheese with the local farmers, before marinating themselves in smoky village bars. During the long, dusty days, they read battered paperbacks and gorged on stolen wine.

Every morning, to stave off the boredom, Hartmann and his four-man tank crew took their Tiger out on manoeuvres, swerving through hedgerows and dodging phantom enemy action. Inside their armoured shell, each of them already felt indestructible, but he drove them tirelessly until each could read the others' minds, and until he was absolutely certain that no one could possibly do it better.

And then he had seen Koenig.

Out of nowhere, in a dusky town square – Hartmann couldn't remember its name – he'd heard his friend's rollicking laughter. A minute later Koenig was stepping out from a crowd, utterly undiminished, crushing his hand and swallowing him whole in a stubbly embrace.

'You made it then, Max. And you didn't take a desk job either.'

Twisting free of Koenig's arms, Hartmann stepped back and examined his boyhood companion. He looked tanned and fit. Over by a packed bar he could hear a group of men singing hymns. A mighty fortress is our God. 'I'd have missed the creature comforts.' He grinned.

'You know your problem, Max? You're too fucking serious.'

'You know yours? You talk crap.'

'Ha. It's good to see you. It really is.' Koenig looked up at the clock on the church tower. 'Tomorrow maybe? A day out?'

'I could get my hands on a car.'

'Sounds promising. It's my birthday, too. I'll be expecting something lavish.'

'Open-topped and a straight run to the seaside?'

Koenig wrapped his arms round Hartmann again, and kissed him on the cheek. 'I met the Führer, Max. He spoke to me.'

*09:34 hours*

Funny that, thought Hartmann.

If he was right, the sun was blazing down on his own birthday this time, with no gifts in prospect, and no waltzing on any clifftops. All around him, sheets of netted camouflage were being rolled back from assault guns and tanks. The last drops of fuel were being shaken from battered jerry cans. Meat rations were being traded for bullets. Hay was being stuffed into lorry tyres so riddled with holes they could no longer hold air.

With every passing minute, as the sky brightened, the scene grew more pitiful. Blackened faces tight with worry; shredded uniforms; and, buried within the ragged chaos, the unknowable split between

28

those who secretly wanted only to survive, and those who dreaded the unpardonable shame of imprisonment.

Few people were expecting victory, whatever they said.

Only two weeks after his day at the seaside with Koenig, the Allies had surged across the same Normandy sands they'd wrestled on. By the time the 1st SS Panzer Division – and Koenig's 12th – had entered the battle zone, it was too late.

During the daylight hours, British planes vaporised them at will. During the night, shocked survivors regrouped and prayed for coherent orders that never came.

Near Carpiquet village, Hartmann had watched Spitfires cutting down infantrymen like corn. It no longer mattered that they fought like cats; that the German tanks were superior; or that Hartmann felt invincible inside his Tiger. Everyone was on his own now. If it had ever existed, the centre was falling apart, and a forest of men was falling back on what was left of their homes in Germany. Along the way, both sides were losing their heads.

Somewhere near Caen, Hartmann's patched-up group of tanks had cornered a dozen Canadian foot soldiers and slaughtered them in a field. Two days later, he'd seen four Germans pulled from a broken-down truck, pushed to their knees and shot through the head. Everywhere, rumours swirled like the fires that burned in every ruined village. On some days it was said they were turning the Allies back. On others – on most – they were crumbling towards oblivion. South of Soliers, he'd helped wipe out twenty British tanks. Behind the German lines, deserters were being bound to trees and executed. As fuel supplies dwindled, tanks were abandoned and torched. A thick veneer of oily smoke blanketed the skies, and every verge was littered with jettisoned machine guns and the dead who had once carried them.

Hartmann shuddered and pulled himself to his feet. From what he could tell there were five working Tigers including his own, plus one commandeered Citroën van and one decrepit old bus. During the night, their section leader had vanished, leaving a befuddled deputy whose hearing had been destroyed by a bomb-blast.

Koenig would have found all this funny. Koenig would have known what to do. But then Koenig was probably dead.

'Unterscharführer Hartmann. Where are the enemy? Which way should we go?'

He turned round. It was the same skeletal teenager he'd trained back in Belgium. 'We've met before?'

The boy nodded and clicked his heels sharply together.

'Do you still think we'll win the war?' said Hartmann.

'Yes, of course. Nothing has changed. We are still Germans.'

Nearby, two dishevelled riflemen were stuffing a wooden handcart with blankets and apples. Another was defecating in full view of his comrades. Sitting in the back of the bus, a young army grenadier was playing a Viennese waltz on a looted violin. On his head was a plain black Frenchman's beret. On his lower forearm – exposed when he raised the bow – was a freshly tattooed heart.

'You're good,' said Hartmann. 'Where did you learn?'

'I taught myself. Can't you tell?'

'What happened to your helmet?'

'I think this suits me better.'

Hartmann moved away. The boy carried on playing. Overnight, two men had died of their wounds and their corpses were being heaved into a ditch under a buzz of flies. From the top of the bus, a wounded paratrooper was scanning the skies for enemy planes. Where his left ear had once been there was a hole, and his neck was crusty with dried blood. Apart from Hartmann, there was no one left to tell them what to do.

'We need to be going,' he said.

To his astonishment, everyone obeyed him. Even the violin fell silent.

*12:00 hours*

By midday, there had still been no sign of the enemy.

Hartmann's tanks had flanked a long narrow lane winding east; three on one side, two on the other. After weeks of sunshine, the rutted dust was easily stirred and by keeping to the edges of the fields

30

they made themselves harder to spot. Between the tanks, in the centre of a tree-lined track, crawled the rest of the ramshackle convoy.

Forty men maybe, Hartmann calculated; fifty at most. Some of them, he knew, were desperate to die fighting: the younger ones, mostly; teenagers with eyes that were dead already. The rest lay awake all night desperately trying to remember their childhood prayers.

By early afternoon, they'd covered twenty dread-filled miles and everyone was still alive.

Without instructions, Hartmann had chosen his route well. Beneath a thick cover of leaves, they'd remained invisible to the Typhoons criss-crossing in the blue above. Whenever he'd heard one, the lookout on the bus had screamed them to a stop. Frozen under their green canopy, the men's eyes widened, engines were stilled and guns bristled from every window until the danger was past.

In the beginning, someone had usually thrown up. Now they were used to it.

Just a few more hours, and the day would cool. Then they'd be out of this baking heat and safe again. Grainy streams of sweat ran down faces crawling with mosquitoes. Every man's head ached with concentration. If only they could just keep going.

At around four, Hartmann called the convoy to a halt where a clear stream bisected the track. Everyone now looked to him as their leader and he was comfortable with that trust. A few yards ahead, their woody lane ran out into open countryside. If they carried on, they'd be horribly exposed. If they waited till nightfall, their pathway towards Germany might be cut off.

'Sir, may I ask? Is this classified as a retreat? Or are we regrouping for some sort of counterattack?'

For the second time that day, Hartmann found himself being questioned by that boy. 'What is your name?'

'Zuhlsdorff. Kurt Zuhlsdorff. Tank gunner.'

'And do you want to get home, wherever that is?'

'Lübeck, sir. But not like this, not as a coward.'

It was a slap, not a real punch, but Hartmann had meant it and a ribbon of blood was running down from the pale teenager's nose.

'Until death, sir,' hissed Zuhlsdorff. 'The last man. Those were our orders.'

But Hartmann wasn't listening. Soon enough the boy would have his wish. Out of sight, he imagined the teeth of a giant trap clenching around them. Stay, or press on. Either way he felt sure they were finished, and already their numbers were dwindling. Through the window of the bus, he could see an abandoned violin on the back seat. The kid with the tattoo had fled. Soon there would be others.

'Fill your bottles and cool down in the brook,' he said firmly. 'We'll keep going until dusk. Be ready in thirty minutes.'

*19:46 hours*

It was a perfect evening when they moved away from their cover.

Behind them, the sun still loomed huge above the treeline, casting their moving shadows long across a breathless sea of corn. Over the golden seed-heads, aimless clouds of tiny insects danced drunkenly in the yellow light. From the forest's edge, flycatchers watched before swooping greedily to feed. High above, in the crown of a twisted oak, a young sparrowhawk preened its feathers, seeing everything and feeling the warmth stretch deep into its bones.

Like the raptor, Hartmann felt alive with expectation. As before, he'd arranged the group into a steel-plated sandwich. Down the middle, the two battered vehicles stuck to the flinty track. On either side of them, leaving a flattened wake of crops, the Tigers drove on.

From his open turret-hole, Hartmann scoped in every direction. Ahead of them, the farmland swelled up to a gentle hill. Beyond that, he could see the spike of a church spire, and a black blanket of woodland. In an hour, maybe two, they'd be safe. But the noise they were making was thunderous, and they were provoking a cloud of pollen and dust that would be visible for miles.

Up on its warm perch, the sparrowhawk twitched its neck and fled. Down below him, in the stewing darkness of the tank cabin, someone was yanking at his leg. It was the radio operator.

'Look behind you, Max. We've got a problem.'

Hartmann would never find out if the bus had broken down, or simply run out of petrol. All the men inside it had been roasted alive before he could ask.

Framed by the setting sun, the five Typhoons had come out of the west, unheard and unseen until it was too late. The first rocket had incinerated the bus. The second and third had melted the dilapidated Citroën in a purple ball of flame. As his tank screamed and wheeled furiously, Hartmann took one look before dropping down and banging the steel hatch shut. No one could have survived. The fiddler had chosen wisely.

'Until death it is then,' he bellowed.

As a boy, with Koenig, he'd enjoyed proving himself as a marksman. All soldiers had to be able to kill. It was the malignancy of purpose he despised, not the process. What was it Koenig had said around that driftwood fire? If we kill more of them, we win? Maybe it really was that simple.

Yanking the radio from his operator's hands, Hartmann barked into the handset, 'Make back for the wood. Keep swerving and stay focused.' He hoped the other four crews had heard.

In a few minutes, the tanks would reach the safety of the forest. Banking quickly, the fighters returned, unleashing a coordinated salvo of rockets. Brown clouds of broken earth and metal plumed skywards from the cratered cornfield. Three of the Tigers shuddered to a standstill.

As their turret lids banged open, two of them exploded. No one came out of either. As the crew of the third stumbled clear, the planes were already heading back. Through his slit, Hartmann could see the five men looking skywards with their hands on their heads. And then, as the Typhoons swooped low, he saw their bodies minced by shellfire.

Two working tanks remained; only four hundred metres separated them from the sanctuary of the forest. Neither of the crews expected to make it, but every second brought them nearer and, for some reason, the Typhoons had not yet come back. And then, from his steel cauldron, Hartmann could see why. Along the edge of the wood, in every direction, Allied troops were pouring towards them.

American, Canadian, British. He didn't know. He didn't care. Panic lashed his innards and the tank whined into reverse. From somewhere, a shell boomed uselessly against its outside. Swinging the turret towards the noise, Hartmann saw five enemy tanks heading towards him.

M4 Shermans. Easy meat. If the second Tiger had survived – if that urchin Zuhlsdorff knew his business – the Yanks wouldn't have a chance.

For the first time in months, he relaxed. Every man inside his tank's putrid cockpit knew precisely what to do. Luck was handy, he'd often told them, but skill was handier. They'd practised for this. They were the best.

'Forward now and hard right.'

The tank lurched and wheeled, rupturing the field in a boiling stew of dirt. Three more shells landed close by. Dirt and stones drummed down on their cage. From the corner of his left eye, he saw a flash. Zuhlsdorff's crew were handy too. Excellent. Four enemy tanks left. Four versus two. Much better.

Spinning back into the cornfield, Hartmann's Tiger accelerated up towards the rise and then turned. The world had gone mad. Over an unbroken crest of trees, furious clouds of rooks were circling across a pink sky.

At his side, an armour-piercing tungsten shell was being rammed into position and his gunner was feverishly calibrating the shot. Somewhere to his left he could hear the other German tank, and climbing towards them – in line formation – were the four surviving Shermans.

It was a terrible pity, but he had no doubt that everyone inside them would soon die. And that he would soon follow.

In the fading light, more tanks and troops were emerging from the wood. So be it.

With a peculiar grace, the gun snouts of both Tigers swivelled towards their enemies and fired. Behind each cacophonous flash, sixty-eight tons of metal lurched back on its tracks. A few seconds later, they unleashed a second furious double salvo, and then stillness.

As the air cleared, Hartmann saw four tangled heaps of metal and a swarm of foot soldiers looking out in the direction of the fading sun.

'I'm truly sorry,' he muttered into the stifling gloom. All of his crew had heard the same thing.

Just one Typhoon had continued flying, defying the dusk for a final shot. Now its last rockets were airborne, hissing low across the ruined corn into the mud-clogged bogey wheels of the two German tanks.

Inside each one, shards of scalding metal ricocheted through thick, oily smoke. Gore-spattered hands reached for the turret locks. Rich harvest air flooded over the spluttering men, and a ring of American soldiers watched to see who, or what, would emerge. Hartmann's driver had scrambled out first into a halo of gunfire and his body had slithered back into the cabin, the double lightning bolts on his lapel saturated with blood. Above his head, Hartmann could feel boots swarming over the ruined tank. Disembodied machine guns were pointing down towards him. He closed his eyes.

Alize, he thought for one last time. Alize.

And then hands were dragging him out and a rifle stock cracked down on his nose. All around him he could smell sweat and tobacco, and as he struggled to stand, invisible boots clattered in, again and again, stomping him down into the filth alongside his crippled tank. Somewhere behind him, he heard gunfire, screams, and then more shots. Four bodies were being thrown alongside him.

Twisting sideways he could just make out the other Tiger, burning furiously in the gloom. Alongside it, four more corpses, and a fifth man, badly beaten, slumped on his knees.

For a moment, their blackened eyes met.

It was Zuhlsdorff, the boy. Two of them were still alive and the killing had stopped.

For a second time, Hartmann tried to stand. When he stumbled, two pairs of hands grabbed his arms and held him up, while another yanked back his filth-caked hair. Through the ringing in his ears, he heard a pistol being cocked.

A gap had opened between the soldiers, and a single figure was walking towards him pointing a revolver. Clean-shaven, rimless glasses, and two stripes. A corporal, thought Hartmann, my Yankee executioner.

Leaning forward, the officer unbuckled his captive's leather holster and let it fall to the ground. He then patted the German's pockets and pulled out the silver cigarette case.

'Nice case. Do you speak any English?'

'Yes, a little.' Hartmann's mouth was full of grit.

'Where are you from? What do I call you?'

'I'm from Munich. Vienna, really. Max Hartmann.'

As they spoke, the American corporal had been rolling the case, distractedly, in his hand. Now he was looking inside it. 'You're SS?'

'Yes I am.'

'Your English is excellent. Who's the girl?'

'She's my wife.'

Turning the case towards the light of the flames, the officer peered closer. 'How old are you, soldier?'

Hartmann smiled; his own private joke. This was how the day had begun.

'Maybe you can tell me,' he said. 'I was born on August sixth, nineteen twenty-two.'

The cherub-faced corporal looked up. 'August sixth?'

Without looking down, the American had folded the case shut, and was stroking its cold silver sheath. With a sudden jerk he tossed it back towards the prisoner.

'Happy birthday, Max Hartmann from Vienna. Many happy returns.'

# August/September 1944
# northern France

Looking back, he could see how lucky they had been.

As calm returned around their ruined tanks, whispered orders had gone from man to man. Two GIs had appeared carrying green fuel cans. Others knelt over the eight shattered corpses, ransacking the pockets for souvenirs. A Luger pistol had been found and was being emptied into the night sky. Scorched belt buckles and weapons were being examined in the firelight, and knives were hacking the silver-stitched SS insignia from every lapel.

When there was nothing left to plunder, petrol was splashed over the dead. Stepping forward again, the bespectacled corporal flicked a match against his nail and tossed it into a dusty puddle of fuel. For a half-second, a flickering purple snake hissed through the corn before wrapping the pyre in a white sheet of flame. When Hartmann tried to turn away, a hand on his face forced him to watch. 'Beats a few birthday candles, soldier.'

After a few minutes, even the Americans had seen enough. One by one they turned from the charred tangle, and walked back down the hill. Ahead of them, along the black edge of the forest, a line of trucks was ticking over noisily. Insects swirled in their headlights as the men clambered in. No one was looking back to check the bonfire, glowing steadily on the ridge. No one wanted to talk about the smell.

Under the flickering lamps of the lorries, the injuries of both prisoners looked shocking. Blood was flowing steadily around a shard of twisted shrapnel which protruded from Zuhlsdorff's shoulder like a coat-hook. His left arm hung uselessly at his side, and the two middle fingers were missing from the hand.

Hartmann's beating had left him unrecognisable. Either side of his blackened nose, his eyes peered from behind horribly swollen cheeks. Blood was visible around both ears, and the pain in his ribs made standing almost impossible. To walk down from the tanks, he'd needed the help of the corporal. To move any further he'd require a stretcher.

'Not far now,' whispered the American. 'We'll get you fixed up real soon. Understand?'

Hartmann nodded. 'It's going to be all right,' he said, turning to Zuhlsdorff. 'They're not going to kill us.'

Slowly, the boy diverted his eyes from his own ruined hand. For a moment, some sort of furious understanding seemed to blaze in them.

'You're disappointed?' whispered Hartmann. 'I get it. You wish you'd died back there with the rest of them.'

Zuhlsdorff's lips mouthed a silent oath. Arms were reaching out from the back of a hospital truck to pull the two men inside with a gentleness which jarred against what had happened back there on the hill.

'Thank you,' Hartmann said quietly as the convoy made its move. Behind them, he could still see the fire and the twisted silhouette of a gun barrel growing paler. And then they were back in the forest and the only lights were their own.

Above the deep rumble of the trucks, planes growled eastwards. Through the flapping oilcloth, Hartmann could see a blizzard of stars. What did they call it? A bomber's moon? He wondered where Alize might be and prayed she'd avoided the cities. Hamburg? Munich? Dresden? God, he hoped not.

Every plane on earth seemed to be out tonight.

Clamping his hands over his ears, he examined the clotted ruins of his face. Through their slits, his eyes could still see. Nothing felt badly broken. Not on his face. He'd got away lightly.

During the next hour no one spoke. For the two Germans, every jolt in the track was an agony of expectation.

Sitting across from Hartmann, Zuhlsdorff was moaning strangely. All around them, their guards were close to sleep. Across their heads, Hartmann could make out lamps within and beyond the forest, together with the soft outline of tents, dozens of tents. Somewhere nearby, a generator was racing and the convoy was slowing to a halt.

'Zuhlsdorff. Zuhlsdorff.'

With a groan, the boy lifted his head. Blood was still pumping out around the metal spike. As he stared down at his hand, the lorry's back flap slammed down and arms reached up to guide him to the ground. A crush of shapes was gathering below them and orders were being relayed along a chain of blurred voices. One of them seemed to be directed at Hartmann, but he couldn't see from where.

'Listen. I'm here. This is an American military field hospital.'

Hartmann turned his head towards the voice.

'My name is Lieutenant Steve Hodges. US Army medical corps.'

Somehow, Hartmann had been eased down from the truck after Zuhlsdorff. Now the voice was behind him.

'We're going to fix you up, and then we're going to move you on. OK?'

Up ahead, the teenager had already disappeared through the canvas door of a huge, camouflaged marquee. From inside he could hear frantic yells rising above a gust of disinfectant. There was nothing he could do, but his knees were buckling, and wet grass was filling his open mouth.

Two days later, he came to in a tent full of light and noise.

Outside, he could hear guy ropes creaking in the sun. Heavy vehicles were on the move and somewhere a panful of bacon was crisping in its fat. Sliding his back cautiously up his pillow, Hartmann surveyed his new billet.

Along each side of the makeshift hospital, there were around forty occupied camp beds. On the ground between lay another hundred or so wounded soldiers, some swaddled in muddied sheets, the rest curled up on blood-soaked stretchers.

Precisely how many of them were still alive was impossible to guess. Every few seconds, through the dazzling gash of the tent flaps, another casualty was added to the crush and each new arrival prompted groans of disappointment. Those who could still move independently shuffled sideways to clear some space. Those who couldn't were squeezed even tighter by the string of uniformed orderlies tiptoeing between the lines.

Away to his left, close to another pair of doors, Hartmann could see doctors bunched around a screaming patient. On the other side of those doors, he guessed, was the operating theatre.

From what he could already see, the two lifeless bodies down at his side wouldn't be needing it. Each was being hastily disconnected from his tubes, wrapped in blankets and carried back into the sunshine.

'Hartmann. You're SS, right?'

He hadn't noticed the doctor approach his bed.

'You've been lucky. The SS normally go on the dirt.'

Hartmann smiled. It hurt. He remembered the voice. Not the face. 'You're Hodges, right? Where exactly are we?'

'You know English. That's impressive.'

As the doctor spoke, he pulled back the grey blanket and pressed his fingers against the patient's bruised midriff. Hartmann winced and twisted in his cot.

'A broken rib or two. Nothing more. You'll be pissing like this for days.' From between Hartmann's legs, the American had rescued a bedpan and was emptying it into a bucket. Most of it was blood. 'Looks bad, but it's a flesh wound compared to most.'

Carefully, Hodges rolled the covers back. The bedspread felt like a steel clamp. 'You've cracked a cheekbone, too. But you'll be out of here in a week.'

'I came in with a kid called Zuhlsdorff. Z for Zuhlsdorff. Shrapnel wounds.'

Hodges ran a finger down the list on his pad. A thousand names, thought Hartmann. And too many of them had been crossed out.

'This isn't the only tent. There's a whole town of them.' Hodges flicked over another page. 'First name Kurt? Also SS? Also lucky. Looks like he's going to be walking out of here with you.'

'You never said where we were.'

Now it was Hodges' turn to smile. He was young too, Hartmann realised.

'No, I didn't. It's a military secret probably. But I can't really see it doing you any good. You're in a hospital somewhere south of Bayeux. About five miles from the coast.'

'Anywhere near Arromanches?'

'I've really no idea. But I could probably find out.'

'Don't bother.'

From behind them, a furious German voice — a harsh parade-ground bark — suddenly terminated their conversation.

Everything in the tent had frozen. By the doors of the operating theatre, a patient was yanking a drip from his arm with one hand while clawing at the face of a medic with the other. As two military policemen pushed through the knot of wounded men, a tray heaped with plasma infusions went crashing to the floor. Foul abuse and spittle were pouring in a torrent from the patient's mouth.

'Jesus. Fuck.' Hodges had turned back to look at Hartmann. 'You'd better translate that for me.'

'He says he's a general. He says he wants to know where the blood is coming from for his operation. Your guys have told him it is American blood. So now he's told them they can only operate if they use German blood.'

'And that's it?'

'Not quite. Apparently it's the blood of an American Jew. Or at least that's what your people have told him. I assume they're lying.'

'Of course they're lying. We have no idea where the blood comes from.'

From across the ward, the shouting had started again.

'Now he is saying he would rather die for Hitler.' Hartmann looked back across. The prisoner was being sedated. 'So what will they do with him, Lieutenant?'

But Hodges was already turning towards another patient. He stopped, wiped his shining brow, and said quietly over his shoulder, 'They'll keep him alive. And he can believe what he wants.'

After five days, Hartmann was back on his feet. It was time to go.

If anything, there were more wounded squeezed in than before and most were in terrible shape. Night and day, the whimpering had never stopped. Nor had the stream of broken young men going in and out of the makeshift operating theatre.

The burns disturbed him the most: the half-melted faces crawling with flies; the red stumpy claws; the eyes pleading through the crusty black remnants of lost faces. That could have been him. Even after dark, Hartmann could feel the guilty heat of their stares. Wherever he was going next, it couldn't come soon enough.

Wrestling his smoke-smelling uniform back on, however, was like prodding a bad memory. For almost a week, it had been bundled in a kitbag under his bed. Buttons had vanished, and a torn pocket drooped from the chest. Inside the tunic pocket, he could still feel the cigarette case, miraculously intact; everything else was ruined.

Never had he felt less like a soldier. If Koenig could see him now, he'd be devastated. Only the glittering telltale insignia on his lapel appeared undamaged, and as he pushed up from his bed the twin S's on his collar were all anyone could see.

All over the tent, heads turned and hushed conversations died rapidly away. Among the chaos of bloodied conscripts, a path was opening which Hartmann navigated in tiny, shuffling steps. Every few seconds he paused to let the pain retreat from his chest, and when he stumbled no one offered to help.

'The ordinary soldiers don't seem to like you – your own countrymen.' It was Hodges again.

Hartmann rested near the dark canvas doors. 'They don't like the badge. They know nothing about me.'

The doctor smiled and put his arm around Hartmann's waist. They were nearly outside and Hartmann could feel the clean blowy warmth.

'We're young. What do any of us know about ourselves?'

At a nod from the medic, a guard unfurled two dingy flaps. Beyond them, Hartmann could see only vivid outlines moving in a slab of scalding light. One more step and he was standing in it.

Lifting his head to the sun, he swayed drunkenly, eyes closed, filling his lungs with air drifting south from the sea. For a moment, he was somewhere else; lifting a child in his arms, or dancing on a clifftop with a gutful of schnapps.

'*Eine schöne Frau, Herr Hartmann*. Your photograph. She's a beautiful woman. Whoever she is.'

Hartmann's eyes snapped open. When he looked back, Hodges had gone.

From the tent behind him, he could hear the familiar murmurs of distress. Whatever happened now, he would not be dying for Hitler. Not just yet, anyway. He'd become aware of an immense city of green. Not just one hospital tent, but thirty or maybe forty, stretching out in neat rows under a coral sky streaked with stray plumes of cloud. In every direction, he could see jeeps and trucks and men, moving purposefully under the smoke blowing from a bonfire of linen. A pair of ambulances went surging past and in the far distance – beyond the edge of the visible compound – something else was moving inside a curtain of dust.

A sharp pain jabbed at his side, and he was limping forward again; no longer alone but in a steady line of fifty or so prisoners who, like him, had been discharged from their beds. No one was walking quickly. That was good. Any faster, and Hartmann was certain he would go down. For the second time that morning, he felt fearful eyes upon his back. The few soldiers who'd been talking before had fallen silent and everyone appeared puzzled by the distant commotion.

'They only kept us alive so they could shoot us.'

A hand was on his shoulder. A familiar voice was pressing in his ear. Zuhlsdorff.

'You made it then,' said Hartmann. He didn't need to look.

'I think those fuckers would have preferred it if I hadn't.'

'Surely not.' Hartmann paused. 'Did you need any blood? Any blood transfusions?'

'Of course I fucking did. I'd have died without them.'

Hartmann smiled. One day I'll tell him, he thought.

'What? What's so fucking funny?'

For a few moments, the older man felt the weight of Zuhlsdorff's puzzled gaze. When it had passed, he stole a glance at his companion.

Defeat had wrought a shocking transformation. Before their capture, the teenager's face had shone with the zealous glow of the righteous. Now his skin was cracked like parchment and every remaining ounce of heft had slid from his body. Across his chest, his left arm lay pinioned in a grubby sling. From its end hung a hand swaddled in blood-soaked strips of bandage. Just his thumb and two fingers remained.

Only the death wish seemed undamaged.

'Don't worry, old-timer. I'll still be able to look after you. I can still pull a trigger.'

But Hartmann was no longer interested. A half-mile from the canvas city, the column had stopped and there were raised voices ahead. Along their flanks, the two lines of guards were now furiously concentrated and every rifle had been aimed at their bellies.

Zuhlsdorff's lips pressed hard against Hartmann's ear again. 'I told you. I fucking told you.'

A handful of jittery Germans had already started protesting, and a guard was snarling back, '*Schweigen. Schweigen.* Shut the fuck up and listen.'

Moving up slowly from the front, two officers with clipboards were shouting out the prisoners' names.

'Don't be such a dumb prick.' Hartmann sighed. 'No one is going to shoot us. It's a handover. We're being passed on. Look.'

Finally, everyone could see behind the wall of dust. From the hospital tent, they had assumed it to be tanks or field guns on the move.

But it was neither.

## 5

It was a river, a filthy river of the vanquished.

If they looked to the right, they could see no end. If they looked to the left, the line eventually vanished in its own brown haze. Every few minutes, shambling ten abreast, hundreds crossed his gaze but not one returned it. Some wore crumpled caps; some sprouted unlit cigarettes from drooping lips; and every wretched uniform seemed several sizes too big for men dragging their feet through a country they had once stormed in glossy boots.

Just once, Hartmann heard fragments of a marching song but it was a lonely voice, swiftly extinguished. Mostly, this was a fearful river flowing north in the silence of its own collective apprehension. Not one of its constituent parts knew where he was going, or for how long he would be going there. SS or regular soldier; it didn't matter here.

'Move. *Schnell.*'

Slowly, Hartmann's own bedraggled tributary was being eased out into the main flow. At least no one here is in a hurry, he thought. I'll be able to keep up.

It was not a long march – a dozen miles, no more – but it took all day. And no one on it would ever forget the smell. By mid-morning, thousands of prisoners were on the move; eyes locked forward, and whatever rag they could find clamped over their noses.

For weeks, fermented by the summer's heatwave, the dead had been rotting where they fell.

Against a red-clay bank, two knelt legless as if in prayer. Another had fallen back against a bole, his expression one of frozen alarm, eyes chiselled out; and, in places, fly-blown limbs hung from the trees.

'Is it any wonder they hate us?' Hartmann had said to no one in particular.

All day long, the men had gagged on the stench. Nothing they could do made it more bearable, and progress was horribly slow. Every few minutes, they were stopped and bullied off the road, scarcely daring to look where, or on what, they might be standing, while convoys of trucks rocked by full of grinning soldiers screaming abuse. Every village they passed through was a crumble of smoking timbers, and during their extended stops, pails of water were passed down a line which had stretched out over two miles of bleached French lanes. There was rarely enough. By late afternoon there had been no food, and resentment was rippling along the column. By early evening, they had stopped once again.

'What's happening?' Hartmann asked the nearest guard.

'You're checking into Hotel Normandy. You won't be here for long. Don't expect a bed.'

Ahead of them was a square barbed-wire enclosure. The surrounding wall climbed four metres high and ran for around three hundred metres on each of its four sides. In places the wire was so slapdash, a man could have walked through the gaps. There were no discernible watchtowers on the outside and no buildings on the inside; just a distant scattering of tents, and more men herded into one space than he had seen since Nuremberg.

Queues seemed to run in every direction, although the scale of the melee made it impossible to discern what the men were queuing for. As he watched, yet more men poured in through the compound's ramshackle gate, and as he inched closer, the crush inside grew even worse.

All around the perimeter, Hartmann now saw a line of bored-looking military policemen. From the backs of two flatbed American army trucks, orders were being screamed in every direction and, one by one, prisoners were being yanked forward from the front of the column.

Suddenly, hands were on him and a hose had been pushed down his back. White delousing powder was filling his hair and his mouth and his trousers were being wrenched down around his knees. More powder was being sprayed around his penis and between his buttocks.

Then, with a kick, he was wrenching up his pants and being steered towards one of the twenty desks which stood between him and the main gate.

In front of him a man in a brown uniform was writing furiously, head hunched down over a pile of notes. When he beckoned Hartmann forward, he did not look up.

'Empty your pockets, Hans.' Near-perfect German.

Hartmann didn't move. The man put down his pen. He was black. Three stripes; a sergeant. Hartmann had never seen a black man before.

'Empty his pockets.'

Alien hands were pulling at his clothes, patting his chest, and sliding between his thighs.

'Just this, sir.'

In the late sunshine, Hartmann's cigarette case glowed as it slid across the desk. Slowly, the black sergeant put down his pen. A sea of grimy faces was watching from beyond the wire.

'This belongs to you? You didn't steal it?'

It was the voice of a baritone, deep and calm. Hartmann inclined his head. The man's skin was extraordinary, like polished wood, and even in a chair he moved with the grace of a cat. It seemed odd, this elegance, considering where they were. After pondering the case for a moment the American picked it up.

'You're absolutely certain about that?'

Hartmann nodded again.

'Don't you speak?'

Two long black fingers were easing the halves of the case apart. From inside, the photograph of Alize was being lifted out and placed face down on the table. Next to it, with precision, the sergeant laid the now empty case, splayed open along its hinge.

'We're not going to hurt you. We're not going to kill you. Soon you'll be leaving France. We just want to make sure you can't do any more harm. So let's play this game. Me first. My name is Leroy Cooke and I'm a sergeant in the United States Army. Now you.'

'Unteroffizier Max Hartmann. First SS Panzer Division.'

'SS tank commander. Hard core. One of the nasty ones.'

'I hope not. No.'

The American scrutinised the file of papers on his desk. Behind Hartmann's back, the line probably stretched for ever. It was better not to look.

From a shiny pack of Marlboros the sergeant shook a single cigarette and placed it in the corner of his own mouth. From a tunic pocket, he pulled a metal lighter, flinted the wick, and closed his eyes as the strands of tobacco caught fire.

'And if you really are Max Hartmann, who might this be?' With his left hand, the sergeant had picked up the photograph of Alize. In his right, the smoky flame of his lighter was still burning. The two were barely an inch apart. 'Is this Mrs Hartmann? Or a girlfriend, perhaps. Maybe some French tart?'

Alarm was suddenly pumping through the prisoner. 'That's my wife. It's my only picture. Please. Don't.'

But it was already too late. In its death throes, Alize's photograph twisted in the American's hands, pluming acid fumes along the length of his arm. As the flames reached his fingers, he tossed the fragments to the floor.

'How does it feel to be a humiliated by a nigger speaking your language?'

Two pairs of hands held Hartmann back, but the fight was soon gone. As his exhausted body sagged, he slid sideways. A few glowing wisps still hovered briefly above the table and the silver cigarette case had vanished.

'You'll see what you want to see,' he mumbled. 'I can't change that.'

'A very dangerous man is what I see.'

Hartmann looked up. 'And burning that photograph is the start of my rehabilitation?'

Somewhere, a mess tent bell was ringing, blown across the camp by a mild evening breeze. Arc lights were popping on, powered by mobile generators. Every prisoner would need to be interviewed. Darkness wouldn't be allowed to stand in the way. The process would continue all night.

'The thing is, Hartmann, I've got to make a decision about you.'

A few scattered fires had been lit inside the enclosure. Tubes of smoke were bending inland on the wind.

'When you leave this desk you'll be classified by a colour: white, grey or black. The whites are the good guys, the conscripts; the sweet guys who probably feel guilty when their lice get zapped; the ones who wished this war had never started. The greys are the soft-in-the-middle guys. The ones who didn't mind joining up, but who sure as hell don't care that it's finished. And then there's the blacks: the bad guys, the killers; the nasty ones who won't stop until they're stopped. And guess what, Max Hartmann?'

'Surprise me.'

The sergeant had picked up his pen but his eyes were back on his papers. 'I guess both of us are black men now, soldier. Next.'

Hartmann felt a hand on his back and he was pushed through the gate into the pen.

At first it was hard to make things out. There were no lights, only a handful of fires coughing bitter fumes but giving no illumination. Almost every tree in the compound had been stripped and burned. Here and there, a match would strike and a spectral face would blink across the gloom. Everything else was hidden. Sleeping men lay every-where, cocooned in their trench coats. Others stood in anonymous huddles, collars hunched, giving way reluctantly as Hartmann inched deeper into the crowd. As his eyes adjusted he could make out faces, but none he recognised, or expected to.

Some watched him intensely. Most turned away from his uniform. The American had been right, Hartmann realised. He was a black man now.

For what remained of the night, he hunched down close to the perimeter wire. On either side of him, dark shapes grunted and shuffled aside. The smell of human waste seemed horribly close, but he was too weary to investigate, or to care, or even to sleep. Nothing beyond his present nightmare seemed real any longer. The only tangible link to his former life had been incinerated.

When it arrived, the early daylight was a relief, bringing light drizzle out of an uncertain sky. Although the pain in his ribs was excruciating, Hartmann had surprised himself by drifting off into a dreamless stupor for a few hours.

Just a few paces away, a line of men was forming by a cluster of buckets. Most were already overflowing with excrement, and those that were not soon would be. Every now and then, in desperation, a prisoner would rip down his trousers and defecate in the grass.

'Horrible, isn't it?' From deep within his coat, the crouched huddle to his left had spoken. 'It only takes a few days and we're animals again.'

A man's head was appearing. The voice was acquiring a face.

'Unless you accept the view – which seems common among our American friends – that we were animals to begin with.'

He was an older man – in his mid-thirties – and not a fighter either. Even in the dawn grey, his uniform appeared kempt, and the two eyes he'd fixed on Hartmann bulged disturbingly behind the thick lenses of his spectacles. Like everyone else, he was unshaven, but the effect felt contrived; as if the stubble – like the parting dividing his sleek black hair – was an affectation; part of a look engineered for effect, to be maintained whatever the circumstances. When he spoke, the voice was cultured and measured, and his words, which were studiously neutral, emerged from a face that was fleshy and well fed.

'Don't be fooled by the wire. We're no safer inside this cage than we were outside it.'

Over by the pails, a prisoner was weeping. His own dirt was on his outstretched hands.

'If they don't move us soon, we'll be dropping like flies. Cholera, typhoid. It's what happens when you put thousands of men in a cage without a toilet. On the other hand, we might be killing ourselves before too long.'

Hartmann followed the stranger's curious eyes across his grey uniform to the lapel.

'Schutzstaffel. You should feel at home. There really are some very bad people in here, very bad indeed.'

Finally, Hartmann felt moved to respond. 'I'm a black prisoner, apparently. You'd better be careful.'

More people around them were waking up. A fight had broken out over by the buckets. One man was down. Two others were kicking his head. A little warmth was beginning to trickle out of the sky. It felt good to Hartmann to be having a conversation.

'You don't look dangerous,' said the stranger, peering out at the crowd. 'But then who does any more?'

'Actually I'm not really sure I ever was.' Hartmann forced himself to turn, and extended a hand. 'My name is Hartmann, by the way. Max. Do I assume that you're a very bad person too?'

'Excellent. Yes. I think that's where all lasting relationships should start: with doubt and suspicion.' The heavy glasses had slipped along his nose, exposing small, dark eyes. 'But as to whether it is true, I must let others be the judge of that.'

He was Wolfgang Rosterg. He was thirty-four years old, and like Hartmann he spoke near-perfect English. Before the war, he'd worked for two years in London. And before that, he'd travelled and worked all over Europe, picking up fluent Polish and French along the way.

'You're rather old for war,' said Hartmann. 'And talented.'

'I am. Both. Thank you. All the more reason to ensure that I win it.'

Back in Berlin, his home was a nineteenth-century villa on the city's outskirts, where – he presumed – his wife and three children were still living. 'There's a very deep wine cellar and we're a long way from any obvious targets,' he told Hartmann. 'They'll go down and get drunk when they have to.'

For four years his work had kept him beyond the fighting until 1943, when he'd felt compelled to enlist with the Wehrmacht. Now, like almost everyone else, he was wondering what happened next. 'I still thought we'd win when I joined up. Bad decision.'

'No one else did. Not by then. Apart from Goebbels.'

'Yes, but I'm not like you, Hartmann. I'm just a soldier. A Feldwebel – a staff sergeant who hung around out of gunshot range and made sure you lot got ammunition, fuel and food.'

'You look well on it.'

'I like a good meal. That didn't make me bad at my job. And the French are fine cooks.'

Two jeeps full of American soldiers were checking the fence. A solitary Hurricane was flying low over the camp. 'So you're a category white prisoner?'

'No, I'm a black actually.'

Hartmann looked puzzled. 'Me, I understand. Why you?'

'I'm not entirely sure. When they questioned me they seemed more interested in my job before the war.'

'And that was?'

'My father is a manager with an industrial chemicals firm. I. G. Farben.'

'I've heard of them. But why would that even matter?'

'I work for them too. It's what kept me out of the war and got me around Europe.'

'I still don't understand.'

'Nor me, really. It's a huge company and my father is a good Nazi, if you like. He uses slave labour, Jew labour, to make pesticides. Zyklon B. We've got factories in Poland. That's what I was selling when I lived in Britain. I told them all this out there at the gate. They seemed interested.'

Rosterg fell silent. He pushed his spectacles back over his eyes and focused on Hartmann. 'We're killing people out there, in the east. You must know that. They've seen photographs of camps.'

'And Zyklon B?'

'Is a very effective killer of parasites.' He paused again. 'And for some reason, they think I'm a criminal. Or the child of one. So I'm a black. Just like you.'

Hartmann didn't ask any more questions. The man unsettled him. Something wasn't quite right. If Rosterg was lying – which he might be – he didn't really care, or understand.

If he was telling the truth, it would be better not to know.

## 6

While the two men had been talking, the camp had woken up. In the chilly half-light, men were stamping the blood back into their feet, and as the sun fought back, the early rain vaporised on sodden coats.

A sullen army of beaten soldiers was standing in its own smell.

Hartmann rose to his feet and shivered. From deep inside his stomach, he felt the forgotten tug of hunger. The last food he'd tasted had been in a hospital tent.

'What do we eat?'

'This way. It's not safe for you here.'

Rosterg led off along the fence. Close to the gate, Hartmann could see the still-feverish line of desks and the delousing station. Beyond them, hundreds – maybe thousands – more prisoners were jostling towards their turn. A little further on, the two men cut back deep into the compound where snaking queues were forming along tracks worn down into the field. Watched by sleepy guards, Red Cross volunteers had set up long trestle tables. At the end of each one, watery porridge was being slopped out into tin mugs. Further along each table there was bread and cheese and what looked like tinned meat.

Hartmann's hunger rolled over in his belly. To feed so many men would take all day. It could be hours before food passed his lips.

'This way, Max. You'll eat, I promise you.'

As they inched nearer the back of the compound, the ground rose slightly. Here, the stumps of a few trees had survived, between which tarpaulins had been hung for cover. Along one edge of the fence, a narrow stream ran weakly through trampled grass. Clean, fresh water. Damp wood hissed hopelessly in a fire pit around which a handful of men sat in mute expectation. Some were smoking cigarettes. All of them had food. He could smell coffee and hear laughter.

'These are the authentic bad boys, Max,' said Rosterg.

He hadn't needed telling. Every uniform on the knoll was SS, and Hartmann could feel the cold stares of the ordinary soldiers as he threaded his way through them.

'No one can see inside your head. It's what you're wearing on your collar that counts. Never forget that,' said Rosterg. 'I can move freely around the compound because I'm clean. I'm Wehrmacht. But from now on, you should stay up here. We'll all be shipped out pretty soon anyway.'

In the corner, where the fence turned, an oil-stained square of canvas had been spiked back to the barbed wire to form a shelter. Beneath it, a dozen men were chatting loudly. Among them he could make out Zuhlsdorff, with his arm still strapped in a bloodied sling.

A tall figure with a square face was peeling off from the larger group.

'Who have you found now, Rosterg?'

With a theatrical bow, the Feldwebel ushered his new companion forward. 'Yet another recruit for your congregation of righteousness, Herr Goltz.'

'He's called Max Hartmann. I know him.' Zuhlsdorff had stepped forward, holding up his mutilated fingers with a grin. 'He turned our tanks away from the front. It's his fault I'm a cripple and a prisoner.'

The one called Goltz extended his hand. Up close, Hartmann could see that he had no eyebrows, and that his hair was completely white.

'Not true, I'm sure. The boy has some sort of fever, perhaps.' The man was like a living ghost. His skin was pale and his pearl-coloured eyes seemed in constant movement. 'It's an affliction, a very mild one. I compensate for it in other ways.'

For an uncomfortable moment, Hartmann clasped the offered hand. 'I didn't mean to stare. I'm sorry.'

'Don't be. If they're feeling brave, people tell me I look like a corpse. But really I'm Joachim Goltz. Unteroffizier. Twelfth Panzers. Very much alive. You want food?'

Nineteen years old at most, Hartmann guessed. An albino, maybe.

Or near enough. The ultimate Aryan. The only eyes he'd ever seen like that before had been those of a husky.

'You can't possibly know how badly. Thanks. And a cigarette maybe?'

Zuhlsdorff was still hovering nearby. From his trouser pocket, he unearthed a fresh blue packet and a bar of Hershey's chocolate. Hartmann seized it gratefully and ripped off the paper.

'That is so good. How did you get it?'

'We trade. We steal. People want our clean water.'

'Your clean water?'

'You can go now, Zuhlsdorff. Goodbye.' With a hand on his shoulder, Goltz steered Hartmann under the cover of the canvas awning. 'Sorry, but I try to keep out of the sun. And Zuhlsdorff can be rather annoying.'

'You've noticed.'

'Light?' The two men sat down, and Hartmann leaned in to the flame of a metal lighter. 'What he said isn't true, is it?'

'It looks easy when you don't have to make the decisions. No, it isn't true. We did what damage we could. We were captured. Everyone here was captured.'

'That's true,' said Goltz. 'And yet these Americans still seem a little afraid of us.'

For a few seconds, Hartmann's head was spinning. The rush from the tobacco had overpowered the sugar, and the hordes in the distance fused into a single green blur.

'How long have you been here?' he asked.

'Four days. It seems the most time people spend here is five.'

'And after that?'

'We think America.' Goltz took the cigarette from Hartmann's hand and inhaled. 'Look at them all down there. Toerags. Cowards. Traitors. Most of them couldn't wait to surrender. But who the fuck's told them the war's over?'

Hartmann remained silent, his eyes locked on the swimming mass of prisoners. Gradually, the stockade had come back into focus, but his thoughts had not. He wanted to be sick, and Goltz's eyes were probing him like needles.

'Of course, the senior officers are kept apart. Somewhere else. Don't know where. Soon, I expect, they'll try to separate SS from Wehrmacht.'

Hartmann looked genuinely surprised.

'You're wondering why? It's simple. So long as the Wehrmacht boys can see us up here, they'll never completely relax. Never quite give up the war.'

'So the Americans won't relax until we're separated?'

'Exactly.'

'And where does Rosterg fit into this? He's Wehrmacht, isn't he?'

'Ears and eyes, Max. Ears and eyes.'

All the next day, Hartmann kept his head down. Exhaustion was common among new arrivals and everyone could see he'd put up a fight. The purple bruises around his eyes were proof of that, and no one questioned his detachment. When he wasn't asleep, he rested back against a fencepost and watched.

Rosterg had been right. The camp had split itself in two.

On the lower ground, around two thousand soldiers milled in amorphous knots. Looking down on them from their privileged corner, a couple of hundred SS wrestled with their own frustrations under the glacial scrutiny of their self-elected leader Joachim Goltz. It wasn't difficult to explain his pre-eminence. At least four people had told Hartmann the legend already.

Like Hartmann, Goltz had fought in Russia, but when he took his tank into battle at Kursk, Goltz had barely been eighteen. By the time he got home, he was a war hero, a wholesale killer and an SS-Scharführer with a chest of medals and a handshake from Hitler.

If the stories were true, he'd destroyed twenty-two Soviet tanks in an hour. He'd also acquired a chilling hauteur well suited to his colourless features, his disarming eloquence and his steady rise through the ranks. As capture loomed in France, he'd apparently closed the hatch on his tank, removed the pin from a stick grenade and clutched it to his chest. Two minutes later, when it hadn't gone off, he was dragged into captivity screaming vile Teutonic obscenities at the Americans whose comrades he had been routinely slaughtering for weeks.

Through half-closed eyes, Hartmann used his time to observe the teenager's operation. It certainly wasn't Goltz's physical strength that drew people around him. Close up, he looked like a consumptive weakling and it was only when he spoke that his presence exuded authentic danger, the promise of which ensured a constant circle of disciples. Whenever he whispered an instruction – or handed down an opinion – everyone stopped to listen. Most of the time, however, no one did very much at all.

It was like sitting in a cage full of buzzards.

Virtually nothing could happen in the compound without Goltz's knowing. Sheltered only by the August sky, private conversations were impossible, and the place was overrun by informants who'd concluded that the SS were a threat they couldn't ignore. Dissent and disloyalty were to be rooted out and punished. Defeatism was a heresy. Anyone who deviated from absolute trust in the Führer was at risk.

Wearily, Hartmann tried to remember what he'd said to Rosterg; too much, probably. Be very careful, Max, he thought. We are turning on ourselves. They will be watching you too.

It was almost dark when he awoke. Even in the thinning light, he could see that the camp's population had been swelling all day. Now, no open ground was visible, and the food queues – if there were any – had been swallowed by the crush. From a distance, the rise and fall of so many heads was hypnotic. Beyond the main gate, the arc lights had clicked back on. He could hear the generators ticking, and periodically a shot rang out above the noise. Keeping order, he presumed. Another red line drawn through a name on a list.

'You ready to eat?' It was Zuhlsdorff. 'Mind if I join you?'

It was odd the way they'd been thrown together again. Odder still how tenacious the boy's curiosity seemed to be. No matter how cold Hartmann's shoulder was, Zuhlsdorff never appeared to notice. Now he was even bringing him soup. Hartmann frowned.

'We're never going to be friends. I'm confused. Why the chocolate? Why the food?'

'I heard what they did to that picture of your girl.'

Hartmann spooned into his lukewarm broth, and ignored him. Food up on the knoll seemed in easy supply.

'Goltz says you're OK. I think he's wrong.'

'Like I give a shit what you think.'

'Listen. If you're feeling up to it, there might be some fun tonight.'

There was meat in the soup. Even half-cold, it tasted good.

'Joachim's bored. He's asked me and you to bring someone in.'

'Bring who in for what exactly?'

'A soldier called Wirz. Heinz Wirz. He's been telling everyone he can't wait to get home. Goltz just wants a word with him.'

'A word?'

'We should go in a few minutes. If you're feeling up to it.' With his teeth, Zuhlsdorff was tearing the foil from another bar of chocolate. It was a test. It had to be. They were checking him out. 'We're to meet Rosterg by the main gate and he'll take us to this Wirz. Are you in?'

Hartmann put down his bowl, and hauled himself on to his feet. 'Just don't go too fast.'

No one stood in their way. Dozing men either rolled aside, or were kicked aside, and as they moved deeper, private conversations died. Even in the dark, their presence emanated threat. When one prisoner grunted irritation, Hartmann slapped the cigarette from his mouth. 'Go to hell!'

Zuhlsdorff looked back with an approving smirk. That would get back to Goltz, for sure. A little easy credit would do him no harm whatsoever.

At the main gates, Rosterg was standing alone in the shadow of a tall post. Beyond him, under the floodlights, the admissions desks were still swamped.

'It never ends, Max,' he hissed. 'Germany is emptying of men.'

As he slithered off along the inside of the fence, the two men followed at a distance.

'We just have to watch his eyes,' explained Zuhlsdorff. 'He'll make it clear which of them is Wirz without giving himself away.'

A nervous pulse seemed to beat through the compound. To Hartmann it felt like a vast herd of terrified beasts, feigning slumber.

Up ahead, they could make out Rosterg's silvered glasses bobbing in the moonlight. He'd stopped. A handful of men was blocking his way and a single furious voice was raised, supported quickly by others.

Zuhlsdorff looked nervously back at Hartmann. 'They're on to him.'

Cunning no longer mattered. Emboldened by darkness, the herd was stirring. A circle of men had tightened around Rosterg. Two of them were pulling him to the ground and a filthy cap had been clamped over his mouth to stifle the squealing.

'Which of you is Heinz Wirz?' Hartmann asked. Hartmann's whisper was lost in the noise of the scuffle and Rosterg was already down. In a few seconds, he'd be torn apart. Hartmann wrestled forward until a gap opened and the beating stopped. Twenty or so soldiers stepped back to look at his uniform. All it took then was a whisper.

'One more time. Which of you is Heinz Wirz?'

No one answered. No one moved, apart from the figure holding the gag over Rosterg's face.

'I'm Wirz.'

'Fuck. I know you,' hissed Hartmann. 'What's that in your hand?'

The soldier unclenched his fist. He was holding a black felt beret.

'Roll up your sleeve.'

'I know you too,' said Wirz, grinning. 'I've a tattoo of a heart. So what? Is that my crime? What have I done? What do you want?'

'We know what you are.' Zuhlsdorff had stepped forward, pulling an iron bar from inside his tunic. As he raised his arm to strike, Hartmann stepped in front of him.

'Fuck you, Nazi. We all think the same here. All of us,' spat Wirz. 'The war's over. We lost. Hitler lost. You can't silence us all. You're on your own.'

'Wrong,' said Zuhlsdorff. 'Take a look.'

Wirz's confederates had already melted back into the black huddle of the camp. When Hartmann glanced round to make sure he was unharmed, Rosterg had gone too.

Standing alone, the boy's courage dissolved. 'Listen. I just want to go home now. That's all. I'm sorry.'

'You left your violin on the bus.'

'Back to my parents. Is that really so bad?'

'Don't panic,' hushed Hartmann. 'We only want a little talk. You'll get back home. We all will.'

'That's not for you to decide, Hartmann.'

'He's a fucking German, Zuhlsdorff. One of us.'

'Please don't tell them I deserted,' whispered Wirz.

'I won't. I promise.'

## 7

When the three returned to the elevated corner, the remnants of a fire were still burning and Goltz was rotating his hands over the last of its flames. Behind him, sitting on their haunches, were another dozen or so men, but it was too dark to see their faces.

'So this is Wirz?' Goltz stood up and placed his right hand under the terrified soldier's chin. 'He's a nice-looking boy. Does he know what he's done wrong?'

'I'm sorry. I'm sorry. Shit. You're fucking hurting me.' Tears were running down the boy's face. The ends of Goltz's fingers were pushing into his neck.

'Sorry? Sorry isn't enough, soldier. Nothing like.'

Hartmann saw nothing of what followed. As Goltz released his grip, a shapeless pack of men slid alongside, and with one grim sideways look the quivering boy simply vanished.

'He just needs a little light training, Max,' said Goltz. 'That's all. We'll soon put him right. Rest those bones. You did well.'

The following morning, over lukewarm coffee, Wirz's fate wasn't even mentioned and Hartmann knew better than to ask. The skinned knuckles on Zuhlsdorff's hand told him enough. Everyone else's silence – and Goltz's absence – filled in the rest.

If it had been a test, he presumed he'd passed.

The kid wouldn't be dead, but his teeth would be scattered around the hill. When, or if, he ever opened his mouth again, the message would be clear. The war wasn't over until Hitler said so. And if Wirz still had any functioning brain cells, he'd be passing the news on to his mates.

Hartmann lay back again and closed his eyes. It was a fine sunrise and even bad coffee tasted good, especially when your ribcage was on fire. Beyond the wire, the bells of a church were clanging. It was a glorious sound. He wondered why that church had survived the shelling, and who was ringing its bells. Out there, he guessed, everything was struggling back to normal.

Farmers' daughters would be pulling flutes of golden bread from fiery ovens. In a few weeks it would be harvest time; by day, every lane would be jammed by wagons laden with stooks of corn, followed by sour red wine all night. Where will we be then, he wondered. All the certainties in his life were crumbling away and somehow the war was getting more complicated, not less.

The enemy was on the inside of the wire now.

'You're awake early, Max.' It was Rosterg, doing his rounds. 'I owe you some thanks for last night.'

Hartmann leaned up on his elbow, steering carefully around the pain in his chest. Through the wire, he could see a Red Cross ambulance pulled up by the gate. Three stretchers, each carrying a body wrapped in a sheet, were being eased into the back. People were dying already, or being killed. If the typhus took hold, this was where it would all end.

'You seem like a useful person to keep alive, although don't think it makes us friends.'

Rosterg laughed. 'We speak English, you and I. We're clever. That makes both of us useful. To everyone.'

'And the boy last night?'

'It isn't safe to ignore people like Goltz. Not yet, anyway.'

'But you're army, you're not SS. Just keep the fuck out of it.'

'I've told you. I'm here to make it through. I've got a wife. I've got children. I've got a life. It's no more interesting than that.'

'I don't think I can do this.'

'You can. You can if you've got something to get back for.' Rosterg smirked. 'Besides, we're all going to be leaving here soon anyway.'

'America?' Hartmann desperately hoped not. If the rumours were true, at least one ship loaded with prisoners had already been sunk by U-boats on its way to the United States. Germans killed by their own. It was insane. Everyone on board had perished, but in the gossip around the buckets, the men had reluctantly concluded that drowning might just have the edge over dysentery.

'Great Britain. The United Kingdom,' declared Rosterg, clapping Hartmann on the back. 'We're going to get there before Hitler.'

Whoever they were, the Feldwebel's sources were impeccable. Daylight had brought a palpable shift in the compound's uneasy dynamic.

Since midnight, no more prisoners had been allowed in. Extra food was being crated in for breakfast, and by mid-morning the pattern of activity around the gates was showing some change. For the first time, British officers had been seen near the compound. The desks were all folded away, and, as the sun peaked, lines of armed GIs started to muster at either side of the entrance.

When the gates were finally dragged open, instructions barked through tin megaphones began to filter across the packed square. Here and there, clapping broke out. Up on Goltz's hill, a lone voice began chirruping '*Sieg Heil*' until it was silenced by a cacophonous drum roll of ironic cheers. Then, in densely packed single file, the first line of prisoners commenced its expectant shuffle from the camp.

Behind them, an emaciated army dressed in rags calmly waited its turn.

It was three hours before Hartmann moved.

Ahead of him, the makeshift holding camp was emptying, soldier by soldier. Ruined patches of grass, strewn with heaps of smouldering wood, were becoming visible in every direction, and across the entire field hung the rank smell of the unwashed. It cheered him to see how many of them were smiling. Grinning teeth flashed from bearded faces grooved by anxiety, and even deep hunger could not hide the spring in the men's steps. The further from home they all went, Hartmann had realised, the closer to home they all got.

For the first time in weeks, it felt glorious to be alive. Patriotic marching songs were bursting out everywhere. Two soldiers were even surreptitiously goose-stepping towards the gate. And then suddenly, with the sky threatening thunder, it was his own turn to inch forward and be ticked off a list, before joining the dusty trail to the coast.

It was so wonderful to be moving.

Somewhere in front of him, Goltz and his entourage had forged ahead, dragging silence in their wake. Behind them he could relax. Out on the road alone, nursing his bruises, it was easy to shuffle anonymously among strangers and the fellow-wounded.

As they had been before, the lanes were choked with military traffic, and the wayside was littered with twisted junk, but there were no corpses and his head reeled with the scent of wild stocks and freshly scythed meadow. Had he craved it, escape would have been easy. Only a handful of gum-crushing GIs guarded their flanks, and the bramble-choked hedges, in places, stood as tall as a house.

'It's tempting, isn't it? Escape?' The words were mumbled, almost incomprehensible. 'But you wouldn't get far. Or at least I wouldn't. Not in this state.'

Hartmann swivelled in their direction. It was Wirz. Or what was left of Wirz.

'How do I look? Do you think my mum will recognise me?'

Hartmann turned away.

'I'll take that for a no, then.'

Only his right eye was visible. The left was lost behind a scarlet globe of swollen cheek. Nails had been torn from several fingers, and his lower jaw appeared to be held in place by a bandage which ran under his chin and over the top of his head. Through the pulpy maw of his mouth, a few cockeyed teeth were still showing. It was a miracle the boy could even mumble.

'Jesus. What did they do? Stupid question. I'm so sorry.'

'I should have kept my trap shut. It's just taking some getting used to.'

'What is?'

'That you lot are more dangerous than the Americans.'

'I'm not your enemy. I'm just dressed like your enemy.'

For an hour, the two men drooped back into silence. They didn't know each other, and, for each of them, marching without pain required intense concentration.

By late afternoon, the light across the fields was still quivering with heat. Deprived of water, dozens of men were dropping in their tracks. Along the line, the morning's optimistic rush had been displaced by stifled, angry complaints.

'Back in the forest, where did you go? When you left the bus?'

'Not far. The woods were full of their soldiers. I only lasted two days.'

'You didn't take your violin.'

'It wasn't mine. I stole it.'

Somewhere up ahead, a single pistol shot interrupted them. A few minutes later, the pair passed an SS man face up in a ditch. Blood was pumping thickly from a hole in his neck. One pale eye was frozen open. At his side, a young GI searched for souvenirs, while another rained abuse on the dead man's head. Both of the Americans were black.

'What's he saying?' mumbled Wirz.

'He's saying that the dead German had just spat in his face.'

'Why is he shouting at the body?'

'He's asking him, "Who's the master race now?"'

Wirz stared into the ditch for a few seconds, pulled out his penis and began to urinate on the corpse.

'What the fuck are you doing?'

A stream of blood-streaked water was splashing down on the dead man's head. The two American soldiers were laughing.

'Last night,' whispered Wirz, pointing at his own face, 'that creep did most of the damage. The weird-looking white one just watched.'

'You know you're dead if they find out.'

'They'll find out,' said Wirz, tucking himself back in.

The pair moved on. No one was singing any more. All the banter had stopped. Nothing could be heard but the clump of blistered feet too weary to march. Leaving the camp had felt like a turning point but within just a few hours the surge of expectation had collapsed. Hands were stuffed in pockets, shoulders were hunched, and every face signalled its owner's despair.

With every bone-tired step, each man could sense another trauma was near. Many still privately expected to be shot. None of them seemed to care. Above them, in growing numbers, deluded seagulls were clamouring in the hope of morsels, and a biting salt wind was building from the north under mountainous clouds.

Hartmann remembered it well. 'Smell that, Heinz. Fill your lungs with the sea.'

Now, the road wasn't just dirt, it was sand, skittering around their boots. Shattered concrete pillboxes dotted the horizon and in every direction the traffic was building. Lorries and trucks thundered past billowing black fumes. Beyond a steep crest of dunes, creamy barrage balloons could be seen tugging at their restraints. Four Spitfires streaked low and loud over their heads, and as the column laboured forward, the ocean finally came into view.

For the second time in my life, thought Hartmann. Had Koenig come this way too? Or might he?

Running east and west, the beach was alive. Tanks spewed from a line of landing craft. Above the tideline, forklift trucks buzzed around huge mountains of crates. A city of massive windowed tents billowed and snapped. Everywhere Hartmann turned, men and machines seemed to be swarming across the sand, and beyond them the sea was peppered with ships from which smaller craft shuttled in relays to the shore.

Looking up, he saw the dots of a bomber squadron moving silently east. Looking down, he saw cranes and low-loaders hauling field guns up off the beach. In ordered lines, untroubled by any resistance, thousands of fresh troops were heading inland. And even from a mile away, their jeers could be clearly heard, carried towards the Germans on the brisk summer wind.

For the next hour, the footsore convoy marched west along the beach. At times, where the sand was soft, progress was painfully slow, but night was coming and the guards goaded them forward.

As the sky pinked, lights came on all over the beachhead. Countless pairs of headlamps flickered up through the dune grasses. Invisible machinery groaned, and foreign voices swirled among the clanking of steel and cable. Soon, the men were scarcely more than inky silhouettes swaying unsteadily in the blackness. To his left Hartmann could still make out Wirz. Since the shooting, they had stuck together. Everyone else was just a smudge in the dark.

'People will smell us before they see us, Heinz.'

But Wirz wasn't listening. Wirz was tuned in to something else. Since reaching the coastline, their march had hugged the edge of the dune hills. Now they were wheeling sharply, and the only thing in front of them was the sea. 'Perfect. They're going to drown us all.'

'I don't think so. That would definitely be more our style.'

For the first time, as the column wheeled, Hartmann could see its full length marked out against the darkening sea; a black serpent slithering across a watery strand. A thousand men? Two thousand men? It was impossible to say.

Beyond the breaking waves, sky and sea were no longer separable. Giant warships seemed to be levitating, not floating, their distant portholes flickering like neat lines of stars. At last, Hartmann could make out where they were going.

Ahead of them, a dozen landing craft had pulled in close to the shoreline and each one had lowered its loading bay doors on to the sand. Icy water was swirling around Hartmann's feet. The tide had turned. Instructions were being screamed in every direction. If there had been a plan, it was dissolving fast in the rush of seawater.

For the second time in that long day, Hartmann awaited his turn.

'We can't stay together. Not for much longer. Understand?'

Wirz nodded. The bandage around his chin was red with blood.

Driven by the guards, the prisoners waded thigh-deep towards the craft. As each one filled, its watertight door rose, and the engines screamed into reverse. Inside, the men groaned disapproval. There was nowhere to sit, they could not see out, and there was no cover over their heads.

Backing into the heaving water, the vessels pitched fiercely, and a rising wind tossed spray over and into the hold. Boat after boat was quickly loaded and dispatched. No one was ticking off names. Segregation had been abandoned. Black, grey or white, suddenly all that mattered was getting these people off this beach and away from the war.

One craft was left; one more metal box to fill. Hartmann looked around. A few hundred prisoners were left at the water's edge. It felt good to stride into the waves, feeling with his feet for the hard edge of the ramp. Behind him, Wirz splashed his wounds and gasped sharply as the salt bit into the exposed flesh. Hartmann leaned back, offered his arm and pulled the injured man up on to the warm steel plates of the deck. When the last prisoner had stumbled in, the hydraulic door closed and the throttle roared.

'We can't be going all the way to England in this, surely,' shouted Wirz.

Every wave sent the luckless passengers lurching, first one way, then the other. And since there was no room to sit, each clung on to his neighbour. Only when the craft had turned, and was navigating away from the shoreline, did the motion settle. Then, through slit holes in each side, they could make out the other vessels, their engines straining against the wind and the current.

'Not to England. Not in these,' said Hartmann. 'To transport ships.'

Almost every trace of daylight had drained away. Black shapes shifting on the water were the only things left: the tell-tale outline of a funnel; the tapered barrels of immense guns. From what little he could see, the water was choked with ships of every size. And as the engines slowed, he found his gaze climbing up the inky flanks of one of them. Looking back down was a line of curious faces.

Somewhere a horn was sounding. Ropes were snaking out of the night on to the deck of their landing craft. Invisible hands were securing warps, and the front ramp was clanking down on to a wooden pontoon.

Now everything made sense. Lashed to the transport ship, the floating raft provided a makeshift jetty for the flotilla which had steamed from the beach. Draped down the side of the transport ship was a wide rope net. Already it was crawling with prisoners from the first boats, feebly hauling themselves to the top.

As the carrier boat rocked in the swell, the net slid sickeningly from side to side. Only a handful of men were moving quickly. Among the sure-footed prisoners, Hartmann had already spotted Zuhlsdorff, climbing fast and doggedly hooking the hemp rungs in his left elbow to protect his ruined hand. Wirz had seen him too.

'You people are indestructible. You're like syphilis.'

Away from the shore, the night was bitterly cold. Nothing mattered now but the net and soon it would be his turn. Around him, the last batch of prisoners stepped on to the floating pontoon and tottered to the side of the ship. Up above, they could hear curses and see the desperate scuffling shapes of exhausted men. For the first time in days, Hartmann's broken ribs thumped with pain. One step at a time, he thought. No heroics. Wherever this ends, it cannot be here.

As a space opened up on the rigging, Hartmann hauled himself forward. He'd eaten well at the camp and felt strong. He was also buoyed by a surge of unexpected vigour. Somewhere, he felt certain, Alize was alive and well. His war was over and an adventure was unfolding which he fully expected to survive.

Grimacing, but moving strongly, he powered upwards and flopped over on to the deck, where soot was falling from the smokestack like black snow. Somewhere deep beneath his feet, a battery of pistons trembled. Snaking across the foredeck, an anchor chain slid weed-glistening from the sea and coiled itself around a giant winch.

Alien voices and bells rang out, and the ship eased away from its mooring. As it wheeled, Hartmann caught one last sight of the beach and then they were building speed towards England. A series of deep shudders rattled from bow to stern, and a stiff breeze began to blow.

Quietly, each prisoner had found himself somewhere to sit. Sailors with blankets were passing among them. Others dispensing water and biscuits. Every square inch of the deck was covered by the grey-green serge of a foreign army, huddled around lifeboats or clinging to the stays. If Wirz had got any sense, he'd have hidden himself away. Very soon, no one would be in a fit state to look for him anyway. As the ship wallowed, men had already begun pushing towards the rail to be sick and a hideous lump was rising fast from Hartmann's belly.

When he bent forward to retch, a mutilated hand tapped his arm. Zuhlsdorff.

'You should be with us.'

Hartmann straightened. The boy seemed to live in his shadow.

'We're over there. We should stick together.'

He could see them now: a dark scrum of grey uniforms, standing in deferential orbit around the bloodless spectre of Goltz. Hard eyes turned his way to watch as Zuhlsdorff steered him between the sleeping bodies of soldiers.

'Look who I've found.'

Goltz stepped half a pace forward. The red glow from a steaming light high on the mast slanted across his face. 'Max Hartmann. You choose unlikely friends.'

'To be honest, they tend to choose me.'

Goltz smiled and leaned forward to poke the lightning insignia on Hartmann's tunic. 'See this? It's not sensible to get too attached to anything else.'

Without warning, the ship lurched sharply to port. A deep groan rose from the darkness and Goltz plunged forward into Hartmann's arms.

For a second, their faces were almost touching. Each man could smell the other's breath. Through the rags of his uniform, Hartmann could feel the eerie weakness in Goltz's body.

'Sleep tight, Max,' whispered Goltz as the two men pulled apart.

'*Heil Hitler*,' said Hartmann.

By the following morning, almost every prisoner on board had been sick. The few of them who had seen the sea before had never been on a boat, not in waves like this. Only a handful of prisoners appeared immune – survivors pulled from sinking German ships. The rest had endured a frightful night of clammy disorientation.

If he sat down, Hartmann felt certain that he would die. Even in the faint morning light, hours after puking away the last dregs of his stomach, he was still retching foul air. Along the edge of the boat, his weakened fingers clutched a cold metal rail. With a furious heave he pulled himself forward until his stomach was tight against the bulwark and he could look down on to the gunmetal-grey sea and feel the cooling bow-spray on his bruised face.

When the ship corkscrewed violently, Hartmann's mouth opened, diesel fumes flooded his nostrils and his empty stomach heaved rotten gas into the wind. He wasn't alone. In every direction – bow to stern, port and starboard – the guard rail was jammed tight with the sorry spectacle of retching prisoners. Whenever the boat pitched, a foul-smelling slick slid from one side to the other which no one made any attempt to avoid. All the men craved now was a sight of land, any land. After so many hours at sea, the will to live had gone overboard with everything they'd ever eaten, and when the British guards circulated with fresh water, no one refused.

'Here. Drink this.'

With an effort, Hartmann turned his shivering gaze from the sea, and took the mug from Zuhlsdorff's outstretched hand. Old blood was scabbing across the bandages. 'Have you pissed in it?'

'I thought about it.'

Hartmann looked away. These past few weeks had thrown them together, but it was an accident, no more. Hopefully England would soon throw all of them apart. Zuhlsdorff's orthodoxy made him far too dangerous.

Under a brightening sky, visibility was improving. From a distant brown smudge, the English coastline was finally filling out with detail. He could make out farms and hedgerows, and the faint pulse of a lighthouse.

As the shoreline drew closer, the swell steadied. Two vertical shafts of sunlight struck the sea either side of their boat, illuminating more ships jammed with ashen-faced men. Beyond that, and behind them, Hartmann knew there were more: a vast flotilla of steel buckets awash with vomit; the same buckets that had carried an invading army south just two months before.

'We're the lucky ones really,' he muttered, turning back to Zuhlsdorff. But Zuhlsdorff had gone, and Rosterg had taken his place. He looked rested, and freshly washed.

'Yes, I agree, Max. Although I'm not sure that's a sentiment it would be wise to share with your new chums.'

The two men looked out across the eastern shoreline of the Isle of Wight. In the morning light, the cliffs shone like new teeth.

'We'll be in the Solent soon. I went sailing there once. Nineteen thirty-six. Took a boat out down the coast to Penzance. Rotten seas. Ended up catching the slow train back all along the south coast.'

A bad knot was tightening rapidly in Hartmann's stomach. Something was wrong. 'Just now. Where did Zuhlsdorff go?'

'You're interested? I rather thought you loathed him.'

'Something's happening, isn't it?'

'I'm afraid you've lost me, Max.'

Wirz. It could only be Wirz. Shit. Hartmann turned his back on the sea and swept his eyes across the foredeck. Nothing.

'Looking for anyone special?'

'Fuck you, Rosterg. Fuck you.'

'He should have been more careful where he pissed, Max. That's a lesson for us all.'

He had to find him. He had to be somewhere. The previous night, he'd watched him climb the net. After that, they'd kept apart. Wirz had known why. Getting back, getting out. That was all that mattered now.

If he could get off the boat, Wirz might just have a chance. On it, he was doomed. But he couldn't hide for long. His face was too mashed. And he was unfinished business. Where had he gone? Dimly, Hartmann remembered that the soldier had headed right from the top of the net, towards the back of the boat. Fewer people there. More places to disappear. In the darkness, Hartmann had turned left, back into the company of Goltz.

Where the fuck was he?

Down each side of the ship, dozing men cursed when he lifted the blankets from their faces. Others simply watched, bemused. Under the fast-warming sun, the deck had begun to steam. The long night was over. Ashen-faced soldiers were heaving themselves up to see the chalky coves and emerald fields. No one wanted to know what the wild-eyed man in the SS tunic was doing. Or why he was muscling them furiously out of his way.

Between him and the stern, there was just one last bundle of men. A few paces ahead, he could see the Royal Ensign snapping on its pole. From each corner of the flag, frayed ends streamed out over the sea. As the ship turned into the wind, the cloth suddenly sagged and then stiffened with a crack. Like a bullet. Every head turned, and Hartmann pushed on. Now only two men were ahead of him.

'Just in time, Max,' said Zuhlsdorff.

Wirz had been bound at the wrists, slung across the rail and hung out over the end of the ship. Only his face and arms were still visible, but there was no sign of life. Either he was unconscious or he was already dead. Stuffed in what was left of his mouth was a black felt beret.

From his bloodied wrists, a long rope ran three times around a thick steel winch and then back into the hands of a soldier Hartmann had never seen before. As he took in the scene, the soldier flicked the line, momentarily relieving the friction on the drum.

Wirz's body yanked downwards and a scream curled back over the side of the ship. He was alive. Just two coils remained.

'Who is he, Zuhlsdorff? Make him stop.'

'That's not going to be easy, Max. Your friend pissed on the face of his dead brother.'

Somewhere far beneath Wirz's dangling legs, the propellers surged hungrily. The soldier twitched the warp again. One coil was left and the only part of Wirz still visible was his mangled arms.

'I don't know your name, but I'm asking you to stop. You can end this now. No one has to die.'

The stranger nodded and released the end of his rope.

For a few seconds, nothing happened. Then, gathering speed quickly, the rope's friction relinquished its grip on the winch. With a vicious lash, the last few feet broke free and followed the tumbling body of Heinz Wirz down over the edge.

By the time Hartmann could look over, there was absolutely nothing to see. Nothing but the seagulls and the line of foamy wake which seemed to be pointing all the way back to Germany.

# Confidential: 3/9/44
## Ref: 456921GH/lkj

*From:  Directorate of Prisoners of War*
*To:     Home Office (various)*

*There has been a lot of speculation. These are the somewhat alarming facts.*

*If you recall, General Montgomery's 21st Army Group expected to take 1,000 prisoners a day by D+10. The actual figure by just D+3 was 6,000 a day; a number that has been swamped by a further 47,000 in June, 36,000 in July and 150,000 in August. Furthermore, in the wake of current engagements, in particular around the so-called Falaise 'pocket', we are anticipating a further 300,000 men to fall into Allied hands by the end of September.*

*Given the staggering volume, it is perhaps no surprise that satisfactory segregation of these prisoners is proving difficult. Recent captives have included significant numbers of highly motivated young SS fighters whose capacity — and wish — to perpetuate their struggle should not be underestimated. SS infiltration of German army groups is common, and there have been countless reports of punishment beatings. We conclude, therefore, that the risk of more serious, sustained episodes of organised resistance is high and growing.*

*There is now an urgent need to review our vetting/interrogation procedures, while accelerating the construction of appropriate secure accommodation in both Great Britain and the United States. Detailed plans for both those needs are attached for discussion in today's working party.*

# 8

## Late August, 1944
## Portsmouth to London

Hartmann stared out across the empty sea.

It would be hours – maybe days – before anyone realised Wirz had disappeared. There'd be no urgency to ask many questions. And without any witnesses, his family could be told anything. Missing in action; believed drowned; shot while trying to escape? Whatever half-truths trickled back, it would come to the same thing. The boy should have been at school, thought Hartmann. Or lying in a field chewing grass. Not a meal for fish in an ocean the colour of gruel.

Apart from himself, no one seemed to have noticed. All over the boat, the mood was lifting. Zuhlsdorff had vanished and two military policemen were shovelling their human cargo into some semblance of order. Hartmann took one final futile look seawards, and followed.

Immense warps were being uncoiled, and a hum of anticipation was building among the drab throng of men. For the first time in twelve hours, the swell had relented. Between the broad banks of the Solent, the waters were flat, and the dark mass of a busy port was closing in on both sides. From every possible vantage point, prisoners jostled for a view; an invading army without a single weapon between them.

Hartmann, like all of them, was astonished. Hadn't the Luftwaffe reduced England's great cities to smoking dust and bones? And yet here, for mile after mile, the riverside thrummed with activity and purpose. Alongside immense destroyers, dense ranks of American merchant ships waited patiently while cranes swung back and forth over holds bursting with cargo. Line after line of windowless warehouses reached back from the quay, and everywhere they looked, lorries and trucks buzzed with ferocious purpose. How many lies had they been fed?

He remembered Koenig telling him about storage sheds full of American butter that had burned outside Portsmouth for days, and how the city's streets had supposedly run with golden fat. He remembered a headline, too; something Goering had said about bombing Britain back to the Middle Ages. Goering or one of those other fat greasy fucks. Whoever, whenever, it hadn't happened. All lies. Fucking lies. Just a few rubble-ringed craters where buildings had been. From this distance, under a perfect morning sky, the place looked unscathed.

Hartmann scrutinised the ruins of his uniform. Unlike us. We won't be quite what they expected either.

'Have you noticed?' Rosterg's arm had slid around his waist. 'None of us ever asks what's happening next. Or where we're going. Or who we're going with. All they have to do is bellow at us and point.'

As the ship drew alongside its mooring, a deep tremor passed through the vessel, and the funnel disgorged one final cloud of filth.

'What did you expect? We lost. It's over. Now we do what they tell us.'

'No, Max. You're quite wrong. It isn't over at all.'

It was always the same with this man; every word he uttered felt like an examination. With men like Goltz, you knew where things stood. Rosterg, on the other hand, slithered around this new world like a bad smell. Even his face was a mystery. Behind the distorting lenses of his spectacles, Rosterg's eyes often appeared misshapen, offering no discernible expression Hartmann could usefully interpret.

'They didn't have to kill him. He'd got the message.'

But Rosterg was no longer listening. With clockwork efficiency, the ship had been made fast to the wharf and a gangplank was being wheeled to the rail. Down on the quayside a mustachioed officer with a polished stick was screaming instructions.

'You see what I mean, Max. They point. We go. Welcome to the great British empire.'

The night before, out on the beach, there had been confusion. Here, there was none. In the Channel behind them, a line of ships heavy with yet more prisoners awaited their turn. Soon they would all be steaming back to France for more. Everything now depended on speed. Urged on by tired-looking soldiers carrying machine guns, Hartmann walked shakily down the wooden ramp watched by a small contingent of flat-capped dock workers.

Two long lines of prisoners soon began to stretch out along the quay. Some still wore their metal helmets. Most sported crumpled military-issue caps pulled low over faces grained with exhaustion. Every one of them looked – and was – desperately young. When the British asked for names, they answered in whispers. Shuffling feet rasped nervously across the concrete. Not one man seemed capable of standing still. They're afraid, thought Hartmann. I'm afraid. We're all afraid.

This time, there wasn't far to march. For a mile, the cobblestoned quay ran straight towards the city. On their right was the oil-flecked sea, slurping back on the ebb tide. To their left, an unbroken wall of warehouses, shuttered by immense sliding doors. As they moved forward, Hartmann imagined a thump of triumph returning to the men's stride. Just so long as you didn't look too closely, they had done it. They were on English soil; a German army heading proudly towards London.

Or somewhere.

Inland, the sky danced with ragged silk balloons for the Luftwaffe bombers that no longer flew and the docks hummed to the industrious scurry of forklift trucks. As the wharf gave way to red-bricked terraces, the men's faces brightened. Standing in almost every doorway, clusters of brightly dressed young women had come to watch the spectacle. Against their drab homes, they looked like spring flowers.

A few yards ahead of him, Hartmann watched as Zuhlsdorff unwrapped his hand and waved it towards the spectators. When he added a blown kiss, a salvo of gestures and abuse flew back in his direction. Puzzled, he turned to his friends. 'What's she saying?'

Hartmann leaned forward. 'She says that even for a German, you've got a tiny dick.'

From so close, every soldier had inhaled the perfume and seen the girls' glossy, scarlet lips. Long after they had passed, each one would remember it. In an army of teenaged virgins, Hartmann guessed, most would be reminded of their mothers. All that came to his mind was Alize.

Over eighteen months had passed since their wedding. Somewhere right now she'd be wearing a dress and stockings. Beneath it, he could picture her breasts and the pale curve of her belly. If there was a child nearby, his child, he couldn't picture that. Better not to try. In any case, the memory soon dissolved.

Ahead of them was a dusty bombed-out patch of flattened ground. Around its edge, rusting iron poked from pyramids of shattered brick. A factory, or what was left of a factory. They'd hit one of them, at least.

In its place stood a crude open cage ringed by clouds of barbed wire. Beyond that, he could see steam rising from a sleek black locomotive at the head of a dozen carriages, maybe more.

In the compound, there were no tents, no fires, and no signs of makeshift occupation. Over the entrance someone had hung a sign: *Welcome to England. Please drive on the left.*

Beyond the gate, a dozen elderly British officers shuffled papers and prepared themselves for the next boatload. Hartmann stepped forward and a painfully thin, middle-aged man rose from a chair to greet him.

'Good morning. How was the crossing? Not too sick, I hope.' Two pips: a lieutenant; sweet-scented hair tonic and an impeccable grasp of German. 'We find most people get their land legs back pretty quickly.'

Not hostile; not an ordinary soldier, much too warm and well spoken for that. An intelligence officer, maybe.

'Someone's given you a bit of a pasting. One of yours? Or one of ours?'

Anxiety swam in Hartmann's empty belly. Fixing his eyes on the black flanks of the train, he stared forward.

'No need for an answer. Purely rhetorical. Don't suppose you'd tell me anyway.'

All through their training, the notion of defeat – or capture – had never once been raised. No one had prepared them for questioning. To have even mentioned the possibility would have been deemed treasonable. Somewhere, unexpectedly, a sleeping grain of patriotic defiance stirred.

'I'm Max Hartmann. That's all you're getting.'

The officer ran his pen down a list of names, and turned a page. 'Max Hartmann? Unterscharführer, First SS Panzer Division? Do you mind if I sit down? I'm rather tired. You all rather blur into one.'

Clouds of steam were swirling around the train's wheels. Two men in blue overalls had wrestled an overhead canvas tube into its boiler. At the yank of a lever, water bulged through it, hissing and foaming as it spilled across the shining metal.

'I'm from Munich, if that helps. I really can't tell you any more.'

The lieutenant smiled. 'It seems there's a fellow missing from your ship.'

A third man had clambered into the train, and the grating scrape of his shovel was followed by a soft whoosh of exploding coal dust.

'Sorry about the racket. It never stops all day. Filthy old things really.'

Hartmann's gaze was locked on the activity around the locomotive; anything to distract himself from what he knew was coming.

'Does the name Wirz mean anything to you? Heinz Wirz? Young chap? Infantryman? Just turned eighteen? I'm told you knew him.'

'Told by whom?'

'So you do know him, then?'

Suddenly, Hartmann felt terribly weak. Who'd seen him? When? He remembered soldiers at the back of the ship but Wirz was fish food by then. So who else? Rosterg? Goltz? It would suit them to have a fall guy; to send out another warning. Or was it that fuck Zuhlsdorff?

No. They wouldn't do that. Not to one of their own. Not yet. The clown behind the desk was bluffing. He'd got no name, no witnesses, no body. Then he thought of Wirz, chewed up by the propellers. There wasn't going to be any body.

The lieutenant was waiting for a response. Hartmann looked down into his eyes and met sadness coming back from a face riven with deep, tired creases.

'We're asking everyone,' said the Englishman. 'Don't look so worried.'

'I didn't know him. I'm sorry that I can't help.'

'That's a pity. You know, I spent a summer in Munich once. Nineteen twenty-four. It was long after the war. I'd got out of the army and I was in a university choir. We sang songs by Schubert in the cathedral. Every day was the same. Endless glorious sunshine. Wonderful. There was a glockenspiel on the town hall. Charming little thing. We'd watch it ring every day at five. You must know it? We took a train across to Salzburg, and I stood in the room where Mozart was born.'

Hartmann looked down at his own boots. From nowhere, a dry wind was bearing the trace of freshly mown grass and in his left toe end there was the beginning of a hole. Two world wars. The man in front of him had seen them both. And it wasn't hatred he was transmitting; it was despair.

'Do you have any idea how much I want all that back?' asked the lieutenant.

'Yes. Of course.'

'And how exactly is that?'

'Because I was married there.'

Behind them the train was ready. One of the engineers was wiping his blackened face on an oily, wet towel.

'Where are you sending us? Am I allowed to ask that?'

Taking his weight with an arm on the back of his chair, the officer stood. 'In the next few hours, most of the people here will be leaving on that train and going to a prison camp. When they get there they'll be fed and watered. They'll even have bloody books to read. You'll be on that train too, but – as the cohort of murdering thugs – you won't be going to that particular holiday camp.'

81

'I didn't harm Wirz.'

'Whatever. You will be taken from here for proper questioning, along with all your charming friends, and after that you might, or might not, find yourself in a camp.'

'May I ask you to do one thing, Lieutenant?'

'No, you may not.'

For a few seconds, the officer peered into the prisoner's bruised face. 'Next,' he shouted, and Hartmann was escorted from his presence.

After that, for once, things happened quickly.

Inside the compound, they were searched and resprayed with disinfectant. A food table had been set up, serving mud-coloured tea which the prisoners drank while the guards marshalled long lines of men along the fencing closest to the train. Every name in every line was checked, and then checked again.

Looking around him, Hartmann could see that his own line was the shortest; no more than a couple of dozen men and almost all of them SS. Most of them had made the journey together from the compound in France. A few yards away he could see Goltz and Rosterg, but there was no sign of Zuhlsdorff.

'You won't find him,' mouthed Rosterg, shuffling closer.

'Why not? Where the fuck is he?'

'He's made a judicious switch of identity. I'm told he's temporarily joined that lot.'

Alongside them, the crowd of Wehrmacht prisoners had swollen beyond the perimeter of the compound. None of them would notice a stranger – all of them were strangers – and by the time they did, neither Zuhlsdorff nor the fate of Heinz Wirz would be of interest to anyone. Among that huge chattering body of ordinary soldiers, only one thing mattered now and it wasn't the anaemic boy with half his fingers missing.

'So much for his noble sense of duty,' Hartmann commented.

'Maybe Goltz wanted him in there. Eyes and ears. I'm not sure. Ask him yourself.'

He wouldn't bother. Everyone knew they were bound for a camp.

None of them cared where. It was a camp, and Zuhlsdorff would probably vanish into penal oblivion like the rest of them.

For the first time in weeks, certainty had re-entered the soldiers' lives, mixed with relief and an absurd feeling of excitement. A few hours before, these same figures had slouched green-gilled on to English soil. Now, wherever Hartmann looked, he could see contented faces. Strangers were forging instant friendships. The long hours of uneasy silence were being blown away by an upswell of happiness, rent with wolf-whistles and laughter, and lifted even higher by the fistfuls of cigarettes handed out with the tea.

Beyond the wire, the black train was wreathed in snarling coils of steam. From his cabin, the driver stooped down to talk with two British officers. After a swift exchange, they stepped back and the engine juddered forward until the first carriage was in line with a crude gateway in the fence. Two explosive hoots of the whistle followed, and Hartmann's line was ordered to board. For a moment, they hesitated, before responding to the command with a strut of defiance.

Across the entire square, conversations swiftly faded. Everyone wanted to see them. A dozen rifles had been trained on the exit, and one by one the 'black' prisoners stepped through the fence and sharply up into their carriage.

None of them had expected this.

Off a narrow corridor, sliding wooden doors opened on to cushioned first class compartments, into which eight prisoners were bundled, sitting four a side, beneath meshed luggage racks and smoky glass-shaded lamps. As he sat down by a window, Hartmann caught his reflection in the bevelled wall mirror above the opposite seats. At least three weeks had elapsed since he'd last seen himself. Now there was a tramp returning his scrutiny. Only his blue eyes still shone. The rest was a grizzled catastrophe of beard and bruise.

With a groan, he slumped back. Outside, behind the armed soldier in their corridor, he could see streams of prisoners heading for the remaining carriages. For the second time that day he was puzzled. According to the British officer, only a small number were

83

being sent for interrogation. And yet hundreds of Wehrmacht soldiers were pouring into the other carriages.

For the first time, Hartmann took a look at his travel companions. Six were SS. The other – the man now staring serenely back at him – was wearing the greasy pullover of a German submariner.

'It's simple. At some point, we'll stop. They'll detach the other carriages, and everyone on this one will be taken on to wherever it is they're taking us.'

It made sense. Hartmann's eyes widened. 'You're a mind-reader.'

'It's a trick you learn on U-boats. When you're not allowed to speak, you learn to hear what a man's thinking.'

He was Josef Mertens. He was twenty years old, and back home his parents worked the fields around the rolling hills of Bickendorf where a childhood in the country had clearly imbued him with monastic calm. Behind his brown eyes there seemed to be no anger, and despite his broad muscular frame the sailor's body language transmitted no obvious threat. Folded across his lap were the huge hands of a man who knew the land. Everything about him oozed levels of self-contentment Hartmann had believed extinct.

All that's missing, he thought, is a prayer book.

'And now you're thinking: why is he here?' Like his face, the young man's voice was gentle.

'You've done it again. Yes I was.' Hartmann's eyes flicked to their companions in the compartment. 'You can see clearly why we seven are all here. SS . . . captured in France . . . landlubbers. So spot the odd one out.'

'It's good to be a mystery.'

Quietly, he told them he'd been a submariner for less than a year. When U-741 had been launched in Danzig the previous December, the farmer's son had been one of its forty-nine-strong crew. A new volunteer, he'd been ranked Gefreiter, just one lowly notch up from an English able seaman, but no less desperate to destroy Allied ships than the officer-aristocrats whose eyes were pinned to the periscopes.

For a few months, it had gone perfectly. In March they'd sunk their first warship, and, back on shore leave in Cherbourg, Mertens had gorged on schnapps for a week. By the time his hangover had gone, U-741's luck had disappeared too.

'We were down there for days when absolutely nothing happened and we'd begun to think we were invulnerable. Everyone does. Even when they got a trace on us, we always managed to escape. Then a few days ago we got sloppy.'

While he'd been speaking, Mertens had scarcely shifted. His enormous fingers remained knotted across his thighs, and when the train engaged gear, sending a deep groan along its entire length, he seemed transfixed, indifferent to the explosive chuffs which filled the train with steam and speckled its occupants with soot.

Once the engine had achieved a fluid rhythm, he resumed. Everyone in the compartment was listening.

'It had been getting scarier for weeks and after their invasion it got worse. We kept hearing of other U-boat sinkings. We should have known better than to cruise so close to France on the surface. Anyway, we got spotted just after dawn by an English boat. August sixth it was. Not sure what type. Frigate? Corvette? The light was poor; we saw it late, and we'd barely started to dive when it hit us with a whole load of depth charges.'

'But you got out?' Hartmann was hanging on every word.

'Pure luck. We weren't deep. I was standing near the hatch. One of the explosions blew it open, and I swam to the surface.'

'Any other survivors?'

'The British waited. They even circled the slick for an hour. But I was the only one.' Outside, the light through the windows flashed green. The train was galloping quickly through a wood of ancient oak.

'The day you were captured. That was my birthday. I was captured that day too.'

'A lot of us were,' muttered a voice in the corner.

'Many happy returns. Belatedly,' said Mertens.

After that, no one else spoke again for a while.

As Hartmann gazed out over the rolling fields, the pieces fell into place. Back in Germany, they'd been reassured that their submarines were a technological miracle, light years ahead of their rivals in the sea. On their own they could win them the war, which meant that Mertens was on the train because of what he knew. Or what the British thought he might know. Poor bugger. He was probably in for a kicking.

But there was something that still didn't fit. U-boat crews had a reputation for being fearsomely loyal to Hitler, like the SS, except in Kriegsmarine blue, but brutality wasn't something he could sense in this tranquil farm boy. Even so, it would be wise to be careful. It was what you were, not what you wore. And that could cut both ways, for good and for bad.

He stood up and eased open the small sliding window. Summer scents blew in over the stinging swirl of cigarette smoke. It was a beautiful country studded with anonymous white-painted stations, the names of which he would never know. Liss. Liphook. Mousehill. Godalming. Each one rendered anonymous to protect this same landscape from men like him. Alongside each one, women worked in huge allotments. Glowing tubs of pink blossoms punctuated every platform, and the rich golden fields were peopled with spiky stacks of corn and men swinging oiled scythes.

For Hartmann, it simply wasn't possible to imagine a war being fought across these placid chalky hills. It seemed inconceivable that Goltz wanted the fight to go on. With a premonitory shudder he turned back to look at his dozing companions.

From the fields, the labourers saw only a locomotive racing away from them under its own glorious cumulus of steam, but the train was like a black worm snaking towards the heart of an apple.

As the morning dragged on, the train became insufferably hot. All communication with the other compartments was forbidden and each compartment was watched by its own armed soldier. There was no food, and only limited water drawn from jerry cans at the end of the carriage. When the prisoners wanted to urinate, they were escorted to the nearest lavatory by a guard. When they got there, they found the doors had been unscrewed and taken away. Endless delays ate at the men's patience. From the angle of the sun, Hartmann felt sure they were heading towards London, but at times it would have been quicker to walk. At Dorking, they'd boiled outside the station for two hours, and in Reigate, clods of horse shit had been thrown through their open window.

By early afternoon, they'd squealed to a halt in a maze of sidings. Above them they could hear transport planes and the shrill trajectory of Hurricanes. Ahead of them on the main line, a gang of men was battling to switch three sets of points. Looking down the train, Hartmann could count nine carriages, each one with faces crowded curiously at the windows. Once the railway workers had scrambled clear, the entire snake switched on to a branch line running along a deep embankment crowded with silver birch.

After a few minutes more, accompanied by a single strident squeal of the whistle, they stopped again. Every face in every compartment – including Mertens' – pressed itself to the glass.

'Where are we?' Hartmann had slid open their door. Outside, along the corridor, the guards were gathering their own kit.

'Outskirts of London. Kempton Park. It's a racecourse, or was.' One of the soldiers had stepped into their compartment. A lifeless cigarette was tucked behind his left ear. 'Now renamed Number Nine Reception Camp. From here, you're only about twenty miles from Buckingham Palace.'

'Number Nine?' asked Hartmann. 'Jesus. How many are there?'

'Don't get too excited. You won't be getting off.'

Now they could see it. Just a brief glimpse of the curved white rails, and the grandstand beyond. But nothing green; not a blade of grass was showing. Instead, a vast city of tents puckered in the breeze where horses normally ran. And behind the now-familiar walls of wire, Hartmann could see German soldiers – thousands of soldiers – milling under the sunshine.

Along the entire length of his train, doors were being slammed open. Low-risk prisoners were streaming out on to the platform. For a chilling moment, Hartmann was certain he'd seen Zuhlsdorff but the crowd was thick and streaming away too quickly to be certain. Somewhere close by, a sledgehammer was pounding at an iron coupling and fresh guards were lining up along the side of their carriage.

'You were right, Mertens. How did you know?'

The submariner shrugged. Without warning, the engine lurched backwards and then forwards again, dislodging an iron chain which crashed loose into the stony ballast. Outside, the phalanx of guards was stepping back from the edge, and the sweltering cough of the locomotive's boiler had resumed.

When the new guards were on board they moved forward, and for the first time that day the train felt light-footed. With only their own carriage to be pulled, they were travelling faster than before.

This time, there were no fields. This time, they were boxed in by dark factories; and then, for mile after mile, they ran on between back yards and gardens, broken by random snapshots of sleeping dogs and red buses and scruffy-looking children playing cricket in parks.

Although he couldn't be sure, Hartmann thought it was a Saturday. Not that it mattered. Like everything else, it was a matter of guesswork; something to occupy his mind. He was also certain that they were still heading straight towards the heart of London. But that, too, was wild conjecture.

Back at the racecourse, he pictured the 'whites' being deloused and searched yet again, checked off a list and sent on their happy way to a holiday camp. Somewhere among them would be his perpetual shadow, clasping a scabby hand, and seething in the silent shame of his subterfuge. If this were a normal world, Hartmann reflected, they would never see each other again.

But it was anything but that. Even the weather was mystifying. On one side of the train, a fierce sun sliced through the city's dust. On the other, bullets of rain carved streaky lines through the dirt on their window. No one in their compartment passed any comment. Since Kempton Park, they had been travelling in absolute silence. Each man, alone, had realised they were in London and was silently preparing himself for an interrogation in which some sort of pain was sure to play a part.

In every direction, they could see industrial buildings and the distant creamy spires of churches. Once, when the tracks rose slightly on an overpass, they had even glimpsed the grey dome of St Paul's, rising cleanly above the unbroken façade of the riverside.

'It doesn't make any sense,' said Hartmann, turning to the others. 'I thought we'd flattened this place four years ago. I thought they were practically begging us to come and put them out of their misery.'

He looked back. He could see a man with an umbrella hailing a cab, and a blinkered pony pulling a wagon creaking with scrap metal. He could see a girl sliding a letter into a scarlet box.

'Perhaps they built it all back up again,' said Mertens.

Another train was rattling alongside theirs. Every seat inside it was taken and the aisles were jammed with standing travellers. Maybe it wasn't a Saturday. Hartmann rested his fingers on the hot glass. Condensation misted around the tips.

As the two lines drew closer, a ponytailed child stared over into the compartment where Hartmann was sitting. When their eyes connected, she too put her fingers on her window. After a moment, she turned to whisper to the woman sitting beside her. Her mother? Her sister? The girl by the postbox, perhaps? Soon, everyone in the entire carriage seemed to be peering at him. At them.

If I could swap places with that girl, he wondered, what would I see?

Hartmann turned sharply away from the thought, catching his own ragged reflection in the grime on the glass. That wasn't him. She wasn't seeing him.

But when he swivelled sideways for a second time, the other train was gone.

## 9

Waterloo Station, a clatter of footsteps and voices.

From the platforms, out of the roiling steam, came a constant stream of travellers. Beneath the giant clock – Hartmann now knew it was 4.17 p.m. – couples kissed their farewells and kitbag-laden soldiers strolled everywhere, dipping down into the gloom of the Underground, or out towards the sun-bright river embankment.

Suddenly to be there, at the heart of London, seemed so extraordinary that Hartmann's vacillating spirits soared; almost alone out of the hell-bent millions, he had made it. At that moment, beneath the bomb-bruised station's magnificent canopy, he and his fellow-crocks were the only German soldiers who mattered; doughty warriors who'd battled to within a spit of Churchill's bedchamber without the energy or the wherewithal to do a damned thing about it.

And who, even now, had not one single clue about where they were going.

'You're smiling.' Goltz had been the last off their carriage. 'What's so funny?' Alongside him, Rosterg met Hartmann's eyes.

Their train was already nosing out of the station. In a day or so it would be back with more prisoners. And after them, yet more, until Europe was stripped bare of German fighting men.

'Not funny exactly, just interesting. I was thinking that very soon there'll be more of us than them on this side of the Channel, more young ones, anyway.'

Goltz looked puzzled. Hartmann pressed on.

'Take a proper look.' He gestured towards an elderly man in a uniform walking his dog. 'Most of the soldiers left in Britain look pretty ancient to me. Like him. He's probably a pensioner or a bank manager.'

'And that's interesting because?'

'Just ask Rosterg to tell you the story of the Trojan Horse. You never know. There might be a medal in it for you somewhere.'

At that moment, however, it seemed very unlikely.

From a distance, they looked like a string of vagrants. Only up close, as they marched across the dazzling concourse, could people see and smell what they were. Even after their long journey the silvered threads of their lightning insignia still sparkled, and from the packed station buffet woozy men emerged clutching pints of ale to watch them pass. None of the locals seemed sure how to react, and when a drunk staggered forward to hurl abuse a clergyman carrying pink flowers held him back.

'Which one of you is Hitler then?' yelled a lad selling newspapers.

'That'll be me,' said Rosterg, in his best cultured English accent. 'But you can call me Adolf.'

At the station steps, two army trucks were already ticking over. As they clambered on board, Hartmann caught his first smell of blackened buildings. Through a crack in the rear canvas, he saw a demolition ball swing, and then, fleetingly, the bold sweep of the Thames across a weed-choked sea of rubble and gutted homes.

Everything seemed so random, so haphazard in its distribution of luck. Along one side of a street, every building had gone. Along the other, geraniums still glowed in neat window boxes. And yet, clearly, nothing – absolutely nothing – had been stopped. The red blood of London's double deckers still flowed along every artery and the city's pavements were a defiant crush of determination.

As they moved through the honking traffic, Hartmann pressed his mouth to Rosterg's ear. The other man, too, had found a peephole in the oilcloth.

'Hitler must have known all this for years,' Hartmann whispered.

'I wouldn't let anyone else hear you say that.'

'His seedy third columnists would have told him long ago.'

'Or they painted only the picture that he wanted to see; the one full of Londoners down on their knees, desperate to embrace the swastika.'

Peering out across the busy streets, Hartmann could see little sign of that. London was just as he had dreamed it as a boy. Big Ben was still standing. The Thames thronged with barges. Crowds were flocking into Westminster Abbey and Kensington Gardens appeared to be sagging under the weight of its flowers.

In his childhood head, he'd ridden these streets before. Carefully, he peeled back more canvas and looked back down the route they were travelling. Soon, surely, their endless journey would end. Over to the right he recognised the Albert Memorial, followed smartly, on his left, by the Royal Albert Hall.

'Mondays used to be Wagner night,' offered Rosterg. 'I'll wager it isn't now.'

They were heading west. There was no doubt about it. Somehow, they'd avoided Buckingham Palace and were skirting the green heart of the royal park. He could see uniformed nannies pushing black prams; a wounded barrage balloon detumescing above the treeline; and daubed across a terraced gable-end, the health benefits of nightly bile beans proclaimed in a huge painted hoarding.

Unless he ate properly soon, he doubted he'd ever need any.

As the park ended, the properties swelled. Immense marble mansions with elaborate balconies rose out of high-hedged gardens, and around every one stood a curtain of spear-topped railings. Finally, the truck was decelerating. With a squeal of its heavy tyres, it swung sharp right.

'We're going upmarket. Kensington Palace Gardens.' Rosterg had caught a glimpse of the street sign. 'This looks promising.'

From a gallop, their progress had slowed to a crawl. Everyone was craning to look down a straight, broad avenue peppered with palaces and punctuated by elegant Victorian streetlights. No other human beings could be seen.

'We must be lost,' said Goltz. 'It doesn't make any sense.'

For once, Hartmann agreed. Since the previous afternoon, they'd travelled from a French beach to the epicentre of the British aristocracy. Goltz was absolutely right. It made no sense whatsoever.

'Just so long as the wine is served at room temperature,' said Rosterg.

Both trucks had stopped. Armed soldiers were slamming down the barge boards, and pinning back the canvas flaps. Two huge iron gates, flanked by sandbagged sentry boxes, were being dragged open. Beyond them, across a golden-gravelled forecourt, was an oak door peppered with iron studs. As they approached, it swung open and the prisoners stepped forward into an oval hallway showered with light from a dozen stained glass windows. Huge oil paintings rose to meet finely tiered cornice work tumbling from a ceiling dotted with plaster rosebuds. A wide staircase cascaded from the upper floors to a broad oaky landing from where a line of five officers stared down at them with statuesque disregard.

The man in the middle was the oldest, and the shortest, with a round, weather-tanned face, and uniform that looked borrowed.

'Good afternoon. Or rather good evening. We often lose track of time in here.' It was the voice of a man in his sixties; cold, but not a trace of accent, like a BBC radio announcer. 'My name is Scotland, Colonel Scotland, and I'm in charge of everything that happens inside this rather splendid building.'

With his arms, he beseeched his audience to absorb the grandeur of their surroundings.

'It's my job to make your stay here as pleasant – and short – as it can possibly be. Whether it meets either, or both, of those expectations will be entirely up to you.'

Hartmann's eyes walked quickly along the faces of Scotland's colleagues. There were three men and a woman: an attractive dark-haired woman in a red suit and skirt. Another two dozen pairs of German eyes were looking in the same direction.

'We call this place the London Cage, and whatever sick private fantasies you harbour, your war is over.' The colonel had taken two steps down the stairs towards them. 'Officially, unofficially, it's finished. Here. Now. Done.'

He paused. An ancient memory seemed to flash across his face.

'Before the last war, I actually worked for Germany, out in Africa.

93

We were all friends then. Now many of my dearest people are German.' Outside, the daylight was fading and turning the coloured glass in the windows to black.

'One day I'd really like to see those friends again, rather like your wanting to see your parents or your girlfriends.'

Hartmann thought about Goltz. The colonel couldn't be more wrong.

'I know most of you are SS, but you each know things that might help end the war sooner. By a month, a week, an hour. By a minute. It doesn't matter. One bomb less. One bullet less. Little things that might save the lives of the people you love.' His eyes seemed to lock on Hartmann. 'Details: names and places, regiments, even bits of idle gossip. Things it really won't hurt you to share.'

Scotland turned, and walked slowly back up to his colleagues. 'My friends here will be assisting you in those conversations.'

'And the Geneva Convention?' Rosterg had stepped forward to speak, and was looking up the staircase.

'We're British. Just help us to help you, and it won't hurt a bit.'

At the side of the atrium, a large door swung open and a dozen immense guardsmen entered the space.

'These gentlemen will escort you to your rooms.'

Later, Hartmann would try, and fail, to remember the route they'd followed next. The building was a maze; a burrow of vast interconnected chambers and vaulted corridors. Not just one mansion but three, rendered with such architectural precision that their own vagabond presence felt like an affront. Through one open door, he'd seen a ballroom lined with gilt-framed mirrors reflecting the shabby line of grey serge as it passed. Through another, he'd looked across to twilight hedges of box laid around bushes pruned in the shapes of mythical beasts. Finally, in a windowless basement room, they'd been ordered to strip and shower in ice-cold water.

While their clothes were searched and bagged, a man in a white coat ordered each of them to bend. Hartmann gasped as rough fingers pushed into his rectum. Alongside him, Goltz stood bolt upright with his back against the shower wall. Naked, his body was the colour of watery milk.

'No fucking way. No fucking way.'

A black boot walloped into his groin. Rough hands were on his neck, twisting his head down into the wet-tiled floor. Another kick swung in and Goltz stumbled forward, locked by two pairs of uniformed arms. One furious gurgled scream later, and the search was over. When Goltz straightened, he smelled of bleach and there was fresh blood running down the inside of his thighs.

'Don't tell me you didn't enjoy it,' said Hartmann.

A hand clamped over Goltz's face before he could reply, steering him through into an adjoining room. Hartmann and the rest followed shivering behind. It was strange, he thought, how men covered their genitals in situations such as this. As if anyone cared, or was looking.

At the door, a red-haired guardsman yelled out their names and handed back their bags of clothes. From each one rose the sour whiff of disinfectant, but there were clean underpants and socks, and although their boots no longer had laces, the smell of battle had gone.

Stumbling against each other, the men dressed quickly. For the first time that day, Hartmann heard laughter. It felt good to be scrubbed; and to smell fresh. The men were relaxing.

When they were lined up against a curtain for their mugshots, no one resisted. One by one, Hartmann watched them wince as the powder flashed. It was comical to see how fierce each prisoner tried to appear. It was tragic how lost and how young they all looked under the clean white spark of the magnesium. As he sat down and looked into the lens, he counted how many of them he knew by name. There weren't many.

Somehow he doubted whether the photographer would know the German for cheese. But he said it anyway.

'*Käse*,' he said, thinking of the other picture that had been lost.

After that, they were fed; eating with the silent intensity of men returned from the dead. Twelve men crammed either side of a huge pine-topped table confronted by piles of fresh-baked bread and hot soup bobbing with vegetables. There was no meat or butter. Instead, there was endless tea and plain biscuits and a packet of Senior Service for every prisoner.

Under a fug of smoke, they leaned back, unsure whether to feel fear or contentment. Through the arched dining-room window, they could see across the gardens to a high wall topped by razor wire and floodlights. Escape wouldn't be an option here.

'We don't actually look very dangerous any more, do we?'

For an hour, until now, Mertens had sat beside him without speaking. Although his bowl had been licked clean he was still clutching his spoon.

'Will you talk, do you think?' asked Hartmann. 'I mean, if they hurt us?'

'Honestly? I don't know. But listen, this is how it will go. They will tell us the war is over, and I don't believe it is. They will tell us they already know all our secrets, and I won't believe that either. They will lie to us and we will lie to them, and then they will let us go.' Carefully, Mertens placed his spoon on the table in front of him. 'Like the old man said. They are British, remember. They'll play by the rules, and that is why they'll lose this war.'

All around the room, blackout curtains were being drawn and a nervous stillness had fallen across the table. From the door, there was an order to stand and the group was led up two flights of stairs into a long dark corridor, broken at regular intervals by white-painted steel doors. Outside the first one, the men were stopped, and a single name was shouted out.

Goltz.

As he stepped forward, the door opened on a featureless cell with bunks. 'It's a fucking shithole,' he screamed before the lock turned behind him.

Halfway down the corridor, it was Hartmann's turn. Another forbidding portal on to similarly bleak lodgings. Inside, just beyond reach, hung a single lightbulb. In one corner was a steel bucket. In another was a small table with a single chair.

Hunched on the bottom mattress of the bunk he could see a figure buried deep inside a blanket, stock still, his face turned to the wall. Now wasn't the time for introductions. As quietly as he could, Hartmann hauled himself on to the top bunk and flopped back with a sigh. Sleep would be swift.

'So tell me about this wife and kid then.' The voice from below was muffled, tired, but joyfully familiar.

Koenig.

It was Koenig.

# Private and Confidential

*From:* *Combined Services Detailed Interrogation Centre (CSDIC)/
Southampton*

*To:* *Colonel Alexander Scotland/6&8 Kensington Palace Gdns/London
Cage*

*Alex,*

*Following on from yesterday's telephone conversation, we have still been
unable to locate the missing German soldier Heinz Wirz. Sadly, this is
unlikely to change. Given the huge numbers of men involved – there were 234
men on the boat that picked him up in France – our interviews have been
severely hampered by time and manpower. Foul play remains a distinct
possibility (he was horribly beaten at the holding camp); however, as you are
well aware, there have already been a number of reported suicides, and prisoner
morale appears directly linked to their proximity to the vicious hard-line
elements within their own ranks.*

*In this context, your next cheery consignment of Hitler's finest left the
south coast this afternoon. Nineteen in total (travelling first class – something
I've never done) and all of them with significant blood on their hands, I'm
sure. They will probably have arrived by the time you read this. Rather you
than me. Pay particular attention to the fellow called Goltz. A nasty piece of
work whose hold over his SS chums can only be linked to his combat record,
given his less than impressive physique.*

*One last thing: it seems a number of SS may have already 'lost' themselves
within the Wehrmacht ranks; planted as spies or moles by chaps like Goltz,
I expect. But then, no one knows more about that sort of business than you.*

*Don't be too rough on them. Queensberry rules, etc.*

# 10

There was no discomfort, no embarrassment. Like children, stifling giggles, they squeezed into the same bed together and for a few seconds they wrestled in a delirious embrace, pushing and punching until tears flowed, and silence followed. Neither knew how, or where, to begin; as if the terrible stew of their memories was better left unstirred.

Gently, Koenig touched a tear on Hartmann's cheek, and watched as it flowed across on to his own finger. 'You see. I told you we'd meet again in London.'

And then his story came gushing out.

Like Hartmann, Koenig had been captured in France a few weeks before. To his shame, there'd been no heroics. Instead, it had been a capitulation of sublime anticlimax. On a country lane near Tournai, his tank had run out of diesel and while his crew wandered off to ransack a roadside farm, Koenig had squatted behind a tree. Minutes later, with his trousers around his ankles, he'd found himself at the wrong end of an American rifle.

'Don't laugh. It was fucking humiliating. When I got back to the tank, they lined my crew up against a wall and shot each one of them in the face.'

Alongside him, Hartmann could feel his friend's body stiffening with rage.

'After that, I tried everything I could to get myself killed. But the worse I behaved, the more pleasure they got from keeping me alive. Category black. Are you the same? Camp after fucking camp, all over France, until two days ago when they dumped me off here.'

There was more – a grimmer version – Hartmann knew. But he'd never get to hear it. Koenig's rag-haired zest was what he loved, not his odious brand of patriotism, however difficult it was to separate the two.

Back in Normandy, everyone had heard stories about the 12th SS Panzer Division – the so-called Hitlerjugend – and he didn't doubt that Koenig's hands would be horribly blood-stained. Or that their views on humanity occupied different galaxies. Strangely, he'd never felt their differences to be an obstacle to friendship. It was for others to worry about the contradictions. To him, it was simple. In men like Goltz, he saw a future to be avoided at all costs. In Koenig, he saw hope; a challenge; a brother. Or he had done, until war crushed it down.

Through the fabric of his friend's uniform the muscles felt rigid with tension, and when Koenig eventually slept, the stiffness remained. I'm losing him, Hartmann realised. I may have lost him already.

A few hours later, when he stirred, Koenig's cheek was still crushed against his shoulder. From a deep recess, high on one wall, light was trickling slowly down towards the bunks, revealing crude swastikas hacked into the painted brickwork. There were names, too, and dates. He could probably read them with his fingers. As he reached over to touch, Koenig woke. Neither man had any idea what time it was, or how soon they would be separated.

Without being asked – or interrupted – Hartmann told his own story; about the tank battle and Alize and the child he'd never met. When he'd finished, Koenig rolled away. 'You're a lucky man.'

'You're not jealous? Or are you?'

There was more light now, and noises outside in the corridor. Hartmann sat up and contemplated the steel bucket in the corner. Reluctantly, he rolled from the bed, picked it up, held it to his thighs and watched the hot stream stir the contents. When he was done, he sat down at the metal table.

Koenig had turned back and was watching him carefully. 'No, I'm not jealous. Why would I be?'

'You seem annoyed. I'd have told you on my birthday. But you didn't ask.'

'None of that matters. Forget it. You just need to know what happens here.'

Hartmann craned forward. His friend hadn't learned much. The previous day he'd been questioned by a British officer and so far there'd been three square meals, but no beatings and nothing that might constitute serious maltreatment.

'Not so much an inquisition as a job interview.' Apart from their morning walk to the interrogation block, prisoners were mostly kept apart, and hard information was scarce. 'The person in here before you just disappeared. I didn't even get to know his name.'

'Disappeared? Or moved on?'

'Prison camp somewhere. No one tells you much.'

'Did you tell them anything?'

'What do you think?'

'Can we write letters?'

'I've no idea. I haven't asked.' Koenig paused, sadly. 'I'm not like you. Who would I write to?'

Breakfast came soon after, brought to them on dull metal trays: two slices of fried bread alongside a boiled egg and sweet tea. A few minutes later, a hatch in the door opened and a hand appeared holding a lighter and two cigarettes. After lighting one, the hand – and the lighter – quickly withdrew.

The two men looked around and then laughed. There was nothing to set fire to.

'Apart from ourselves,' said Koenig. 'And we're barely fit for kindling.'

'Remember that fire up on the clifftop?' Hartmann was pushing the smoke out through pursed lips, forming silvery halos in front of his face. 'You made me dance in my pants.'

Koenig grinned. He was blushing. The door crashed open. Two guards hovered in the corridor. A third entered the room and signalled Hartmann to follow. Each of them was immense, crag-like, carrying a long, thin polished stick capped by a worn silver ferrule. Calmly, Hartmann rose, crushed the still-glowing tab under his foot, and stepped out of the cell.

'Take care, my friend,' whispered Koenig. 'Look after that pretty face.'

All along the corridor, other prisoners were being pushed from their rooms. Ahead of him, in the sickly yellow light, he could see Mertens and Goltz, but no sign of Rosterg. It was a huge place. He could be anywhere; in a hot foam bath or a suite of rooms nibbling caviar with the colonel. Nothing would have surprised him. Wherever you dropped Rosterg, he looked like a man who would thrive; like a virus, but less pleasant.

After two turns in the labyrinth, they could see daylight and feel the breeze blowing in through a narrow outside door. A sharp right turn took them into the garden, where they snatched at the fresh air like parched travellers. Behind the thick curtilage of garden maple the sun was struggling and the air was still cold.

Only Mertens, the seaman, looked untroubled. The rest shivered in single file as their feet crunched the lavender-edged footpath along the front of the three old buildings. Close up, they were even more magnificent; a glorious creamy cluster of Victorian extravagance entered through a portal fit for a pharaoh. As they were herded back inside, Hartmann noticed a number six on a fat column by the oak door, and an overweight bulldog sniffing around in the thick growth of shrubs. How perfectly British it all was, he thought.

With an arm on each elbow, he was steered across the chandeliered hall and down a flight of stone steps into a musty windowless room with ceramic white bricks and a rusty iron handle. In the middle of the space were two chairs, one placed either side of a large wooden table. Unaccompanied, he walked towards the table and saw three sheets of paper.

Two of the pieces were blank. At the top of the third were three handwritten words. Hartmann stepped closer to read them. *Meine liebe Alize . . .*

With his heart bouncing, he picked up the paper and slumped back into the chair.

# 11

'Max. We know so much about you.'

A voice from behind, a woman's voice.

Hartmann straightened and fixed his gaze on the far wall. In the shadows to his left, he could feel a warm presence. When she spoke for a second time, she was much closer.

'I'm sorry this is all so theatrical. It wouldn't be my choice at all.'

Hartmann looked down again at the three words on the paper. None of this was possible. War was chaos; a billion billion fragments of random chaos. How could they know him or anything about him?

'You've never met your child, have you?' He could see her now, an outline finding form. 'I expect that must be a pretty good reason for staying alive.'

Now she was in front of him, taking a seat, perusing a file of notes and smoothing down her skirt. She looked much prettier than the previous night; auburn hair stretched back in a bun, a pale hourglass neck and kind, green eyes. Not a red suit this time, but a tartan pattern skirt, a delicate pink blouse, and a ruby brooch. The only make-up was on her lips.

'It really doesn't look very good for you, does it, Max?' She flicked deeper into her file. 'A man goes missing on a boat. You're one of the last men to be seen with him. A bunch of SS brutes run amok in a French camp. You're part of the gang.'

She stopped, tilted her head. For the first time, there was eye contact. 'That's better. Now we're getting somewhere.'

Hartmann averted his face again. She was far too beautiful.

'Don't be shy. I can't imagine what you'd say that would surprise us. We already know what regiment you were in. We know where you're from. We know names and troop dispositions and tank numbers. We know your tanks have got no fuel and that your entire army has lost the will to live. We know how the war's going to end – which is badly, for you – and I know you'd dearly, dearly love to talk to another human being.' She drew breath. 'And I thought you might like this back.'

Reaching between her feet, she pulled a silver cigarette case from her small handbag and set it down on the table between them.

'It's yours. Take it.'

Hartmann reached across, feeling the cold gloss of the metal in his hand.

'Now let's talk,' she said.

It was extraordinary. He'd never heard German spoken so seductively. After Hitler's ravings, he'd thought his language contaminated beyond repair. But this woman spoke like an angel.

'If you know so much already, how can I possibly help?' he said. He was rotating the silver case and passing it from hand to hand.

A smile spread across her face. '*Touché*. You see, your English is perfect, far better than my clunky German. I'm Helen by the way. And it's a pleasure to meet you.'

After that, they talked.

She was Helen Waters. She was twenty-three, and her childhood had been spent in France, the daughter of a career diplomat whose peripatetic household had always rung to the babble of foreign tongues. When invasion loomed, she'd been sent back to Brighton – to Roedean – but when the girls there were evacuated north, she'd charmed herself straight into Cambridge. Three years later she'd strolled out again with a double first in languages, and a job with Army Intelligence.

'You're a spy?' Momentarily, Hartmann had forgotten where he was.

She laughed, a soft, conspiratorial chuckle. 'I'm afraid not. I don't have the courage to be a spy. Secret ink and firing squads. Not my cup of tea at all. Intelligence, they call it. Something of a misnomer in my case. Would you like some tea, by the way?'

Without waiting for a reply, she pushed back her chair and walked behind him. He could hear whispering – a second deeper voice – and then she was back.

'Listen. I'm here to try and get this war finished.' The gap between them had narrowed, and she was looking hard into his face. 'A thousand little pieces of information added together can make a difference. But if it's ten thousand or a hundred thousand imagine the lives we could save.'

Hartmann knew what she meant. Sooner or later, the flailing rump of his brainwashed army would make a stand and bring her invasion to a bloody standstill. Somewhere in a wood, or the ruins of some nameless town, they'd turn and fight and people would die. He'd already seen what a few dozen lunatics with tanks could accomplish.

But she was wrong too. They all were.

'You can't stop men like us,' he said. 'We're not the same as you.'

'We wondered if the cigarette case was looted, by the way; stolen from a dead British soldier, perhaps. Please tell me we were wrong.'

'You were wrong. It's my father's.' Nothing he told her would change a damned thing, nor would a million fragments of loose gossip. The British had never understood. You couldn't conscript brutality. You had to breed it.

'Tell me what you're thinking.'

Hartmann rolled his eyes to the ceiling. The room was stifling, and the light was buzzing strangely.

'Did you kill Heinz Wirz?'

'Of course not. The opposite. I tried to help him.'

'You were the last person seen with him.'

'Maybe in a way I did kill him. Does it matter?'

'You feel guilty?'

Hartmann shrugged. It was too complicated to explain.

'Are you married, Helen?'

'A boyfriend in France. Fighting you.'

There were a dozen heavy footsteps behind him, and a stout figure was sitting down alongside the woman.

'Milk? Sugar?' It was the man who'd introduced himself as Colonel Scotland, the man from the welcoming party. 'You two seem to be getting on. Good.'

Hartmann's expression was blank. The thread was broken.

Through the walls, he felt sure he'd heard a fairground organ piping, the muffled waltz of a carousel. The tune seemed familiar. It must be coming from the park. When he closed his eyes, he saw children on golden horses. And that melody; it was a Strauss tune, definitely.

When he opened them, it was gone, and an anaemic mug of tea steamed between him and his two interrogators. He looked across at the woman. Helen.

'You heard it too. Am I right? Was it Strauss?'

Something had shifted in the room's chemistry, as if a playground game had suddenly acquired teeth. Under the table, he imagined his hand on her knee, and how that would feel.

The colonel had slid the three sheets of paper back across to Hartmann's side of the table.

'How do you know my wife's name? Who told you I had a child?'

'You could write to her if you wanted. We could help.'

'You wouldn't send it. You don't know where she is.'

'Nice watermark. See?' The colonel had picked up the top sheet and was holding it to the ceiling light. 'It's amazing what you can find in anything if you look hard enough.'

'How the fuck did you know? Have you heard from her? Fucking tell me.'

Gently, Scotland spread the three blank pages in front of the prisoner. The backs of his hands were leathered and creased. 'Tell me. Do members of the German SS routinely share a bed?'

It was like an electric shock, a bomb-burst.

'You and the prisoner Koenig seem very friendly. Very friendly indeed, I'd say. All that pillow talk and moonlight clifftop revels.'

Until a few hours ago, Koenig himself hadn't known Alize's name. Wherever the British were getting their information, it wasn't Koenig. Rosterg maybe? But then Rosterg knew nothing about Koenig. And he'd never told Goltz anything he didn't have to. Somehow these people were inside his brain, scooping out his secrets with bayonets. Either that or they'd heard every word he'd said since he stepped out of the lorry.

'Exactly, Max. Exactly. We've been listening to you. We've been listening to all of you. From the sad deluded fantasies of your comrades to the moving saga of your very own love life.'

'Fuck you all.' Hartmann rested his forehead on the cool surface of the desk. He could hear the Strauss again, a faraway lifeline sinking deeper.

'The technology is primitive but it just about works, and what we don't hear, we glean from those who are sensible enough to talk to us.'

'Stool pigeons.'

'I think of them as modern and progressive intellects.' Scotland snapped upright. He reached his arm forward and touched Hartmann's back. 'Much as you are, I think.' Without waiting for a reply, the colonel pushed his chair back abruptly and stood. 'Perhaps you just need a little time on your own to reflect.'

As he passed behind the woman, she stretched up for a whispered instruction.

'Or a little civilised persuasion, perhaps?'

Hartmann didn't move.

'Either way we'd like your help. And in return maybe we can find out where this woman of yours is hiding.'

The door slammed. He was gone. Beneath its greasy sheen, Hartmann's tea quivered. Neither he, nor Helen, appeared to be breathing.

'They're not traitors,' she said, finally. 'The traitors are the ones who do nothing.' She nudged the writing paper closer to Hartmann. 'If she's alive, we can get a letter to her.'

'Only if you give me a pen.'

'Things are rather different in the Cage, I'm afraid,' she said. 'Let's have a little talk.'

## 12

How long had she been gone?

There was no clock, and no window, and his grasp of time had been slowly eaten away by the war. Life was what mattered, not its mundane calibration. At a guess, he'd have said five hours. But his stomach told him more. Since the eggs, there'd been nothing; just the one rancid brew he'd drunk cold through a skin which had stuck to his tongue.

The chipped enamel mug was there in front of him now. Its stain-streaked insides were the colour of wet peat, and for want of anything better, he drained out the last bitter drops and slammed it down.

'I need some food. What's happening?'

Then again, louder.

The sound of his own noise rang off the clammy plaster; an echo which yielded no reaction. Behind him, the reinforced door remained resolutely still. He looked up. A large moth was banging against the blaze of the room's single filament. In the room's emptiness, he could share the panic of its wings.

An ancient sediment of dust was falling through the beam and a stray zag of light branded itself painfully inside his right eye. Hartmann blinked sharply, stood up, and walked to the door.

'You can't do this. You cannot do this to me.'

He placed both palms against the steel. It was solid, cold, and beaded with condensation. Since whenever he'd been brought there, the cell had become stifling. With his temple resting against the damp metal, he could trick the droplets on to his face. It was like a game. If he twisted his head at the right moment, they ran into his mouth. If he got it wrong, they ran off his chin.

Bored, he turned round and weighed up his new universe. It was a rectangular box formed by four brick-lined walls little more than a few strides wide, longer one way than the other. Ten foot by fifteen, with a wooden floor and a ceiling designed for short men. Men like Scotland, he thought. There were little Hitlers on both sides.

On the table, beneath the buzzing lightbulb, the three blank pages looked back at him. He could fill three hundred telling her what was in his head, but three would do for a start. He just needed that pen.

He sat down. And then he paced again, hugging the walls and dragging his hand along the chill surface of the tiles. Twenty rotations one way, then twenty more the other. Somehow – and probably not by accident – the room was getting unmanageably steamy. Standing with his back against the door helped, but his uniform had grown heavy with sweat and the heat was making him weak.

'Please. I need some fucking air.'

Six hours, seven hours, twelve hours. All his bearings were in pieces. Maybe the entire day had gone. Maybe he was into the next one. Outside there would be bats, bearing down on dreaming flies. Unless he'd been shipped out, Koenig would be back on his bunk wondering what had happened.

If he was jealous, why was he jealous? What did he want? What did he feel?

Somewhere, the questions lost their way and he sat down yet again, pushing the paper to one side, and dropping his head down across folded arms. Above him he could sense the insect, still magnetised by the yellow light of the tungsten. Both of them were trapped, but sleep was coming and there would surely be food in his dreams.

At first, Hartmann didn't hear the boots in the corridor outside, or the door open, or the furious order to wake up. For a happy moment he'd been gone – a few seconds, no more – but the hand across his face spun him round into the spitting breath of a guard. He could smell stale smoke, feel nails tearing at his skin. Behind him, he sensed another voice: instructions. The hand retreated across his forehead, and yanked him fiercely back by the hair.

'You don't eat. And you certainly don't sleep.'

Hartmann's nose slammed down on to the hard wood. Through a watery eye, he could see spots of blood on the paper. As his vision cleared, he heard the door clunk heavily behind him. In front of him, standing to attention against the far wall, a lone guard was looking straight back across the table. Outside the bulb's bleak cone of light, it was difficult to make out his face. To the German, he was no more than a dark blur, bereft of telling detail.

'I don't suppose you speak.'

The large shape by the wall didn't move.

'No, I didn't think you would.'

In the weeks ahead, Hartmann would remember little of what followed, only the vague and never-ending sense of vacuum devoid of those distinctive things around which memory normally coalesced.

From time to time, water would appear in his filthy metal cup, but he had no certain recollection of how it got there. Since there was no dignity in begging, he had soon stopped asking for food. All he truly craved was sleep, but as the forgotten hours accumulated, it was clear that this simple blessing would never be countenanced. Whenever his eyelids shuttered down, the silhouette stepped forward menacingly. Whenever his head drooped, he was woken. At the beginning, a warning shout was enough. But as the hours stacked up, and his body screamed louder to be shut down, only a boot or a slap would pull him back.

'I can't stay awake in this heat. I can't.'

On the single occasion he tried curling up on the floor, the experiment ended abruptly with a kicking. In desperation, he toured his mind for information, certain that he knew nothing that would be of any value.

'What can I tell you?' he wept. 'I don't know anything.'

As he entered the second day, the hallucinations began.

From beneath his feet, pink steam seemed to be seeping between the floorboards and the bloodied face of Heinz Wirz could be seen howling inside the lightbulb. After that he lost all command over his mind, and surrendered to its meanderings.

There was a black GI ringing the hour on a town-hall clock, looking out across a square full of blazing tanks. From inside every bonfire came the screams of burning women. There was a British officer offering him a cigarette from a silver case full of yellow butterflies. When he opened it, and turned towards Hartmann, the man's face turned into a young girl's and was blown away like sand.

Sometimes, amid the madness, there was clarity: Alize on her belly in a dusty attic; Alize asleep at dawn and the smell of baking bread on a spring morning. But on the rare occasions his mute ravings made sense, he cried uncontrollably. And the only thing that would release him from his despair was sleep.

Almost two days had elapsed when the woman – Helen, was it? – returned.

At first, to Hartmann, she felt like another phantom. In his madness, the silhouette against the wall appeared to have softened, and when it stepped forward it did so in a different shape. This time he wasn't required to flinch. Finally, he felt safe enough to close his eyes.

When he opened them again, she was still there, and on the table between them, alongside the blood-spotted paper, was a pen.

'It's Helen, right?'

'You can sleep now,' she said quietly. 'After that we will talk.'

'And if I still have nothing to say?'

Gently, she picked up the pen and turned it in her fingers. 'Then we will start all over again.'

# 13

Hartmann's disconnection from his own world was complete. There were no clocks, no watches; only the now remained.

For a few solitary hours, he'd been taken to a narrow cell containing a single mattress where the dreamless slumber that followed was so profound he might have been dead. When he was woken it was like being winched painfully into the light from a deep, black well.

Every neuron of his body felt damaged. For the first time in days, the throb in his ribs had returned, and the ache behind his eyes made him gasp. At his bedside, he found a bowl of porridge and a cup of something sour and black. With his blackened fingers and then his tongue he tore at the sticky oats until nothing remained. The lukewarm coffee he sipped like wine, feeling the lift from its caffeine and the relief from his thirst.

When he was taken back, she was still there. This time the room seemed lighter, cooler, and Hartmann could smell her perfume as he walked unsteadily towards the table. As he took his chair, their eyes engaged. She was wearing a caramel-coloured blouse and a Celtic cross nestled in the hollow of her neck. Just before she spoke, her head tilted to the left, and the cross slid across her white skin until it was hanging free.

'May I say something?' she asked.

'I'm not really in a position to stop you, am I?'

'You look like shit.'

They had laughed, and then, finally, they had talked.

To Hartmann, every morsel he disclosed felt vapid and inconsequential. Whatever she asked, he answered truthfully, and when it was over she gave him the pen.

He told her about his father and his recruitment through Hitler

Youth. He told her about Russia and morale and he told her about their tanks. When he became tired, or emotional, he was allowed back to his cell. When he returned, she was always there waiting, immaculate and calm. On occasions, there were questions he couldn't answer.

'Why are you in the SS?'

'I don't know. Because it seemed exciting. Because my father wanted it. Because it was too terrifying not to be,' he had replied. 'Look. It was simply what you did. And the uniforms were amazing. Admit it.'

Sometimes there were questions which made him weep.

'Which do you hope it is? Boy or a girl?'

And because it was a conversation, the German had questions of his own.

'Do we mystify you?'

'You don't,' she had told him. 'But the rest of them do.'

'Do you torture all your prisoners?'

'You haven't been tortured. We stopped you sleeping for a few days. That's all. I imagine I'd have been treated worse in Berlin.'

Gradually, he'd fathomed what she was hunting for, and that behind every one of her thrusts lay fear.

To the Allies – embodied by this girl – it seemed incomprehensible that Hitler's mighty Wehrmacht would crumple so easily; somewhere there must be another army, poised like a rat trap. Why else would she ask so many questions about numbers? What other reason for her fascination with the quantities of living men? Only when they'd put a number on their foe, and subtracted the dead and the captured, would the British know the scale of the threat.

And when Hartmann flagged, she probed elsewhere, seeming haunted by the thought of secret technologies that would turn the war back round.

'Are you aware of any special building projects?'

'No.'

'Any unusual transportations or railway movements, or no-go areas?'

For a moment Hartmann thought again about Rosterg's mysterious Zyklon B and the camp he'd seen from the train outside Munich. But it was guns and planes she wanted, not politics. And if Hitler had a miracle up his sleeve, he'd honestly never seen it.

'I saw German soldiers trying to get home in stolen Citroëns. I saw officers pushing prams full of loot. Unless those things count as secret weapons, you should be all right.'

When their conversation lost its way, Hartmann studied the girl's shining maze of hair, sucked hard at the sweet air which surrounded it. In those rare silences it felt as though they were the last two people alive. No noise penetrated their private space from the outside; the fairground steam organ had stayed quiet. To Hartmann, it was as if they alone represented the entirety of war; as if five years of insanity had simply come down to this: two civilised young adults jousting wearily for supremacy with no clear understanding of how or when it might end.

'It's strange, but I've probably spent more time talking to you than to my wife.'

Helen straightened her back and looked up. Her skin was paper-white with exhaustion.

How many other monsters was she interrogating? He pictured Goltz and Mertens and the endless lorryloads of venomous lunatics who would follow. Any one of them would wear down a saint.

Even now, she was scrutinising him through bloodshot eyes. It wasn't a job for a woman. It shouldn't be a job for anyone, he thought, and shame flooded his soul.

'For God's sake, don't cry again,' she said.

'Sorry. I think you still owe me some sleep.'

'I'm not sure I'm allowed to say this – it's probably a hanging offence – but I've enjoyed your company.'

Hartmann wiped his eyes. A week-long beard burned the back of his hand.

'You're in a mess but you're a good man too. Don't let anyone ever tell you different.' She had closed her file, and was standing up. Under the light, Hartmann saw the shadowed curve of her breasts, and turned away.

'Is that it then, Helen Waters?' he said, his eyes locked to the floor. 'Do we shake hands? Do I get paid a fee? Can I go home now?'

He was aware then of her aura at his side; an offered right hand, tiny, with nails like shining fish scales.

'We shake hands.' Her face had been transformed by a huge smile. 'But you don't get to go home just yet. Sorry.'

Clumsily, Hartmann rose to fold her fingers in his. 'A little kiss maybe? Oh, don't panic. I'm only joking.'

He sagged when she was gone. On the table were the three pieces of writing paper and her pen. Hours later, when they came to take him away, they found two crumpled balls rolled into the shadows and one short message across the top of the single blood-spotted sheet that remained. *September 6th. London. My dear Alize. I am a good man. Don't let anyone tell you different. All my love for ever. Max.*

Much later, when they led him back, Koenig was asleep, a glowing cigarette still dangling from his left hand. Hartmann carefully detached it and put it to his own mouth. As he dragged deeply, he studied the face on the mattress. It looked guilt-free like a young boy's – a lifetime younger than Hartmann's – unmarked and fringed with wild blond hair. Gently, he rolled a few loose strands between his fingers.

Hartmann envied the fathomless depth of Koenig's slumber, the precisely syncopated rise and fall of his chest. Lacking faith, Hartmann's nights had become a series of jagged reefs, with dreams like rocks around which it was often impossible to navigate. When he was a child, all his night-time worries had dissolved with the dawn. Here, the onset of daylight simply made them worse.

He sat down quietly by the small steel table, twisting the dead stub under his boot. A few feet away, Koenig had started to snore. It was good that he was sleeping. Hartmann needed a little time. Something odd had happened back in that room.

However hard they tried, Koenig would have told these people nothing. Now, Hartmann needed his friend to believe that he'd been equally resolute. Not that he'd known anything of value, or given them any information they didn't already know. It was all just a game, as Mertens had predicted.

From the crumpled pack on the table, he rattled a fresh tab loose and turned hopefully towards the door. If he was lucky, there'd be a friendly guard with a light.

As he stood up, the cell was shaken by a thunderous bang, followed less than a second later by another matching detonation of sound. In the same moment, up over the rooftops, there was an immense rush of solid air, followed by one sustained note of glorious silence, and then the distant clatter of panic.

Back at the front, he'd lain beneath his tank during countless bombing raids, feeling the soil quiver along his spine. He'd watched the fields and flaming forests turn themselves inside out. But this was different. Two deafening cracks, but no explosion, no alarm bells or sirens.

Through the walls he could hear men running. There'd be little chance of that light now. He turned back towards the beds. Koenig was still sleeping.

For the rest of that night, Hartmann waited.

With his fingers, to pass the time, he traced out the graffiti etched into the ceiling. Girls' names and anonymous heresies; the crude outline of a cock pissing over a passable likeness of Hitler. Clearly, he wasn't alone. Not everyone slept so easily with their secrets as the child below him.

On the wall by his head, several pairs of large breasts had been rendered in stunning detail. It was tough for all of them to live without that. Even back there with Helen Waters he'd felt himself harden. In the military hospital he'd seen it too. Everyone masturbated and not always in secret; one last filthy memory before who knew what. But not here, though. Not right now. Outside, beyond their cage, something had changed. Even in the darkness, Hartmann could sense it.

As the hours passed, he tried to picture sunrise over London, seeing a pale light on an oily river sliding through a city exhilarated by war. All night he'd heard keys in locks and stifled protests, heavy footfall and furious Bavarian oaths. Prisoners were being moved. Apart from Koenig, no one in the entire complex appeared to be sleeping. When their own door finally slammed open, the faces of the guards were grey.

'You. Down. You, fucking wake up.'

Four of them, big men, shoving, shouting, prodding Koenig's curled back with machine guns.

'Now, not to-fucking-morrow. Wake up and stand up. Both of you. Now. Now.'

As Hartmann lowered himself to the floor, Koenig spun furiously, fists clenched, to face his captors. A tangle of hair was stuck across his brow.

'Don't. Please don't,' Hartmann whispered as their faces met.

Koenig's mouth opened and shut silently on his own words.

'Finally,' said Hartmann. 'A little common sense.'

All along their corridor, the same scene was being repeated. Unhappy prisoners were being pushed from their cells and out through the network of passages towards the gardens. As they retraced their steps – stone flags yielding to polished oak floorboards – Hartmann glimpsed sunlight spilling down through a dense perimeter of trees. It was later than he'd thought, mid-morning, maybe, and from somewhere hidden within the maze, there was the smell of bacon frying.

'My God, that smells good.'

Koenig ignored him.

Hartmann tried again. 'Sausage. Sauerkraut. Fried potatoes. Don't tell me you're not interested.'

'Bollocks to that,' hissed Koenig. 'They were listening to us. Everything we said. All of us.'

'Yes. I know.'

'Did you talk? Did you tell them anything?'

'Did you?'

'Of course I fucking didn't.'

Hartmann clasped his friend round the shoulder. 'Trust me. I told them nothing they didn't seem to know already.'

'Good man,' said Koenig. He looked sheepish. 'They even knew we'd got pissed together on the cliffs.'

'Embarrassing, I know. But it's not likely to win them the war.'

There was no bacon for them in the dining room, just cindered bread and porridge on a line of trestle tables. As the men surged forward, Hartmann watched their reflections in a wall panelled with huge mirrors. Kings had probably feasted in this place, he thought. Now look at us, tearing at morsels like wild dogs.

In a few seconds, everything was gone apart from their appetites, and as the men fell quiet he glanced around. There was something distractingly familiar about the scene. Across the table, either side of the pale face of Joachim Goltz, a line of bowed heads was being washed by the sunlight from four vaulted windows. It was like a painting of the Last Supper he'd seen somewhere; Munich, probably. How peculiar that this should feel so similar, and how utterly inappropriate.

'Are you a grass, Hartmann?'

The silence around them thickened. Goltz was turning a piece of burnt toast in his fingers while he spoke and a clock was chiming awkwardly in a distant room.

'Only if telling them my middle name will win them the war.'

'But are you really one of us, Max? Can I call you Max? You don't seem like one of us. Or was your best friend Zuhlsdorff wrong?'

From close behind, Hartmann sensed a guard stepping forward, but he had moved too fast, wrenching up his shirt to turn his skeletal white torso in Goltz's direction. From a welt on his ribcage, purple bruising pulsed out across his chest like spilled wine. Beneath it, just a few inches from his navel, the botched surgery around his Russian bullet wound was still horribly visible. 'Full name, rank, number. Fuck all else. OK?'

By the time he was pushed back down, Goltz was grinning. 'I was joking, Max.' He didn't look as though he'd been joking.

Like a supplicant, he reached both hands across the table; that painting again. 'You're a clever man. What's your theory on the noises in the night?'

There wasn't time to answer. All around them orders were suddenly tumbling through the room. 'Get up. Get up. Get up.'

As they scrambled to their feet, chairs tumbled backwards,

spilling puddles of half-drunk tea out across the tops of the uprooted tables. Finally, with unexpected clarity, Hartmann could remember the way; along past the golden ballroom and into the hall of paintings. This time there was no reception committee, just more soldiers with guns and sticks, shepherding them out to the leafy driveway from where Hartmann looked back. In his life, he'd rarely seen such a dignified building. And yet nothing he'd seen had ever looked less suited to its current purpose.

Two lorries had already gone. The main door on to the marble stairway was closed. Across by the sandbagged sentry posts, the last dingy-looking truck stood rumbling under the broad green canopy of the avenue. No one had asked where they were going. No one would have told them if they had.

When the canvas flap was rolled back down, the men were plunged into darkness. Sitting opposite each other in silence by the tailgate were Hartmann and Goltz.

'Buck up, you two. We're going on another mystery tour.'

Rosterg. Unmistakable, even in the lorry's murk. Hartmann hadn't seen or heard of him for over a week.

'What do you know, Rosterg?' asked Goltz. 'Or rather, what don't you know?'

'A great deal to please you, my friend.' The engine had been turned on. Black exhaust fumes were rising up through the floor. 'Those two explosions we heard last night were rockets.' Rosterg was bellowing now. 'Big new beautiful German rockets.'

'That's why everyone is so scared?'

'Exactly. I think we heard them go through the sound barrier.'

'And they're moving us because?'

'Because the British don't know what might hit them next.'

None of the prisoners asked him how he knew. They were too busy cheering to care. Five minutes later, when the truck jerked back towards the city in a bilious cloud of diesel, the war felt as though it was theirs to win.

As they bounced away, Hartmann felt the sweaty clamp of a hand on his thigh.

'You see. We're still in this.' Goltz grinned. 'Everything to play for.'

Hartmann appeared to nod, but said nothing. From somewhere close by, he was certain he'd caught the reedy refrain of a fairground waltz.

'That's better, Max. You look happy. You should be. We all should be.'

Yes, he was smiling. But Goltz would have killed him if he'd known why.

Max and Hartmann was all there was. There wasn't, and never had been, any middle name to give.

# Private and Confidential

*From:* *Helen Waters*
*To:* *Colonel A. Scotland*

*Once again, I cannot overstate my appreciation for your allowing me to take that two-day break from the interrogations. I don't know why, but dealing with this last batch left me exhausted and it was lovely to be out of the city, especially in this glorious and cheering weather. Everyone is talking about the rockets, however, and everyone is very worried what will come next.*

*No doubt you've done this already, but it would be wise of the War Office to keep an eye on SS-Scharführer Joachim Goltz. An hour in his company left me chilled to the bone. He has a faintly messianic air about him, and nothing short of a handwritten instruction from Hitler will ever persuade him to yield.*

*Among the others, I found Erich Koenig to be the most mystifying, alternating between long periods of silence and incoherent rants about Russian partisans. From what I could see, he was only anything like normal in the company of his cellmate. As you rightly remarked, there's a whole other story there, methinks. But no time for that, I'm afraid. Maybe in another life!*

*However, on the plus side — and it's a huge plus — I feel confident we may have 'turned' a couple of those men in our direction. We shall see, but I have high hopes.*

*Thanks again.*

*P.S. Sadly, still no news of Jim's fate.*

# 14

## September 1944
## London to Devizes
## (Camp 23)

On the train they behaved like children on a school trip; every playground song, every bawdy ballad from the barracks, bellowed out until their voices cracked and the obscenities fizzled out in jubilant laughter.

Rosterg had been well informed. In Paddington Station, as they were hurried across a ghostly midday concourse, they'd heard the incomprehensible shouts of newspaper boys and craned their necks to interpret the headlines.

'What are they saying, Hartmann? You're the clever fucker.'

The British were calling it a V2, and in a charmless London suburb three innocents had been vaporised. It was hardly a glorious new front, but after two dispiriting months the development felt like a conquest.

Rockets – even the British couldn't stand up to rockets.

'There's got to be more. We need to know more. What else is there?' insisted Goltz.

'Nothing. Unless I buy a copy. And that might be problematic.'

All morning, they'd felt the sour loathing of their guards, of the entire city. As they boarded the train, an elderly porter had put down two suitcases, cleared his throat, and emptied its contents over Koenig's back. 'I'll give you first class,' he'd muttered.

Now, stretched out inside one of Great Western Railway's carriages, the mood of the prisoners had soared. Something in the air was shifting. Even Hartmann could feel it. More than the others, he had grown attuned to the mood of his captors, and for the first time since France he could feel doubt.

If there was one rocket, there'd be more. Maybe the three dead pensioners in Chiswick were just a start. Maybe the sky would soon be dark with rockets. A hundred rockets. A thousand rockets. It seemed unlikely, but the thought drew him to the window. Under a broad umbrella, a man holding a briefcase was kissing a woman in a dark green suit. A shower of rain was pricking holes in the grime on the glass. Once again, no one had told them where they were going. He relaxed back. Somebody, somewhere, would have a plan.

There were eight compartments in the carriage, and each one was absurdly comfortable. If they were full, that meant around sixty prisoners. At best, he knew where around half of them had come from. It wasn't a mystery he'd dwell on. Living in ignorance was a prerequisite for any sane soldier. Being a prisoner wasn't so different.

This much he knew: Britain was over-endowed with unused first class carriages and unwanted Germans. When they got there, he'd know where it was. Before then, he'd ride the drunken mood of victory until it sagged.

'I know you're happy, Koenig, but please don't sing,' he muttered, closing his eyes. 'Or you'll get us all arrested.'

After that, they stopped just twice. Once, alongside an orchard, where a red-faced boy shovelled apples through their window. Then again, for two hours, in the dripping black of a tunnel where, finally, the men had fallen silent. From the cracks between the sodden brickwork, pale fingers of calcite pointed down to the track, and when the locomotive eventually pulled out into the light they were in yet another station. Everyone looked at Hartmann, who shrugged. 'I haven't a bloody clue.'

'Camp Number Twenty-three, Devizes,' said a voice from the corridor. 'If you're lucky, they'll have put the roofs on.'

Since London, their train had slid under darkening skies alongside stubbly fields. Now, as the prisoners massed on the platform, grumbles of thunder prowled overhead and rain began coughing from the jaws of rusty drainpipes. Nearby, big band music was seeping between the misted double doors of a station buffet out of which two girls had tottered to stare insolently across at the Germans. One was holding her nose. The other was patching up her lipstick in the mirror of a compact. Behind them, a half-empty passenger train was being flagged clear to leave. Hartmann glanced up at the giant station clock. If it was right, it was 5.27 p.m. For a moment he thought about leaping aboard. No one would have stopped him. No one seemed bothered that they were there.

'I get the feeling we've lost our novelty value.'

Hartmann swivelled round to see Mertens looming over his shoulder. For a huge man, the submariner moved like feathers. He was right, though. The town seemed utterly unmoved by their arrival. Around its stone cross, in the redbrick market square, the bank clerks and grocers had long since totted up and scurried home. Rain spun noisily down black grids and from the doorway of a pub – the White Bear – two solitary drinkers hooted crudely in Hartmann's direction. From somewhere behind him, the girls from the buffet whistled back. Apart from a few swishing cars, and a jeep loaded with American soldiers, nothing else on the street was moving.

The good people of Devizes, it appeared, were not stirring from their wireless sets for the arrival of the SS.

Out of habit, the prisoners had drifted into their marching formation, watched by a handful of distracted GIs and a dozen middle-aged men wearing ill-fitting British army cast-offs. Most of their escort carried guns fixed with bayonets, but none with any conviction; and only a clutch of sodden policemen on bicycles seemed in any way focused upon their task. As the group began to move, two of them pedalled upfront, periodically blowing their whistles, while their caped colleagues scouted the flanks, clutching truncheons. Head down against the horizontal rain, Hartmann slouched on.

Within a few minutes, houses had given way to harvested fields and bramble-thick hedgerows. A few strides ahead, Goltz appeared to be goose-stepping alone through the deepening puddles in just his socks. In the evening light, his skin looked grey.

'It's a punishment. Apparently he tried insisting on a lift from the station.'

Hartmann glanced to his left. The lean figure of Rosterg had fallen in alongside, where he was calmly wiping the rain from his spectacles with a monogrammed handkerchief. When they were dry he hooked the arms back over his ears and beamed. His uniform, although saturated, looked fresh. His whiskers, unlike everyone else's, appeared miraculously trimmed.

'You read it well, Max. We've been left in the hands of bank managers and grocers. All the young ones are probably in Germany drinking my claret.'

Ahead of them, carried on a flurry of wind, a bell came clanging. A few seconds later, a military ambulance rounded a bend, spitting muddy grit over the men.

'We must be close,' said Rosterg, removing his glasses again. 'There'll be trouble if they haven't run my hot bath.'

'To be closely followed by a round of golf and à la carte with the camp commandant?'

'Indeed.' Rosterg smirked. 'But not golf, Max, please. Billiards.'

A few steps ahead, one of the British guards had stumbled on the steep wet verge. As they passed him, in softening light, Hartmann offered an arm. The soldier declined. 'I'll be fine. Not far to go now. Better move along unless you want a whack from a copper.'

'You really have got a soft spot for losers, haven't you?' whispered Rosterg.

Even at dusk, it looked enormous. On both sides of the road, brand-new huts stretched back in seemingly endless rows. Fieldsful of giant tents crouched around parade squares fluttering with Union Jacks and in every direction – under generator-powered spotlights – more buildings were being wrestled into place. Rippled sheets of corrugated iron stood in huge silver piles, and dumper trucks loaded with bricks heaved themselves across a churning lake of mud. As the rain eased, steam began to rise along a line of shiny-backed Nissen huts.

There were sturdier barracks too – immense turreted veterans of older wars – and all of it, this whole swarming campus, appeared swaddled in billowing curtains of vicious barbed wire beyond which Hartmann could see thousands of men, heads down, streaming towards the canteens for their suppers, followed by the eyes in the towers where the big guns were primed.

From the road, Hartmann could make little sense of it. It would be days before he did. Only then, fully armed with hearsay and his own observations, did the epic scale of Camp 23 sink in.

Several thousand prisoners had got there before him, and the total was rising constantly. Every day – in the early evening – a few hundred more would march in from the station. Every morning, before it was light, a smaller number were clandestinely shipped out. No one seemed to know where or why. Troublemakers, some said. The wounded, said others. No one really cared. Food and fags were what mattered, closely followed by information.

And with every new arrival came yet more fuel for the rumour machine. Camps were being thrown up everywhere, it was said; hundreds of them; camps like small cities; camps in Scotland; black camps for killers; all of them leaking like sieves and the British countryside supposedly alive with armed fugitive Nazis.

At the entrance to the camp, a lone sentry box guarded each gate-post, and a small wooden office block provided shelter for a handful of uniformed men. From inside, a kettle could be heard whistling. No one seemed in a rush to come out into the rain.

When a brisk-looking sergeant finally emerged clutching a mug of tea, there was a swift head count, an exchange of damp pieces of paper, and the wooden gates were dragged open. Beyond them, through a single line of twelve-foot wire fencing, Hartmann could see soldiers waving their arms.

'This way. Look sharp. *Schnell. Schnell.*' Down a gravelled path, under orange sodium lights, they were pushed towards a shower block. 'Strip, wash, and then through there. Leave your clothes where they are.'

As the men tiptoed into the water, guards rifled through the stinking pile slicing off metal buttons and Nazi insignia. Souvenirs. Items to trade.

'That's my fucking uniform. You've no right. You've no fucking right.'

It was Koenig, snarling naked under an icy cascade. Two military policemen were dragging him out by the arms towards Hartmann.

'You speak English, right? Tell us what this Kraut fucker is saying.'

Koenig's eyes were wild. Shorn of his uniform, he looked helpless, weak.

'He says he's never been so clean. He thanks you . . . and can he keep his cap?'

'You're a lying cunt.' The men let Koenig go. 'Tell him his stuff's going on the fire.'

After that, there were no more indignities. In place of SS grey, they pulled on two-piece prison suits, cut from rough military cloth. Sewn on to the back of the mauve jacket and the left leg of the matching trousers was a large black disc. In the pockets of each were three unexplained metal tokens.

'I met Hitler in that uniform, Max,' mumbled Koenig, stretching out his right hand. 'He shook that. I touched him.'

'I know. You told me. Hands like an artist.'

None of the others was speaking. Humiliation had rendered them mute.

During the meal which followed, not even Rosterg dared fracture the silence. At one end of a deserted canteen, they sat across tables replete with food: serving plates tottering with bread and brutish chunks of orange cheese; rock-like dumplings bobbing in tureens brimming with fatty broth.

So much food – more than they'd seen for months – and to begin with, as always, they had ripped into it like fifty or so frenzied animals. A few minutes later, very little of it had been eaten. First our souls, now our stomachs, Hartmann realised. Everything about us has shrivelled.

It had been a long day. When they were herded outside, nothing much else was moving. Spotlights flickered across the wet metal roofs but the huts were dark and the residents silent. In his head, each man was trying hard to cling on to his bearings: a lamppost, a manhole cover, a chimney, anything. Knowing the way back might be useful, but the night had come early and there was nothing much to see; just the silhouettes of their guards, the neat lines of identical arched Nissens, and the first stars pricking the forested horizon.

Finally, at what felt like the camp's black heart, they'd entered a second compound. More wire and more huts, built in pairs and staring across at each other like accusing twins. At the third one on the left, they stopped. There were two small windows either side of a crude wooden door set in a semicircle of brick. A number six had been painted in black on the wooden doorframe and neither its door nor its windows were locked.

'This is it. Home sweet home.' A soldier had stepped forward and was gesturing for them to enter. 'What were you expecting? The Ritz?'

No one moved. A few more drops of rain stirred on a sharp swirl of wind.

From the back of the group, Goltz was pushing through. 'I'm knackered. Let's stop dicking about.'

As he wrenched open the door and stepped in, a rancid draught blew out. Men in barracks, from Dresden to Devizes; the same flatulent stink everywhere.

Followed by the others, Goltz pushed on into the darkness of the block. Down each side, sleeping men were stretched out on bunk beds. 'Just find a space,' he said. 'We'll see who they are in the morning.' If anyone was awake – which they were – they didn't speak.

For once, indifferent to the swampy air, Hartmann could have slept for ever. Since his capture, every day had seemed never-ending, and a thin blanket on a doughy mattress felt like luxury. He had pushed Koenig ahead of him, and the two of them had taken a bunk at the end furthest from the door. Within seconds, Koenig's snores were swelling the hut's glottal chorus, while Hartmann's legs had embarked on their involuntary nightly dance.

When the twitching eased, and the dreams began, they were rotten ones. He was suffocating in a giant swastika. He was being thrown out of a plane, bound naked to Alize. He was standing alone in a vast field full of blazing torches. But even when he stirred, troubled by the distant nag of his bladder, Hartmann slumbered on.

# Private and Confidential

*Diary entry:  HQ, Salisbury Plain and Dorset District (POW directorate)*
*Date:          13 Sept. 1944*

*At 23 POW Camp Devizes, additional facilities have been put in hand to meet the new commitment — i.e. 7,500 German POWs in permanent residence. It is expected this could be accepted by 30th Nov. 44 as follows: in covered accommodation: 6,170; in tents: 1,330.*

*Furthermore, the District Command has authorised the provision of a further 46 Nissen huts to replace the single tentage at present in use. Three working parties, each of fifty German POWs from Camp 23, have been organised by HQ under escort to work on public highways, a helpful expedient in removing the large deposits of mud brought on to the roads by tracked vehicles which have led to the cancellation of local bus services.*

*Urgent note: SS — and other black-grade prisoners — are in no circumstances to be granted access to these work parties.*

# 15

It was still dark when the bugle blew. Distant at first, but then closer and loud, a shrill coda to a sleep cut short.

As the men surfaced, subdued conversations began, building quickly to a curious buzz. Outside, someone was banging the hut's glossy metal skin repeatedly with a stick. Inside, legs were swinging down off beds and a string of men was dashing for the door. Everyone, like Hartmann, had slept in his prison clothing. Everyone, like Hartmann, was desperate for the lavatory. Without waking Koenig, he slid on his boots.

The hut was full. Twenty bunks each side; eighty men in total. No wonder the place stank. During the night, a handful of buckets had served as latrines and no one seemed in any hurry to empty them. Instead, the prisoners were filing out into the sharp morning air where a thin beading of dawn was visible beyond the perimeter wire.

Hartmann filled his lungs. It was five in the morning maybe, certainly no later than six. Across the whole camp, dingy security lights were still glowing on their concrete stalks. Shapes were becoming clearer. Seven more identical huts in his compound alone; over six hundred prisoners.

Black discs were everywhere, like holes in the men's backs; a sea of black holes bobbing towards the concrete toilet blocks intent upon only one thing. And among them, the loping adolescent form of Kurt Zuhlsdorff.

Hartmann spotted him first. 'How perfect that we should meet up again in a shithouse.'

'I know that voice.' Zuhlsdorff's eyes squinted against the low, rising sun. 'My old friend, the patriot.'

'Were you on a mission, or did you just fancy a cushier number?'

'Fuck off, Hartmann. I missed you. They rumbled me. I couldn't keep away. All right?'

'Piece of advice, Zuhlsdorff.' Hartmann pointed at the younger man's ravaged hand. 'Next time you go undercover, wear gloves.'

Inside the icy latrine they pulled down their pants and took a seat. Along an entire wall, twenty men sat over an open drain which ran out through a wall. As the river of waste flowed beneath them, schoolyard comments flew around the block.

'There's not much to amuse us here, Max. Seeing who generates the day's biggest turd represents a high point in our routine. You should do well.'

Hartmann cast around for some paper.

'We get issued three sheets a day and most people save it to keep diaries or write letters.'

'So what do we use?'

Zuhlsdorff held up both hands, revealing the puckered stumps of his lost fingers. 'When you're done, the sinks are over there.' He grinned.

Hartmann groaned. Lately, his bowels had felt as if they were full of rocks. Without any paper, maybe that was a blessing.

With an awkward hitch of his trousers, Zuhlsdorff stood and moved towards the row of sinks. After a few more seconds of futile heaving, Hartmann gave up and shoved his filthy hands under a trickle of cold water.

'Remind me,' he said. 'Back at that military hospital, you told me you'd had blood transfusions.'

'That's right.' Zuhlsdorff had stood up straight to wipe his wet hands on the seat of his trousers.

'Anyone ever tell you where the blood was from?'

'What's your fucking point?'

'My point, Zuhlsdorff, is that they were using Jewish blood, drawn from the pumping heart of a real-life American Jew boy GI.'

'You're lying. You're fucking lying.' Zuhlsdorff's shoulders had slumped, and in the toilet block's feeble light his skin looked grey.

'Maybe I am. But you'll never be sure, and that makes me happy. Great start to the day. See you around, my friend.'

Back at the hut, Hartmann poked Koenig awake. The bugle was blowing again and the new arrivals were floundering towards the door. Zuhlsdorff still hadn't emerged from the latrines.

'We eat when they've counted us,' someone was explaining.

Ahead of him, he could see Goltz and Mertens, distinct shapes against the brightening windows. Beyond them, marshalled by British soldiers, a line was forming on each side of the grassy rectangle between the eight prefabricated dorms. Everywhere he looked, hundreds of men were slouching into position. Each one sported the two giant black discs, and as the sunlight finally broke clear two British officers bellowed into the silence.

'Att-en-tion.'

No one moved. Hartmann's chest was pounding. The tinny drone of the bugle had stopped and a halyard was pinging rhythmically on a flagpole. Witnessing Zuhlsdorff's collapse had been good. He'd forgotten what elation felt like.

'ATT-EN-TION.'

The officers were standing back to back now, pale-faced. One of them had his fingers clamped over the pistol holstered to his belt. The other already had a service revolver in his hand. Both looked utterly lost. All around them, the prisoners were slowly raising their right arms in a stiff-backed salute. When a solitary voice rang out a '*Sieg Heil*', it was immediately joined by more, until every man – including Hartmann – was spitting out the mantra; a hoarse crescendo of hatred that rose above the entire camp like a sullen cloud.

'*Sieg Heil. Sieg Heil. SIEG HEIL.*'

And then a shot, followed by more shots, and then nothing.

'Don't worry. It happens just about every day.' An unfamiliar voice from behind in his ear. 'They do their thing. We do ours. Then we can all go away and feed our faces.'

Hartmann resisted the temptation to respond. Loaded weapons weren't fun, even when they missed. Hut by hut, name by name, the prisoners were being ordered forward to be checked off. When his name came, he was ready. At last the guards were satisfied, and the men were dismissed. Only then, as they flooded off towards food, did the tension slacken. Barely an hour had passed since reveille, and already Hartmann felt exhausted.

'I'm Heinz Bruling, by the way.' It was the voice from roll call. 'Mind if I join you for breakfast?'

Hartmann shrugged. It was too early for small talk with another zealot.

'Step on it a bit, and we'll get to the front of the queue.'

Ahead of them, prisoners were jostling to get through green-painted double doors into the long flat-roofed canteen.

'There's always plenty,' Bruling explained, 'but it's usually cold if you get in last.'

From inside, the crisp smell of fried food was pouring out of the kitchen. Despite his recalcitrant bowels, Hartmann's appetite quickened. The bottom end would look after itself. Eventually. Right now, the top end badly needed attention.

As the queue stuttered closer, the fatty fragrance became over-whelming. Along one entire wall, greasy-smocked orderlies stood watch over steaming tureens. Calibrated helpings of creamed rice for every man. A dollop of jam. Two plums. Four slices of fried bread. The ubiquitous sweet tea. And yet more cheese.

Behind him, the low rumble of expectation seemed to stretch right back into the courtyard. It was his turn now. He picked up a chipped enamel plate and pushed it forward. Nothing happened. A dripping ladle of porridge hung motionless over his dish. 'You've forgotten something, pal.'

Hartmann stared back at the server helplessly.

'They want paying.' Bruling had returned, clutching a tray covered in food. 'Somewhere in your clothes? The three metal discs?'

Hartmann felt inside his trouser pockets. The ragged tokens, seemingly hacked from a tin can, were still there. When he handed one across, his plate was filled.

'You surrender one for each of the day's meals and then tomorrow morning you get them back and start again. Unless, of course, you want to trade them. You'd be surprised what people will swap for second helpings.'

Hartmann doubted whether he would. He also doubted whether he'd ever grow tired of being fed like this.

The two men took seats at the end of a long trestle. For a few minutes they ate in a state of trance-like concentration. Everyone in the room was doing the same, heads studiously bent and spoons scraping. Hartmann finished first and watched Bruling mopping up his porridge with a crust. He seemed different, somehow; less gaunt, and much less wired. Like all of them, he was horribly young – early twenties, no more – but his thinning hair framed a round, bookish face, and his manner lacked the obligatory tribal snarl.

'Is it always this good?' Hartmann asked.

'Three times a day. I've never eaten better.' Bruling took a measured sip from his tea. The room was jammed tight with men. 'The Tommies hate us, but we're soldiers too,' he explained. 'That means we get exactly the same rations as them. Bacon, cake, biscuits, everything. Those are the rules. Whatever else happens in here, you'll never be hungry.'

'You sound like an old hand.'

From his tunic pocket, Bruling dug out the remains of two battered cigarettes. He lit both, and passed the longer one to Hartmann. His hands were pale and undamaged.

'You came last night, right? I watched you come in. We've been here three weeks. All of us in that same hut as you. All rounded up together. All sick as pigs it ended so soon.'

For fifteen minutes, they swapped stories under a stinging fog of service tobacco. Bruling was bright. Three years before, he'd walked out of a Hamburg university, preferring *Mein Kampf* to mathematics. He'd fought in Russia, then France, earning promotion to Rotten-führer – section leader – somewhere along the way. Belonging to the SS, he said ruefully, had felt like a calling more than a duty.

Inwardly, Hartmann grieved. 'You don't seem to fit the stereo-type,' he said quietly. 'I'm disappointed.'

Not long after that, they left, drifting out under still-warm September sun. The Rottenführer had been right. There were two more daily meals, each one just as substantial as the last. But in between them, Hartmann quickly realised, there was absolutely nothing.

Forgoing Bruling's offer of company, he'd paced his new world alone. Eight Nissen huts, a toilet block and the canteen building lay inside a compound the size of a football pitch. Around them was a badly constructed wire fence, slung between evenly spaced concrete posts no more than ten feet high. Along the top of the fence, barbed wire ran from corner to corner. Along the bottom, shovelfuls of earth had been slung hurriedly across the mesh to hold it down. On Hartmann's first lap, he'd nudged it loose with his foot.

On his second, he'd opened a gap big enough for a fox to crawl through.

On his third, he scuffed the hole shut.

No one had seen him. And from what he could tell, no one had been looking. Carefully, he scanned the compound. Security was laughable. A couple of dopey-looking guards by the gate set against the hundreds of bored young SS killers stretched out on the grass, or back in their bunks murdering time.

They've put us all together, he thought, when they should have driven us apart. They're feeding us up, and making us strong again.

Bruling had looked so fit there'd been a bonfire in his eyes. Soon Goltz and the others would be re-energised, and everywhere he wandered Hartmann heard the same conversation. V2. V2. V2. The war was swinging round. Prisoners one day, kings the next.

Faith was surging back through men programmed to believe in their own invincibility.

# 16

By the end of the day, he had a much sharper idea of his new world.

His first impressions had been right. The camp was huge. Four independent compounds surrounded by their own wire sat within a further outer fence. One enormous compound for the Wehrmacht soldiers, smaller ones for the Luftwaffe, the officers and the SS; each fully segregated from the rest, and each one growing fast.

Such as they were, the guards seemed to be a peculiar mix of old-school British officers and toothless veterans, supplemented by the miscellaneous Americans who'd been left behind in the Normandy rush. Every single one of them, he suspected, would rather have been fighting.

'There's one other thing you need to know,' Bruling told him later over a bowl of mutton stew. 'All the other prisoners can apply for work off the camp. Farming, ditch digging, road repairs, that sort of stuff.'

'And because we're category black, that's not allowed?'

'Correct. We're the only ones with absolutely nothing to do. Except eat and get pissed off.'

After that, the evening seemed interminable. Another tense roll call had preceded the third meal, following which the men were restricted to their huts until lights out at 9.30 p.m. As darkness fell, groups of men playing cards reached for their bedding. Games of chess were left abandoned. Huddled conversations withered and died.

Propped up on his top bunk, Hartmann looked down the full length of the hut. It was strange, but for the first time in weeks he'd had a good day. Zuhlsdorff was still brooding alone somewhere. Koenig was refusing to eat, and had sulked in the hut between roll calls. Goltz was off circulating furiously, but their paths had not crossed. Left alone, under the sun, he'd felt almost normal. Staring up at the clouds, serenaded by a blackbird, he'd remembered who he was. Not just POW No. 15298. He was somebody's husband, somebody's father, and those twin certainties had unlocked an anomalous rush of joy. Even the cherub-faced Bruling had noticed.

'You seem happy,' he'd said.

'Do I? Remind me how it looks.'

Now, under the metal skin of the hut, having removed only their shoes, each prisoner had entered a grim, private race against the cold. Most still wore their caps, and unless sleep came quickly they'd shiver all night in their single blankets. Once the lights had clicked out, the building filled with new sounds: coughing; the clatter of urine in buckets; the rustle of a horsehair mattress and the eerie creaking of the roof as it contracted beneath a star-crammed sky. If we're still here in December, Hartmann thought, we will all freeze to death.

Long ago, under a tank somewhere, he remembered craving the sanctuary of absolute silence – war's impossible dream. But even here, in the night's stillness, he could make out the thud of distant trucks and the laboured engines of bomb-heavy planes.

Maybe it wasn't happiness. Maybe it was hope. Against all logic, he felt certain that Helen Waters had sent his note and that someone would be moving it on from one bomb-crushed address to the next until it found her.

Next time, he'd write more. Next time, he'd tell her he was coming home.

A few bunks away, someone had started babbling in his sleep, a high-pitched voice like a terrified child's. Someone threw a boot and the whining stopped. Hartmann turned and corkscrewed into his blanket. Deep within his groin, sharpened by the cold, his unemptied bladder was whispering again.

Every few minutes, the hut's two far windows glowed in the light spinning round on the guard tower. If he counted the flashes, maybe he could bore himself to sleep. But after fifty or so, the whisper was a scream. Somehow he had to reach those buckets. As he eased down on to the hut's concrete floor, he tried to picture where they were:

halfway down on the left; a dozen paces along into the cacophony of wheezing. That was it. Hartmann picked up his boots, clutched his testicles and inched forward, feeling for obstacles with his feet.

Something ripe-smelling was horribly near. As the tower light flashed again, he saw it: a steaming pail, crammed with black water and faeces. He lurched back, rocking a second bucket hidden in the shadows. Something warm sloshed onto his trousers. Hartmann retched. Both buckets were full. He had to get outside. Upended chess pieces were rolling on the floor. Disturbed sleepers were bawling furiously after his phantom silhouette. A few more steps and he was out, hands on the side of the hut, wrenching open his flies.

He stood up, relieved, and stretched back with a shiver. Dew was forming on the grass already, sparkling under a black helmet of stars. Feeling better in the open air, Hartmann pulled his coat tight and walked out beyond the latrine block towards the wire.

Looking back from a slight knoll, he could make out the geometric shape of the camp and follow the spotlight as it swung lazily across the square-shaped SS compound. Between the fence and the toilet block he was completely invisible. Unless someone came looking, he could stay there all night. With his back against a concrete stanchion, he hunched up against the cold and filled his lungs. A raw northerly wind was carrying the rustle of distant trees, and with it the plea of a solitary owl. After a minute, he stood up and walked cautiously along the inside of the fence towards the canteen.

At the midway point, he kneeled down. In the friable topsoil, his shaking fingers located the bottom of the wire. Within a few seconds he had freed a section the width of a man. He took a long, deep breath. What was he doing? He'd only come out to relieve himself. Now, for the first time in days, his guts had started to move.

He could stand, turn round, and go back. He could forget all about this and eat three huge meals a day until someone put him on a boat home. Except that he wouldn't. He would see where this went. No one else would need to know.

With both hands, Hartmann held the lower edge of the fence and pulled upwards until a space had opened into which he could crawl.

One quick glance over his shoulder, and he was through. No gunfire. No dogs. No voices. Only the timpani of his heart. He was alive. His mouth was crammed with dirt. But he was still alive.

Slowly, he came up off his knees. Directly in front of him was another identical fence running parallel to the one he had just scrambled under. Between them was an overgrown no man's land, around six feet wide, running away on both sides like a corridor through the darkness. Beyond the second fence he could distinguish the outline of more huts – huge huts – similar in shape but four times bigger than his own. As he tried to count them, the arc of a second guard tower light began moving quickly towards him. He froze. The beam advanced, rippling on the apparently endless rows of tin roofs before spinning out towards the fence. Certain that it would find him, he raised his hands over his head. The white ellipse of light was tracking speedily across the sodden grass. Any moment now, they would see him and shoot.

He closed his eyes. Nothing happened. When he opened them, the pale disc had swept harmlessly on. Five minutes later, Hartmann was still watching. This time, he would keep his eyes open. Behind him, the light over his own compound seemed to have packed up altogether. At its closest, this second beam fell yards short of the fence. Wherever the corridor went to, it was completely unguarded. Whatever he did, no one would see him.

Squatting down in the long grass, Hartmann composed his thoughts. How long was it since he'd left the hut? Ten minutes? An hour? If anything, the sky had darkened. No trace of dawn yet. No need to head back. Tucking his cap into the wire as a marker, he turned left and walked quickly along the gap between the compounds.

If nothing else, it was something to do.

# 17

After that, he went out every night. Sometimes he wandered. Sometimes he merely watched.

Without his secret excursions, he would have been crushed by the routine, and by the bitterness which now polluted almost every exchange. On the rare occasions that they spoke, his conversations with Koenig were short and cold. Beyond the curtain of darkness, he was alone and Camp 23 was his to explore.

Within a week, he'd drawn a clear mental map of not so much a prison, more a German city, spreading fast across the autumnal Wiltshire fields. By his own crude reckoning, six new huts were going up daily, most of them for the newly arrived Wehrmacht prisoners who whistled in cheerfully through the main gates every day around dusk. The smaller structures housed eighty men. The new ones were like massive warehouses, each providing shelter for six hundred, maybe more. After navigating the wire corridor which kept the groups of prisoners apart, Hartmann put the camp's population at six thousand.

Six thousand.

Under the moonlight, around the fringes of their huts, groups of Wehrmacht prisoners kicked footballs listlessly until boredom drove them back to their bunks. Elsewhere, Hartmann hid and listened as a fledgling choir found its voice behind metal walls. During the nights that followed, it grew more confident, launching full-throated German hymns across the stillness of the camp. No one stepped in to interfere, and as each song reached its climax, muffled applause burst out all over the giant army compound.

After a few trips, he was staying out longer and penetrating deeper. Inside the main perimeter wire, close to the main gates, was a deserted parade ground. On the other side of the wire were the brick-built quarters of the guards into which they retreated every night. Beyond that, he could follow the fitful shadows of night traffic, enjoying glimpses of the wooded countryside beyond.

Apart from the desultory spotlights, and the 24-hour watch posted on each of the four compound gates, security seemed to evaporate soon after curfew. With familiarity came the realisation that escape would be easy, and once the idea had drawn breath, there was no shifting it from his thoughts.

Inside the SS huts, the atmosphere was increasingly rank. Creeping back into his bed each night, Hartmann sensed the poison like a pressure shift in the air. With no news to sustain them and the inescapable joylessness of their days, morale had crashed. Even in their sleep, the men looked tense. Except for the daily name-checking, the relentless meals, there was nothing for them to do; nowhere for them to go. It was a hollow into which Goltz had poured himself with masterful aplomb.

After displacing Bruling as the self-appointed leader of Hut No. 6, he'd wasted no time in asserting his total command over the occupants of the other seven huts. There'd been no formal coup; Bruling had merely deferred to the formidable cocktail of combat legend and mobster-in-chief with which Goltz charmed his new world. Even the listless Koenig had been impressed, and wherever their leader now wandered, he, Zuhlsdorff and Mertens were never far behind.

At mealtimes, their arrival in the canteen guaranteed a dip in the luminous chatter. Away from it, they ensured that the continuance of the war – and victory – remained uppermost in every prisoner's thoughts. If there was dissent, no one voiced it, and even Hartmann felt compelled to raise his arm during roll call. For whatever reason – despite the incident in the shower – Goltz had shown no hostility towards him. And for the sake of his health, Hartmann was determined to keep it that way.

In the middle of the third week, the wind swung round to the south, lifting the mood with a soft surge of warm air and blue skies. Whenever they could, the men eased out into the sunshine, or shambled in groups around their pen.

'You and Goltz seem close.' It had been several days since Hartmann had sought Koenig out. There was an awkwardness between them neither had experienced before.

'Do we? Maybe. I like him. He talks a lot of sense. Is that an issue?'

'I'm still your best friend though. Right?'

Koenig had nodded. 'Sure.'

The two of them had reached the fence behind the toilet block. Somewhere in the distance, sand and gravel were grinding around inside a cement mixer.

'I need to tell you something,' Hartmann had whispered. 'I just need to know I can still trust you.'

Koenig had smiled – his old smile – and slid his arm round Hartmann's waist. 'Charlie and his Orchestra. Of course you can.'

'See here. Look.' With his right foot, Hartmann had scraped away a small bowl of dirt, exposing the ragged bottom edge of the fence. 'I go out every night. I know every inch of this place. I could get you out. Me and you. I'm talking about escape.'

'You must be fucking joking.' Koenig had stepped away, pulling his arm back.

'Why would I be? This place stinks. We're all slowly dying here. You know that.'

'Because we're stronger together, maybe? Because you'd get killed for nothing?'

'I've a kid somewhere, Erich. I can't wait.'

'You were going to go without me.'

'That's not true. I've not even started to work this out.'

The two friends had parted moments later. That night, bad weather stormed back again, penning all the men behind their iron walls.

Koenig had made himself invisible, and for the first time in days Hartmann chose not to slip out of the compound after darkness. Not that night, nor the next three. Something felt wrong, something was stirring, and so he ticked off the hours playing endless games of patience, while forcing away memories of the violinist's mangled face.

Outside, drumrolls of squally sleet fed icy pools of slush.

On the fourth night of rain, he watched nervously as Goltz swept into the canteen with his entourage. No queuing; no scruffy metal tokens either. Shaking the drops from their sodden uniforms, they'd strolled to the head of the line, filled their plates, and taken the table kept exclusively for them. Among the group, to Hartmann's surprise, was the bookish face of Heinz Bruling. When their eyes eventually met, Bruling put down his knife and fork and walked cautiously across to where he was sitting.

'I can't join you, Max. I'm with them.'

'Yes. I saw. I'll be careful what I say.' Hartmann paused to swallow a mouthful of cake. 'I never had you down as Goltz's type.'

'He's not so bad.' Bruling laughed. 'What else is there to do in this shithole anyway?' He looked back to check his chair was still free, and dropped his voice. 'Look at us. We could all go mad in here. Goltz might wake us up a bit.'

Hartmann glanced away sharply. A bucketful of cutlery had crashed to the floor. As always, there'd be another mind-numbing wait while the guards counted the knives.

'There's a meeting later. Goltz wants you there.'

'Any idea why?'

'Nothing to do with me, Max. We're Schutzstaffel, remember. We don't ask questions.'

When he left the canteen, the rain was coming harder, cascading between the corrugated ripples of the Nissen huts and backing up around the hastily laid concrete foundations. Inside, a line of rusty drips had surfaced along the seams of the roofs and bunks had been dragged aside to dodge the leaks.

As he ran to Hut No. 6, Hartmann heaved his jacket up over his head. Either side of the door, the black windows stared at him like two rheumy eyes. Behind them, the block felt cold and damp. Apart from himself, there was only one man there.

'You're still wearing your uniform, Rosterg. How come?'

Rosterg peered down at his tunic. Damp streaks were spreading out from his epaulettes. Drops of rain clung to the round metal buttons, and he was still wearing the soft calfskin boots he'd been captured in.

'A welcome privilege, Max. That's all.'

'Which you earn for doing what exactly?' Since their walk from Devizes Station, Hartmann had seen nothing of the older man.

'You and I are lucky. We can speak English. Not everyone does. A place like this needs an interpreter. Let's say I've made myself useful.'

Hartmann grinned. The man was indestructible, forever sliding mysteriously between the cracks; no less sleek in the squalor of a transit camp than he had been in the baroque splendour of a London palace.

'What's this all about, Rosterg?'

'Absolutely no idea. Some sort of lecture, perhaps?'

Even here, with his spectacles misted over and his hair shining wet, the man's composure seemed perfectly intact. With a wordless bow towards Hartmann, he busied himself with the task of drying his perennially wet glasses. When he was satisfied, he pushed them back along his nose, and sighed.

'Blind as a bat without them, Max.'

'So how do *I* make myself useful?'

'That's not so easy, I'm afraid.' Rosterg inclined his head, indicating the black roundel on Hartmann's leg and back. 'I'm not SS. I'm a pen-pusher. I don't represent the same threat to civilisation that you lot do.'

'And if I was wearing a different badge, would that make me less of a threat?'

'Quite possibly. But I'm not really sure how we find that out.'

Outside, the wind was firing pellets of sleet against the windows and water was wriggling between their feet towards the door. Rosterg stepped carefully to one side and eased himself down on the lower half of a bunk.

'Not what you're used to?' asked Hartmann. 'Need to keep those nice boots dry?'

'Oh, do stop bleating. As it happens, I slept the first night under canvas. And yes, I slept the next night in the officer hut, which is where I still am. So what? Someone has to work out the system. Someone has to be on the inside. You can't fight what you don't understand.'

'So help me understand, you clever fucker.'

Hartmann listened carefully. To ensure discipline, each of the four compounds had its own leader and management group. Above them all in the prison hierarchy was the Lagerführer – the self-appointed spokesman for the camp's entire prisoner population.

'He's the one who talks to the British camp commandant when we've got any issues. Food, medical supplies, bedding, that sort of stuff. He's the one who needed someone who spoke various languages, someone who knew British ways. Me, in other words; the perfect fit, as always.'

'So you're this Lagerführer person's bumboy?'

Rosterg sighed. 'Whatever happens here, I know about it.'

'And the Lagerführer. Is he SS?'

'No. He's army. A major. Walter Bultmann. Between you and me, he's a little faggot – a pussy, a pushover.'

'So where does Goltz fit in?'

'There are five Wehrmacht soldiers to every one of you SS types. If all of them accepted that the war was truly lost, people like Goltz would be powerless. You'd be overwhelmed. It's the faint possibility that Hitler might win that keeps them so afraid. I suspect Goltz wants to keep it that way.'

'You're saying doubt makes us – him – strong?'

'Precisely. Nothing else.'

In the gloom, something hard had torn loose on the roof. A line of bolts connecting two iron panels had sheared, and cold air was pouring in from a fading crescent of sky.

'Still think you'll get back to that wine cellar, Wolfgang?'

'That's all I think. What about you?'

Hartmann didn't answer. Beyond the walls, he could hear the stomping of puddled feet and the ringing laughter of Koenig. It was terrifying how quickly their relationship had deteriorated. Since their brief conversation by the fence, not a word had passed between them, and Koenig's surrender to the compound's darker elements seemed complete. Sitting down across from Rosterg, Hartmann watched the door peel back in a spatter of rain; Goltz first, then Bruling, Zuhlsdorff,

Koenig and the impassive form of Josef Mertens closing the night out behind themselves and a few whose faces he didn't know. No one else was coming, and Koenig was doing everything he could not to catch Hartmann's eyes.

'We need to sit,' barked Goltz.

A damp semicircle was hastily formed around a single empty chair, lit from overhead by an electric light. Behind them, Hartmann withdrew his face from its glow. With luck they might forget he was there. Beneath his backside, he could feel the misery of waterlogged bedding. A few poor souls wouldn't be sleeping well tonight. Rain was running everywhere and the ends of his fingers were yellow with cold.

For a few empty minutes, as the group settled, Goltz was the only thing moving. No one had yet occupied the empty chair and the only sounds were the drip-drip from the ceiling and the furious hissing of water on a hot bulb. From the far side of the hut Zuhlsdorff appeared to be staring furiously in his direction.

'Someone seems to be missing. One of our guests.' There was a mangled scraping of wood on concrete. The wet slap of Goltz's footsteps had stopped. 'Are you still with us back there, Max?' His voice was as lifeless as his skin. 'Is there anything you might like to share with us?'

Hartmann stiffened. They knew. They knew. And now they could all see him, shrinking further back from the light under the creaking woodwork. One by one, they were standing and shouting, but panic had rendered Hartmann deaf and the room had fallen inexplicably silent. In mute horror, he watched as Koenig rose from his chair and stepped forward to sit next to his friend.

Hartmann shivered and tightened the blanket around his shoulders. The night's cold had burrowed itself into his marrow.

'I told them, Max. What else was I going to do?'

# 18

It was impossible to know who was hitting him. Everything had happened so horribly fast. Cold pairs of hands had pulled him down on to the floor, dragging his jacket over his face. Booted feet were stamping on his back; a piece of wood – a chair leg maybe – was being used by someone to club his head and neck.

Zuhlsdorff would be one of them, for sure. He could feel the venom. He could hear the juvenile glee in his grunts. Mertens too, probably. Just so long as it wasn't Koenig. Please. Please, not Koenig, he thought.

If he rolled over he'd see them, but all that mattered were his ribs, and so he curled down deeper until he could taste the foul wet dirt of the floor.

'On the chair. Put him on the fucking chair.'

The beating stopped at once. Someone was dragging him by the arm. He could feel the slender outline of the chair, and then a second pair of hands yanking him up and round until he could sit and straighten his uniform, push back the bloodied hair from his eyes.

Zuhlsdorff was standing to his left, breathing heavily. He had a splintered wooden stave in his one good hand. Koenig was sitting calmly on a bunk looking down at a space between his feet.

'We need a talk, Max. A short talk.' Goltz had pulled up a chair. He was so close that Hartmann could feel the odourless warmth of the other man's breath. 'Your friend tells us you're planning to leave us.'

'He's wrong. It's not like that.'

'Escape was never part of our training. It's not who we are.'

'I got curious. I found a way through the wire. Nothing was planned.'

'Time and again you disappoint me, Max.'

'Are you married? Have you got any children?'

There was just enough time for him to protect his head before Zuhlsdorff brought the club down hard on his exposed fingers. As he fell forward, Goltz clamped his hands around his neck and held on until the screams gurgled away.

'You're making a mistake. I'm sorry. It was a fantasy, never a plan.'

A weak smile drifted across Goltz's face. He removed his hands and placed them side by side, palms up, on his thighs. 'Gentlemen of the jury, our prisoner thinks I may be making a mistake. What is your verdict? Raise your hands if you think he is guilty.'

Hartmann stared at the motionless figure on the bunk. Three hands were already in the air – Zuhlsdorff, Mertens and Bruling – but Koenig's arm had not yet moved.

'If I may intercede for a second . . .' From the far end of the hut, Rosterg had stepped calmly under the light and placed his hand on Hartmann's back. 'Although I'm really not sure why you invited me, I'm wondering if your man here might be more use to you in one piece.'

'This had better be good,' spat Goltz.

Rosterg shrugged his shoulders and smiled apologetically. 'You want influence. Correct? You want to – shall we say – police the attitude of those less committed to this war than yourself. Correct?'

As Rosterg spoke, Goltz had risen to his feet and turned his back on Hartmann. 'This place is too soft, too easy,' he muttered. It was as though he was talking to himself.

'I agree. They feed us well. No one is complaining.' Rosterg looked up at the leaking roof. 'Well, not much, anyway.'

'That has to change now.'

'And how would you have it changed?'

Hartmann's pulse was racing. He didn't know why – or care – but Rosterg was battling to save his life.

'What's all this got to do with him?'

Goltz had spun back round, and was rocking from side to side in his own weak shadow.

'Calm down,' Rosterg went on. 'Just tell me what you want. That's all I'm asking.'

'All right. I want every German in this camp fighting the war again. I want to know everything that is going on here. Every fucking thing. I want an SS man living in every hut in every compound. I want to know what people are saying and thinking. I want to know if there are escapes planned. I want to know about guards. Who they are, where they're from. How many there are. How many times a day they take a shit. Every fucking thing. So, Rosterg, you tell me how this piece of shit helps.'

No one in the hut had ever heard Goltz speak for so long, and the effort seemed to have rendered him breathless. In the flickering glow from the bulb even Rosterg's tranquillity had wavered under the onslaught.

'I'm waiting, clever dick. How does he help?'

Hartmann pushed back his chair and leaned forward, awaiting Rosterg's reply. Zuhlsdorff's arm was still hanging hopefully in the air.

'You want your men in every compound. But only he knows the camp inside out. You want to be able to move your men around as you see fit, but only he knows all the weaknesses in the system. You want control but you're stuck here. You want brains and he's got them.'

'If I hurt him, he would tell me all those things anyway.'

'Was it really such a crime? Curiosity? Use his knowledge. Turn his folly into your strength.'

No one had noticed, but the wind had eased, leaving a tinny clatter of rain falling undisturbed on the roof.

'He's right. I can help you.' Hartmann had pulled himself up. A torn black roundel was flapping on the back of his jacket. 'I was bored. Daydreaming. Really, that's all.'

'He's lying! He's a fucking snake!'

'Put your hand down now. Now! That's an order.'

Zuhlsdorff lowered his arm. The wooden club rolled away under a bunk.

'Hartmann lives,' said Goltz. 'And that's an order.'

150

## 19

Within a day or two, it was as if nothing had ever happened.

Morale in the compound was soaring. Hartmann had been unexp-ectedly invited to join Goltz's inner circle and his friendship with Koenig had been patched up over a shared jam sandwich.

'I was angry. I thought you were going to abandon me.'

'I wasn't going anywhere. Not yet anyway.'

'But you'd have taken me?' As always, the canteen had been boiling with heat and noise.

'Yes. Of course I'd have taken you.'

'Then I'm sorry.'

But there was neither the time nor the inclination to go deeper into what had occurred. A fever of planning had erupted behind the wire walls of the SS compound.

Inside Goltz's head, Hartmann's unique knowledge of the camp had mutated into a single, all-consuming objective: to gain control over the entire prison population by swapping SS prisoners with men from other compounds. And since the seed for the plan had been planted on the night of the 'trial', Hartmann's misdemeanour appeared forgiven.

Nevertheless, if he was going to survive, it would require round-the-clock concentration. At best, his continuing presence in the compound was fragile, and he felt no inclination to gatecrash the many huddled discussions which went on around him. Curiosity and disloyalty were far too easily muddled – he knew that now – and he would speak only when invited to.

Several things were common knowledge, however. Two prisoners in each of the three neighbouring compounds had been persuaded – by Rosterg – that their 'best interests' lay in an open-ended move to the SS compound, during which time their beds, prison uniforms and identities would be taken by six members of the Schutzstaffel. No one knew how he'd done it, not even Goltz. Like most of Rosterg's affairs, the process was shrouded in mystery. All that mattered was that it had been done. But Hartmann fully understood.

Wherever they'd been, he'd watched Rosterg making himself useful; drawing strength from the numbers who leaned on him. Studied closely, it was easy to discern the man's languid aristocratic bearing; much harder to discern the steely pragmatism which under-pinned it. Rosterg was a showman who took risks, around whom dangerous rumours seemed in constant orbit: that he was a homo-sexual; that he'd supplied intelligence to the French resistance; that he was a millionaire, a deserter and a Jew. No doubt he'd heard them all and was bent on drowning the stories in a whirlpool of mutual dependency. Goltz needed him; the British needed him; the Lager-führer needed him. Just so long as he was useful, no one really cared who or what he was.

Hartmann, on the other hand, was readjusting to his sudden unnerving elevation. Koenig's betrayal had cut deep. It was good that they were speaking again, but the episode had left him dangerously isolated. As never before, it was time to play the dutiful patriot and commit himself fully, and vocally, to the mission's successful outcome. No one must know – especially Koenig – that the reasons for his enthusiasm differed markedly from the plan's architects, and that getting work on the other side of the fence was all that mattered to him now.

'He would have killed you,' Bruling had informed him, exactly a week after the beating. The two men were standing side by side at the washbasins. 'You've been allowed in because of what you know. Not who you are.'

'I'm more than aware of that. But I wasn't trying to break out.'

'I believe you. It's exciting, don't you think? Really exciting.'

A thin, cold lather was dripping off Hartmann's face. Pinpricks of blood were showing on his chin where the dulled razor had torn out his whiskers.

'A beautiful plan, Max,' continued Bruling. 'It's going to be our camp, at last.' Within the next few days, a pair of SS infiltrators would be smuggled into each of the Luftwaffe, Wehrmacht and officers' compounds, to 'restore Nazi values and re-establish military back-bone in the camp'. With Goltz's blessing they could identify traitors, dish out any necessary punishment, or pass details of serial offenders back for more intensive 'rehabilitation'. He called them his 'beautiful Rollkommandos' – raiding parties – and at Goltz's own insistence, Hartmann's name was one of the six.

'We are still an army,' their leader repeatedly told them. 'We should behave like one.'

There would be blood, Hartmann was certain of that, but not on his own hands. Not if he could help it. Bruling had told him there was work off the camp for low-risk prisoners. Work on the farms. Work on the roads. If he could survive in his new identity, Hartmann would be able to volunteer. Whatever happened, he was keeping his fists in his pockets.

'It is set,' Goltz finally revealed. 'You go tomorrow after lights out.'

They were all thankful it had stopped raining. Even by German standards, the British weather could be soul-destroying, but after two days of incessant murk a little warmth had returned again, allowing the men to lay out their filthy, wet mattresses on the hot tin roofs while they gathered, between meals, in countless whispered huddles.

No one had made any secret of the coming swap, and the identity of the six volunteers was widely known. Around the huts, each was already a hero and the mission had sent the collective mood soaring, boosted yet higher by the latest news from Rosterg. Hitler's new rockets were apparently falling on cities all over northern Europe and a secret German army was massing in the Belgian woods. Unconfined joy rose in the camp like the warm steam from their bedding.

With just a few hours to go, Hartmann found a spot by the fence, sat down and looked drowsily out across his compound. Leaves were falling from trees he couldn't see, and a faraway siren was screaming. Above him, the sky was clear. No planes. No rockets. It was probably just a factory hooter, sending sweaty-faced workers home at the end of their shift, back to their wives and their women.

'Everyone seems happy.'

Hartmann turned sharply. Koenig was sitting down next to him.

'It's normally you waking me up, Max. And you were snoring.'

'I wasn't asleep.'

Under the slanting autumnal light, Hartmann was startled to see how vibrant his old friend looked. Camp life had transformed all of them, but Koenig's carbonated bounce had been fully restored and his eyes flashed mischief above the familiar broad grin. 'Are you thinking how gorgeous I look?'

'The other night. If Goltz had forced you to choose would you have put your hand up?'

'Come on, Max. Get over it. I told him about your wanderings for your own good.'

'Meaning what?'

'Meaning people ask questions about your attitude. Meaning, now you're one of us.'

'I'm alive, I suppose. That's something.'

'It's fun, Max. Come on. It's like when we were kids.'

Hartmann frowned, and returned his gaze to the huts. It was true. Everyone did look happy. Hundreds of shirt-sleeved men were dreaming again.

A dusty-black butterfly landed on his arm. When Koenig placed his hand alongside, the butterfly stepped across on to his finger.

'People will hate us in there,' said Koenig. 'Germans will hate us.'

'I know. I'm getting used to it.'

'At least he's put us together. The old team: you and me and a few thousand enemies. What could possibly go wrong?'

From its perch on Koenig's thumbnail, the butterfly stretched its wings and then stepped off into the void.

# 20

That night they were the first pair to leave.

Along each side of the hut, every man stood from his bed to applaud. Even Zuhlsdorff raised his right arm in salute, following Hartmann with his eyes as they walked between the bunks.

When they stepped outside, the noise followed them. Within seconds it had spread to the other huts, a gruff chorus rippling out across the camp. From its furthest edge, a spotlight wheeled sharply in their direction, framing two men walking innocently towards the latrines. For a few moments it tracked them before moving on across the rooftops, illuminating a solitary bat gorging on a cloud of moths.

In the shadow of the toilet block they waited. Only when the chanting had faded could they think of moving on. With their backs pressed to the wall, Hartmann stole a glance at his friend. The boy's adrenaline was running so hot, he could smell it.

'Calm down, Erich. Go easy.'

Through the ragged fringe of distant trees, a half-moon was rising. Koenig's eyes seemed ablaze in its light.

'Let's go, Max,' he hissed. 'I can't stand the smell of shit here any longer.'

Hartmann counted to three. He could feel Koenig's hand pressing on his shoulder.

'Now. Now. Now.'

One more second for luck.

'Come on, Max. Now.'

A deep breath, then together they stepped forward to the fence. Clutching the wire, with their faces jammed against the cold mesh, they waited again. Somewhere in the nearby fields, a dog was howling furiously on its chain. Farm animals. Pets. Nothing more than that. No one had seen them. They could move on.

Hartmann's confidence was already rising. Until tonight, this had been his secret world and back inside it he felt secure. Ten paces to his left he reached down and exposed the old gap at ground level. In less than a minute they had both shimmied through.

'Brilliant, Max. I'm impressed.'

Hartmann put his finger to his lips. 'Sssh,' he mouthed. The British had a point. Careless talk cost lives.

Turning away from his friend, he walked quickly along the mazy wire corridor towards the Wehrmacht compound. Behind them, the other two pairs would soon be setting off on their own missions to terrify the airmen and the officers. It wouldn't pay to dawdle. Every ten paces, he placed a short stick in the ground.

Everything was just the same. Away to his right, the spotlight from the second guard tower was still falling hopelessly short. Ahead of them, he could hear the glorious swell of the soldier choir. '*Stille Nacht*'. Silent Night. Of course. How perfect. Winter was coming.

No time to listen tonight. A few more twists and they were alongside the wire which embraced the seemingly countless huts of the vast German army compound. At the tenth concrete post from the corner, they stopped. Beyond the fence, two silhouettes were slouching towards them across a broad grassy swathe of open ground.

'The tenth post. That's what Rosterg said. This must be them.'

'Miserable-looking fuckers,' said Koenig.

As the figures drew closer, Hartmann could see why. These were not volunteers. They were tearful children with terror engraved on their faces. Neither looked as though he could lift a rifle, let alone kill a man with one.

'You are Hartmann?'

The voice was barely audible, a descant squeak from the taller of the two prisoners. Closer up, they looked like brothers; the same downy hair, the same deep-set eyes.

'Stupid question, I suppose. Sorry.'

As he spoke, the second boy had dropped to his knees and begun pulling dirt away from the bottom of the fence. After a few moments he looked back up and nodded. Again, it was his taller companion who breached the silence.

'You want us to come through now?' On their own side of the wire, the two SS men were already hastily removing their clothes. Koenig cursed. 'Of course we fucking well do.'

When all four men were stripped, Hartmann and Koenig dressed quickly. Rosterg had done his work well. The swapped uniforms were a tidy fit; clean, too, with the freshly stitched yellow discs of low-risk prisoners on the regulation mauve jacket and trousers.

'Look at us, Max. We've been rehabilitated.'

But Hartmann wasn't listening. Neither of the two prisoners had moved. Each was still shivering in his pants, not daring to touch the discarded outfit at his feet.

'We need your names,' he said. 'You need to dress.'

'I am Karl Eschner. And this is Walther Sieber. We were both Panzergrenadiers.'

Koenig stepped forward menacingly into the boy's space.

'Sorry. I meant we are still both Panzergrenadiers.'

'And your hut numbers?'

'Walther is in seventeen. I am in nineteen. Easy to remember. Same as our ages.' He turned round and pointed. 'Over there. Quite close to each other.'

'Look. I know you're scared, Karl. But you have to wear this.' Hartmann had picked up his own prison suit and was handing it across.

'What will happen to us in your compound?'

'Nothing. I absolutely promise you. Nothing. You've been chosen because you're loyal. Not because you're in trouble.'

'Do you think we will ever swap back?' The boy's voice was breaking with tears.

'Yes, we will. Of course we will. I just don't know how soon. Now dress.'

At Karl's side, the boy called Walther had already pulled on Koenig's clothes. Soon all four were ready to go. The choir had stopped. It was getting late and the two young soldiers still looked reluctant to move.

'You are Max Hartmann now, Karl. Remember that. And your friend here is Erich Koenig. Where you're going . . . however crap you're feeling, you always walk tall. You don't slouch. OK?'

The trace of a smile had appeared on Eschner's face. Koenig and Sieber were shaking hands.

'Follow the sticks in the dirt. Someone will meet you at the other end. Hut Six. The cold one.'

With a kindly pat from Hartmann, the boys left, eyes down and running for the telltale wooden markers. If he could, Rosterg would look out for them. Just so long as they kept quiet and remembered their new names. Hartmann turned to Koenig.

'I'll be Karl. You can be Walther. The younger one.'

'Fine by me, Karl.'

Ten seconds later – with two yellow moons glowing on the backs of their tunics – they were standing inside their new compound.

# 21

It would be a long week before Hartmann got outside.

For both of them, life in their borrowed skins required adjustments neither had anticipated. After the bellicose austerity of the SS compound, they awoke in a softer world, a place of kitchen-sink contentment.

In almost every physical way, Hut 6 and Hartmann's new residence of Hut 19 were identical. Outside, the sun bounced off the same curved sheets of corrugated iron. Inside it, another eighty young men slept out their nights on cold, rickety bunks.

By day, life was divided between metronomic roll calls and meals. And by night, the prisoners shivered and snored and masturbated just the same. However, when he looked deeper, it wasn't difficult to identify what separated his former berth from this new one. He could see it in every face. He could sense it in the wooden toys that the POWs whittled for their children. In the matchstick ships in bottles, and the slippers crafted from cardboard and sacking; in the choirs and the football teams; in the ukulele bands and the boxing tournaments; in the thriving black market; in the night classes in physics and shorthand; in the blackout sheets being used as blackboards.

If there was satisfaction that their war was over, Hartmann never heard it spoken. And yet the incontrovertible evidence for it was everywhere, in the way these men walked and talked and in their rustic yearning for peace.

Goltz could send in a battalion of Rollkommandos but he'd never change a thing. V2 rockets. Secret weapons. Counterattacks. No one here cared, or not enough, anyway; not yet. If necessary, they'd swear their loyalty to Hitler and proclaim their willingness to die. Some would mean it. Most wouldn't. In France or under the sea, death had already skirted far too close. Here, the food was good and the war was lost, and however many heretic noses Koenig flattened, he wouldn't shift things an inch. At best, the two infiltrators could sow doubt and denounce a few noisy waverers. In reality, Hartmann concluded, Goltz's mission felt like an imbecilic waste of time.

Just for appearance's sake, while it lasted, he would peddle the Nazi hard line. It would be suicidal not to show willing. These days, you never knew who might be watching.

By dawn on his first day, the word was already out. In the toilet block, he'd been blanked; every pair of eyes snapping quickly away whenever contact was made. As he'd tidied his bedroll and walked to the 6 a.m. roll call, the collective icy shoulder had persisted.

Temperatures overnight had plummeted, and each man on the parade ground was desperate for his fried bread and tea. Three lines ahead, he could make out Koenig's thick curls; one of two thousand souls, maybe more, streaming into formation. Even the wounded were being guided into position on their crutches.

When the last prisoner was in place, the bugle stopped. Military policemen with sheets of names began working backwards, line by line. As they drew closer to Koenig, Hartmann saw his friend stiffen and then turn, glancing quickly over both shoulders. He's looking for me, Hartmann realised. He's forgotten who he is.

'Hamann.'

'Present.'

'Rottlander.'

'Present.'

The guard had stopped at the end of Koenig's line. 'Sieber.'

No one spoke. The unanswered name remained hanging in the sunless air. Grey vapour was rising from damp uniforms and the only sound was the stamping of bloodless feet. All around Koenig, heads were swivelling.

They'd been stupid. Of course. Why hadn't they expected this? Sieber's friends were looking for him among the vast block of faces.

'Sieber. Walther Sieber.'

Come on, willed Hartmann. Come on. His fists were balled uselessly at his side.

'Present.' Koenig's voice, quiet and catching in his throat.

'You are Sieber?'

'I am. Present and correct.' Stronger now. And louder.

'Wake yourself up, lad,' bellowed the British soldier.

Koenig's head stayed bowed. No one had betrayed him, but everyone knew. A few minutes later, as the torrent of men surged towards the canteen, they sought each other out.

Hartmann spoke softly. 'It makes no difference. It was never going to be a secret for more than a few hours.'

'I was right. They fucking despise us. Why?' On every side of them, the rush of men pressed silently on, faces forward.

'Welcome to the new Germany.'

'What exactly is it we're supposed to do here anyway?'

'Make sure they're more frightened of us than they are of the British. It shouldn't be difficult.' Hartmann was looking intently at his friend. 'But that doesn't mean you have to hurt anyone. Being seen around will be enough.'

Koenig looked doubtful. 'Just a little rough stuff, maybe?'

After that, they had joined the line of men clutching their priceless meal tokens.

But it was lonely, lonelier than Hartmann had ever imagined. Wherever he wandered, the air curdled around him.

During the day, when the weather was fine, the huts emptied and the compound crackled with energy. Fence posts became goalposts. Huts became impromptu nets over which wooden sticks were tossed between teams howling with laughter. Huddles of men listened as the camp newspaper – printed, written and edited by the British – was read aloud to hoots of derision and disbelief. From every corner rose the unrestrained buzz of chatter and from every word of it, Hartmann was excluded. Even his most gentle, stumbling overtures were resisted.

On his second morning – as reveille sounded – he'd climbed blearily down past his shivering bunkmate in the darkness. As always, every trace of warmth had fled in the night through the wafer-thin roof.

'It doesn't get any easier. Maybe we should soon be asking for stoves.' Wrestling on his stiff boots, Hartmann had momentarily forgotten they were different. In the blackness, a half-sleeping body turned towards his voice.

'Who are you really? What's your name?' A shape, a bundle. Still too dark to make out a face.

'I know yours,' said Hartmann. 'You're Juncker, I think. I'm Karl Eschner.'

By the same evening, the bottom bunk had been stripped of bedding and abandoned. Whoever had occupied it was gone. On the wall above his own bed, a dark cross had been daubed on to the metal in human shit and two dead rats had been left on his pillow. Calmly he'd carried them to the latrine bucket where they were still floating the next morning. It was irksome, but he could live with being compared to the Black Death.

'That's fucking disgusting,' Koenig swore when Hartmann told him.

'Don't, Koenig. Please don't.'

Two days later, Juncker had been found beaten unconscious. Both his arms were broken.

As the week progressed, Hartmann had enjoyed being in the company of humans again – albeit as a spectator – and his sleeping had dramatically improved. Sometimes, during the long dark evenings, he eavesdropped as the soldiers read letters from home to each other. And although the nights were getting colder, his dreams had returned and Alize was in all of them.

It wasn't something he could explain, but she felt closer now, as if the possibility of being reunited was a thought finding its time. For weeks, months – years – he'd gone into almost every day expecting to die. Hearing the soft voices of his fellow-prisoners sharing their clumsily penned expressions of love had unlocked a prospect he'd held in quarantine for too long.

Maybe the glorious weather helped. Since the night of his trial, the camp had sizzled under what the British called an Indian summer, and as autumn knocked the skies seemed stuck in blue. For a few precious hours each day, it felt like August again. By midday, with their backs against the huts, it was warm enough for the men to strip off their shirts. But after dark, with the first frosts biting, the men counted the hours until dawn.

On the afternoon of his seventh day, Hartmann's hut had received a visitor: Wolfgang Rosterg, sweeping in out of the sun, with a handkerchief clutched to his brow.

'Too hot. Too hot,' he'd said to no one in particular.

Alongside him was a shorter man, turning to fat, wearing the uniform of an army major; the Lagerführer, Hartmann presumed. Walter Bultmann, Rosterg's 'little faggot'.

Observing them together, it wasn't difficult to work out the command structure. Before speaking, the major always consulted his aide for advice, and while Rosterg's eyes seemed to penetrate every visible corner of the room, Bultmann's face wore a look of perpetual disengagement. Even when his lips were moving, it felt – to Hartmann – as if Rosterg's words were coming out.

'Good afternoon, men. Another lovely day and two bits of news.' Someone towards the back of the hut was sniggering. 'Firstly, we've brought you this week's copy of the camp newspaper. And secondly, we can tell you that from the beginning of October, we've persuaded the British to install two stoves in each of the huts.'

The cheering was as loud as it was sudden. As fists thumped the roof, Rosterg stepped in front of the major and held up his hands for silence. While the din subsided, he took off his glasses and wiped the sweat from the frame. When they were nudged back into place, he was looking directly at Hartmann.

'We should add that the newspaper is written by the British and that every word of it may be a lie. Despite what you might read in there, our fine comrades in Europe might be turning this round.' The clamour in the hut had receded. 'And when you get your stoves, do please try not to burn the furniture.' Immediately the hut was shaken by joyous uproar. 'Thank you, Hut Nineteen. The major and I have a lot of people to tell. Enjoy the sun while it lasts.'

A few minutes later, when Hartmann slipped outside, Rosterg was waiting for him.

'You're growing a beard, Rosterg. It suits you.'

'You noticed. I'm touched. Life here seems to be suiting you too. You look well.'

As they spoke, the two men worked their way to the rear of the hut.

'We haven't got long, Max. I really shouldn't be seen in your company.' From hut after hut, they could hear cheering. News about the stoves was spreading fast. 'As you'll have realised, they're simple people. They want to carve wood, not dig tunnels.'

'Listen. I owe you a thank you.'

'Don't flatter yourself, young man. Your peregrinations have done us all a favour. Goltz would have exploded without this.'

'What do you tell him?' Hartmann asked. 'Not the truth, obviously. If he knew what they were like . . .'

'The same things I always tell him: that when it comes to it, soldiers will follow orders; that they might be simple, but they're not fools.'

'I want to ask a favour.'

'You need to be very careful. That moron Zuhlsdorff loathes you.'

'I still need a favour.'

'Everyone needs favours.'

'I want to get out.'

'Really? You surprise me. I thought you might have learned your lesson.'

'Not escape. I don't want to get shot. I want to dig ditches. I want to work outside. I want to come back at night with blisters on my hands. I want you to get me on a work party.'

'You want to go out and come back in? You're serious?'

'Correct. At least to begin with.'

'Nothing could be easier, Max. You won't be popular, but consider it done.'

'Thank you. And, for the record, I'm not exactly popular now.'

# 22

Hartmann knew what he had to do. Rosterg had briefed him well.

All week he'd watched carefully as truckloads of prisoners rolled out of the camp after roll call, returning footsore and tanned eight hours later. From a distance, the selection process had seemed entirely haphazard, but armed with Rosterg's reassurances he felt ready to give it a go.

'Promise me you'll come back,' Koenig had pleaded over breakfast.

'I'll come back,' he'd reassured him. 'And I'll bring you some smokes.'

Everyone understood the game, even the guards. Happy prisoners didn't make trouble, and contraband – provided you could either eat or smoke it – made them happy.

Outside the wire, where life was governed by ration books, the locals looked enviously at the food mountain being shipped into the camp each day. And every day, in the spirit of rapprochement, a little slice of that mountain trickled back out again.

Walking away from the canteen, Hartmann could feel the bacon in his tunic pocket. Twelve rashers stolen by his friend, and from the smell, not too recently. Almost every prisoner on the work parties would be the same. Cheese and meat going out. Tobacco and maybe a drop of Scotch coming back.

A few hundred miles away, mused Hartmann, we are tossing grenades at each other. Here we shake hands over a sausage and a Senior Service.

On the parade square, prisoners were massing around the wire either side of the main gate. Beyond it, he could see lorries, and a line of flatbed trailers hitched to tractors. On previous days, around two hundred men had been selected for outside work. Today, as always, there were ten times that number hoping to get lucky. Very few of them were talking and a mood of hunched concentration hung over proceedings. Each was a player in a desperate lottery and every pair of eyes was locked on the large boards being hung on the fence ahead of them. Earlier, over breakfast, selected prisoners had each been given a numbered metal disc by their hut commander. If the same number was chalked on to a board, they'd be attached to a work party. If it wasn't, someone else would get their chance tomorrow.

Hartmann had found his at the bottom of his tea and had no idea how it had got there. Now it was in the palm of his hand. A three had been crudely scratched into the tin. Over the crush of heads, he could see guards furiously copying numbers on to the boards from their lists. Every one provoked a cheer, and exultant prisoners were pushing their way to the front.

A new board was going up. A plump soldier was looking down at his sheets of paper and lifting his chalk. A three. Hartmann unclenched his fingers and checked again. He was going out. Out. Across the width of the square, crestfallen men were turning back towards their huts. Alongside him, twenty lines of jubilant ones – twelve in each – were having their discs checked under the eye of a handful of policemen on bicycles.

'Group One, ditch-digging . . . Group Two, hedge-cutting . . .'

The camp gates had been dragged open. In single file, the prisoners were marching out to their transports. Hartmann could feel his pulse galloping. A policeman was blowing his whistle. He was next.

'Group Three, apple-picking. That's the green tractor over on the right.'

At that moment, nothing had ever felt better. Sitting on a trailer, legs dangling from the side, there was no war. Along the straggle of hedgerows he caught the loamy scents of late summer between black wafts of diesel. Much further away, behind distant teams of Clydesdales, he could see seagulls scrapping above the ripe dark narcotic of freshly ploughed fields.

Closing his eyes, he remembered the train journey from Southampton. And further back, the frowsy scent of stocks in a Munich garden. Opening them, he saw twelve pairs of legs happily swaying and just one soldier on a motorcycle following behind.

When the tractor stopped, the men were led between the drooping boughs of a vast orchard, where empty boxes and a few patched-up stepladders were waiting for them. Stretched out in a broad line, each man worked silently down his own allotted row, stretching up for the swollen fruit, lost for those minutes in the depths of a deep green tunnel. Only when they reached the field's edge could they ease their backs and enjoy the soothing drift of the open country before turning back inside their canopy of leaves. After four hours, when a whistle summoned them to a lunch break, all of them were exhausted.

Under an oak tree, along the edge of a stony lane, Hartmann watched the breeze stirring a soft storm of thistledown. Somewhere behind him a green woodpecker was laughing. Reaching back, he pulled two plump blackberries from a spiky straggle, popping one in his mouth and crushing the other between his fingers. Fascinated, he watched as the tiny purple explosions spattered his face with bitter juice.

A few yards away, their guard was sitting astride his bike aiming his rifle at imaginary planes. From around a curve in the lane, two figures were approaching, accompanied by a small, yapping dog. One was a girl, carrying a basket. The other, an elderly man, relied on a long, crooked stick. Wiping the sticky drops from his face, Hartmann sat up quickly and waited.

She was sixteen, maybe less, with strong, bare legs and glossy black curls falling across the shoulders of a simple white dress. To the twelve young men now watching her, in their sweat-darkened prison garb, she seemed like a visitation. And when she stopped in front of them and smiled, no one had the remotest idea what to do or say.

'I know you can't understand me but my name is Alice. This is my grandfather, and we've come to say thank you for helping us on our farm.'

The men shuffled uneasily. The dog – a Jack Russell – was trotting among them twitching its nose in apparent disgust.

'We've brought some home-made lemonade, and some bread.' The girl peeled back a muslin cloth from one half of the basket. 'We've also got a few things you might like to take back.' Pulling the cloth away completely, she revealed packs of cigarettes and a handful of ring-bound notebooks. 'I don't suppose any of you speak English?'

'Yes. I do.' Hartmann stood up, wiped his hand, and offered it first to the old man and then to his granddaughter. 'This is most kind. You have a beautiful farm. I'm sure we're all very pleased to be able to make things up to you.'

After that, the trading began. Within minutes, almost every prisoner had completed his exchange and was swigging contentedly from a stone bottle. Warm, crusty loaves were being torn apart. Cigarettes were being shaken from their boxes.

'They'll need a match,' Hartmann said politely. Their guard, he noticed, was now looking studiously in the wrong direction.

'Of course.' The girl turned to her grandfather, who passed over a box of Swan Vestas. 'No need to give them back. They're easy to come by.'

She looked down. The dog was sniffing dementedly around Hartmann's leg.

'He can smell meat, I think. You're the only one who's done no business.'

He felt his tunic pocket. He'd forgotten. The bacon was still there. 'I'm not sure you've got anything I want.'

The girl – Alice – smiled, and glanced sheepishly at the old man. It was too cruel that they shared a name. 'What do you want? Try me.'

'A pencil. Your paper is no good without a pencil.'

'Anything else?'

For the second time that morning, Hartmann was conscious of his own heart; the steady pump of a warning. 'That you help me by sending the letter I write to Germany.' He looked round. The guard was swiping a clump of nettles with a stick.

The girl's brow creased, and she tugged at a loose hair on her cheek. 'It's all right. I won't tell him. But you already have a right to send letters. I'm sure you do. You don't need me for that.'

Hartmann wondered how much he should tell her. 'It's complicated.' The bacon was hanging limply from his outstretched hand.

'What's she called?'

'Alize. It's German for Alice.'

When the whistle sounded, Hartmann tucked the notepaper into his jacket. Four hours later, when the sun had dipped behind the trees, they were allowed to stop. All around them, towers of wooden crates swayed under the weight of their labours.

Elation had given way to weariness. No longer working, the prisoners found themselves shivering under a clearing sky. Hartmann would return tomorrow. The others might not. He could feel the sharp edges of the token between his fingers. There were benefits to being feared. No one would ever dare ask for it back.

He wondered if that, more than the cold, was why the men had fallen silent, or whether their hours of freedom had depressed them. What was it his father said? Sometimes a morsel was harder to digest than a mountain? As the camp drew nearer, he looked up and back. A single star had broken cover in the east. Road dust glowed in the yellow beam of the guard's motorcycle.

'First time out? You'll need to go easy on those blisters.'

Hartmann looked to his left. Another face he'd forget, barely visible. For a thousand reasons, he felt no inclination to talk.

'I think I'd kill myself if I couldn't get out. Most of us here are the same.'

'You don't hand your work token back?'

'Not for ages. People are lazy. They'd rather have the cigarettes than the graft.'

The tractor had stopped. Beyond the gates, the prison camp stretched out under a battery of lampposts. Smoke was rising smoothly from the roof of the barracks.

'I've worked every day for two weeks. I could live in this country when it's all over.' They were inside now, and the prisoners were slipping off towards the canteen. 'Maybe I'll see you tomorrow.'

Hartmann didn't answer. No point. By the next day, everyone on the work party would know who he really was – or who he really wasn't. And where he was from.

After that, no one would speak to him again.

*From:  4th Wiltshire Home Guard*
*To:    Chief Constable, Lt Col. Sir Hoel Llewellyn KBE, DSO, DL*
*Date:  1 Sept. 1944*

*We have been informed by the local police inspector that we are to stand by in the event of trouble arising with Prisoners of War.*

*Will you kindly advise if the Home Office may be approached for loss of earnings, injuries sustained (if any) and subsistence allowance in the event of a turnout? Also, will the assistance of outlying companies be sought in view of the very small area controlled by this company?*

*The Home Guard will be most willing to assist in any way, but – as must be abundantly clear – we are limited both by our numbers and by the physical capacity of many of our volunteers.*

*Currently there are no reasons to fear any unwelcome 'activity' at Devizes, but we are told there are elements there who may prove troublesome in the future.*

*Regards, etc.*

# 23

The following morning, after breakfast, Koenig disappeared into the kitchen, returning with fistfuls of sausage.

'You could get out too,' Hartmann told him.

'Not interested. Not just yet, anyway.'

There wasn't time to ask why. All around them, men were surging down the camp's concrete pathways, and lines were already forming in front of the chalkboards. Hartmann saw his own number going up last, causing another flotilla of despondent faces to turn away yet again. He felt a wave of raw anger coming from the prisoners jostling back. Pockets of men were jeering and the token felt hot in his hand, making him clutch it even tighter. He was learning to live with the hate. It might not be fair, but he was going out again.

'Fucking Nazi cunt.' Hands were on his back, pushing. A boot had swung into his shin, hard. 'Fuck off back where you came from.'

As he stumbled, a fist bounced off the back of his head. 'Screw Hitler.'

There were shouts from the wire – English voices – and when he straightened his back the crowd had drifted away. Whoever they'd been, if their names ever reached Goltz, they were dead.

Ahead of him, the gates were being opened. No policemen today. It was probably a Saturday. Everyone on the trailer had seen what happened. When he tried to climb on board, no one would let him.

On the road behind, he could hear the approaching burble of a motorcycle. As he stepped aside, it pulled up with a spray of dirt. Astride it was the same young guard from yesterday, with the same decrepit rifle slung over his back.

'Norton four-ninety? Nice,' said Hartmann.

The driver grinned. He looked about sixteen and his teeth were black. 'Hop on, Kraut. It isn't far.'

Like the day before, he worked alone all morning, staving off hunger with stolen apples. Overnight, his muscles had tightened, and a dull ache was pulsing in his leg. The boxes seemed to fill more slowly. But after a few hours, once the morning mist had burned away, he found a steady rhythm, working hard to push away the possibility that the girl might never come back.

Around noon, the whistle sounded. Immediately, Hartmann looked both ways up the lane. No one in sight. He retrieved his tunic from the side of the field and walked stiffly towards the oak tree for lunch. As he sat down, he could smell it: the peppery bite of bratwurst, the taste of home.

'They've eaten it all.' It was the guard, still lining up his sights on phantom targets. 'They don't seem to like you right much, do they?'

Hartmann smiled. You could get anything in a war if you knew how. Someone would surely come. He needed it to be her.

He wasn't alone. Everyone in the work party seemed tense. When the dog finally appeared, driven frantic by the smell of meat, they relaxed. Once again, the guard took himself off, nodding politely to the girl and her grandfather as they passed on the lane. Hartmann sat up. She was wearing a red dress, and her hair was tied back. Her eyebrows, he noticed, were thick and black like a man's. It wasn't hard to imagine her naked and so he did. When she found his face in the shadow of the tree and smiled, a rare tingle of delight passed through his groin. Later on, like all the men there, he would relieve it.

'I'll sort out the others first. Is that all right?'

'Of course. There's no hurry.'

He felt confident. She would not have let him down. After a few minutes, her basket was empty.

'Hello again, Alice.' Behind her, the rest of the work party were lighting up, no longer interested. 'Have you got something for me?'

The girl's grandfather had disappeared. Without asking, she sat down beside the prisoner, smoothing her dress carefully along her thighs. 'Yesterday you said it was complicated. What's complicated?'

A large plane was landing somewhere nearby, followed quickly by another. It felt uncomfortable to be having this conversation in a Wiltshire field with a teenager he didn't know.

'You're SS, aren't you? You're not a soldier like them.'

'What makes you think that?' He could feel her eyes walking all over his face. He didn't want to look.

'Because you're not the first I've met. There've been others like you who've come out.'

'Like me? How are we different?'

'Mostly the others seem a bit happier. Does that sound silly?' Her grandfather was limping back towards them with a box full of eggs.

'Have you got my pencil?'

'Why don't you trust the camp to send your letters?'

'I'd trust you more.'

'I'll give you the pencil if you show me a picture of your Alice.' She was flirting. Her head was thrown back, and her knees had parted slightly, forcing the red dress up across bare legs. When their eyes locked, she grinned. A stalk of grass hung like a dare from the scarlet smear of her mouth.

'I don't have a photograph. Not any more.' He could still smell it, twisting and burning.

'Tell me what she looks like, then. I'll bet she's not as pretty as me.'

Hartmann wondered what would happen if he put his hand between her legs, if he sought out her wetness. Even the thought felt suicidal. Dizzied by it, he stood up awkwardly and jabbed his hands in his trouser pockets. 'I've got a sausage here for you, Alice.'

Her laughter was a glorious girlish thing, a high-pitched screech which rang across the sombre fields. As she stumbled chuckling to her feet, Hartmann reached out and slipped his fingers around her wrist. Against the gritty leather of his own skin, hers felt smooth like ancient driftwood. When he released it, he was holding the stub of a pencil.

'The horrible truth is that I remember less and less about her,' he whispered.

'Bring me the letter,' said Alice, still smiling. 'I'll post it on one condition.'

'What might that be?'

'No more sausage jokes.'

The rest of the day passed quickly. All afternoon, words swirled in Hartmann's brain; promises and declarations of love which dissolved in his quest for the perfect phrase. When the trailer dropped them back at the camp, he was too absorbed to notice anything unusual. There'd been a little more space on the wagon, but he'd thought nothing of it.

'You've done it again, you fucking moron.'

A white-faced sergeant – wearing a uniform that looked two sizes too large – was yelling at their solitary adolescent guard.

'Count them again, fuckwit. You left here with twelve. You've come back with ten.'

It wasn't unusual. The whitecaps called them walkabouts, the low-grade escapees whose curiosity drove them to wander. At worst, they slept rough for a few nights, throttled the odd chicken, and tried ringing Germany from a telephone box. At best, they made for the pubs in Devizes where they pleaded with the bar staff for a pint of beer. If they were lucky, they'd manage two before the military police rolled up. If they could play the piano, they'd get a rum thrown in as well.

And yet to Hartmann, the camp's indifference to its own security seemed dangerously misjudged. There were insufficient guards; the perimeter wire was patchily constructed; and the prevailing ethos of gentlemanly trust felt like a mismatch against brutes like Mertens and Zuhlsdorff. Every day, hundreds more prisoners were arriving, and every day, a handful wandered out of the main gates unnoticed, often sauntering back in for their tea around dusk.

'Sorry, Sarge. They must have jumped off on the way back.'

The place was a joke. When the absentees were rounded up by the local constabulary, they'd be hauled back for two weeks' solitary and basic rations. As he crossed the parade ground alone, Hartmann glanced up at the two guard towers. Only one of them was manned. Worse than a joke.

Clutching the pencil in his fist, he pushed open the door of Hut 19. At each end, a huge black stove was roaring out heat. Bultmann

– or rather Rosterg – had been true to his word. Climbing up on to his bunk, he caught an echo of the farm girl's fragrance on his fingers. His hand slid beneath his waistband. A minute was all it would take, less probably. No, Max, he thought. Priorities. Letter first, that later. *My darling Alize ...*

It was impossible. This was why he'd written so little in London. There were a hundred questions – a thousand. He could list them all, one by one. Where are you? How are you? Who are you? Or he could chronicle his own experiences in carefully sanitised headlines. But he was alive, well fed, warm – and she ...

The worst of it was not knowing; not knowing her and not knowing anything about her current circumstances. At that moment, she might be stumbling through blazing rubble pursued by Soviet rapists. She might be strung out on a road with a child and a million dead-eyed refuges.

Ten thousand questions. *My darling Alize ...*

In frustration, he pummelled the side of the hut with his fist. The metal felt warm. No one would shiver tonight.

*My darling Alize ... If you got my last letter you will know I was alive in September. If you get this, you will know I am still here. Better than that, I am safe and uninjured, and have every reason to believe that I will make it back home in one piece. With all my heart, I pray that you can say the same ...*

He stopped. It was true what the girl said. Most of the army prisoners wrote home every week, but so far very few letters had come back. Everyone had their theories, but no one knew why. In the army compound, he'd heard some people say that their letters were never sent in the first place, and in the SS compound, writing of any kind was deemed unmanly.

Using the farm girl was a risk, but it got round the censors and gave him a chance.

*If she has been true to her word this has been posted by a local girl called – guess what? – Alice. So there is still kindness in this world despite our best endeavours. By my best guess it is now early October. The weather has been fair, and I am in a prison camp near a town called Devizes. The food here is plentiful and the guards behave decently. Time passes slowly, I'm afraid, but*

*I shouldn't complain. There are no bullets, no shells, no bombs, and pneumonia is probably my biggest danger. The rain here is worse than home!*

The light in the hut was fading. In the centre, around the stove door, he could see a perfect square of orange flame.

*I wonder constantly if we have a child, and if we do what he or she looks like. Beautiful, like you, I expect. Remember those days in the attic? We hear rumours about the war, but nothing more so I can't even guess when we will meet, or how all this will end. But I promise you this. I will come back with no guilt, no shame and no secrets. It is hard sometimes but I am still trying to be a good man, someone a child might be proud of! Stay safe. Stay close. Stay true. Stay mine for ever. One day when you look towards the sunshine it will be me walking towards your arms. So wherever and whenever, please know this. I WILL find you. All my love. Max.*

It would do. Between Alize and him, three vast forces were fighting for a continent. If his letter slipped through, it would be a miracle. Folding it carefully, he fashioned a crude envelope from a second piece of paper and addressed it to his father's house in Munich. She wouldn't be there, but it was a start. Someone might find it and pass it on. A chain of kindness, that's all it would need; a chain of hands through the ruins of Europe starting with a teenager in a Wiltshire cornfield.

Hartmann sagged back. The unfamiliar heat had risen, making him feel drowsy and calm. When he awoke, eight hours later, he was still clutching the letter. Outside, a thunderstorm had broken, clattering rain down the sheets of iron. During morning roll call, spikes of lightning danced around the camp, releasing an earthy smell which clung to the men's noses.

'Like mushrooms,' Koenig had said, as they wandered to the canteen.

But Hartmann hadn't been listening. The only thing that mattered now was his letter. Idly, he traced circles in the condensation on the dining-room window. Beyond it, he could see prisoners splashing hopefully towards the gate through the sodden darkness. Something felt different – askew.

'You can have my breakfast, Koenig. We'll talk later.'

At the doorway he checked his pocket. The letter was still there. Although the rain had stopped, the air felt saturated, and the camp was swimming in brown water. Out on the farm, he knew, the fields would be turning to mud. Ditches would be flowing like rivers. With a feeling of dread, he turned towards the main gate.

Ahead of him, he could see the familiar crowd of hopeful workers. Twelve-strong work parties were already heading off on trucks. Even the policemen were there, helmeted and hidden under dripping blue oilskins. He was wrong. Everything was normal. A number three board was up on the wire, and his trailer was waiting.

Somewhere to the west, there was a last exhalation of thunder and a smudge of brightness had broken through the clouds. As the tractor edged away, it lurched violently in a water-filled pothole, cascading water over a furious policeman.

That was when Hartmann noticed. There were three motorcycle guards, not one. And the black-toothed adolescent wasn't among them.

During the previous two days, he'd laboured in sunshine. Today, the earth sucked at his boots, and however hard he worked the cold never quite left him. Up on the lane, the guards seemed on edge, prowling restlessly with their rifles cocked. There was no banter, but the prisoners seemed happy in their silence. Without the sun it was impossible to gauge the time.

When this was over, he decided, a watch would be the first thing he bought. Hunger was a useful clue, and he was starving, but it could never replace a clock. Somewhere up in the clouds, he could hear planes buzzing. It was also starting to rain again, a steady drizzle from a drooping sky.

Hartmann stood up and stretched his shoulder muscles. Close at hand, he could hear the girl's dog yowling, and from the end of the lane a sound like an angry wasp. Another army motorcycle, moving fast through the puddles.

As it drew nearer, the three guards on the lane stiffened. Across the width of the orchard, the other prisoners had stopped to look. Some were already emptying their pockets of stolen rations. The rest were stepping forward in expectation of a command. Everyone around the field had sensed the rising bubble of panic. For a moment, the soldiers conferred, and then the shouting began.

'Up here, you fuckers. Now.'

Stumbling through the sticky mud, the prisoners assembled on the puddled lane.

'There's twelve, there's twelve,' someone was shouting. 'Get them on the fucking trailer, quick.'

Hartmann hung back. She could come any minute. Where was she? What time was it? Everyone else was ready to go. The three riders were gunning their engines.

'Get on the trailer, Kraut.'

'I need to take a crap. Give me a minute.'

'We don't have a minute. Get on the trailer, or we'll shoot you.'

'We're all hungry, you bastards. Can't we at least have some food first?'

He heard the click behind him. They meant it. For some reason, everything had changed. Two of the guards were bustling forward. Around his feet, he felt the snuffling nudge of a warm presence. The girl's mutt had come for its scraps.

'Let me feed the dog, at least. OK?'

With his back to the soldiers, Hartmann put his hand in his tunic and bent down. There was a collar and it was tight. Maybe – just maybe – that would do. When he stood up, the dog was still growling.

'Jesus. What did you give it?'

'I had a sausage in my pocket,' said Hartmann.

Even from a mile away, he could see something was wrong at the camp.

From every direction, the work parties were returning. Fraught-faced officers with loudhailers were barking orders, and the perimeter roads seemed clogged with mud-caked trucks. Although the rain had finally stopped, dusk was coming early. Every light around the wire had been switched on, and the giant spots on the towers had swung into action.

As he came through the gates, Hartmann could see hundreds of prisoners massing on the parade square, flanked by a single unbroken line of armed soldiers. There couldn't be a hut that hadn't been emptied. More and more POWs were pouring out. Soon the hundreds would be thousands, very few of whom were speaking. From such an extraordinary congregation, Hartmann suddenly realised, there was very little noise.

Just a few yards through the wire, Koenig was waiting, his face wild-eyed with excitement. 'Fuck. I thought I'd never find you.'

Not since the rallies had they seen so many Germans in one place. On the parade ground, robotic spears of men seemed to disappear in every direction, each one facing the same way.

'What's happening?'

'Last night. There was some sort of escape attempt.'

'People walk out of here every day. It's easy.'

'This was different. This wasn't someone desperate for a pint or a quick fumble.'

'Who was it? Goltz? Anyone we know?'

'Two airmen. Luftwaffe. Definitely not SS. Both shot and killed.'

'And that's all we know?'

'We know it was early this morning. Before dawn. And that no one seems sure how they got out.'

It was two hours before they moved or spoke again. The camp's collective punishment was to stand in silence until further orders. If anyone had expected an official explanation, none came. Rumour would have to suffice.

In the distance they could hear doors slamming and the drumbeat of heavy footsteps. Beds were being dragged into the open air. Manholes and septic tanks were being probed. Search parties were rampaging through every hut.

He needed to know more. And quickly. Where was Rosterg when you wanted him? A British officer was yelling out hut numbers. Block by block, the prisoners were scampering back to their billets. The word was already out – no evening meal. Instead, they'd spend their time sorting out the mess. And after that a few games of rummy before lights out at 9.30. Hartmann envied them. Alone on his top bunk, listening to the crackle of the stoves, he sensed an unbridgeable chasm between their world and his. No one was concerned about the escape or the dead pilots. It was the lost meal and the confiscated cigarettes that hurt most.

'Max. Wake up.'

He'd been dreaming. A girl in a red dress. In a hotel room.

'Come on. Come on. Wake up.'

His eyes opened stickily. In the thick black of the hut, a hand was jerking his arm.

'It's me. Koenig. Shake your bones.'

Someone had left the wood burner door open. Backlit by the embers, he could make out Koenig's face, smell the rank tobacco on his breath. Someone else was there too. A second shape. Hartmann rolled over and lowered himself quietly to the floor. 'What the fucking hell do you want?'

'We've got to leave. Now. Get your boots on.'

'You're crazy. Leave and go where?'

'It's Goltz. He wants us back.'

Down by the glow of the fire, Hartmann's eyes had adjusted. The other person. It was the tall boy – Eschner – still wearing his prison black.

'You. Jesus. Are you alone? Where's Walther? Where's Sieber?'

In the weak light, the boy looked a hundred years old. 'Just me. There is no one else. Sieber's dead.'

# 24

## 16–19 October 1944

The airmen had built the tunnel well. But it still hadn't saved them.

Between the toilet block and the double outer fence there was just ten feet of open ground. To line the walls, they'd used sacking stolen from the farms. To hold back the tide of earth, they'd purloined timbers from the half-finished huts springing up all round the edge of the camp.

Pilots and engineers, Hartmann presumed. Practical men.

While Goltz fantasised, they had got down on their knees and dug. Now two of its architects were cluttering a morgue and the guards were closing in on their escape route. From all directions came the echo of boots and voices. Every hut was being revisited and torn apart. Every manhole was being wrenched aside.

Through the line of ventilation holes above the toilets, Hartmann could see the first milky traces of dawn. It seemed strange to have invested so much time in a tunnel when the camp itself was a sieve guarded by incompetents. Digging out was scarcely less risky than walking out through the main gates. Perhaps it was an airman thing. Like everyone else he'd heard wild stories about RAF escapees. Why was it that fliers had such an unlikely compulsion to dig tunnels? Right now there wasn't time to find out.

Dawn pinks were filling in the shapes around him. Rust-stained sinks along a wall, and the familiar line of buttock-sized holes perched over a filthy open drain. Two prisoners – men he didn't know – were lifting a narrow section of the long wooden seat. Beneath it the gulley appeared wider, and clean.

'Don't worry,' one of them was saying. 'We diverted the sewer. No one shits over this end.'

A living smell, not unpleasant, was filtering up around their feet, fused with the caustic tang of disinfectant. Hartmann's admiration was rising.

The tunnel's engineers had simply followed the route of a pipe that was already there. A week's work, maybe two, and they'd enlarged it sufficiently for a prisoner to crawl through.

A dozen questions flooded into his head. No time for any of them. Somewhere nearby – only a hut or two away – a door crashed open. More beds were being turned over. An indignant squeal of protest ended abruptly with a thud. On every side, he was conscious of hard-breathing soldiers and the clatter of rifles on metal buttons.

For a final time, he looked down. The draught from the tunnel had blown out his candle. Close by, a single match scratched into life.

'I think we'd better go, Max,' said Koenig.

Just a few hours before – was that all? – they had been woken by the shivering boy. Back there, in the half-light of the stove, Hartmann's blood had turned to slush. At his side, Eschner's ghostly face was saying it again.

*Sieber is dead. Sieber is dead.*

The same three words, the same icy breath.

'How? Who? What the fuck happened?'

Eschner had looked at them both in turn. His SS prison uniform – Hartmann's uniform – was stained and torn, and in the hut's deathly stillness they could hear the clacking of his teeth. Koenig passed him a blanket.

'I . . . I found him in the toilet block. God, it was horrible. Tonight. A few hours ago. Less. Just hanging there and his eyes were open and . . . fuck . . . he was dead. He was fucking dead. Sieber was dead.'

Koenig's hand clamped round the boy's face. A few feet away, the dry joints of a bunk were creaking. Koenig's hand clamped round the boy's face. 'You're shouting. Don't shout. We can fix this.'

A rank smell – like sour cheese – seemed to be seeping from Eschner's skin.

'You're saying he'd hung himself? In my fucking clothes?'

Eschner nodded. There were tears running down his cheek on to Koenig's hand.

'I ran out. I was scared. I found Goltz. I woke him up and I told him.' The boy swallowed, and wiped his face on a blackened cuff.

'Go on.'

'Goltz disappeared with a few others for a few minutes. When he came back he told me to come here. He said you'd know what to do. He said he wanted you back.'

'And Sieber? What happened to him?'

Eschner looked up at Koenig, and then back to Hartmann. A tremor of cold pulled him deeper inside his blanket. 'I came straight here. For all I know, he's still hanging from a joist.'

He wasn't the first. There'd been others.

Everyone in the camp had heard the stories. When the darkness became unbearable, a few strips of knotted blanket was all it took for the young lads who saw dismembered body parts in their nightmares. Just a few seconds jerking their legs over space, and they were free.

'I'm sorry, Karl,' Hartmann said. 'I promised that you'd be safe.'

'He seemed all right at the beginning.' Eschner's words were coming in short jumbled gasps. The boy seemed to be shrinking before their eyes. 'It got horrible in there. Some people were horrible in there. You told us we'd get back.'

'Who, Karl? Who was horrible?'

'I never knew his name. The one with no fingers.'

Koenig's hand was pressing on Hartmann's shoulder. 'We have to get back, Max. There isn't time for this.' He pushed his face close to the boy's. 'Strip. Let's get this done.'

Everything was exactly as it had been. Slipping out under the army compound's fence, the two men moved easily back towards their own huts. At the spot where Hartmann's feet had first disturbed the wire a torn black roundel hung from a spike of metal above a ragged hole big enough to crawl through.

Over to his right, he could make out his old hut. Motes of ash were rising from a black chimney flue. Rosterg had sorted stoves for the SS too. Cosy times, indeed. Directly overhead, he could trace the pan-like outline of the Plough, and follow a line up its blade to the North Star. Where had he been the last time he'd looked at the stars properly? Russia? There'd been a full moon that night too.

Turning away from the smell of woodsmoke, he hurried towards the squat brick bunker of the lavatories.

'You're kidding me,' groaned Koenig, stumbling alongside. 'Goltz will kill us.'

They didn't need a light. Sieber's body was still there; utterly motionless, one half in darkness, the other whitened by the moon. His one visible eye was twisted upwards towards the makeshift noose. Beneath it, the boy's tongue hung obscenely across his chin and the contents of his bowels were still dripping from his bare feet.

'He's not wearing his boots. Why would he walk across here without his boots?'

Koenig wasn't listening. He was staring at the corpse. Rocked by a faint zephyr, it was turning gently away from the moonlight. As the face slid into blackness, Sieber's dulled eye appeared to swivel in Koenig's direction.

'Jesus. How am I going to wear that now? It stinks.' He grabbed Hartmann's arm, pulling him urgently towards the fresh air. 'Come on, Max. He's fucking dead. That's all that matters.'

Koenig was wrong. Sieber could badly hurt them all. Whatever happened now, his body mustn't be found. Not in their camp, anyway. Goltz would be working on that, for sure. In the meantime, only Hartmann would wonder how he'd died. Maybe he had strung himself up. Somehow he didn't think so.

'Shall we knock?'

They were standing at the door of Hut 6. Inside, they could hear the low drone of voices. As they stepped through, it stopped, and a dozen faces turned from the nearer stove. Side by side, Hartmann and Koenig walked towards the heat. A tall figure – Mertens – peeled away from the fire-watchers to greet them.

'Look what the cat dragged in.' Zuhlsdorff was holding up his maimed hand in salute. Applause was circling the hut. With a shuffle of feet, the circle widened, and the pair stepped close to the wood burner where more faces sharpened in the crackling light.

Bruling was there, offering a gentle nod of recognition, and further back, a pair of detached silver discs seemed to be floating in the darkness: Rosterg, Hartmann presumed. Nothing would be discussed without Rosterg.

Only one of the group was sitting: Goltz. Not on a chair, on a wooden box from which he rose slowly and stepped forward to shake their hands.

'Welcome home.'

Inside the stove, pine sap was boiling and popping like gunfire. Above it, a line of wet clothes was turning crisp in the rising current of warm air.

'You've seen Sieber?'

Koenig looked uncomfortably at Hartmann. Hartmann nodded. 'What happened to him?'

'It's a mess which we are dealing with. As we speak, he is being cut down; his SS prison black is coming off and his army colours are going back on.' Goltz stopped abruptly. He seemed even more pale, unwell. Agitated. 'His body will be returned to the army compound and strung up from a ceiling in his own latrine. In so far as anyone cares, it will look as though he killed himself there.'

It was perfect. No one would investigate another suicide. No one would care. One less mouth to feed and – eventually – a formal letter home. If there still was a home.

'What happened to him?'

'You've seen what happened to him, Hartmann. He died.'

'Was it Zuhlsdorff?' Hartmann looked towards the space where the teenager had been standing.

'Listen. Sieber isn't the fucking problem any more. Sieber isn't why we're here.' Goltz clicked his fingers. Rosterg stepped forward. 'Tell them. Quickly.'

'Gentlemen. Good morning. I'm afraid we don't have long.'

The flames in the stove were dying. No one moved to replenish it. There was no wood left to burn.

'Please don't ask me how I know, but there are now over three hundred prison camps in Britain. At a conservative guess, that means there are three hundred thousand men like us scattered around the country. That's not counting the ones who've been shipped across to America. Or indeed the ones arriving in the Channel ports today, tomorrow, the day after. New camps are going up everywhere. Overnight, sometimes. The entire system is stretched to breaking point, and the British are trying to react to a problem they never properly anticipated.'

'The point, Rosterg. Get to it.'

'The point is that I hear things. I read things. Bits of paper, telephone conversations. Further north, there's already been trouble. Riots, breakouts. Shootings. No one is segregating the new arrivals properly any more. Black prisoners. White prisoners. All mixed up. That's good for us, very bad for them. But there's something else too.'

'V2 rockets?' asked Bruling.

'Still falling everywhere. But no, not that.'

'What, then?'

'Some of the most recent arrivals are saying the Allied invasion has stalled.'

Someone was coughing violently. Only the air around the fire was warm. Away from it, the damp seemed to drip from the hut's iron bones.

'You make it sound like a surprise . . .' Goltz had heaved himself to his feet again. 'But it isn't. Not to me. None of this is an accident. We're in this shithole because the Führer wanted us to be here. Here. In this exact place. We didn't lose back there in France. We let them think they'd won. It was always part of his plan . . . let the British sail us to Britain. Let the British heal our wounds and feed our bellies. Let the British keep us warm.'

In the centre of the group, the stove was cooling quickly. Pulling his crate closer, Goltz sat down once more and wrapped both hands around the lukewarm pipe. His voice, which had started strongly, had fallen to a murmur.

'We are merely instruments in a plan of absolute genius, two sides of a brilliant trap. On one side, we have strong men all over England. On the other, we have our armies hidden in France and Germany and Belgium. Every one of them – like us – is growing stronger every day. And, my friends, guess who's caught in the middle?'

Goltz unlocked his stare on the gathering. Every glowing face was entranced. A beatific warmth seemed to have enveloped the entire frozen huddle. As if by magic, meaning had been miraculously pulled back into their lives.

Hitler had delivered. Hitler had everything under control.

Goltz is insane, thought Hartmann. They are all fucking insane. On a bunk by the door, a lone voice was singing 'Deutschland, Deutschland Über Alles'.

Goltz raised his right arm over his head, put a finger to his lips. The singing stopped.

'An army in a cage cannot fight. We need to get out. We need every prisoner in every camp to get out. Not in ones and twos but all at once – everywhere. And then what happens? Then what happens?' This time he didn't halt the singing or the stamping of feet. 'Then together we march on London.'

In the swirl of euphoria which followed, Goltz made his way to Hartmann's side. 'We need to talk, Max. You and me.'

Outside, they crouched around a single cigarette. There were noises over by the wire; stifled curses and awkward breathing. Sieber's body was on its way back home.

'The pair shot yesterday. They weren't ours. They were Luftwaffe and we knew nothing about their tunnel.'

'But you had two men in there. How come they didn't know?'

'Maybe we're not as popular as we thought.'

Hartmann hesitated before he spoke. 'What you said in there. Do you truly believe all that or is it just bollocks?'

'Think of the carnage if we can get out.'

'Apart from you – apart from us – no one wants to get out.'

'In a few hours, the guards will find that tunnel and destroy it. I want you and your lover-boy to go through it before that happens.'

'We're on a bloody island. Where are you expecting us to go?'

'You're a bastard, Hartmann.'

'It's a fair question.'

'I want you to find out what's round here. Planes. Runways. Vehicles. Weapons. Troops. Tanks. I want to know where we are. I want a map inside your head. And when you've done all that, I want you back here. Alive and in one piece.'

'So we break out, and then break back in again? Brilliant.'

'Like I said, Max, you're a bastard.' Goltz flicked the stub of the cigarette away into the darkness. 'But now just do what you're told.'

# Order of the Day No. 1*

*Men of the Freedom Movement*

*The hour of liberation has approached and it is the duty of every German to fight once more, arms in hand, against World Jewry.*

*I demand of every German man to fight for his Fatherland without hesitation.*

*It is the duty of every leader of the Freedom Movement to fight as a German and not wage the fight like a plunderer and murderer.*

*I call upon and demand all men to stand by their colours faithfully and bravely.*

*Circular discovered in a routine search of the Devizes Wehrmacht compound, October 1944.

## 25

Hartmann's candle had yellowed back into life.

'I think we'd better go, Max,' said Koenig.

Everything in the previous hour had happened in such a rush.

After a few fraternal hugs, they'd slipped back into the darkness, half-running between the walls of wire until whispered voices guided them through a hole into the airmen's compound. Someone – he guessed it was Rosterg – had prepared the ground well. In the murk of the night, black silhouettes had helped them to their feet and steered them to the tunnel entrance.

Now they were alone. Nowhere to go except forward.

'Are you listening? I think we should go.'

In the creeping half-light, Hartmann felt in his pocket. With his fingers he could clearly trace the monogram. WR. A handkerchief. Rosterg's secret parting gift had been a handkerchief.

'It's time.' An unfamiliar voice again. One of the Luftwaffe prisoners – urgent, scared. Hartmann's wits snapped back into shape.

'How long to get through? What's on the other side?'

'Not long. It comes out inside one of their sheds. There are clothes there. Now go.'

Down at his feet, Koenig had already dropped into the gulley, and was holding his own candle into the darkness ahead. Protecting the flame against the flow of air, he crawled forward until there was room for Hartmann to clamber in behind.

As their eyes adjusted, they noted the carefully crafted staves and the hessian walls: skilful, expert work. The airmen had built their tunnel well.

From the latrines they could hear running water and toilet seats slamming down. Even the British wouldn't be in a hurry to look into this place. Tapping Koenig on his boot, Hartmann shuffled quickly after him towards the icy source of the draught.

It wasn't easy to stay quiet. In the confined darkness, every breath seemed to explode and every thrust of their bodies seemed to echo like an avalanche. After two minutes they were sweat-drenched and exhausted. After two more, Koenig stopped and stretched up into a wide vertical shaft, pine-scented and roofed with faint bars of early light.

'It's a fucking dead end,' he spat.

Loose dirt was cascading over Hartmann's blackened face. Brushing it away, he wriggled awkwardly into the space until the two were standing face to face.

'You should take a look in a mirror,' said Koenig.

'And you should keep fucking still.'

He needed to think. He didn't need Koenig's oddly timed sense of fun. On his secret night-time excursions he'd covered most of the camp, and although it was incomplete he'd a rudimentary picture of the entire place in his head.

If it was right, they'd passed beneath the fence and were under a firewood store. If it was wrong, they could be anywhere. Holding his breath, he pushed both hands hard up against the wooden ceiling. Nothing moved, and the noise sounded hellish. He tried again, this time with Koenig's muscle backing him up.

'What the fuck are we dealing with here?'

'It's a trapdoor.' Hartmann was trying desperately to synchronise their efforts. 'Whoever built the tunnel cut this door out of the floorboards. I think someone's piled logs on top of it.'

Finally, it was lifting. Enough space had opened up for Koenig to scrabble through and clear away the timber. Seconds later, Hartmann heaved himself into the confines of the woodshed.

From the far reaches of the camp they could hear bugles. Soon the counting would begin. And soon after that, all hell would break loose, or at least the worst kind of hell this ramshackle place could muster.

'We've an hour at most. After that it will be too light to move.'

Koenig nodded. Already he was feeling his way around the hut, delicately pulling back resin-sticky logs, looking for anything they could use.

'I can smell rats,' he muttered. 'I hate fucking rats.'

Hartmann could smell them too, the rotten acid of leaking vermin.

'Just keep looking. They told us there were clothes. We're going nowhere dressed like this. After that we need to cover the trapdoor again with wood.'

In the seam of light around the hut door, he was unfolding Rosterg's handkerchief. A whiff of cologne spilled from its pressed creases and the cotton blazed white against his filthy hands. With Koenig's back turned, he pressed its softness to his face and drew the sweet smell of orange into his lungs.

When he pulled his hands away, he saw it, black and clear. Rosterg's gift wasn't just a scented gateway to a lost world. Rosterg's handkerchief was a lifeline.

'I've found it. I've got the stuff.' Koenig was emptying a sack on the floor between them. The Luftwaffe had been thorough. Several pairs of worn workman's trousers, a selection of collarless shirts, woollen jackets, lace-up boots and caps.

'And I've got our way out of here,' said Hartmann, tilting the fabric until the image of a simple map was clear, traced carefully in black ink. Alongside a sketch of their hut were the words: *Change here. Wood collected twice a day.*

Rosterg's handiwork was meticulous, precise and unambiguous.

Apart from a couple of warehouses and a narrow military road, there was absolutely nothing between them and what – rendered in Rosterg's steady hand – appeared to be a vast swathe of trees. In the top right-hand corner of the cloth was an arrow marking north and the words *Pass auf*.

'Don't worry,' Hartmann muttered. 'We'll watch out all right. Take a good sniff of that, Koenig.' He tossed over the scented handkerchief. 'And choose yourself an outfit.'

They looked credible in their clothes. From a distance, they would pass.

Back home, pre-pubescent farm workers were being bundled off to die at the front. Here in England, agricultural labour was still sheltered from the fighting, and no one would wonder why two scrawny young labourers were out walking through the fields.

To vanquish his lice, Koenig's flaxen curls had been sacrificed to the stove, and the returning stubble appeared grey. Few would have guessed he was blond, and with luck no one would get close enough to see the blue pools in his eyes.

In the event that they did, Hartmann's linguistic skills would be their first line of defence. And if that let them down, Koenig's temper would be their second.

There was a large wooden latch on the inside of the door. Hartmann lifted it gently and squinted through the widening gap. Two jeeps were crunching slowly down the gravelled road clearly visible on their map. Each was full of soldiers. As a faint morning mist dispersed the beam from their headlights, the men's voices drifted to the wood store. American voices, talking about girls.

'Losers,' mouthed Koenig.

As the sound of the jeeps receded, Hartmann eased out of the door and scanned both ways. Nothing. The camp's familiar rhythms had already been dislocated. No one would be worried about replenishing the wood baskets. Not when the search parties came looking.

'You ready?'

Koenig was grinning. Hartmann took that as a yes.

In a few strides, they were over the track, pelting between the two huge storage buildings. Looking back, Hartmann could see the outline of a large wooden barn, standing tall against the outer fence of the camp. They'd done well. The door of the wood store was closed, and Koenig had covered the false floor with lumber. If they were lucky, it would never be found. Now only teamwork would keep them ahead of the search.

A few yards ahead of him, Koenig was stretching out towards the wood. When he pulled up for breath, Hartmann whistled and waved him back.

'We go together, and we do our job. Understand?'

'Yes, boss. Sorry.'

193

'We need to know what's in these.' Hartmann gestured to the windowless warehouses. 'You take that one. I'll go in this.'

The doors were on rollers; immense sliding plates which ran from ground to roof. Leaning his weight against one end he pushed, hearing the low rumble of the wheels as they ground heavily in their tracks.

A crack of blackness opened, wide enough for a man to wriggle through. Hartmann stopped. There was a tic pulsing in the corner of his left eye. No one was coming. Neither the whistle nor the quake of the door had done any damage. With a final glance around, he stepped inside.

Quickly, the shapes began to make sense. Army trucks, brand new, parked nose to nose and receding deep into the shadows on either side. Under his fingers, he felt the smooth green paint above the nearest wheel arch, noticing the white star on each door and the unsullied bulk of the tyres.

A familiar smell – that of damp canvas – hung in the cavernous space, reminding him of youth camps and night rallies. Feeling his way carefully forward, he entered the gap between the flat-fronted radiators and started counting. By the time he reached the far wall, he'd counted twenty five-ton trucks. Every lorry door that he tested was unlocked. And when he kicked against the fuel tanks, they sounded full.

'Good news, Max.'

Hartmann spun. His palms were prickling with terror. There'd been no noise. He'd heard no footsteps.

'Fuck me, Koenig, you prick. I could have killed you.'

'Relax. It's exactly the same in the other warehouse. A whole load of mint American trucks ready to go.'

'Maybe Goltz isn't as dumb as he looks.'

'Not a bad start. We've only been out five minutes.'

Less than that, reckoned Hartmann, and already it was feeling like the longest day in his life. Judging by the light, the sun was up but hidden behind a drape of weak cloud. From the warehouse door, they could see the ragged fingers of the treeline, a half-mile away at worst.

One dogged sprint and they'd be there. No turning back after that.

On his shoulder, he could sense Koenig's puppy-like straining. Somehow Hartmann would get him through this. For a last few seconds, they listened. No more jeeps. No noises at all. After easing shut the sliding door, they were off, zig-zagging through long grass before diving into the soggy mounds of leaf-drift beyond the dark edge of the wood.

At first, all they could hear was the thudding of their own blood. Months of inertia had left them unfit, and their lungs rattled with phlegm. Lying side by side, they fixed their eyes on the twiggy lattice of the forest canopy. Five minutes. Ten minutes. Fifteen minutes passed. Neither man moved.

As their discomfort eased, woody noises drifted down on pale folds of sunlight: falling leaves and the gargle of startled pigeons; and from somewhere unseen, the piping of a lone curlew criss-crossing the glossy brown ingots of the ploughed autumn fields.

'Listen. Over there. Beyond those bushes.'

Something was moving nearby. They could hear footfall and the crackle of dry leaves. A gunshot – then another – echoed through the undergrowth. Above them, a flock of pigeons launched themselves in a panic of clapping wings. A light-brown shape was moving towards them, its edges softened by the thick tangle of undergrowth. Suddenly Koenig was on his feet and laughing.

'It's a deer.'

The shape sprang back on its hind legs and froze. A young female, wide-eyed and terrified.

'We're going to have to eat, Max.'

'Don't be ridiculous.' Hartmann stood up. The deer bolted and the forest fell still.

'What about the gunshots?'

'Farmers. Shooting rabbits. Or pheasants maybe.'

'I think we need a plan, Max.'

'I think we do,' said Hartmann.

# 26

All that day, they familiarised themselves with their hiding place.

Within a few hours, they had mapped the forest perimeter, found natural springs and constructed a simple shelter on its western fringe. If they could evade capture till nightfall, then their chances would improve, just a little.

Even from the wood's deep cover, they could sense the hue and cry. The entire army was probably looking for them. Or what was left of it. Every church tower was ringing its bells, and when the wind swung they could discern the crooning of hounds and the urgent growl of military traffic.

If they possessed any tactical advantage, it was the madness of their instructions. Most escapees in their position would be heading for the English Channel. They, on the other hand, were still rooted within earshot of the camp. No one would be expecting them to stay so near.

The forest felt huge. It was also the safest place to be. Along the northern edge, a country road ran steeply up from a sleepy village of soft yellow stone. There, they'd seen mossy-thatched roofs and smoking chimney pots, and beyond them the lonely contours of the North Downs, tracked by sheep and riven with prehistoric workings.

In every direction they'd seen lorries ferrying search parties, and further around, where the trees stood along a sharp, grassy scar, they'd looked across fields to isolated farms, sensing the northern outskirts of Devizes beyond, and remembering their walk through the rain from the railway station.

Two girls, the glow of a public house, and Goltz in his socks.

'How long is it since you were captured?'

Hartmann had to think hard. For the first time that day, the sun had broken loose. In a few moments, it would be gone and already there was a pepper-dust of stars.

'It was my birthday. However long ago that was. Years, months, I don't know. Maybe two months.'

A mile away to their left, clusters of subdued house lights were popping on. Now that Goering's bombers had stopped coming, the blackout was relaxing and the sirens had mostly fallen silent. As a precaution, people kept their lights low – dim-out, they called it – but no one really expected the Heinkels to be back.

For the British – in the skies, at least – the war was almost finished, along with the enforced darkness of the Blitz. From their hideout, Hartmann wondered if these islanders were right, or whether Goltz's apocalyptic babble had some awful seed of truth.

It seemed so long since he'd cared who won. Two months? After his capture, all that had mattered was Alize. But something had lurched. Without fully comprehending it, he'd slipped between the two sides, and was perilously poised, drifting, like the houses in the black valley beneath them, from the darkness towards the light.

'I'm starving. You should have let me throttle that deer.'

'Over there. That's Devizes.' Hartmann's finger pointed south, along the spiky line of the trees. 'We can get food there. Coats. Maybe some money. Maybe steal a car. We might even get a beer.'

'A beer would be good. You're crazy.'

'Maybe. Maybe not.'

'Why would we want a car?'

'I heard planes – military planes – when I was working on that farm. Taking off and landing. There's an RAF base near here, I'm sure of it. We should find it.'

'And the car?'

'Means we can go faster than a truck full of men trying to shoot us.'

'Only if I drive.'

'Not a chance.'

They set off two hours later, rigid with cold. Since nightfall, a damp, squally wind had flayed their shelter, and as they walked stiffly down across a wet meadow the showers turned to hard rain. Unable to see their feet, the two of them slithered and fell. Water seemed to be bubbling out of the earth and startled cows thundered heavily from their path.

After five minutes they were saturated, but the field had levelled, and a hard-worn path could be seen running straight towards the town. Behind them, they could make out the ridge of the hill, and the dark cut of the forest. Without a word, they turned right, hurrying along the exposed narrow track until its flanks grew thick with hawthorn. Ahead of them they could see the weak glow of Devizes; they could smell the smoke from its coal fires and a clock was ringing the hour. Ten strikes. Most of its people would be sleeping, or ramping up their fires for the night. Normal things, boring things; a few last minutes with a book or an hour by the wireless.

Hartmann envied every last one of them. All he had now was this strange night drawing them out of the dark fields on to an old stone bridge.

From its low parapet, they could see a channel of water stretching in either direction. Slender narrowboats clogged its banks, with an oil lamp burning behind almost every curtain. Not a river, thought Hartmann. It was almost certainly a canal running towards the Irish Sea one way and straight into London the other.

'Slow boat to Hamburg?'

Koenig didn't respond. Crossing over the bridge first, he could see terraced houses alongside a straight asphalt road and, at the far end, the comfortingly squat outline of a church.

'That's it,' said Hartmann. 'There'll be a vicarage. Priests always have food. We make for that.'

Embedded in a wall on their right, they passed a scarlet postbox. A little further on, what might have been an ivy-wrapped school or a hospital. They were almost there. They could see the clock face in the tower. And then they could hear voices. Loud and getting louder.

'*Scheisse.*'

Koenig turned and spun back. Hartmann was on his heels. A narrow alley ran off the main road, partly hidden by a rambling privet hedge. Squatting down, there was room in the blackness behind it for both men. Several pairs of footsteps were coming towards them. Two people, maybe three. All of them were singing.

'They're pissed,' whispered Koenig. 'You can smell it from here.'

At the entrance to the ginnel, the group stopped. Only one of them was singing now. 'God save our gracious king.' The others were fumbling by the verge.

'This one's for you, Adolf.'

There was a loud, ringing laugh, followed by two spouts of hot urine shooting through the bushes.

'And this one's for Hermann Goering.'

In his hiding place, Koenig lurched forward. He couldn't rise. A hand clutched at his collar, and an arm was wrapped around his chest. When their eyes met, Hartmann shook his head furiously.

'*Nein*,' he mouthed. '*Nein*.'

Sooner or later, Koenig would get them both killed. But not here. Not like this.

Already, the drinkers were moving away towards the bridge. Another song trailed in their wake alongside a warm cloud of steam.

'You should have let me throttle them. I've got a boot full of enemy piss.' From the shadows, Koenig heard a low chuckle. 'Button it, Max. It's not fucking funny.'

For another minute, stiff with cramp, they waited. More lights were going out in the nearby houses. Further away, someone was lobbing stones in the canal – the same drunks, probably – but their boozy clatter was receding, and the town felt dead, deserted. Overhead, the clouds had dissipated and the windless cold of an early frost was gathering, clutching at the escapees' damp clothes and chilling their toes.

In a few more strides they were standing alongside a church wall lined with yew. Behind it they could make out the delicate buttresses of the nave, and beyond the square tower a stony path leading from a roofed gate towards a large detached house. Led by Hartmann, the two men threaded towards it.

A Union Jack looked sadly down on them from its pole and soggy flakes of confetti clung to the flagstones. As they drew closer, the vicarage took shape, hunched quietly behind shuttered windows. By the front door there was a bicycle, and a pair of black wellingtons stood guard over an iron boot-scraper.

Nothing appeared to be moving, outside or in. And if there was life there, it was still.

'Frontal assault or round the back?' asked Koenig.

'Kitchen door. But only if they've left it open.'

The night was too young for brute force. Every sound would carry for miles. Even the pebbles crunching under their feet sounded awful, but since each was compelled by a hunger he could no longer contain, neither man could be bothered to remove his boots, and whatever reserves of caution they'd had were exhausted.

Passing an outside toilet, and a shed steepled high with coal, they approached a sturdy red door at the rear of the property. Out of habit, they stopped, just briefly, to listen and look. Not even an owl. The entire world had switched off.

There were two broad stone steps and a bell-pull in the wall. Koenig climbed the steps and turned the large cut-glass doorknob to the left. With a gentle push, the door swung open smoothly, releasing a warm gasp of air and, with it, the smell of food.

Inside, the light was feeble – just one small candle left burning – but it was enough. In the centre of a bleached pine table, damp tea towels concealed three freshly baked pies. On a flour-dusted worktop there were apples, eggs and a jug of lukewarm custard. Against one wall, heat was pumping out of a coal-fired range, and the marble shelves of the kitchen's pantry were lined with beef dripping, cheese, cake and bread.

'You're on fire, Koenig.'

Water droplets were ghosting from their heavy jackets, together with the sickly smell of wet wool.

'It's as if we're in a fairy story or something. None of this feels real.'

Koenig pulled back a chair at the table for his friend. 'In which case, you must be the handsome prince.'

For a few minutes, they ate in silence. Cold had sharpened their appetites. But it had also dulled their reason. When they were full, they sat motionless, enjoying the heat on their skin and watching the silent dance of the candle wick.

Outside it felt darker, as if the nearby church was sucking up the light. Inside, the scalding metal clinked and the two men's eyelids drooped.

Neither of them heard the hall door open behind them nor felt the subtle drop in temperature. What they saw was the sudden agitation of the candle.

And by then it was too late.

## 27

A light clicked on overhead and a tall blur edged into the kitchen with its back against the wall.

Momentarily dazzled, Koenig was already blindly pushing back his chair. At his side, Hartmann's hands were fumbling on the table for a knife.

As the shape moved in front of them, they froze.

'What the devil do you think you're doing in here?'

It was a man, an elderly man, holding a shotgun. Around his shoulder was a leather bandolier full of cartridges.

'Not your typical look for a country doctor, I agree, but these are strange times.' With a flick of his rifle, he motioned for the two to sit back down. 'How do you like my housekeeper's baking? I do find she makes a rather fine rhubarb crumble.'

They could see him clearly now, a wiry man in his seventies with a full grey beard and a pair of half-moon spectacles perched on the tip of his nose. Despite the hour he was dressed in a brown tweed suit and mud-stained brogues. Apart from a few wild grey tufts around his ears, he was completely bald.

'I was out shooting earlier, actually. Thought I'd seen something up in the woods.'

As he spoke, the man worked his way around the space, filling a kettle from a brass tap and placing it on the stove. While the water boiled, he opened a caddy and measured out four teaspoons of tea into a pot.

'One really should warm it first, I know. Do forgive me.' Throughout the procedure, the gun had remained expertly crooked in his left arm. As the tea mashed, he arranged three china cups and saucers on the table. 'No sugar, I'm afraid. I think it all went into the custard.'

Finally, he sat down. With the shotgun across his lap, he leaned into the light and strained the peaty brown tea into each cup. Close up, Hartmann could see the man's hands were shaking, and he could smell whisky on his breath.

They hadn't woken him; he'd been awake. The fellow's eyes had the dead glaze of a man who couldn't sleep.

'Help yourself to milk. I take mine black.'

Neither of the Germans had moved.

'Are either of you going to tell me who you are?' Two dark tea leaves had escaped through the sieve, and were circling in his cup as he stirred. 'It's patently obvious what you were after. But I'm deuced if I know where you've come from.'

While he spoke, the man's watery gaze seemed to drift towards a sideboard. Beside a letter rack, there was a large black telephone. In the candlelight, Hartmann hadn't seen it before. Now it seemed to be staring back at them like a dare.

'If you don't speak to me soon, I suppose I'll have to speak to somebody else.'

It was Hartmann who broke the silence, in English. 'You don't need to ring anyone. We'll leave now.'

He stopped, searching quickly in his head for a story. 'We've been working on the farms, earning a few bob where we could, but there are so many prisoners doing it for nothing now, they don't need us.'

Even to his own ears, the words sounded incredible, as if they were coming from far, far away.

'We were hungry and soaking wet and then we saw the vicarage. We shouldn't have done it. Really sorry.'

The man's eyes narrowed. 'I'm a doctor. Not a vicar. This is a surgery, not a house of God.'

With deliberate care, using both hands, he sipped from the edge of his cup. When he placed it back down, tea spilled out on to the saucer.

'My job is to keep people alive. Their job is to prepare people for death. What we share is a fondness for ridiculously big houses and a liking for good food, notwithstanding the privations of war.'

'We saw the church. We just assumed . . .'

'Wrongly. So tell me. Where exactly in Germany are you from?'

Somewhere deep within the house, a mechanism was clicking and a chain was sliding down past a pendulum. From the dark oak cabinet of a standing clock, the soft sound of a bell reached into every dusty corner, before triggering twelve deeper chimes from out in the graveyard, bell on bell, until the day was officially declared done.

'How delightfully hammy! Like a bad movie.' The doctor clapped. 'Shall we speak in German or English? I'm equally happy in both.'

Hartmann looked across at Koenig. His face was blank, unreadable. So far, he hadn't understood a word. Later on – if they got out of there – Hartmann would tell him what he'd missed.

'I was born in Vienna. Grew up in Munich. My friend was born in Bremen.'

'And is that where you're trying to get to now? Munich?'

Outside, a heavy lorry was moving slowly down the street. They could see its headlights flickering among the trees and feel the vibrations in the floor.

'Yes, I suppose so. I'm not sure. We didn't really think. We just saw a chance and we got out.'

'The camp are saying that you're SS. Highly dangerous. Not to be approached. Should I be worried?' Nestled in his arms, the shotgun seemed to glow and streaks of oil glistened along the length of its barrel.

'Do you know if there's anything of Munich left?' Hartmann asked.

'I'm afraid there's not much left of Germany at all.'

'And Cologne?'

'Pretty much wiped off the map, I hear. Like everywhere else over there. Terrible business. But then you did rather start it all off.'

In the silence that followed, both men felt the sadness that flowed between them.

'Do you know someone in Cologne?' asked the doctor.

'I don't know,' said Hartmann. 'I might do.'

Through the kitchen door into the hall, he could hear the rhythmic tutting of the clock, as if the very house itself had a heartbeat.

'Your bombers gave up on the job rather too quickly. We, on the other hand, seem to have got something of a taste for it.'

'My wife was going there for safety. I was married just before your invasion. Last time I saw her she was pregnant. If they're alive, I have a child I've never met.'

'I'm very sorry.' The doctor leaned back on his chair and stretched an arm out towards a side table. 'I think we all need something a little bit stronger, a drop of Scotch, perhaps.'

As he poured, the two prisoners watched as if hypnotised. Three small glasses, each one filled to the shimmering brim. When they bent down to smell, the vapours scorched their throats. When the first drops touched their lips, the heat burned deep down into their boots.

'*Prost*,' said the doctor.

'*Prost*,' replied the two in unison.

With a polite clink they drank, quietly and slowly, savouring the moment and feeling no necessity to speak until every drop had been drained.

'Will you ring the camp now?'

'I will not.'

'But we are in your house. We are your enemy. What will you do?'

'We have something in common,' answered the doctor. 'I also have a child in Germany. And like you, I don't know if he's dead or alive.'

There was whisky left in the bottle. He picked it up, and divided what remained between the three of them.

'He's RAF, you see. Gun crew. Shot down on a raid in the summer. Some of the other planes saw parachutes. Three parachutes, maybe four. So in all probability, he's in a German prison camp. Just like you. I just don't know where. And I don't know for sure.'

'What's his name?'

Even as he asked the question, Hartmann felt shamed by its pointlessness. War had turned his existence into a series of unfinished sketches, a black canvas of fragments whose only connection was Hartmann himself.

He would never know whether Sieber had tied his own noose. He would never know the doctor's name, or find out what happened to his son. He would never know if Eschner got home, or whether the girl Helen had been reunited with her own missing boyfriend. War didn't lend itself to neat endings – or fairy stories – and his life, like that of every soldier, had the qualities of a length of rope, being merely a thread anchored to absolutely nothing at each of its ends.

'He's called Christopher. He's probably about the same age as you.'

The last of the Scotch had gone. So, too, was its glad promise of deliverance.

'You should be angry. I don't understand why you're not picking up the phone.'

'Because if my son escaped, I would hope someone in Germany might treat him like this. Give him a chance. Show him some respect. Point the way home.'

The empty glass was still in his hand. With his eyes closed, he held it to his nose and inhaled. 'There are so many different ways to be brave.' The words were almost inaudible, a private notion breaking free.

'And now, my young friends, it is time for you to go.'

The glass slammed back on the table, and in the same movement he was up and moving towards the hall. 'My wife will be wondering where I am.' He turned towards them for the last time. 'I'll leave you to make your own way out.'

'You never told us your name.'

'You'll find the keys in the bread bin.' He was gone; a pair of footsteps padding softly away.

A final whisper. 'Good luck, soldier. I hope you find your child.'

## 28

It was a wrench leaving the house.

The alcohol had eroded their energy. The kitchen was still warm, and outside the temperature had plummeted. On the doorstep Koenig stumbled awkwardly and the cold sparked a surge of irritation. Listening to the two men inside had bored him to the brink of sleep. For ten minutes he'd endured a conversation that meant nothing. And now Hartmann was hurrying him out with heat still pumping from the range.

'What was all that about? You seemed to be getting on well.'

Hartmann opened his hand in front of Koenig's face. There was a knot of car keys inside. 'Interested now?'

'We're stealing his car?'

'He gave us his car.'

At best, Hartmann calculated, they had twenty-four hours. After that, the doctor would surely report it stolen. Passive assistance was one thing; active collaboration was another. Even saintliness had his limits.

'What kind of car are we looking for, Max?'

'I'm not expecting we'll get much choice.'

It was good that Koenig was awake again. Back in the kitchen, Hartmann had sensed his friend's fuse burning down. Even as a child, Koenig's world only made sense in black and white; them and us. Questions and doubt merely stirred his devils, and the galaxy into which Hartmann had drifted – riddled with both – was beyond his comprehension. To Koenig, the doctor was the embodiment of a culture he'd been taught to despise.

Not even a slice of pie and a glass of Scotch would ever change that.

'Let's hope it's a Rolls-Royce. No one will suspect us in one of those.'

Around the front, they found it. A stubby dark saloon parked on the doctor's driveway. Even in the meagre light, they were bemused by its dowdy practicality; all tidy and brisk like a banker in a black city suit.

'I think it's an Austin of some sort,' said Hartmann. 'Odd little thing to look at.'

The doors were unlocked and they clambered in.

'Small point.' Koenig grinned, running the steering wheel through his hands. 'But if you're going to drive, you're sitting on the wrong side.'

Hartmann handed him the keys. To the front, through a wide open gate, he could see the main road heading away from the town. Somewhere to the right, he assumed, was the lane back to the canal bridge. Behind them, hidden by trees, must be the centre of the town and beyond that – somewhere – was the camp.

Once they were moving, he felt certain the geography would make sense. Back in the youth camps, it was always Koenig who tinkered with engines while Hartmann pored over maps. In his mind's eye, he could see an airbase, and his inner compass told him it was north. If they could get the doctor's car going, north was where they would go.

'Making any sense?'

The interior of the Austin was black. Blindly, Koenig's fingers were exploring every inch of the dashboard. 'I've got the key in the ignition. Just looking for the choke and the starter pull.'

Hartmann wound down the passenger window and leaned out. There were bad memories in cars. As a child, he'd been incurably travel sick and the smell of petrol and polished leather seats always brought the nausea heaving back.

At his side, Koenig was beaming. 'Choke out. Starter located. Here we go.'

Three convulsions of the engine was all it took. As the petrol fired, a toxic cloud spewed from the exhaust, and the motor held strong in a comforting chug. Every bolt in the chassis seemed to be vibrating, but there was no weakness in the sound. The British had built well. Ugly, but well.

Koenig pushed the choke halfway back, and the juddering eased. With a wrench, he located first gear, took one glance at his passenger, and slipped out the clutch. If anyone had heard the engine, they'd think the GP was going out on an emergency call. No one would be looking for two Nazi killers in a mud-spattered Austin Ten.

Somewhere behind them, Hartmann felt sure the doctor would be watching, but when he checked, the house looked merely abandoned.

'Ready?'

Hartmann pointed ahead, and the car crunched slowly out across the pebbled driveway.

Slipping carefully between two ornamented gateposts, Koenig stopped at the edge of the road, wincing as the brakes rasped. Nothing was moving and the windscreen was already fogged with their breath. Using Rosterg's handkerchief, Hartmann wiped away the droplets until they could see.

Every streetlight was dead, and the houses were still. From the front of the Austin, a weak yellow glow was coming from its shrouded headlamps. Reaching down into the footwell, Koenig was scrabbling for another switch.

'There won't be one. Don't bother. That's as much light as you'll get. Look around you. No one drives at night. Blackout rules. There's no magic switch.'

'So what are we doing in a car, mastermind?'

'Let's just drive, shall we?'

Koenig was right, though. Up in the woods, they'd been safe. Here they were exposed to every twitching curtain. On either side, along narrow streets, the wet pavements were lined with shuttered shops, and to each of them, in the town's stillness, the car sounded like a tank.

Even with a map it would have been tough, but the British had hacked down most of their road signs years ago. If they could some-how feel their way out of the town, their chances might improve, but not by much. Somewhere out there, search dogs would be yapping. And dogs didn't lose their sense of smell in the dark.

'The canal we saw back there, I'm sure it's on our right. If we can get back across it, we'll be out in the country lanes. This thing won't sound so hellish out there.'

'Assuming you're right, which way then?'

'I'm guessing, but the canal must run along an east to west line. So if we drive up and away from it, we'll pass the camp somewhere to our right. After that, we can sit tight and listen. With any luck we'll hear where those planes are taking off.'

'It feels strange that we're not trying to get home,' said Koenig. 'Don't you think?'

'Yes, I do,' answered Hartmann. 'But I didn't think you would.'

Another pair of slitted headlights was moving towards them on the opposite side of the street. As the vehicles crossed, Koenig rammed his foot on the accelerator.

'Fuck. Army lorry.'

Adjusting his mirror, he could see a blaze of red brake lights, followed by the roar of an engine reversing.

'They're turning round, Max. I think it might be full of soldiers.'

'There'll be more. There's bound to be.'

'Does it matter? They'll never catch us in this.'

'Not if the good doctor put any petrol in it.' Petrol, thought Hartmann. The fate of the world would be decided by petrol.

In his wing mirror, he could see the lorry's headlights, but they were already shrinking back, two distant white spots getting smaller. Koenig's foot must be flat to the floor. Unless the troops had radio – which he doubted – they'd need to find a telephone box. And by that time, they'd be safely up there on the Downs.

'Ease it down a bit. Quickly. Quickly.'

Down to his left Hartmann could see the dark path of the canal. He could feel the road rising and make out the black-painted swing arms of the lock gates. Koenig's boot returned to the accelerator. The car shot over a low bridge, and the town thinned swiftly to where thick tangles of hedgerow squeezed them tight under an archway of trees.

'Not so fast,' Hartmann shouted, straining to be heard above the Austin's screaming engine.

Just a few months before, they'd raced through a maze of French lanes in an open-topped staff car, drunk on friendship and victory. Now they were fugitives in the English countryside, slipping deeper

210

into the bosom of their enemy. After a sharp bend by an ivy-smothered ruin, the road narrowed and the faint glow of the town was all gone.

Somewhere along the way, the tarmac had given way to dirt. Stones clattered the undercarriage, and filthy spouts of water ran down the windscreen. From inside, Koenig leaned forward, urging the wipers on. But when the spray cleared, he was still blind. Out in the viscous Wiltshire night, their headlamps were almost useless. Beyond the shape of the road, hemmed in by steep grassy verges, they could see nothing. And with every comatose hamlet they crawled through, and every random turn, the two were moving closer to just one thing: the daylight.

'We're lost, aren't we?' Koenig's voice sounded weary and his hands were clenched tightly around the top of the steering wheel.

'I've got a rough idea. We need to find some height. If we could get on a hill, I'm sure I could work things out.'

'This is crazy.'

'Yes, it is.'

They drove for another hour, slowly and often in accidental circles. There were no other cars and on three occasions they passed the same village pub. As their eyes grew accustomed to the impoverished light, a few reassuring fragments emerged. Not every signpost had been melted down for bullets. Alongside a barn wall they were cheered by one that told them they were halfway between Devizes and Chippenham. There were village names too – Bromham, Chittoe and Bowden Hill – and for a short time the black presence of a river Hartmann felt sure was running west.

'Is Chippenham north or south of Devizes?' asked Koenig.

'North. It has to be.'

But Hartmann wasn't sure, and Koenig's pronunciation didn't help.

Finding higher ground wasn't easy. Roads climbed, and then dipped away suddenly. Views were often obscured by stranded clumps of trees, and there were countless dead ends; tracks that terminated in fields or, worse still, squalid farmyards rocking to the sound of furious sheepdogs.

'We should sleep maybe, Erich? One at a time? You first?'

Koenig brought the Austin to a halt alongside a derelict mill. They could make out sodden blades and the hulk of a giant wheel, slipping into a mossy race. Up ahead, the road appeared to rise promisingly towards an escarpment.

'At the first sign of light we carry on up there and see what's what. OK?'

But Koenig was already asleep, with his head slumped forward on his hands. Around his mouth, a crescent of condensation was fanning out across the windscreen, and as the engine cooled Hartmann watched the rise and fall of his companion's back with envy. A bed would be nice; a bed with white cotton sheets. Anywhere free from the sickly emetic of warm leather and fumes. With his left hand, he fumbled for the door handle and kneeled on the grass. Sick was rising through his chest, a bitter worm of acid. Deep breaths, deep breaths. The childhood mantras came flooding back, forcing his lungs to open, filling his tubes with the cold, clean moorland air.

As the nausea passed, he straightened and walked to the edge of the runnel. Stooping down to it, he cupped his hands and brought the water back to his face. Rinsing the bitter taste from his mouth, feeling the icy ripple inside his chest.

Although there was still no moon, the cloud was thin, and a milky glow seemed to be leaking through; enough to discern the shape of the horizon and the scattered flicker of distant farms. Soon enough the morning would colour it all in.

He sat back down again – with the door left open – and wondered what time it might be. In the town, the clock had chimed twelve times. But was that one hour ago or five? Next to him, Koenig hadn't moved. Only the breathing was altered; much deeper now, with the low murmur of a snore.

Eventually, the cold would wake him. Every trace of the car's clammy heat had fled and its bone-hard seats were not made for comfort. Away in the trees, a tawny owl was watching them. And somewhere far beyond that, Hartmann heard a train and pictured it sliding south under a hood of white steam, pulling carriages overflowing with letters to Germany.

A little after that, he woke.

At his side, Koenig was rocking backwards and forwards, with his arms crossed tightly over his chest. The ends of his fingers were white. Out of the side window, Hartmann could see the first flickering of morning sky changing quickly from luminous grey streaks to ragged shreds of orange. Down in his boots, his feet felt like frozen blocks, and the crystals of their breath had formed icy ferns on the glass. Leaning forward, he scraped clear an opening in front of Koenig's face.

'There's been a frost. Are you OK?'

Koenig shook violently. It was probably a yes.

'We need to drive up there.' Hartmann pointed in the direction the car was facing. 'Hopefully we'll get our bearings. And then we need to lie low for the rest of the day.'

'And then what?'

'Then tonight – if we can find it – we recce the airfield like we've been told, and head back to the camp.'

'Simple.'

As the engine turned, a lone pheasant screeched ahead of them up the lane and clattered to safety. Within seconds, heat was flowing across their legs.

'This is crazy.'

'So you keep telling me,' said Hartmann. 'And yes. It is.'

For a mile, the track wound upwards, through high pasture dotted with grazing sheep. Instead of a hedge, they were flanked by water-filled cuts, and beyond them the countryside tumbled away shapelessly; an indecipherable code of lines and hollows lacking any obvious or memorable feature. When the way forward suddenly melted away into the lifeless bracken, Koenig stopped.

Apart from a few defiant red-berried rowan trees, the landscape looked dead, but it was light enough to see a narrow path leading forward, and the two men took to their feet to follow it until they could climb no further.

Behind them, the horizon was vivid with sediments of colour. Towards the still-dark north, they could already see a muscular crest of bare hills, and the slash of a main road running towards them. If there were towns, they were concealed. Here and there, a few buildings clustered in misty hollows, but Devizes was obscured by woodland, and the wild sense of emptiness was enhanced by the bleat of a lapwing.

'Let's give it a few minutes.' Hartmann was feeling encouraged. From the direction of the growing light, he'd worked out south, and knew where they'd come from. The forest they'd hidden in just twenty-four hours before was now clearly visible, and behind that must be the camp. If he was right, then the orchard he'd harvested had to be somewhere to the east and not too far away.

Narrowing his eyes, he peered towards where he thought it must be.

'What are we looking for, Max?'

'Listening for. And looking. That airbase I mentioned.' He pointed away from the rising sun. 'If I've got this right, then it's somewhere . . . over . . . there.'

Koenig saw it first; a wedge-shaped speck, drifting down low over the skyline until it vanished.

'Look, Max. Look.'

A few moments later, another, rising steadily this time from the same place, until they lost it in the cloud.

'Hear anything?'

'Too far away.' Hartmann's gaze was concentrated on a single tiny point. 'But they were definitely planes.'

'How far away, do you reckon?'

'Ten miles? Maybe less?'

For a few minutes more, they watched in silence. But there were no more planes. As much as he could, Hartmann tried to picture his way there, visualising how this same world might look from down in the valley. Getting to the main road running north would be the key. If they risked the backwaters again by night, they could be lost for days.

Turning round, they saw a dazzle of sunlight playing on the car's chrome bumper. The temperature lifted, and the sun rose strongly against the black edge of the land. Every second on the hill would be dangerous now – Koenig was already rattling the car keys – but Hartmann hung back.

Soft morning light was rolling out in every direction, catching on the rain-drooped webs and the faraway windows. Reluctantly he followed his friend's black footprints in the dew towards the chesty cough of the ignition. At the car door, he took a final look around.

'We've got an hour or two before we need to hide up. Let's get as far as we can.'

'Is that it? Fuck me. Is that your only instruction?'

'There was a line of hills to the north of us. If we get on that road we saw, we skirt east of those, and—'

'And we do all of that this morning? Before people are about?'

'We do what we can. The planes were landing somewhere behind those hills. If we got lucky we'd be there in an hour. Nowhere's far. Let's do it.'

Koenig snarled and then laughed. 'Maybe I'll drive a taxi when this is all over, Max. A black one, that is. In London.'

It was easier getting down. They were soon back among the tangle of narrow farm roads which had perplexed them both before. Under the climbing sun, everything made sense and there were fewer mistakes.

When they passed the pub, they turned back. When they saw the road sign, they kept going. Neither worried any more if they drove along the same stretch of road. Everything was trial and error, an enjoyable child's game they were unravelling, step by step.

'We should stop soon,' said Koenig. 'That main road we want. It can't be far away.'

When they'd started off, the roads had been deserted. Now there were tractors moving, hard-worn wagons heading for the fields heaped high with steaming manure. In between there'd been cars. Not many, but enough to worry them, and from every one they'd felt the curious upward glance of the driver.

'This is the doctor's car, Max. Everyone will know something's wrong.'

'A little further. Just a little further.' Hartmann was distracted. A short while back, the shapes of the fields – the configuration of the tracks – had seemed familiar. If he could see the oak tree, the one where they'd sat between shifts, the one where they'd met the girl, he'd be sure.

'Shit.'

'What is it?'

But Koenig didn't need to elaborate. Hartmann could already feel the engine jerking as it sucked on the last fumes in its tank. He could feel the power fading as Koenig crashed down through the gears and scanned the road ahead for a refuge.

In a few seconds they'd be stranded. It was a miracle they'd even got this far. Even for a doctor, fuel would be like gold dust, black market gold dust.

Twenty. Fifteen. Ten miles per hour. The speedometer was in freefall.

'There. There!'

Hartmann had seen it first. On his side, a huge open barn with an arched iron roof and a short track leading in from one end. As the car lurched, the engine died, and the tyres churned in the dirt. Koenig swung hard left. Momentum was all he had left, just enough for him to force the steering wheel back hard the other way.

Walking speed, no more, but they were in. All around them, huge yellow bales rose to the curved corrugated ceiling.

When they opened their doors, the sweet smell of drying hay was overpowering.

# 29

They had been lucky.

It was a darkly warm place they'd found and the chill in their bones had been supplanted by such a profound need for sleep that neither could resist it. Unusually, Hartmann succumbed first, sitting bolt upright in the passenger seat with his head lolling uselessly to one side. For a few moments, they were resting shoulder to shoulder as their lungs emptied and filled in apparent unison.

'Are you asleep?'

It was a girl's voice and Hartmann was sure he must be dreaming.

There was a soft, small hand now on his arm, tugging impatiently at his filthy jacket. 'It's you. I remember you. Wake up.'

Not a dream. He could smell clean, soapy skin, something glorious.

'You wanted paper and a pencil. You gave me bacon. It's you. I know it is.'

Alice.

Hartmann snapped forward, wincing at the stiffness in his neck. He'd known they were near that farm. It was her. The girl he'd met on the work party. Dark curls and strawberry red lips.

Alice.

'You still got a sausage in your pocket for me, soldier?'

She was kneeling on the car's muddy running board. The door was half open.

'You looked like a couple just now. That one had his arm round you. I thought it was a girl you were writing to. Not a fella.'

Hartman swivelled to look at Koenig. His eyes were already blinking slowly awake, blearily readjusting to the light.

'What the fuck?'

'It's all right. I know who she is.' Hartmann returned his gaze to the girl. 'I don't think she's a danger to us.'

Koenig would kill her if she was. Sadly, he knew that. And so he told him the story.

'If she's such a good friend, maybe she can get us some food. Maybe some cigarettes?'

'Can you?' Hartmann translated.

The girl nodded and grinned. 'Of course I can. This is a farm. In the country we don't go short.' She stood up then, and smoothed her dress – the same dress, the same impartial body language. 'I'll be as quick as I can.'

'How did you know we were here, by the way?' Hartmann asked.

'I didn't. My dog did.'

It was there now, fidgeting at her feet, licking her outstretched hand, the black-patched Jack Russell he'd fed in the rain.

'That other time, when you didn't come, I tucked the letter under its collar.'

'I know. I found it. It's gone. Just like I told you. Is he SS too?'

'Does he look as if he is?'

'I'll go and see what I can find.'

There was a narrow gap in the bales. Hartmann watched closely as she sucked in her waist, turned sideways and rustled through. They'd been better than lucky.

'What were you two talking about?' Koenig sounded curt, unhappy again.

'Nothing. Food. She's bringing us something to eat.'

'You trust her. You're quite sure that's all?'

'Absolutely sure.' He'd met her twice and she'd never even asked his name. Of course he wasn't sure.

'If this is a farm, there'll be petrol.'

Sometimes it was the way Koenig said ordinary things that scared him. Until they were gone, no one on this farm would be safe. 'We'll eat, see what we can find, and then leave after dark.'

It was well over an hour before she came back. By the time she did, they were jumpy. Beyond their wall of bales, they'd heard military transports: a convoy of some sort, followed by the heavy thump of marching boots. Twice, there'd been planes overhead sweeping low in the direction they'd been driving.

As they waited, the daylight had begun to weaken, stirring their doubts and sharpening their impatience. Food would be good, but they needed to go, and the night was closing back in fast. When she finally returned, the girl said little, sensing their unease.

'I've brought what I could.' There was a chicken leg each, half a loaf, and a few biscuits. 'No ciggies. Sorry.'

While they ate, she stood and watched. In among the towers of hay, it was almost dark and a cockerel had started up in a neighbouring field.

'We need petrol,' Hartmann told her. 'Not much. A gallon, maybe.'

'You'll get me killed.'

'We'll be gone then. You won't see us again. I promise.'

When she left this time, both men followed. Clear of the barn, the light was stronger and a little colour was still in the sky. Checking to see they were behind her, the girl skirted around the barn and across a wooden stile into a wide farmyard fringed by crumbling outhouses.

Hartmann followed the sway of her hips. In the middle was a water pump, dripping into a chipped enamel bucket. On one side they could make out the farm itself, solid and ancient with a cracked oak front door and smoke rising from two spiral chimneys. Directly opposite was an open-fronted garage. Inside it, they could see a blue tractor and a small black car.

'It's my grandfather's,' whispered the girl. 'He hasn't used it since the war started.'

She was bouncing from one foot to the other, tugging at her hair and casting nervous glances back to the farm.

'I'm not helping you any more now. I have to go.'

Koenig was already over at the car. It was another Austin. Hartmann could see him rooting around for a fuel can and a rubber pipe.

'Will you tell anyone?'

'Never,' she said.

He stepped towards her, took her chin in both hands, and kissed her lips.

'Thank you,' he said.

But she was already gone, sprinting across the yard, and heaving on the huge brass ring of the farm door. As it opened, she didn't look back. When it banged tight behind her, Hartmann was still standing in the space she'd vacated, although the girl's sweet cloud was gone with her.

'Phsst. I need you.' Koenig was brandishing an empty can. A length of filthy black hosepipe was already hanging from the fuel tank of the Austin. 'Get your lips around something useful for a change. You suck. I'll hold.'

Wearily, Hartmann bent to the task. After the first foul mouthfuls, a steady purple trickle began to flow. As the can filled, they could hear its ascending note, and within a few minutes it was bubbling freely from the cap. Beyond the shelter of the garage, a fine rain was greasing the courtyard and, apart from one upstairs window, every room in the house was dark.

'I know what you're thinking, Max. But you're married. And tonight you're with me.'

Uneasily, they stepped out of the shadows and walked quickly back to the barn. Once the petrol was in the tank, Koenig tried the ignition. Underneath the bonnet, the battery lurched weakly. Unless the fuel pumped through quickly it would die. A couple more tries. That would be it. He tried again. Nothing. He thumped the wheel in frustration. 'Fucking fucking British engineering.'

One more time. Still nothing, and the battery almost dead.

'Shit. The choke.' He'd forgotten the choke.

Koenig yanked out the black knob, pulled the ignition and held his breath. The fuel seemed to explode under his feet. Oily black exhaust poured into the car, making him retch. Around the back, he could hear Hartmann heaving back the bales. Dizzily, he slipped the Austin into reverse and eased away from their hideout. If he stalled it, they were finished, but the engine held steady, and Hartmann jumped in alongside.

'Nicely done. We'd better park it on a hill next time.'

If anything, the headlamps were more feeble than before. To save the battery, the men drove on in darkness, and whenever the road split they stopped for Hartmann to look for clues.

Soon they would hit the northern artery they'd seen from the hill. He was certain of it.

Whenever the road rose, he caught glimpses of movement crossing the landscape ahead: telltale flickers and sounds, search parties returning home and troops moving towards the coast.

An hour later, they'd found it; a wide metalled highway running at right angles to their junction. There were no lights, and while they waited and watched, there were no vehicles. The only sound was the steady thump of an engine they no longer dared to switch off.

'We turn left here,' said Hartmann eventually. 'If I'm right, we should hit another road running west in about four miles. After that, we start looking for the airfield.'

'How do you know all this?'

'I don't. It's a feeling. And if I'm wrong, we're fucked.'

'Makes no difference, Max. We're fucked either way.'

They turned left, and crept slowly north, only dimly aware of the flinty hills reaching out on either side. Even in warm sunlight, the ancient dykes and standing stones would have been invisible to them. Each man had his eyes on the road, and only twice did Hartmann discern the shadows of older times; three smooth tumuli rising over a wet ditch and a lone cock-eyed Roman milestone.

Nothing passed them. Nothing came towards them. At the bottom of a long, straight incline, there was a second junction. And less than a minute after that – on the north side of the road – they could make out aircraft hangars, huts, and the end of a short, grassy runway.

After cruising past it twice in both directions, Koenig veered left up a steep, stony track and brought the car to a halt. 'Is that it?'

Hartmann didn't answer. Something wasn't right. Outside, he could hear the exposed tail of the exhaust pipe hissing in the rain.

'I was expecting bombers, fighter planes. Spitfires. There's nothing there. Max?'

'We don't know that yet. We don't know what's down there.' He could feel Koenig's impatience like a bad smell in the car. 'Switch the engine off and get some sleep. We're knackered. We'll see things more clearly in the morning.'

# 30

All the following day, they watched.

Once again, their run of good fortune had held. Through the front windscreen, the dawn rose warm over ploughed fields broken by grassy knolls. Ahead of them, a natural screen of sapling ash provided cover. Behind them, an empty expanse of heathland rose in folds to a ridge lined with stooped hawthorn trees. There were no barns, no houses and no buildings.

Less than a half-mile away, once the light had strengthened, they had an uninterrupted view of the RAF camp as it stirred.

From a row of pale-grey hangars, small planes were being wheeled into neat lines by boiler-suited mechanics. One by one, they took off, usually with a crew of three – two sitting up front, one behind, and each flier dressed in a grey uniform.

By mid-morning, around thirty planes were in the air and ten more were being readied for take-off at the end of a long grass strip running parallel to the road.

'Trainee pilots,' said Hartmann. As he spoke, one of the aircraft slewed skywards, clipping the outer branches of a large oak tree. 'And not very good ones either. Trainee wireless operators, too. No other reason why there'd be three in each plane.'

'They're not just planes. They're Percival Proctors. If you'd paid more attention at your briefings, you'd have known. You'd also know they're not fitted with any weapons.'

'Fucking bravo. I'm impressed. Can you fly as well?'

'Two lessons in a glider once. I'd give it a go.'

'I might just take you up on that,' said Hartmann.

By nightfall, they were ready.

Although they both felt weak, the prospect of action seemed to stir them. For almost twenty-four hours, they'd hidden inside their metal box. They were filthy, they stank and they were bored.

As the pair edged slowly down towards the camp, their military habits returned. Without discussion Koenig led, gliding smoothly across the ground in a low crouch and gesturing with sharp signals when he needed Hartmann to stop or follow.

Just a few minutes before, they'd been warm and dry. Here they were soldiers again, electrified by instincts which informed every movement they made.

At the side of the main road, they dived face-first into a wet ditch and listened. Three unmarked army lorries passed, travelling west in a slow convoy followed by one solitary motorcycle.

After that, nothing.

'Five more minutes,' Koenig whispered.

Still nothing.

Each could feel the wet ground soaking up into their clothes. Neither of them cared. A few seconds would see them across the tarmac. Koenig's mouth formed a word, soundlessly. NOW. And again. NOW.

He was up then, running doubled over, with Hartmann on his heels, crashing into the bushes which had taken root around the fence before dropping down to his haunches, spit and foam around the broad moon of his grin.

'What's so funny?' whispered Hartmann, crouching alongside.

'You've grown a beard,' said Koenig, reaching out to stroke the black stubble around his friend's face. 'I hadn't noticed before.'

From the fence onwards, the older man took the lead. Keeping low, the two followed the perimeter fence anticlockwise away from the main gate. Through the mesh they could make out a jumble of huts and four huge hangars, but there were no guard towers, and from what they could see, no guards either.

'This is hilarious.'

'What is?'

'It's only three days since we were breaking out of a place like this. Now we're breaking back in.'

And still not a shot aimed in their direction.

'What are we looking for, Max?'

'A way in. A gap. A bit of loose wire. Anything.'

At a right angle in the fence, by the edge of the runway, they found it. A fallen branch – knocked down by a hapless, and probably dead, learner pilot – had crashed through the wire, ripping a hole big enough to walk through. On the other side, the base appeared to be sleeping.

They stepped through.

This time, they followed the fence on the inside, feeling the way with their fingers until they were both standing at the rear of the first hangar. Over their heads, the back wall rose forty feet into a starlit sky. In front of them was a green-painted metal door. At a nod from Hartmann, Koenig stepped forward and turned the handle. It was unlocked.

'We've hit the jackpot, Max. First trucks, now this.'

Plane after plane stretched out in perfect drill-square lines. On the fuselage behind their open cockpits they could see the RAF roundel and every single one had been painted in camouflage stripes.

'Close, but not quite,' muttered Hartmann.

There were no fighters, no transport planes, no bombers. Whatever Goltz had been hoping for, he doubted this would be it.

'What do you think their range is?' He was running his hand over the glossy black cone of a propeller. Without waiting for an answer, he stepped up on to the back of the starboard wing, and clambered in behind the joystick.

Luminous dials and switches seemed to be swimming in the darkness. There were straps and cables, and the awful sweet smell of polish. Through the tilted front window he could see the sky, framed by the gaping open doors of the hangar. In his hand, the joystick felt stiff and cold. He had little idea what it did, and no idea how to use it.

The compass, he noticed, was pointing south-east.

'Four, maybe five hundred miles on a full tank.' Koenig had climbed up the other wing, and slipped in beside him. 'This is cosy.'

He reached forward and grasped the co-pilot's stick.

'Germany is that way.' Hartmann pointed straight forward.

'We wouldn't make it. We'd come down somewhere in the Baltic Sea.'

'We could get to Holland. Antwerp. Brussels.'

'We don't know how to fly it.'

Hartmann felt the smooth leather of the crash bar. All day they'd watched these things come and go. They were training planes, stripped down and simple. It couldn't be that difficult. A few knobs, a few levers. If they could just get it off the ground.

'You said you'd flown gliders. We could try.'

'We'd get blown out of the sky.'

'I could try, then.'

There was a moment's hesitation. No more than a heartbeat, but Hartmann had felt it.

'Fuck, Max. No. No. You're in a war. You're still in a war. You can't fly. What the fuck is wrong with you?'

Koenig never got his answer.

From the back of the plane, both men heard the bolt being drawn back, allowing a brass cartridge to slip into the oiled breech. When the bolt slammed back down, they heard the man – very English, very hesitant and seemingly alone with his rifle.

'Put your hands up now and get slowly out of the plane.'

Koenig glanced across at Hartmann, who was already standing up with his hands over his head and stepping down and out of the plane. From the wing they could see the outline of the guard. He looked old – older than them – but his gun was pointing straight at their bellies and as they clambered on to the hangar floor it stayed that way.

'Over there.' There was a tremble in his voice. 'Over by the doors where I can see your faces.'

As they walked ahead of him, Hartmann ran through their options. It wasn't all bad. They were alive. There were no signs of any other guards. There were two of them, one of him. They were in civilian clothing, and he might not link them to the escape. And Hartmann could speak good English.

If Koenig followed his lead, they might get through. But Koenig was an unknown quantity. And silent fortitude wasn't one of his virtues.

'What the fucking hell do you think you're doing?'

Play it humble, thought Hartmann. Talk very quietly.

'It looks bad, I know. We were looking for petrol.'

His English – to his own ears – sounded wretched and implausible. The words felt as though they were knotted in his throat.

'Petrol?'

'Our car. It's back there on the main road. We ran out. You know what it's like.'

'Where's your petrol can then? And where are you from? Not you. Him. The quiet one.'

'Listen to me. The can's back there. We just sat in the plane for a laugh. Bad idea. Really sorry.'

'Not you. I want to hear him.'

But all he heard was his own breath driven from his lungs by the charging shape of the silent German. As Koenig smashed into him, the guard felt his own chest collapse and sensed his rifle clattering across the concrete floor. Something rank and feral was overpowering him.

He could smell its evil desperation in the bony fists breaking his nose and cracking his teeth. He could hear it in the grunting stab of words that made no sense and the hatred which was sinking him deep and deeper, and he knew he should have gone back for help or killed the pair of them while he could.

'No more. Stop, Erich, stop.'

Koenig's fury had been so terrifyingly swift that Hartmann had been paralysed by its sudden ferocity. Down in the shadows of the hangar floor he could hear the mangled pleading of the Englishman, like a wet, soft moan; and he could see the black piston of Koenig's arm pounding into the crumpled black shape at his feet.

'Enough.'

Hartmann reached forward, seizing a raised fist and yanking back his friend's head by the hair. As Koenig turned, there was a furious growl of resistance and his eyes blazed. In that moment, Hartmann wrapped both arms around him and clung on tight.

'No more. That's it. Relax. No more.'

From the cold floor, they could hear the beaten man's ragged bloody breaths. Koenig's scrawny body seemed inflated to twice its normal size, as if possessed.

'Has it gone? Are you OK? Can I let go?'

Koenig nodded. There were specks of blood on his cheeks.

'If you kill him, we'll hang. Just like Sieber. And there's no reason to kill him.'

'It's all right. It's passed. You can let go. I won't hurt him any more.'

Koenig shook his shoulders free, and took a step to one side. He was panting heavily, and his eyes reflected no light.

'There'll be others, don't you think? Someone will come looking for him.'

'We need to go.' Hartmann was already walking away.

'Wait. Hang on. Just one thing, Max.' Koenig had spun back and was crouching down over the twisted shape of the British guard.

'For God's sake, no. No.' Tilting his head back, Hartmann stretched his eyes up to the arched ceiling of the hanger. Stars were showing through a narrow strip of glass. He felt tired and beaten, an old young man still fighting a war he'd never truly been interested in. He felt dizzy too, and as he stumbled, his hand found Koenig waiting for him in the semi-darkness.

'Careful, Max. You were nearly gone there. Too much excitement.'

'You haven't killed him?'

'No. Promise.'

Hartmann let go of his friend's arm and stood up straight. His head was clearing.

'I just thought we might need these more than him.' Koenig was wafting something under his nose: a box of matches and a fresh pack of cigarettes. He could smell the tobacco. He could already imagine the first hot coil of smoke travelling into his lungs, and the glad prospect steadied him.

Behind them, he could still make out the guard, but they'd moved away and it was no longer possible to see whether he was breathing. 'You didn't kill him?'

'I didn't kill him.'

There wasn't time for more. Soon enough, when they were

caught, he would find out. Before then, Hartmann presumed, there was a little more of their absurd race to run.

Within a few minutes, they were back in the sodden ditch alongside the road. No ambulances, no frantic truckloads of trigger-happy soldiers. At the top of the track, the doctor's car was just as they'd left it, and when they freewheeled down the hill, it jerked obligingly back into life.

'Left or right?'

Koenig was at the wheel. The sickly warmth of the engine was refilling the car. For once, Hartmann didn't know what to say. In front of them was a main road. But he'd virtually no idea where it went. Or from where it came. Another aimless night of freedom might be about as good as it got. Looking across the road at the square block of the hangar, he thought of the man bleeding out on its concrete.

Miracles didn't happen if you were dead.

'Go right,' he murmured. 'Back the way we came.'

They were lost within minutes. Every road sign had been stripped, and their sense of direction foundered in the black bowels of the Wiltshire countryside. Three times they drove through the same village, struck by the giant grey stones that circled it and by the unutterable darkness lurking beyond its boundaries.

Strange humps and hills seemed to flank them at every turn. Church steeples rose like daggers through the haze of woodsmoke which hung over every sleeping hamlet. There was no traffic; there were no midnight stragglers; and to Hartmann, it felt as though they had surfaced in an ancient land, stripped of its present troubles and stalked by invisible ghosts.

When the petrol finally ran out, neither had spoken for over an hour.

'What now, maestro?'

Hartmann didn't reply. Through his window he could see a pointed grassy hill, rising sharply up from the roadside. The only sound was the engine, winding down like a dying clock. He opened the door and stepped out into thick grass shiny with dew. Another early frost was coming – he could feel it on his cheeks – and the sky was sparkling with faraway light.

From the boot of the car, he fetched the petrol can and a blanket. It was good that they hadn't damaged the doctor's Austin. Apart from the mud, it was fine.

'We're going for a walk.'

They didn't stay on the road for long. Turning sharply away from a scattering of houses, Hartmann found a footpath heading south across a fast-tumbling brook, and then up towards the sharp ridge which cleaved the pasture from the sky. At the top, they stopped, panting from the effort and clouded in their own mist.

In front of them was a long, grassy mound of earth running back from a cluster of huge stones. As their eyes adjusted, they saw a gap, an entrance, and when he investigated Hartmann felt the cold draught of a grave.

'It's a burial mound with some sort of entrance chamber. If we're lucky we'll be able to wriggle inside it.'

'You're joking.' Koenig tugged at Hartmann's arm. Hartmann pulled it away. 'You're not joking.'

'Let's see if there's any wood around first.'

There wasn't much; a few gnarled branches snagged with sheep's wool, a damp wooden box and a broken fencepost.

'If we need more, we'll look later. Now give me the matches.'

With a shrug, Koenig handed them over. Hartmann dropped to his knees between the two biggest stones and crawled slowly out of sight.

'Pass me the wood and the blanket, then the petrol can.'

From the inside his voice sounded distant, unfamiliar.

'I'll get the fire lit, then you come in as well. It's not bad. Honestly.'

Koenig sighed. Between the cracks in the rocks he heard a match fizz and die. Hartmann's voice came back, muffled like before.

'I've splashed the blanket in what was left of the petrol. Only a few drops. I just need one to catch. The fucking matches are soaked.'

There was a whoosh then, and a spouting of flames from the hidden cracks in the mound. Koenig sprang back. Wisps of burnt fabric were drifting skywards, along with the sharp smell of singed hair.

'What's happened? Are you all right?'

'Come in. Come in.'

Koenig took one nervous look behind and obeyed.

Hartmann had been right. It was a bearable spot. By the light of the fire, he could make out a ring of mossy uprights supporting the immense tilted slab over their heads. Underneath them, the ground was dry, and there was just enough room to lean back and watch the smoke wriggle its way out into the night. As they settled, Koenig reached up and ran his fingers along the wet underside of their roof.

'It's probably been there a few thousand years,' said Hartmann, his eyes locked on the glowing pile of wood. 'I doubt it will fall on you tonight.'

After that they were quiet for a while, enjoying the warmth and the murmuring of the wind. In turns, they dozed or nursed the fire, eking out their precious wood as it hissed at them furiously from its bed of hot ash.

'Are you awake?'

Koenig's eyes were flickering, half-open, half-closed.

'Have you still got those cigarettes?'

'Sure.' He lifted up his right buttock, and reached into his back trouser pocket. 'Are you OK with flat ones?'

Hartmann laughed. Koenig had always made him laugh. Back on the clifftop playing band music. They'd roared together then. From some dusty shelf in his memory, he summoned the tune – a swing tune – and began to hum.

'Remember this? You and me? Love's young dream?'

Koenig smiled, lit two cigarettes, and passed one across. 'Yes, I do. But you got married. Broke us up. I remember that too.'

'I wasn't aware we were a couple.'

A loose end stirred in Hartmann's memory. Some throwaway remark from Goltz. You and your lover-boy, he'd said.

'You never had a girlfriend, Koenig?'

'Never had the time.'

'You had the time. You had the uniform. I bet the girls were drooling over you.'

'Nope.'

'Not even in Russia? Or France? They had wagons full of tarts back there if you wanted them.'

'Diseased hags, Max.' A smouldering twig had fallen across Koenig's foot, and he kicked it angrily back into the fire. 'We were there to kill them, not fuck them.' He took a last deep pull on his cigarette. 'Or did you forget?'

'Look. I fell in love, Erich. It wasn't something I planned. No more than the wedding, or the kid that I've never seen.'

Neither spoke for a while then, and as the flames shrank, the walls around them appeared to shrink too, drawing them closer to the fading heat, and to each other.

'My father would have disowned me, I think,' mumbled Koenig. 'His little boy had to be a hero. A good soldier. No distractions.'

'You were good at it. You found it easy. I never did.'

'It was fun. Always. The camps were fun. The uniforms were fun. The fresh air. It was our world and we were making it right. Better for us. Better for our parents. You thought that too. Don't ever say you didn't.'

'You've been in France. You've seen this country. What can we offer them that would make them so much better? Nothing.'

'You can't talk like that.'

'Where do you think all the Jews have gone, Erich?'

'Have they gone? I don't know. How would I know?'

It wasn't Koenig's fault. Hartmann knew that now. Their parents were to blame, that entire generation of imbeciles with their pushing and shrieking and clapping. Germany had never been so happy, that's what they said. Germany had never been so great. They said it on the wireless. They said it on every wall. They said it until you could crawl and walk and talk and fight and couldn't possibly think any other way. And once they'd thrown in a little fear – a dash of terror – the evil came naturally – so naturally, it felt ordained and good. Nothing to be ashamed of at all.

Just put on the uniform, my son. It will absolve you of all crimes. All the Führer asks is that you defend what he has built. Until the last one of you is standing.

'Max.'

'What?'

'Let's go home. Tomorrow. Let's try and get back.'

'Seriously?'

'It's what you want. That's enough for me.'

Inside their tomb, the fire had gone out and a weak dawn sky was showing between the stones. Stiffly, Hartmann uncoiled himself and crawled outside. Food was what they needed most, but a little dry wood might buy them some time.

They had no money, no papers, no map. And Koenig would change his mind when he woke up.

Stretching his back, he saw a white coating of frost glittering out across the Downs, and when he moved forward the turf crunched under his frozen feet. The sun wouldn't rise for an hour, but there was light enough to look back down in the direction of their abandoned car.

Something was moving towards them.

For a moment he thought they might be sheep, strung out in a line across the fell. But sheep didn't talk. And sheep didn't carry rifles.

'What is it? What are we doing?'

Koenig had joined him, shivering and pale from the cold. When he followed the line of Hartmann's gaze he saw thirty men, maybe more, advancing towards them in the strengthening light.

'No time for breakfast then?'

Hartmann laughed, and wrapped his arm around Koenig's shoulder. 'Did you mean it? What you said back there?'

'What did I say, Max? I don't remember.'

# Confidential Witness Report

*27 Training Group RAF Yatesbury*
*Confidential Witness Report*

*I am a flying officer stationed at No. 2 Radio Flying School Yatesbury. On 21st November 1944, I arrived to find breakfast had been cancelled due to an incident during the night. Military security personnel were already combing the site for escapees, and a 48-year-old part-time military policeman was reported to be in a critical condition following a savage beating by a gang of German POWs.*

*Some attempt appeared to have been made to enter – and possibly start – one of the planes, but this would have been impossible as they require the help of ground staff using a mobile heavy duty power supply.*

*All of us were made aware that a number of small groups appear to have successfully broken out of Devizes camp in the past few days, just as they have from numerous camps up and down the country. All leave has been cancelled nationwide after a Luftwaffe prisoner was found attempting to board the ferry from Anglesey to Dublin. I am told he had broken out of Camp 184 on 17th November, and reached Holyhead on the train via Birmingham and Liverpool. No one seems quite sure how.*

# 31

## Late November to mid-December 1944

As they stumbled down the hill, a growing audience of men was waiting. Along the roadside, troops were tumbling from a line of trucks. They could make out radio noise above the sound of racing engines, and a platoon of armed men was jogging awkwardly up towards the ridge.

Apart from a few desolate sheep, every living eye was on the two tramps coming towards them, shoulder to shoulder and somehow radiant in the breaking sun.

There's nothing else up there, Hartmann wanted to tell them. No hidden army. No spies or secret weapons. We are it. However ruined we look, we are the sum total of your enemy – filthy, hungry and weak. And too bone-tired to care. In his back, he felt the disgruntled prod of a rifle, then another.

'They're feeling humiliated,' he whispered to Koenig. 'This won't be pleasant.'

But Koenig was already being dragged away to the open back of a lorry. And as Hartmann watched, he too was surrounded by a ring of menacing faces and hauled on to the cold metal flatbed of a canvas-topped army truck.

Outside, a hand banged on the tailgate. He could feel the prop shaft turning, and see the light shut out as a wide cloth flap rolled down from the roof. Even before the first rifle butt smashed in, he was hunched, his head pulled into his chest, his knees drawn up to protect his groin.

In the darkness, it was impossible to count how many were beating him, or know whether they were British or American. From every direction there were boots and fists. When he twisted from one, he rolled into another. Later on, blinded by his own blood, he recalled a hard wooden cane slashing at his neck.

The guard, he thought. The guard must be dead.

Finally, bored by his lack of resistance, they stopped. Sensing that it was over, Hartmann allowed his mind to wander over his body for damage. No teeth missing; just the same set of war-battered ribs which felt like hell and a face that was starting to bulge in all the wrong places.

For a second time, there was banging outside. Two more silhouettes were clambering in out of a blaze of light and suddenly they were moving. Up through the gears, two opposite lines of swaying figures sitting either side of their captive, oblivious of the thin bead of blood which ran out under their boots across the floor of the wagon until it curdled unseen on a rusty hinge.

When the canvas flap gusted up, he caught a glimpse back down an endlessly straight road towards a lake of mist. Stretched out along it, he could count the train of army vehicles and one black car – an Austin – pebble-dashed with dirt. Seeing it there, Hartmann's swollen face began searching for a smile that wasn't possible.

It had been quite an adventure, he thought. He'd sort of enjoyed it.

It was funny now he could see things in daylight. The two of them had travelled virtually no distance at all, lost in a gigantic maze of their own confusion.

When the truck stopped, he was half asleep. A chorus of excited voices was nagging at him, and hands were pulling at his jacket, shaking him awake. His left arm was numb, and when he sat up it drooped uselessly at his side. As the blood flowed back, he flexed all his fingers and felt the mess around his eyes.

There was dirt in the wounds, but nothing was broken and he could see. Once the bells stopped ringing in his ears he'd be fine. Hopefully, Koenig had come through it too. If he'd mustered any resistance, he'd quite probably be dead.

Outside, a fresh line of soldiers was unhinging the tailgate. The loose flap had been tied back, revealing a throng of brown serge twisted in his direction: a hundred armed men or more, unsure whether to be jubilant or scared.

Beyond the flotilla of parked trucks, he could make out turreted redbrick barracks, and beyond them, the familiar wire outline of their camp. They were back at Devizes. A gap was opening between the soldiers; three British officers with pips and peaked caps alongside a bored-looking American in pressed combat fatigues. The American was smoking a cigar.

As best he could, Hartmann stood upright and stared into space.

'Well, you've given us the run around, and that's for sure.'

It was one of the British officers.

'I presume you must be either Max Hartmann or' – he looked down to consult his papers – 'Erich Koenig. Would I be right?'

'I am Unteroffizier Max Hartmann.'

It had been a long time since he'd spoken his own name.

'Of the First SS Panzer Division?'

Hartmann remained silent. Nothing he wanted to say would have made sense.

'No matter. You've been a very naughty boy and will be treated accordingly. Four weeks' solitary confinement. Behave yourself, you'll be out for Christmas. One fart out of place, and you'll discover that we've lost the key. *Verstehen Sie*? Do you understand?'

Hartmann wasn't required to answer. His jaw hurt too much anyway.

As the posse of officers stood aside, six stern-lipped guards formed a circle around the prisoner and escorted him through the camp's main gate. Already, the jeeps and trucks were starting to move away. Soldiers were dispersing, and easy chatter was flowing again through the thinning ranks.

When he twisted back hoping for a sign of Koenig, his escort closed in tight and pushed him on across the empty parade square. Away to his right he could see the Wehrmacht compound, where every inch of fence was lined with curious onlookers.

It was a fine day. They'd be enjoying the diversion.

He thought of Eschner, and hoped he'd be watching. Then he thought of Sieber strung up above a wooden bench. A few cheers had

236

begun echoing across the quadrangle, followed by a solitary '*Sieg Heil*' around which more voices coalesced.

Soon, it seemed to Hartmann as if the entire camp was yelling, a stubborn roar which made his guards scurry even more quickly in the direction of the cell block, a long single-storey building with a flat concrete roof and six barred windows either side of its one hulking door.

When it closed behind him, the noise was gone. So too was his escort.

He was standing alone in a small square reception area, illuminated by two single lightbulbs hanging from a concrete ceiling blotted with damp. In front of him was a narrow wooden desk manned by two frozen-looking military policemen.

By a tiny margin, it was warmer inside than out – a very tiny margin. Somewhere Hartmann couldn't see there had to be a heater, but the men were still wearing heavy coats and fingerless gloves, and the walls behind them sparkled with condensation.

After five minutes, they still hadn't acknowledged his presence and the pain in Hartmann's chest was getting worse. Without taking his eyes off the desk, he tried shifting his weight from one frozen foot to the other. A hot knife seemed to enter his belly just beneath his ribcage.

He heard a loud gasp – his own – and he was falling forward on to his right knee, bracing himself with an outstretched arm as the stone floor rose up to strike his face.

He couldn't see all of what happened next. Another door was opening. The two MPs were helping him through it. He could hear heavy bolts being slid one way, then the other. He could hear the clink of keys and the dull echo of voices, and then a cold like no other, a physical assault of bad air tearing through his wet clothes and driving deep into his bones.

With a shudder, he came to. Ahead of him was a long corridor off which he could see six cell doors, two of which were open. At the end where he was standing, there was a small open area, big enough for a tap, a tin bath, a small wooden chair and a bucket.

'Strip.'

One of the two guards had spoken. He didn't know which. He hadn't even looked at their faces.

'Get that filthy shit off your back.'

Hartmann didn't need telling twice. Any new clothes had to be better. As he tossed his sodden jacket to the floor, lumps of dirt and hay broke free of the collar. When he lowered his trousers, the smell of blood and smoke – and something far worse – made him turn away in disgust.

Against the sudden whiteness of his naked body, his hands appeared alien and black. With his rough fingertips, he felt the tight knot of his old bullet wound, and then the darkening cancer of the morning's bruises.

He was all right. It was too cold to bleed. He was going to be all right.

Covering his genitals, Hartmann crouched and waited. From behind him, a clank of metal, and then water pouring down hard over his head.

'Oh my God. Oh my God.'

It was warm water. Not cold. Warm. He gasped at the forgotten pleasure. A hard block of green carbolic had been pushed into his hand. There were footsteps behind and more water and he was scrubbing down his legs and his arms, pummelling the grime out of his hair and looking down into the blood-streaked pool of grey sediment swirling around the drain hole between his feet.

Whenever he thought it was over, there was more water. Not until he was clean did the magical supply of buckets cease, and then – in an instant – the cold returned.

'You put these on now.'

One of the guards had gone. The fellow that remained looked familiar. Or at least his teeth did.

'You gave me a lift on your bike. To the field. Remember?'

'I got bollocked for letting two prisoners wander off. I've not been on it since.'

Hartmann limped forward. There was a vest, pants, thick woollen socks, and a regulation prison suit with black roundels which he pulled on as quickly as he could. The clothes were warm and his old boots had been wiped clean, but the damage in his chest made it impossible for him to reach down to tie the laces.

'I'll do that. Sit back.'

'That's kind of you. Thanks.'

He was just a boy, much younger than Koenig, and even thinner than Hartmann. His face was covered in red spots.

'I won't be much help to you after this.' The guard's eyes flashed along the corridor. 'You ready?' He clamped Hartmann's arm and guided him into the corridor. To the German, every detail suddenly seemed critical. Along the left-hand wall, there were six metal-framed glass windows just above head height. Opposite each one, on the right, was a cell door with a hatch that only opened from the outside. The doors were solid metal, painted grey, and the first four were closed. Apart from the squeak of their footsteps, there wasn't a sound to be heard, and when they got to the fifth door the boy stopped.

'This is it.'

Hartmann was looking into his new home. From somewhere, weak sunlight was dropping on to a metal-framed bed and three neatly folded blankets. There was no heating and no furniture. His only luxury appeared to be a bucket.

'Do I get a shower every day?'

The boy smiled. Hartmann took that as a no. It was time to go in. Three paces took him to the far wall. When he turned, the door was swinging shut. On the other side of it, two giant bolts were sliding into place. After that he heard a key clicking smoothly around its levers. Then a face appeared in the hatch.

'Night night.'

The hatch closed. It was probably no later than midday. Looking up, Hartmann saw a single lightbulb shining at the end of a tiny length of flex. Not enough to hang himself with, too far away for him to reach his fingers into the mains.

Easing himself carefully down on to the bed, he unfolded a blanket and wrapped it around his shoulders. He lay back. His pillow had the feel and smell of wet paper, and for the first time in days he felt hungry. Very hungry.

There'd been nothing substantial since the doctor's kitchen.

And no one had said anything about food.

He needn't have worried. During the first week, he saw little else. Three times a day, the hatch slid open and a pair of hands passed through his meals. Twice a day, after breakfast and lunch, the hands returned to remove his dish and spoon.

When he tried to start a conversation, the hands flapped him away, and after a few failures he gave up trying. Life in his cell was proving tolerable enough without it. The food was good, and provided he kept still – and fully clothed – it was pleasantly warm inside his triple cocoon of wool.

Even better, the cell block was cloister-quiet. Every night – he'd no idea when – the light was switched off at some hidden central point, and every morning it was switched back on again before his breakfast. In between, he took guilty delight from the silence which embraced him.

The only sounds were the ones he made himself: the pacing shuffle of his feet; the scraping of the hot stew from his plate; the days scratched off on the musty wall with the end of his spoon. Mostly, however, Hartmann simply slept, feeling safer than he had done for years.

By the end of the first week, the pain in his ribs had eased and his bruises had ripened into a reassuringly gangrenous yellow. Although still physically weak, he felt nourished and refreshed and his thoughts were clear. He would have welcomed some fresh air, but none was on offer. Instead, he walked his tiny floor, and – as the aches subsided – he lay back on his bed to devise a series of simple exercises, lifting up his legs to work the wasted muscles in his belly, thankful that there was no mirror and glad for the extra warmth that the effort always generated.

On the morning of the eighth day, Hartmann tried again to speak to his captors. As the hatch opened, he pushed his face into the gap instead of his hand.

'Listen. You don't have to talk to me. Just take away this bucket and bring me a new one. That's all I'm asking.'

Through the hole, he could hear a tray being put down, questioning voices, keys sliding around a metal ring. When the door peeled open, the corridor seemed dark and the two shapes, although human, were indistinct.

'Bring it here. Slowly. Please, please don't fuck about.'

It was the younger guard's voice, high-pitched and West Country, almost shy. Leaning in behind him was an older, coarse-looking man, a sergeant, sporting thick non-regulation sideburns.

The older one wouldn't have said please.

Hartmann held up his arms peacefully and walked to the end of his bed. Carefully, he gripped the handle of the pail, feeling the brown liquid sway as he took its weight. Stuck away in the corner, the smell had been tolerable. Stirred by his movement, the contents broke free.

'There. There. In the corridor. Give it to the kid. Don't pass it to me.'

He put one foot through the door and set the bucket down. As he did so, he looked left and then right. The other five doors were closed. By the guards' feet there was a wooden tray carrying six bowls: four empty, two full.

He had neighbours, quiet ones. He picked up one of the filled bowls. 'I see it's busy in here.'

A large hand in Hartmann's chest was pushing him back towards his bed. The unexpected pain made him yelp.

'You need to tidy up, soldier. You've got an important guest.'

Someone was walking towards them. A rasp, not a thump, leather soles not rubber ones.

'People don't normally get visitors in here. You must be very special.'

The two guards were blocking the doorway. The footsteps had stopped and Hartmann's heart was palpitating. Someone important, they'd said.

'You've got fifteen minutes.'

For a short moment, the doorway was clear. The only sound was the two unhappy soldiers, the young one retreating with his cargo of effluent, the older man bending to pick up the tray. Whoever was waiting out there, Hartmann felt certain it could only be bad.

His eyes hadn't moved from the corridor.

It was there now – the poison. He could smell it.

'You do seem to have a remarkable aptitude for survival, Mr Hartmann. Would it be acceptable if I impinged on your solitude for a few moments?'

Not Goltz. Thank God.

'Do I have any choice in the matter, Herr Rosterg?'

'Well done. I'm flattered. You remembered me. But then who wouldn't?'

Hartmann's guest stepped into the doorway. He looked as if the fabric of his uniform had been personally washed and tailored for the occasion.

'You're admiring my boots again, Max. Quite right. Comfortable, but not warm. Even the best things have a downside.'

Rosterg entered the cell, pushed the door shut, and sat down next to Hartmann.

'You look pale, my friend. Who were you expecting?'

'Not you.'

'Relax. I have cigarettes And I could probably get you books, if you were interested?'

'Yes to both. Thank you. And how the hell did you get in?'

'You've got human rights, Max. At least that's what I told them.'

From a breast pocket, Rosterg magicked a petrol lighter and a full packet of Senior Service. He lit one and passed it across to Hartmann. 'I can leave you the cigarettes. Not the lighter. You'll have to ask the guards for a light if you want more.'

A cockroach was crawling along the edge of the floor near Rosterg's foot. 'Within limits, I think they'll look kindly on requests.' He twisted his boot hard on the insect.

'Everyone seems to have a price,' mumbled Hartmann. The first two puffs had made him feel dizzy.

'Civilians get hungry in wars and soldiers have food. It isn't difficult. You've done it yourself.' Rosterg examined a round wet stain on his right sole. The cockroach was still alive, spinning helplessly on its back. 'That's how you got your notebook and pencil. Remember?' He lowered his foot again and smiled, sensing Hartmann's shock.

'There isn't much I don't find out, Max. It's like you said. Everything has a value. To a hungry man, information is merely cheese.'

He slid an arm around the prisoner's shoulder and pulled him closer.

'Now tell me. Do you still have my handkerchief?'

After that, they talked quickly and quietly, sensing the limits of their time. Every detail of Hartmann's escapade was exchanged, from the warehouses full of brand-new trucks to the hangars packed with trainer planes, from the lie of the land to the condition of the roads.

By omission, there was no mention of the doctor or the girl at the farm. For reasons he didn't fully understand, Hartmann felt both would be rendered safer by his silence.

'This is all for Goltz, right?'

'You two weren't the only ones. He's had people out all over the place. He's building a picture. All very impressive, I must say.'

'With a view to what? Breaking out at the head of a prisoner army?'

'Something like that. You know what he thinks. Britain is a shambles. We are the master race. Et cetera. Et cetera. He thinks this whole dismal country is there for the taking. And no one argues with him now. He's got his spies everywhere and that's made him untouchable. But who are we to know better? Maybe he has a point.'

'Is he serious?'

'He's always serious.'

Sensing that their time was up, Rosterg rose smoothly from the bed. They could both hear the guard returning with a clean bucket.

'He's deranged,' said Hartmann. 'He'll get us all killed.'

'It's not bad in here, Max. A little wallpaper and you could make it rather nice.'

Hartmann chuckled. There was something in Rosterg which he'd grown to like. 'Before you go, one last thing. What happened to Koenig?'

'He's fine. He'll be out of here when you are.'

Rosterg stretched out a toe and put the still-spinning insect out of its misery.

'He needs to watch that temper, Max. You got lucky back there. The sentry at the airstrip didn't die.'

'That's good,' sighed Hartmann. 'I'm glad.'

Eight days later, Rosterg was back with a copy of *Great Expectations* and two fresh packs of cigarettes.

'I'd bring you more but the cells are full and everyone wants the same. Not books, cigarettes. No one else wants to read. There's absolutely no competition for those.' Idly, he riffed through the pages of the Dickens. 'I was rather pleased when I found this one. The title seemed to suit.'

After that, he came almost every day, and although the visits were never long, Hartmann grew to cherish them. The older man was witty and well read – an accidental soldier, not a Zuhlsdorff or a Bruling.

Back in Berlin, he had a fine house with a library and a career he was desperate to resume. He had a wife, a nanny and three children who played in a room beneath shelves stacked with records. He had a season ticket for the Philharmonic, and although he liked to talk, never for a moment did Hartmann feel that they'd established a friendship. Their conversations were like innocent swordplay, and although his erudition was entertaining, Rosterg's mastery of evasion reduced every exchange to a playful game. A cold man surrounded by colder men for whom he felt nothing. Accepting that, Hartmann took what he could from their meetings; and whenever he saw an opportunity to, he pushed.

'I've still never really understood why you ended up designated black with wretches like us. You're a staff sergeant, an NCO, a behind-the-lines logistics person. You're not SS, and you don't exactly exude menace. So why?'

'You've asked me this before. I don't really know.' Rosterg's cigarette was pinched artfully between the tips of his thumb and forefinger. 'My father's a Nazi. The company we both work for makes chemicals. I guess that made someone nervous. Or just curious.'

'In Poland, you said. Pesticides?'

'Yes, among other things. It's a huge company. But I really really don't know. That's my father, and it's a long way away. Perhaps someone simply took a dislike to me. Or made a mistake.'

'Do you talk to everyone in the block like this?'

'Only you. No one else really interests me. I'm not sure why you do, really.'

Rosterg was polishing his glasses. When he put them back on, his eyes looked troubled and his voice had dropped in register.

'Listen. You'll find it very different when you get out of here.'

'Different better? Or different worse? It's certainly got to be noisier.'

'Goltz has been busy. He's had nine people on the outside. He knows a lot.'

Along the corridor, two doors were slammed in quick succession.

'I've spoken to every one of the men who got out,' Rosterg continued. 'And Goltz was right. It's a shambles out there. The country's half asleep.'

'The British must know that, surely. They must be mad to let you near us.'

Rosterg rubbed the tips of his fingers together, as if counting banknotes. His eyes were gleaming. 'You won't be able to dodge this when you come out. You won't be able to stay detached. It's too dangerous. You saw what Goltz was like before. Now he's foaming at the mouth, talking about air drops from Germany and storming down to London in stolen tanks.'

'He was saying all that when I last saw him. What's so different?'

'What's different is that he's had your eyes on the outside. What's different is that he has information.'

Rosterg tugged at Hartmann's arm, reading doubt in his face. 'I'm not telling you because you're a friend. I don't have friends. I'm telling you because he asked me to.'

'He asked you to?'

'You're one of his gang now. He's expecting you to be a big part of all this.'

Hartmann reached for another cigarette. 'I could stay in here. I could refuse to come out.'

'That won't happen.'

'It's strange, but I've been here all this time and the British still haven't questioned me.'

'Oh, I expect they will, Max. Just a matter of timing, I'm sure.'

The air in the cell had grown bitter with fumes. Sealed off from the outside world, the only sounds were their own voices.

'Time for me to go, Max, I'm afraid. Next time – if there is one – I'll try to find you a copy of *Bleak House*.'

## 32

There were no more visits. For whatever reason, Rosterg's credit with the jailers had run out.

Deprived of the stimulation, Hartmann's morale sagged. Without company, time slowed and his imagination prospered in the vacuum.

Back at the beginning of his confinement, he'd welcomed the isolation. Now he merely fretted about how much longer they would hold him. At least on the outside he'd be able to gain some control over events, and according to his wall calendar there was just one week left to go.

So far, however, no one had told him when he would leave, or if he would leave. Every morning, the light clicked on. Every night, it clicked back off again. Three times a day, when the hatch slid open, he got food. Twice a day, if he shoved out a fag with his empty plate, it got lit. Beyond that there was nothing.

Six days left. Five days. Four. Three. Beyond his walls the weather had changed, and his nights were now broken by a desperate battle to stay warm.

As much as he could, he sought sleep by reliving his time with Alize. But when sleep came now, it was Goltz, not his wife, who was usually waiting.

And when that happened, he tried Dickens.

On the twenty-eighth day – early December by his own reckoning – Hartmann awoke in good spirits. Few things in prison were ever assured, but the officer had said four weeks, and the British were nothing if not punctilious. During his confinement, he'd been well behaved, and there seemed no reason to expect an extension.

When the overhead bulb sprang on, he was already sitting expectantly on his bed swaddled in his blankets. In front of him, scraped into the masonry, was the record of his days.

Just to be sure, he counted them again. Twenty-eight. Without question.

All over the wall, there were similar markings left by previous inmates. Almost every one of them stopped at twenty-eight. Somewhere along the same corridor, he imagined that Koenig, and maybe others, would be similarly poised.

For the past few days – with no hard evidence – he'd detected an infinitesimal shift in the air, like the physical tightening that always accompanied fear. The disembodied hands at the hatch now belonged to strangers; there was a feeling of urgency in the faceless footfall; and when it came, his food was jammed angrily through the hatch.

When the door was finally opened, it was dark outside, probably late afternoon. Along the corridor, the windows were black and the lights had been left off. Sandwiched by two guards, Hartmann was marched towards the sealed door into the reception area. Like all the doors, it could be bolted and locked from either side. When the leading guard knocked it was pulled open, and Hartmann was bundled through into the warmth. There'd been changes since his arrival. An old oil stove was pumping out heat in a corner, and there was a small artificial Christmas tree on the desk.

There wasn't time to enjoy either. Papers were being quickly checked. Unfamiliar faces were flicking glances in his direction. It was different. He was right. More soldiers. More guns. Not so much jumpy as watchful. Overhead, he could hear rain drumming on the concrete roof, and from the streaks on the glass it looked like sleet.

'This way, Hartmann. You're going to need this.'

The voice was refined. It wasn't a soldier's. The speaker was wearing a long brown woollen coat, and his features were obscured by the shadowed brim of a trilby hat. In one hand he had a waterproof army cape, which he proffered to Hartmann. In the other, he held a cane-handled umbrella.

'Where am I going?'

The door on to the parade square had been opened. Wet snow was swirling under the lights which surrounded it.

'Someone wants a chat. No need to worry. An old acquaintance.'

They walked quickly – with no escort – back towards the main brick-built barracks. In a first-floor window, Hartmann saw the silhouette of a figure watching them approach. When it turned away, he saw the curves of a woman. He wiped his eyes and looked back. Nothing, a phantom. He was being ridiculous.

Freezing rain was pouring over his face from the peak of his oilskin. He checked again; still nothing, but now they were right up against the barracks, and the man was steering him in and up a set of narrow stone stairs. Aware only of their soggy clip-clop, Hartmann followed blindly, turning left along a gloomy passageway towards a single yellow trapezium of light falling from a wide open door.

On the edge of it, he stopped. The water running down from his cape formed a black circle around his feet.

'This is where I leave you. Enjoy your little reunion.'

Hartmann didn't watch him go. Just so long as he stood still, he could sustain the insane possibility that his wife was inside that room. But since that was madness – and he knew it – he stepped forward until he could see a slim figure waiting patiently for him in one of two leather armchairs.

'Hello, Max,' she said, rising from her seat with an outstretched hand. 'Take that thing off and hang it up over there.'

The green eyes, the ruby brooch, the diplomat's daughter. He remembered everything except her name.

'It's Helen. Don't worry. I'll forgive you. Please, let me help.'

'I thought you were someone else. Sorry,' he mumbled. 'Prison sends you slightly mad.'

'I'm sorry too,' she said. 'But that's a common reaction.'

As she drew close to take his cape, Hartmann reeled. Nothing was quite so gloriously intoxicating as the smell of a woman. After months of squalor, her fragrance seemed so sweet he could scarcely breathe, and whenever she moved it stirred invisibly around her like a night garden in summer.

Just for a few drunken seconds, he was lost. But when their fingers briefly touched he stepped quickly aside and sank into the soft, cold leather of the second armchair. Mentally, he surveyed himself before looking again at her. His nails were ragged and rimed with filth and a ripe, unpleasant smell seemed to be rising off his clothing.

'I'm a wretch. I'm sorry. If I'd known it was you I'd have changed.' He crossed his legs and shielded his eyes with his hands. 'Is this a social occasion? Or is there something particular you'd like to talk to me about? Helen . . . Waters, isn't it?'

Helen sat down close to him. On a wide desk behind her was an Anglepoise lamp – the only illumination in the room – which she twisted slightly until the light was no longer directly in Hartmann's eyes.

'Better?'

He nodded distractedly. As she'd taken her seat, her skirt had risen, exposing a smooth expanse of silk.

'You remember me?' She spoke the same seamless German laced with English public school.

'You accused me of killing the boy on the boat and then you tortured me. I'm hardly likely to have forgotten.'

'You had a few sleepless nights. I don't think we can class that as torture. Not by Gestapo standards. No one forced you to talk. We had some good conversations. Didn't we?'

Hartmann didn't know the answer. Whenever he'd thought back to London, there'd been worrying blanks. After the sleep deprivation, his interrogation had left nothing but fuzzy pictures; a set of feelings, rather than distinct memories, laced with the nagging insinuation of disloyalty.

'I was hallucinating. Did I tell you anything useful?'

'Of course. Everything is useful. You were very cooperative.' While she spoke, she was searching the contents of a slim, cardboard file. 'Do you know how many Germans have died since our last conversation, Max?'

Hartmann shrugged.

She pulled an official document from the file.

'Not just in France. Not just military personnel. I mean German citizens. Women, children, helpless old people? Would two hundred thousand sound like an acceptable guess? Is that a price worthy of your silence?'

'I told you what I knew then. I'm a soldier.' His voice was barely audible.

'Not forgetting all the other people you've butchered since last time. Homosexuals, Jews, cripples. Tens of thousands. Millions maybe. Want me to go on?'

'I've butchered no one.' Hartmann's face was pale with distress. 'Soldiers only know what they're told and make up the rest. Just like you.'

'Yes, but I've not seen you for a while, Max.' She looked down again at her notes. 'And I gather you've been on your travels. So maybe you know things now that you didn't know then.'

'I got bored. I went for a drive in the country.'

'We know it was more than that.'

'I'm a very dull prisoner of war. Don't be ridiculous.'

'Tell me about your lovely friends. Tell me about Joachim Goltz.'

She looked at him then, her red lips lifting mischievously at one corner. In that moment, it felt as if the temperature in the room was falling, and that he was falling too, down into a room full of giant roulette wheels. Red or black, ace or king, Hitler or Churchill. Soldiers were gamblers, whichever side they were on. Eventually, all it came down to was the odds.

He felt her eyes on him, waiting.

'You told me I was a good man once. Remember?'

'I really believed that. I still do.' She pulled two envelopes from among her papers and passed them across. 'However, this might prove a rather good test.'

Hartmann knew what they were without looking. Deep down, he'd known they would never be sent. On the outside, each one had been scarred by the red ink of officialdom. Inside, he found his own writing, rain-streaked and barely legible across two delicate pieces of wartime paper.

At the top of each page, Alize's name was still clearly visible. *No guilt, no shame and no secrets.* He'd written that for her, not for these people.

'You lied. You promised.' Hartmann tossed the letters into the darkness of the room.

'Calm down and listen. You wrote twelve words on that first letter which we deemed not to be serious, and since the second letter was not sent through normal channels, it constituted a breach of security. I'm truly sorry. But if you'd approached it like every other prisoner, there wouldn't have been a problem. Maybe if you help us now, we could do better.'

'I'm supposed to trust you now? I don't think so.' Hartmann rocked forwards with his arms folded tightly across his waist. 'The girl at the farm? Jesus. Did she give you this?'

'No one gave it to us, Max. It was posted somewhere near here and picked up by the censor.' She smiled. A small mystery had been solved. 'A girl on a farm? She shouldn't be too difficult to find. You were wrong, you see. I knew you'd be able to help us.'

Hartmann squirmed. He'd said too much. 'There is no girl. No one helps people like us voluntarily. Not unless they're scared. There is no girl. Just talk to me. Don't go looking for anyone else.'

The young woman patted her hands on her thighs. Both of them had felt the decisive shift of power.

'We drank tea together in London last time. Shall we do that again?'

Behind her on the table was a small handbell. When she rang it, an orderly entered the room and took her request for tea. 'With biscuits if you can find any,' she added as he left.

Through the window, Hartmann could see a white tube of light moving towards them across the mossy slates of the rooftops. As he watched, it grew wider, revealing the rain slicing steadily through its beam.

'I could draw the curtains,' she said. 'Would you prefer that?'

'It doesn't really matter. No one can see us.'

When the tea came, it was served in delicate leaf-pattered cups on matching saucers, with a jug of full-cream milk.

'You know, if Alize is still alive, she can easily find out if you're safe.'

Hartmann was listening. The tea was sweet, even better than a cigarette.

'We send lists of captured Germans back to Berlin through the

Red Cross every day. Those lists are widely distributed. If she's looking for you, she'll know.'

'That's a lot of ifs.'

The tea was hot, too, and the roof of his mouth felt scorched. Conscious again of his grime-stained hands, he placed the saucer down on his lap.

'You told me before you had a boyfriend in France.'

'I'm like you. No news. Lots of people here are waiting for news.'

Hartmann thought again of the doctor's son, and Sieber's parents. The woman had drawn her knees together and light was strafing back over the tops of the buildings.

'You see, we're not so very different.'

The spotlight was returning. This time he noticed the loose strands of her hair, backlit like burning filaments of phosphorus.

'We both need this war to end as quickly and painlessly as possible.' Leaning forward, she took Hartmann's empty cup and placed it with hers on the table behind. 'Only it seems to us – to me – that some of you just don't want to admit defeat. Take this place, for instance. Devizes. Far too many coordinated escapes, Max. Far too many strange rumours.'

'Is that why you're here? Or is this merely a social visit? Obviously, I'm deeply flattered if it's the latter.'

'When you broke out why did you make no effort whatsoever to get home?'

'Who says I didn't?'

'People saw you. The car was noticed. Did you really think your doctor friend would keep quiet? We know exactly where you went. We know exactly where the other prisoners went. We've also got a pretty shrewd idea why.' She drew her palms together as if in prayer, and pressed them against her lips. 'Please. You can help me, Max. I'm sure you want to. I'm sure you can. Absolutely sure.'

'We got lost. I don't know about anyone else.' As he spoke, he wondered who else might be listening. 'I keep telling you, we're prisoners of war. Our fight's over.'

'Oh dear, Max, that's so very disappointing. I'm really not that stupid.'

For the first time, Hartmann studied the woman properly. Without her even moving, the smell of her perfume had remained strong. No, she wasn't stupid. She was a British intelligence officer groomed at Roedean.

She was calm, clean and cunning in ways he didn't have the energy to fathom. She was civilisation and order: he was chaos, an insignificant junior SS officer schooled by Nazi brownshirts for a war that had been lost. Looking at her now, it was her absolute stillness that he admired; the feeling that her calm grew from roots in a landscape he'd been programmed to destroy.

Downstairs, there'd be others just like him waiting their turn. Not one of them would tell her a damned thing.

'Is there any way you could find out about Alize? Even if it's just to say she's alive?'

'It's hard now, even harder than it was before. I'm sorry. Your fault, but Germany's in a mess.'

'There's no reason I could trust you anyway.'

'Sometimes you have to do the right thing. You can't always get something back.'

This time, when the spotlight returned, he noticed a clock on the wall between a framed picture of the British king and a large engraving of some Napoleonic battle scene. The hands were pointing to twenty past nine. Somehow, the knowledge felt stolen, his own enjoyably innocent secret.

'Will you be talking to my friend? Erich Koenig?'

At that moment, it was all he could think of to say.

'I'm afraid Koenig has gone. You really should choose your so-called friends with more care. He's what we call a bad egg, a deeply unpleasant and unstable youth.'

'Gone where? I was told he was in the same cell block as me.'

'Come on, Max. You're stalling. You need to help me here. Something bad is brewing in this place which is going to get people killed, people on both our sides. Forget Koenig. You're better than him.'

'Actually, I'm not sure what he is.'

Hartmann wanted to explain, to justify their association. But she was right, and that hurt.

'I promise you he's fine – feeling a little cold maybe – but then who isn't? We've sent him north to a new camp in Scotland.' She gave him a look which he took as a warning. 'I'd try to steer clear of it if I were you.'

'Because?'

'We're filtering people out. Bit by bit, we're isolating the wheat from the chaff.'

'I'm afraid some of your English expressions mean nothing to me.'

'Try this one. It's where we're sending all the shits. We're calling it Black Camp Twenty-One.'

Soon after that, Hartmann yielded.

There was more tea and there were biscuits. There was even some dry and crumbling cake.

When he was eventually taken away, he noticed the clock on the wall for a second time.

It was just two minutes short of midnight.

They had been talking for a very long time.

## 33

They didn't return him to his cell block.

When they took him outside, the sky was alive with stars and a hard frost was digging in. All across the parade square, dull patches of ice were already forming. They'd need salt on those before roll call, he thought, or someone would get hurt. He was accompanied by two immense soldiers on either side, and apart from their boots there wasn't another noise in the camp. At the back of his throat, the air felt like fire. Forget the British. The cold would be their biggest enemy tonight.

A few weak slivers of smoke still rose from the huts, but the fires inside were long dead. He should have told the woman to order more coal. Most of the prisoners here had already come through a Soviet winter. None of them would want to hang around for another like that one.

The endless shivers were Goltz's best friend.

A little fuel might save everyone an awful lot of trouble.

After five weeks away, Hartmann felt disorientated. But even at night, he could see how far the camp had spread. A few sodden tents still remained, but beyond the older Nissen huts a line of new warehouse dormitories extended out into the darkness and the camp floodlights shone on a gang of uniformed men patching a short section of perimeter wire.

At the entrance to the SS compound, the group stopped. Through the fence, he could see the eight iron-roofed huts running up to the brooding silhouette of the latrine block, all terrifyingly familiar. Out of earshot, his two guards were talking in low voices to a lone sentry. He heard the words 'German bastard' and stepped slightly away. Already, his conversation with the English woman seemed like a trick of the mind.

'You know where to go. Hut Six. Now fuck off.'

Hartmann slipped between the men, and walked unaccompanied

into the compound. As the gate closed behind him, the temperature seemed to drop. Or was that just him? Wherever there was light, the air shivered with frozen crystals, and the cold reached so far up through his boots that his teeth ached.

On the threshold of his old hut he stopped, remembering the first time he'd stood there. Back then, it had felt like some sort of ending. Now he knew it had been anything but.

With a lurch of dread, he turned the handle and went inside. Apart from a few disembodied snores, the place was hushed and the concrete floor felt like ice. Only the old blackness was there to greet him, nothing else, and by the time he climbed up into his bunk he was shaking uncontrollably.

The next morning, when the men began to stir, Hartmann couldn't be sure whether he had slept.

For years, his nights had been the same. As a child, he would insist that he never slept at all, but when challenged to say how he'd passed away the hours, he could offer no explanation. The time had gone, but he didn't know where. It was a mystery, just like his dreams. Everyone else forgot theirs, but Hartmann always insisted he could remember every one he'd ever had.

Underneath their blankets, human shapes were twisting reluctantly in the darkness. Somewhere far away, a lone trumpet was blowing reveille. Down the full length of the block, men began to emerge fully clothed, fumbling for the buckets. In a moment, they'd all begin their bitter trudge to the washroom, the lucky ones clutching the blunt razor blades they'd traded for a meal, the rest content merely to hack at their beards with makeshift scissors.

From what he could see, every bunk was full: eighty frozen souls.

If Black Camp 21 existed – if Koenig and others really had been shipped up there – then there was no shortage of replacement prisoners, most of whom had the haunted demeanour of orphans.

'They're getting younger, Max. They're even making me feel old.'

The voice had come from beneath him. When he leaned over he saw an arm hanging casually from the bunk. At the end of it was the glow of a cigarette. The missing fingers told him all he needed to know.

257

'We've been expecting you back. You've become something of a legend, you and your bumboy friend.'

'Koenig. He's called Koenig.' Hartmann ignored the jibe.

'I hear he's been sent away. He's going to miss all the fun.'

'I can't wait.'

'Listen. That shit you told me about the blood . . .' Zuhlsdorff had stood up close so only Hartmann could hear. 'It was a joke, yes?'

Hartmann rolled back on his bed with his hands behind his head.

'Tell me, you fucking pig.'

'It was a joke, Zuhlsdorff. Ha ha.'

From the deep end of the hut, they could hear a poker raking over dead ashes, followed by a single furious shout. Suddenly a hundred or more fists were pounding the cold iron sides of their building.

'It happens every day. Protests like this. All over the camp. There's not enough fuel and the days are getting shorter,' bellowed Zuhlsdorff, as he kicked at the bedframe in time to the beat. 'Sometimes the Tommies come in and wave their guns, but they're just as cold as we are. Everyone's freezing to death, Max. We get a little coal for the evenings, but it's not enough.'

He drifted away to join the others in some indecipherable tribal chant, a baritone roar of defiance from which no one, including Hartmann, was exempt. He'd heard it before, numerous times, but this was uglier, and as the noise built he watched their faces, set hard and steely-eyed like the recruitment posters of the beautiful youths in grey helmets he'd once admired along the walls of Munich railway station, each one staring east under a black flag boasting two ragged lightning strikes. *Waffen SS. Eintritt nach vollendetem 17. Lebensjahr.*

You can join when you're seventeen. Seventeen. No wonder Rosterg felt old.

Almost as quickly as it had risen, the chanting fell away. A line of men was filing out through the hut door, and a bitter draught was forcing the stragglers up on to their feet. Over the camp, the sky was slowly shifting to purple. Another two hours would pass before the sun heaved itself over the eastern horizon, bringing light but precious little heat.

Wherever Hartmann looked, the prisoners were thumping life back into their feet and blowing hard into their hands. In thirty minutes' time it would be roll call, and after that breakfast, the canteen, warmth. Even here, behind barbed wire in an alien country, the men embraced routine. Very few of them, Hartmann realised, had ever made a single decision for themselves.

They behaved like children because they were children. Without a leader, they'd be sunk.

Like everyone else, Hartmann was shuffling towards the exit, past the joyless barrel of the stove. A few yards ahead of him, a stooped giant appeared to be moving in the same direction. Mertens the U-boat man. He was still here.

When they'd first met it had been difficult to picture him in a submarine. Alongside him now, the rest of them still looked like dwarfs. The fellow was a behemoth, a solitary giant walking alone with his thoughts. Some sort of farmer, Hartmann remembered, and he could sense that now in the fellow's inscrutably distant air.

'Max. My old friend.'

A hand had reached out and locked around his wrist. Hartmann turned to his right. The grip was harder than before – and more calloused – but the voice was unchanged.

'Sit down a moment. You'll only have to queue for a sink if you go outside now. Or shit yourself waiting.'

In the weak glow of electric light, Goltz looked exultant, excitedly patting a space on the edge of his bunk into which Hartmann slid.

'Rosterg came to see you? Did he tell you much?'

'I don't know. How much is there to tell?'

'Make a note in your diary, Max.' The words made no sense. And his breath – like everyone's – was still rank.

'I don't have a diary.'

'December twenty-fourth. Christmas Eve,' he hissed. 'We're going out.'

Hartmann wasn't sure whether to laugh. But then no one ever seemed to laugh much around Joachim Goltz.

No one seemed to laugh much anywhere.

Outside in the freezing December mist, it wasn't hard to see why.

For the rest of that day, Hartmann ticked away the hours. In solitary confinement, he'd become a master of wasted time. Between roll calls and meals – which he pushed away listlessly – he crawled on to his bunk and turned away from the card games and the chatter.

For the first time in his captivity, his appetite had gone. There was too much to think about, and none of it was good. The woman had mentioned Black Camp 21, but now that he thought about it, he didn't even really know where Scotland was, and he doubted anywhere could be as cold as this.

During the few hours of daylight they'd had, a hard fall of snow had obliterated all trace of the sun, and by the time the hut door was banged shut for the night he'd not said a word to another person since breakfast.

From his perch, he could see that the stoves had been lit. Somehow, enough fuel had been filched to get them going again, for an hour or so, at least. Along the ceiling, black flue pipes were beginning to clank with the heat. Wherever there was space, wet hats and boots had been squeezed behind them to dry. Here and there, a few candles were burning and – to his surprise – a paraffin lamp had been placed on a box between his own bunk and the door.

In the spread of its light, he could see that the hut was almost empty. Hartmann sat up. The only inmates left were congregating near the stove at the far end. The rest, it seemed, had been sent away, and prisoners he didn't recognise were slipping in from outside to take their place.

Fear zipped along his back. Not again. No one would save him for a second time.

And yet everything was just like before. Bunks were being moved around to form a large square around the stove. A hush of anticipation had fallen over the entire space, broken only by Zuhlsdorff's coughing from the mattress below – the same disturbing hack he'd heard all over the camp.

Listening to the boy's convulsions, you could easily believe the rumours that the sickrooms were overflowing with victims of a mystery virus which was decimating every compound. But very little spread faster in a prison camp than a lie, and bogus epidemics and fuel shortages played perfectly into Goltz's hands.

Nothing would suit him better now than a collapse in camp morale.

'Don't worry, Max. This isn't about you.' Rosterg had entered the hut, whispering his message to Hartmann as he passed.

'No? Definitely?'

'Absolutely not. Relax. They like you.'

Unburdened, Hartmann slid from his bunk to join the other prisoners further down the hut. If there was a meeting, he was presumably expected to be part of it. Finding a gap in the makeshift wall, he kneeled close to the stove and began pushing tiny nuggets of coal though the opening at the top.

From what he could see, around forty men had crammed into the space. Apart from the low crackle of the fire – and the rasp of melting slush across the roof – the hut was virtually silent, and it was a full five minutes before anyone spoke above the murmur.

'Gentlemen, I think it's time we got this going. Each of us has taken considerable risks to be here, and it would be a major setback if any of us were caught on our way back to our proper huts.'

A flicker of firelight was playing on the golden frames of Rosterg's spectacles and for the first time ever – to Hartmann's ears – he sounded horribly nervous.

'I don't think it's an exaggeration to say that what we will be discussing tonight could be a turning point in the entire war, or that any failure to maintain absolute secrecy will cost you your life.

'As we are all well aware, the walls of these places have ears, so have absolutely no doubt that we will find out if you talk out of turn. Do please think about that very hard.'

Rosterg turned and gestured to the rotund figure sitting on his right. Hartmann had seen him once before, back in the army compound: the Lagerführer.

'I'll now pass you over to our camp leader, Major Walter Bultmann.'

As the major rose to his feet, everyone present felt a dip in the mood. Like all the officers, he'd been permitted to continue wearing his full German military uniform. Not for him, or his kind, the full force of the oncoming cold, or any of the other mundane deprivations of prison life.

Everyone knew how they lived. Everyone had seen the heat rising all day and night from the chimneys in the officer compound. Everyone had heard the stories about free-flowing brandy and chocolate.

'Thank you, gentlemen. Thank you.'

Watching the major steady himself, Hartmann wondered if Rosterg's warning had been aimed squarely at this man. The Führer's contempt for his own senior officers was the one opinion that Hartmann shared, and if Goltz ever did break out no one else had quite so much to lose.

It didn't help that the major's insipid voice sounded tired and shorn of conviction. Or that, at forty-four, he was more than twice the average age of his co-conspirators.

'Well, it's good to see you all here. It really is. Around this stove, we have the leaders of the four compounds. Welcome to all.'

A few drops of sweat were running down the sides of his ears. His face had turned bright pink.

'I've not much to say. Just a couple of things, though, before others go into the details. Firstly, as you know, this is not my personal operation. In the position that I hold, it would have been impossible for me to plan anything without the British finding out. So please don't interpret my distance as a lack of commitment. Others have taken the lead role in this endeavour, and, when victory is assured, they will be thanked. Secondly, it's vital that we all understand that this is about the entire camp. Not just a handful, not just the SS, or the Luftwaffe, or the Wehrmacht. This is about all of us. Everyone. When the call comes, we're all going out together. Thank you. *Heil Hitler.*'

In the square of bunks, a few backsides shuffled uncertainly. He was expecting us to clap, thought Hartmann. But no one had moved. After a moment of acute discomfort, the major sat down, grateful for Rosterg's proffered handkerchief as yet more perspiration squeezed beneath the leather band of his cap.

If nothing else, Bultmann had made sense of the gathering. Representatives of the entire camp were gathered around the stove. Goltz wasn't just leading out his trusted SS cohorts. He was taking the whole damned prison population along with him, whether they wanted to leave or not.

'Thank you, Rosterg. Thank you, Major.'

Stirred by the heat, the air in the hut seemed to thicken. Hartmann couldn't see where he was standing, but Goltz had started his address.

'At the beginning of this war, we said we would fight on until victory or death. That was the pledge we took.' There was a catch in his voice, as if he, too, was still battling against a cough. 'Thanks to the brave efforts of many of you, I believe victory to be very close at hand.'

Finally Hartmann had located him, standing slightly back between two of the bunks. There was a grim smile on his face and his voice was growing firmer.

'Some of you probably think all this is mad. But that would be a serious mistake. All around us is weakness and cowardice and fear. Now is the perfect time to exploit it.'

On either side of him, Hartmann felt the rustle of approval as Goltz moved forward into the centre of the group.

'When better to take this place down than Christmas, when the guards are half pissed, half asleep and dreaming about their old age pensions?'

From the darkness by the door, there was a whistle of approval. Goltz turned towards it with a grin and lifted his arms.

'For some of us, the price of this famous victory will be death. For the rest of us . . . our prize will be London.'

In that moment, his audience exploded. If there were guards listening, no one cared. Every man in the room had been rendered invincible, and when order returned, even Hartmann was not immune to his own fascination.

For the next two hours, the plan was outlined in fine detail.

Each compound was to form an elite fighting company of a hundred and fifty men. After darkness on Christmas Eve, these four companies

— sub-divided into smaller sections of ten men apiece — would move on different targets.

One was to break out and seize the army trucks located by Hartmann and Koenig. Another was tasked with overpowering guards in the main barracks and seizing every functioning weapon in the camp. The remaining two were to take control of the gates and gun towers before moving on to the American tank depot which one of Goltz's numerous escapees had reportedly found nearby. The rest of the prison population would be expected to storm the wire at all points until the entire camp was under German control.

'When the world is opening its Christmas presents,' Goltz declared, 'we'll be flying the swastika over this shithole!'

Everyone had questions, and to Hartmann's astonishment Goltz seemed prepared for them all, even his.

'There are thousands of men here. When will they be told?'

'At the last moment, Max. Maybe an hour or two before we go. The more people who know about this beforehand, the greater the chance of detection. Everyone can see the British are already worried about something. Next.'

'We found planes at an airfield. How do they fit in?'

'There are pilots in this camp, as you know. We'll fly two planes out to the east coast to meet up with U-boat crews. The submarines will drop off weapons and special forces. If there are planes with sufficient range — which I know you doubt — they'll be flown to Holland to liaise with the two airborne divisions that will be standing by to parachute in troops and supplies. The runway you found will be held at all costs for future landings.'

'And once we're out, once we've filled up the trucks with men and helped ourselves to these tanks, what then?'

Hartmann checked himself. He was starting to sound too doubtful.

'We're less than a hundred miles from London. We can be there in a few hours. Before nightfall on Christmas Day, I believe that is where we will be. And now, I think you must all return to your compounds.'

As the meeting broke up, Hartmann turned back towards his end of the hut. Leaning against the wall, close to his bed, was Heinz Bruling.

'The mathematician from Hamburg. Did I detect your hand in any of that?'

'Calculations and odds. Of course. What's not to enjoy? I told you Goltz would shake things about a bit.'

'Yes, but will it work? How does he know there will be submarines? Where does all this stuff come from?'

'He's been busy. A lot of thought has gone into this.'

'That isn't what I asked.'

Since their very first meeting, Hartmann had felt there was something wrong about Bruling; something ill-fitting. His mousy hair was too thin, his brain was too big, and however hard he tried to conceal it, he always came across like a scholar.

'You and I are together on the night,' Bruling said, ignoring his questions. 'We're leading the raid on your trucks. Hopefully you can remember where they were.'

'You're nuts. Do you know that? None of this is real. It's a fantasy.'

The door at the end of the hut had been flung open. No one was listening to their conversation.

'Out there, they just want to sing their carols, whittle some crappy presents, and have a quiet Christmas. They want letters from home, not fucking machine guns. You haven't shared a hut with them the way I have. They won't do what you say. They don't want to be vaporised on some crazed march on London. They just don't.'

'That won't happen. We'll be safe from the air. The British would never fire on us. They won't risk civilian casualties.'

'And you know that for sure because of mathematics? Right?'

'I don't want to live in a world run by Jews, Max.'

Hartmann's response was his back. As he scrambled on to his mattress, he was doing some calculations of his own. If the meeting had gone past midnight, he was guessing it was December 10th.

December 10th.

Only two weeks left to Christmas Eve.

# War Diary/Army HQ
## Salisbury Plain and Dorset District

*Today (8 December) an interrogation team working at Devizes camp has discovered what is reputed to be a large-scale plot of the German POWs to break out. A POW named —— is the informer.*

*The break is timed for Xmas Eve or New Year's Eve when a relaxation on the part of the guards etc. is hoped for. In broad outline, the plot is to overpower all guards, seize all arms, including tanks and lorries, and proceed to a nearby training airfield. The first suitable aircraft are to be flown straight to Germany where two Airborne divs are to be mobilised in support of the prisoners.*

*The whole is then to develop into an attack on London.*

*It should be noted that many of the prisoners – notably the black prisoners – are given to extreme flights of fantasy, brought on by boredom and (more recently) by cold.*

*Please advise what action if any.*

# 34

Overnight, it snowed again.

While the men slept, a sharp wind had driven spindrift under the eaves and around the window frames. In places, the snow had settled – on the damp blankets and the frames of the beds – and until they touched it the waking prisoners thought only that the wind had disturbed the ash in the stoves.

A few hours later it was still there. Only when the evening's coal ration had arrived would the hut be sufficiently warm to melt it, and even then a few wisps would linger on for days in the hidden corners.

During the next twenty-four hours, though, no one thought much about the cold. For the first time since their capture, the occupants of the eight huts in Hartmann's compound were back on a war footing, and the buzz of expectation had eliminated all other preoccupations.

One by one, each prisoner in the SS compound had been told what he would be expected to do. No one was permitted to discuss his role with anyone apart from the ten-man section to which he'd been assigned. Even the company leaders – of whom Bruling was one – were ignorant of the identities of the others.

Around the huts, where the men huddled to trade cigarettes, paranoia and curiosity cancelled each other out. Everyone had questions, but no one had the courage to ask them. Not even Hartmann could break through the steel wall of silence. Beyond Goltz, he imagined there would be other ringleaders whose identities he would never know, and the palpable air of mystery had merely amplified the men's high expectations.

Over breakfast, it had been an unexpected relief to see Bruling again, in the mess, sitting alone. Much as he despised him, the fellow's company was intriguing, and as Hartmann weaved through the crowd of men towards him he was pleased to see a space where he could sit.

'I was waiting for you. Eat up quickly and let's go.'

A few minutes later, the two men left together, crossing swiftly to the rear of the toilet block at the top end of the compound. As Hartmann looked on, Bruling slid away an iron manhole cover, reached down, and drew out a sack knotted with a string. Inside it were two sets of prison uniform. The roundels on them were yellow, not black, and they stank of wet earth and urine.

'Septic tank. Not even the Tommies look in here. Swap your outfit. Quick. Quick.'

Hartmann didn't need telling. It was too cold for hanging about. 'What the fuck are we doing?'

'Our orders are to secure those trucks. We need to recce. Practise. Rehearse. We need to know how we're going to do it.'

Bruling was standing stark naked, hidden by the brick gable of the washroom. Without clothes he looked pitiful and fleshless, like a ghost.

'Now that Koenig's gone, you're the only one here who's actually seen them.'

'We got to that warehouse through the Luftwaffe's tunnel.'

'And the tunnel was found, which is why we have to find another way out.'

For a moment, they stood and examined each other in their outfits. Hartmann didn't think he'd ever seen a man who looked less like a soldier than Bruling, or met a man more determined to prove that he was one.

'Will you finish your studies when all this is over?'

'We'll have a whole continent to run by then. There won't be time.'

Seconds later, they were scurrying along the same trail he'd once broken alone in the dead of night. Nothing had changed. Whatever the British were doing to strengthen the perimeter had not been extended to the fencing which segregated the four groups of German prisoners from each other.

Holes were evident everywhere, and the loose section he'd so meticulously concealed was flapping uselessly in the chill northerly wind. If anything, the gap had got markedly larger. A few weeks before, he'd still needed to crawl to get through. Now it required little more than a stoop. It seemed strange, as if their captors had pulled back to allow the prisoners free run of the entire place.

'This feels wrong.'

He was standing up, dusting the snow from his knees. Bruling was right behind him. Rabbit tracks ran away from them in every direction.

'Surely they must know we've been moving around like this.'

'Of course they do, but they don't care. Maybe at the beginning they did. But this place is too big now. They haven't the manpower to worry about what we do to each other. It suits them that we police ourselves.' Bruling steered his gaze beyond no man's land towards the rooftops of Devizes. 'The outer fence is the only one that matters to them now.'

'And that's the one we're going through on Christmas Eve?'

'Correct.'

Hartmann led on again, keeping low over the frozen ground. Away to his right, he could see the army compound. A cluster of prisoners was playing rounders outside Hut 19, his old hut. He could hear the thwack of a bat, and a ball was being chased towards the fence by a gaggle of overheated adolescents.

'It's all right,' hissed Bruling.

The ball had come to rest near the two men. When one of the boys spun on his heels, the rest followed, leaving the ball where it had fallen. Hartmann stretched his arm under the fence and picked it up. With a grunt he threw it high and saw it drop down within reach of his silent audience.

'It's as I told you,' he said, turning back to Bruling. 'They're happy to watch the war finish from here. They don't want any of this bollocks. They need to go back to school. Like you.'

'That's not how they'll feel when we win, Max.'

'But you can't win without them.'

'Since when did they have any choice?'

'We're not in Germany any more. They can do what they want.'

'Inside this wire, we're in Germany.'

Hartmann's head ached, just as it always did when he talked to these people. In so many ways, he envied them. Choice was lonely.

Choice was excruciating. In the beginning he'd tried so hard to believe in the Reich. He'd worn the clothes, he'd sung the songs, and he'd failed.

Now the only certainty in his life was the uncertainty he felt about everything.

'Not being sure is what distinguishes us from animals.'

'What the fuck are you talking about?'

Bruling wouldn't understand. None of them would. Doubt was good. Choice was healthy. It was just a question of timing.

A little further on, they reached the outside edge of the Luftwaffe compound. On the other side of the wire, three prisoners were already peeling back their own weakened section of fence. As they scrambled through, he noticed that one of the men had bolt-cutters, and that all of them had clearly met Bruling before.

As he stood to one side, the four locked arms in a fraternal embrace. Schutzstaffel, he assumed, yet more of Goltz's murderous undercover goon squad. No wonder the British were content to keep their distance.

In full daylight, the compound looked huge; forty Nissen huts in perfect lines, maybe more, housing both air crew and Kriegsmarine prisoners. Across the open space between them, every inch was teeming with men, each one moving constantly to stay warm.

'Over there, the two warehouses. Out towards the line of trees.'

Hartmann was pointing. He could see the log store where he and Koenig had emerged. He could see the narrow track between the shed and the trucks, and now they were closer he remembered the foul smell of the tunnel and the sweet secret of Rosterg's handkerchief.

'What happened to the tunnel, Bruling?'

'They found the far end when the wood supply ran out. Cold weather. There weren't enough logs left in the shed to hide the hatch. Apparently they filled it with concrete.'

'It would have run under our feet right here. I never realised how short it was.'

The five men were standing in the narrow gap behind the latrines. Between them and the outside world stood the wire wall which isolated the Luftwaffe compound from the other three, and the double fence which now ran around the entire habitation.

'We wouldn't have used the tunnel even if it was still intact,' said Bruling. 'Far too slow for what we'll need to do. We'll have over a hundred men to deal with. Getting out in ones and twos wouldn't work. We need numbers and surprise.' He gestured towards their three silent escorts. 'That's what the cutters are for.'

Hartmann scanned the space beyond the perimeter fence, trying hard to think like a soldier. Assuming it was cut in advance, it would still take five minutes to get all their men through. After that would come the lung-bursting sprint across horribly exposed ground to the warehouses, where they'd face the challenge of getting the trucks started. Assuming, that is, the trucks were still there.

'Are you sure about all this, Bruling?'

'I will be.'

Even Hartmann was impressed by Bruling's attention to detail. All around the camp, he assumed, there would be others similarly absorbed by the challenge Goltz had laid down. Some would be working out how to reach the weapons store; others how to activate unfamiliar American tanks.

For the handful in the know, the camp was a whir of secret calculations. For everyone else, the only thing that mattered was Christmas.

From almost every direction – at all times of the day – the sound of choirs could be heard. Every hut was planning its own carol concert, and the camp was a fever of letter-writing. Crude handmade cards were being dispatched to parents, girlfriends and wives. A handful of Christmas trees had been provided for the canteens, and a generous supply of holly was circulating everywhere except the SS compound, where the approaching festivities were regarded as both a distraction and an abject waste of time.

The men who knew about the plot had reached a simple, practical conclusion.

If it came off, the camp would be deserted on Christmas Day. If it didn't, no one would be in the mood for a sing-song.

Two days after their first recce, under night-time conditions,

Hartmann and Bruling walked their route once again, moving much more quickly under the protection of darkness. Away to their right, they could heard the strains of 'Good King Wenceslas'. *Fails my heart, I know not how.*

How appropriate, thought Hartmann.

By the time they reached the spot looking out towards the warehouses, they were breathing hard and chilly with sweat. Nothing beyond the double fence was moving. There were no passing vehicles, no dog patrols, and the camp's big floodlights lacked the wattage to reach so far. Instead, there were electric lights bolted to each of the concrete posts, twenty feet apart and left on until dawn.

'Fucking hell. It's bright,' whispered Hartmann. Bruling was wiping his brow with his cap. Even in the shadows, the top of his head was shining. 'You'd better get that back on. You look like a lighthouse.'

Bruling laughed quietly. Right now, they could walk an army out through the fence and no one would trouble them.

'When will you have the wire cut?'

'Not until we get here on the night. No point in risking it before.'

'Three fences? The compound and the double perimeter wire?'

'Another mathematician. Correct.'

'You could make it easier. Get the men through the hole in the compound wire we came through. One less fence to cut.'

'That hole's too far from the warehouses. We need the shortest line to get everyone through quickly,' said Hartmann. Bruling was right. The more time they spent moving across open ground, the more likely it would be they'd be killed. 'Do you still think all this will work? Honestly?'

'Do I think we can all get out? Yes. Do I know what will happen after that? No.'

'What if the tanks don't exist? What if they don't find any weapons? We'll all be shot. Have you thought about that? What if this is all just in Goltz's head?'

'Did you make up the trucks?'

'No. Of course not.'

'So why would anyone else make up the tanks?'

'To ingratiate themselves? To cover their tracks? Because they were afraid? All sorts of reasons.'

'There's nothing out there to fear. Rejects and geriatrics. Nothing else.'

'No one else we can see,' said Hartmann. 'Not quite the same.'

Ten minutes later, they were back at their own hut. After the snowfall of three days before, the weather had improved, and when they opened the door the place felt tolerably warm. The light was strong from the overhead bulbs and a rowdy game of poker had drawn a crowd of spectators around the stove.

Battle fever, he guessed. Testosterone. The human body's chemical alternative to schnapps. Only normal people went quiet before a battle.

'Don't get settled in.' Rosterg was striding quickly out of the hut. He looked flustered, pale, and as he passed Hartmann he drew him back out under a salmon-coloured sky. 'We need a quick conversation, I think.'

Behind them, there was a huge roar. Someone had just won himself a month's worth of extra meals.

'He shouldn't get too excited.' Rosterg had lit two cigarettes and was passing one to Hartmann. 'He'll probably never get to eat them.'

'What's this all about? You're making me more nervous than I already was.'

A small group of prisoners had spilled noisily from one of the other huts. Everything felt charged, restless. Even the air seemed wrong, unseasonably mild, with every trace of winter momentarily in retreat. The pair moved out of sight, two dots of glowing ash suspended in the black shadow of the hut.

'I hear things, Max. Idle chatter. The Lagerführer speaks no English and I'm allowed certain freedoms. People forget that I'm there. And if they don't, they certainly forget that I can understand them. Sometimes they even leave things lying about. Which, naturally, I read.'

'I know all that, Rosterg. So what?'

'I think we – that is, the German army – might be about to stop the invasion. Rather, I think that there's a serious winter push coming soon. Could be tomorrow, the day after. Now, for all I know. But soon.'

'Seriously? You believe that?'

'Belgium. Luxembourg. France. The Allies have seen some significant troop build-ups apparently. Panzers. Lots of Panzers dug in around the forests. Aerial photographs. Some of the new prisoners have been boasting, too. All very vague, but the British are worried, which means things for us here have changed.'

'Goltz doesn't want to wait, does he?'

'Exactly so.'

Hartmann rocked back against the curved wall of the hut. The metal burned cold through his prison jacket. 'How early?'

'We're going out after dark tomorrow. Goltz thinks everyone is ready. He's calling it the war's northern front. He's convinced the Allies won't know which way to turn.'

Both their cigarettes were finished. Hartmann reached out hungrily for another. Sometimes it felt as if the war could be measured out in cigarettes.

'We both know this is insane, don't we?' he said.

'We do.'

'What will we all do if we get out? Who's going to feed us? Where are we going to sleep? It's madness. It's a game. It's not been thought through. They're not going to let us drive to London. We'll be slaughtered. Wasted. No fucking guns. No fucking point. No one outside this stinking compound is interested.'

'Rather too loud. Max. Unwise.' Rosterg placed a hand on Hartmann's shoulder. 'You're not going to stop this. You can't pull out. Yes, he knows it's a gamble. He also just happens to think it's his duty. A strange notion, but there you have it.'

Hartmann waved his arm vaguely towards the rest of the camp. 'Everyone out there is looking forward to Christmas.'

'They'll be told tomorrow. They'll have a few hours to acclimatise.'

'Then what?'

'Well, if you all do your jobs, five thousand prisoners walk out of the gate.'

'And you, Rosterg? Whose side are you really on? Tomorrow night, where will you be?'

'Right behind you, Max. Now, goodnight.'

Left alone, Hartmann began to shiver. Either it was colder than he'd thought, or the news had left him in mild shock. With Rosterg gone, there was no prospect of another smoke, and he was desperate for nicotine, or a stiff drink, preferably both.

If he went back inside, there'd be a cigarette – he was a hero, after all – but if he saw Goltz's face, there was a strong chance of being sick. A little longer in the fresh air might just clear his head.

Coming out from the shadows, he walked on to the worn grass which ran between the two rows of huts. All the other insomniacs had returned to their beds, and the only sign of life was a faint orange glow in the guard hut by the gate which led out into the rest of the camp.

With no conscious purpose, he began moving towards it. Maybe he could charm a cigarette out of the sentry. Maybe he'd get himself shot. What did it matter? As he drew close, he could make out the outline of a solitary soldier through the window. He had a paperback book loosely clutched in his hands, and his rifle was leaning up against a free-standing paraffin heater. Even from a distance, Hartmann could smell the warm fumes. Another few minutes and the soldier would probably be fast asleep.

He knocked on the closed door and stepped away. From inside, he could hear the gun falling, and a chair being pushed back hard across the floor. Moments later, the door slammed open and the muzzle of the rifle appeared, swinging wildly from side to side. Out of sight, Hartmann could hear the soldier's short, hard breaths. After a few more seconds, he could see his face peering out, spot-damaged and white. It was the young guard from the apple-picking detail, the lad who'd brought him the buckets of warm water in the cell block.

Hartmann edged forward to face him, his hands over his head. 'Listen. Don't panic. Don't shoot. There's no danger here. I just wondered, can you spare a cigarette?'

The boy turned, recognising him. Hartmann smiled. 'Are you the only guard they've got?'

'Go back, back to your hut. Please don't make me shoot.'

Behind the soldier's back, Hartmann could see a calendar on the inside wall of the hut. Pictures of girls in red swimming costumes, and the numbers struck through with a pencil. Thirteen numbers. Tomorrow was a Thursday. December 14th.

'You don't seem to have many mates, Kraut. Same as me.'

'Don't they ever give you time off?'

'Tomorrow. First in a month. I'm getting my motorbike back too.'

'Sounds like fun. Can I come?'

'Yes, it will be. And no, you can't. Now fuck off back to your hut.'

# 35

By four the next day, it was already dark.

In a week's time, it would be the winter solstice, and the camp had never looked more anaemic. All day long, a sullen bank of cloud had hung over the entire place, and the electric lights which circled the fence had burned yellow in the speckled fog. On the flagpole by the main gate, the Union Jack had given up. There was no rain and no wind, and the daylight hours passed so slowly, it felt to the prisoners as if time had actually stopped.

Inside the eight huts of Hartmann's compound, the men were counting down the minutes and not one of them could keep still. Games of chess lay abandoned. Listless groups paced in circles outside. Small talk had become almost impossible and half-hearted conversations floundered on the strict requirement to reveal nothing.

Every individual knew what he had to do and with whom. Beyond that, the soldiers were chained to their secret orders, and forbidden from asking what they each desperately wanted to know.

If it felt odd waiting for a battle without weapons, no one said so. Self-belief had never been an issue for the Schutzstaffel, and everyone was glad the deadline had come forward. Most had masked their faces with dirt. A few had even daubed swastikas on their cheeks in their own blood.

To pass the hours, like most of the men, Hartmann had wrapped himself up in his blankets. Sometimes, he slept. Mostly, he simply watched his fellow-prisoners through half-closed eyes, and like all of them he felt charged with expectation.

Beneath him, Zuhlsdorff coughed and snored on without stirring. For three days, the two men had barely spoken and Hartmann liked it that way. The boy was a murderous cretin. Losing a few fingers had been too good for him. Somewhere down the line there'd probably be a firing squad for all of them, and with a bit of luck Zuhlsdorff would be ahead of him in the queue.

That way he'd be able to watch.

At precisely 6.30 p.m., it started.

'Brave comrades, it is time.'

No one said anything, but Bruling sounded scared; he was saying the right things, but saying them like a schoolteacher.

'The other huts have their own jobs to do. Some of them may have already started. We have ours. You know what it is. Now let's go and do it. *Heil Hitler*.'

Later, Hartmann would always wonder why they weren't stopped at that exact moment. Under a starless sky, the sheer volume of men on the move was absurd. In the four corners of their compound, huge groups were massing for action. Every moment, he expected to hear gunshots. No amount of stealth training could conceal the chaos.

From every direction, Bruling's company surely looked – and sounded – like a herd of suicidal elephants threading single-file towards a catastrophe. One pair of sharp eyes was all it would take and they were finished.

As they shuffled past the bulk of the army compound, Hartmann looked across at the huts. There were lights in a few of the windows, but nothing appeared to be moving. The whole place seemed fast asleep.

A rising. Goltz had promised a fucking rising. Where the hell was it?

At the very least, prisoners should be starting to congregate. It wasn't even bedtime. He checked again. Not a flicker. Either they hadn't been told, or they weren't interested.

Ahead of him, Bruling's men had reached the spot by the outer defences they'd chosen a few days before. Another thirty Luftwaffe prisoners had swollen their ranks. As Hartmann pushed forward to the front, Bruling passed him the pair of stolen bolt-cutters.

'You feeling OK, Max?'

Men with blackened faces sat tensely on the grass. Every pair of eyes was on the double wire and the warehouses beyond.

'There's no one out there. I told you we'd be on our own.'

'No one we can see.'

'We go together. You cut and I'll pull. Like we agreed. All right?'

'Terrific.'

But Bruling was already gone, squirming on his belly to the fence. When Hartmann crawled alongside, the lower edge of the inner section had already been pulled clear of the soil. At Bruling's nod, he started to cut, working upwards and then across until a gap had been opened that was wide enough for three men to walk through side by side.

Behind them, in the darkness, the watching company was practically invisible. No one would move until each of the three fences were breached.

Horribly aware of their own breathing, the two shuffled forward. Every snip sounded like a cracking branch. Another nod, another rapid sequence of cuts. They were tight up against the second fence and Bruling was tugging it back to make room for the cutters. This time, the wire was thicker and every cut required more exertion. At times it took two of them to apply sufficient leverage, but the men worked well together, and their progress was swift. After five minutes, only the last fence stood between them and the trucks. Just a few more snips and they'd be through.

Hartmann breathed heavily in the silence. Sweat was stinging his eyes, and he ran the inside of his arm across his forehead to clear it. Just for a moment, something had felt wrong, as if a false note had been struck somewhere in the chorus of the night. Tuning his ears to the darkness, he scanned left and right. Nothing. Maybe he'd imagined it.

Bruling was already busy pulling away the final doorway for his men. Little more than a sprint was left between them and the trucks which would take them away from there. He raised a triumphant fist back towards the company of men who were charging down towards the gap.

And then the arc lights came on.

Shocked by their sudden exposure, the prisoners halted. A dark snake of army vehicles was roaring along the track which ringed the camp. Hartmann and Bruling were running back, heading for their three ragged holes as the night around them was ruptured by the sound of diesel engines and cocked rifles.

With every step, Hartmann felt certain he would die. He could feel the beaming eyes of the jeeps behind him and hear furious, incomprehensible voices. Surely someone soon would let a round fly. Any moment there'd be a bullet ripping into his back. A stride ahead of him, Bruling was pushing back through the fence. Arms were reaching forward to pull him clear. Seconds later, they had grasped Hartmann too and he was turning to see what was happening.

It was as if the troops had sprung from the earth. Around twenty vehicles were massed in a blockade between them and the warehouses. Many more were still moving in the direction of the main gate: armoured cars, jeeps and lorries bristling with weaponry. Along the outside of the wire, a line of heavily armed soldiers was spreading out at measured intervals. Every one of them was wearing a red beret.

Fucking hell, thought Hartmann. Parachute regiments, the heavy squad.

'They fucking knew,' panted Bruling. 'They were expecting us.'

But there was no time for a discussion.

Out of nowhere, a squally wind had blown up, drawing sleety rain on its edge. From the far side of the camp, there were single gun-shots, followed by longer bursts of machine-gun fire. From every direction, there was furious unintelligible yelling, and Hartmann could see prisoners in their hundreds surging out of their huts towards the perimeter wire.

All discipline had collapsed. In the darkness, it was no longer possible to say where anyone had gone. Bruling had vanished, and his company was dissolving into the night, each man finding his own way into the huge groups stampeding towards the camp's outer fence. Either voluntarily or under duress the huge silent army was mobilising. If they could find a weakness – a gap – Goltz might still pull this off.

At the army compound, Hartmann ducked left under a ruined section of wire and headed towards Hut 19. The rain was coming even harder now. Searchlights were criss-crossing the night sky and an expectant hum seemed to be building; a low background roar centred on the area around the central parade ground. All around him, prisoners were streaming towards it in a state of expectant curiosity. As yet, few of them looked in the mood for a serious fight.

'Max, what the hell are you doing here?'

It was Eschner. He'd found him.

'It's a long story. What have you been told?'

'That we'll be home by the weekend.' Eschner examined Hartmann mock-seriously, and then laughed. 'No one has told us much. Some sort of mass breakout?'

'How did you get out of the compound?'

'I walked. Like everyone else. The gates were open and the guards seem to have made a tactical withdrawal.'

'You should have stayed in bed.'

'Not an option. We've been ordered down to the wire. Seemed sensible to do what we're told.'

'There's rather more to it than that. Do you want to take a look?'

A small plane was flying directly overhead. Hartmann could see the outline of its cockpit and the lights on its wingtips. Not far behind it was a second plane. At a rough guess, both were heading east.

It wasn't possible. Surely.

'I wouldn't miss it for the world. Lead on.'

Since hearing the gunfire, the mood of the prisoners had changed. Curiosity had morphed swiftly into fear then rage; the swell was now a growling, leaderless charge. Up against the fence, the crush was already five deep and more prisoners were arriving all the time.

From what little Hartmann could see, every guard stationed inside the camp had fled. Wooden sentry huts were being ransacked. Heaters and chairs were being carried away. Desks had already been smashed up for firewood, and random bonfires were hissing in the downpour, piled high with stolen papers and files.

With Eschner behind him, Hartmann steered a path through the chaos towards the parade ground. Away to his right, beyond the wire, the ring of red-bereted soldiers seemed to extend the entire way around the camp. Behind the troops, extra floodlights were being wheeled into place, creating a blazing white corridor within which countless men were now milling.

Inside, only a few doubters had held back. The rest were transformed into an unexpected mob, hurling rocks and abuse and standing nose to sodden nose with their enemy.

'They'll be terrified, paras or not,' said Hartmann.

Everywhere he looked, the camp's pathways were being ripped apart for makeshift weapons. A relay of men was passing lumps of concrete to the wire where they were broken into smaller missiles and lobbed over on to the heads of the soldiers. Already, in places, the prisoners had torn at the fence with their hands, pulling it back until the posts lurched, inspiring the men to surge forward against the wild barking of the dogs, furiously, randomly and without any regard for consequence.

'I was wrong,' Hartmann muttered. 'All it took was a spark.'

'They've given us an enemy,' said Eschner. 'That's the only thing that's changed.'

He was right. You couldn't fight what you couldn't see. 'I thought you'd all stay in your beds. Stick to your carols.'

'You people think it's all so simple. It isn't.'

As Eschner spoke, a lamp crashed down off the fence, sparking wildly as it shattered inside the camp.

'You're not the only ones who went into this war wanting to win. It's just that we're better at knowing when we've lost.'

For the second time, Hartmann heard gunshots, distant pops against the rising wall of sound. 'So why all this?'

'It's an impetuous rush of blood. No more. We'll all regret it in the morning,' said Eschner, grinning.

The two men had reached the parade ground where the wind had strengthened and swung, driving sleet across the prisoners streaming towards the main gate. Once the adrenaline subsided, the men would quickly freeze. If this madness still had a chance, the prisoners would need guns, and they'd need them quickly. But where was Goltz? Where were any of them?

Tanks and rifles, that was the promise. Instead, there were sticks and stones and a saturated throng massing aimlessly in the puddled shadow of the old four-storey barracks. Hard against the fence, the men were packed so tightly they could no longer turn round. Strange waves seemed to ripple through the crowd as the heads leaned first one way then another like stalks of black corn.

As more prisoners pushed from behind, the weight of the crush intensified. High-pitched shrieks of protest could be heard from the front, climbing above the deep bellow of discontent. Taking care not to get sucked in, Hartmann and Eschner hung back, seeking a better view of what was happening.

Inside the old barracks, curious faces were peering out from the rows of barred windows. Higher up, along the edge of its turreted rooftop, they could see rifles aiming into the crowd. Down at the main gate – ten yards to their left – two tanks were rumbling into position, side by side, with their immense green barrels lined up on the prisoners. On either flank, three open-backed army lorries were standing ready, and sitting on each was a two-man crew behind a tripod-mounted Bren gun.

'It doesn't look good, does it?'

Even in the lashing rain, there was something about the way Rosterg carried himself; imperious, never flustered. As he moved through the confusion, people gave him space and his voice revealed no trace of alarm.

'I gather you had a welcome party over there. I'm surprised they didn't shoot you.'

'What about everyone else? What the fuck's happening, Rosterg?'

'Bruling is telling everyone the guards had been tipped off, that they were waiting for you to come.'

'You've seen Bruling? Is he all right? He just vanished.'

'Yes, I've seen Bruling. In the same place I saw Goltz and the rest of them.'

Rosterg stepped aside. Another stream of prisoners was elbowing its way to the gate.

'They've all been rounded up, Max. No one had any more success than you did. No one got beyond the fence. Reception parties everywhere. Anyone deemed to have been a ringleader is being taken away.'

'No tanks? No planes?'

'Nothing, I'm afraid.' He turned to survey the crowd. 'Unless you count this bunch of headless chickens. Rather a good turnout, actually.'

'We heard shots.'

'Warning shots. Just a few looseners over the bows.'

'What about you? Will they come for you?'

'Possibly. Possibly not. It depends how fast their brains work.'

'And me?'

'I'm quite sure they're already looking.'

Hartmann turned to Eschner. The boy's face looked grey with fatigue. 'You should go now. Whatever happens, you don't want to be with me.'

'In a minute. I want to see this.'

In the glare of the floodlights, over a thousand faces were turned towards the fence. If they knew it was all over, few of them cared. There was too much momentum now, and this was already a night they'd remember.

From the drenched huddle of men, a fresh storm of rocks was flying up and over the wire. A lone voice chanting 'Deutschland, Deutschland' had been joined by hundreds more, driven on by the tribal pounding of cold feet. Through the racket, Hartmann could hear a British officer screaming instructions. Stones were raining down on his men.

'Hold your fire. Hold your fire.'

A few feet away, German prisoners were spitting insults, and the fence was rocking in its foundations. One concerted effort and it would be down. All across the parade ground, there was a deep moan, followed by a sustained mass surge on the gate. Right down the line, Hartmann could see concrete posts starting to lean. Yet more missiles were falling, and a paratrooper had gone down, blood pouring from his scalp.

Along the base of the fence, the earth seemed to explode in a curtain of dust. Tiny shards of stone flew in every direction, lacerating the men's faces and slicing through their clothes. When the shocked prisoners looked up, a second volley ripped into the ground.

This time, there were screams. One man was holding his hands to a shattered eye. Another was looking dazed, as a huge crimson patch spread outwards from his groin. By his ear, Hartmann felt a whistle of air, which was followed by a soft, low thud. Eschner was down, clutching his thigh, and slick sheets of blood were flowing around his fingers.

'I'm all right. I'm all right.'

'Let me look.' Hartmann pulled back the boy's hands. There was too much blood to see.

Rosterg was reaching in his pocket for a handkerchief to pack the wound. 'He'll get looked after, Max. We're finished here.'

'Jesus. You and your fucking hankies.'

'Just leave me. I'll be fine.' Eschner had rolled on to his side. His voice sounded strong. 'Go. Go.'

As the soldiers prepared to fire again, the crush around the gate began to thin. Men with stretchers were already picking up the wounded, and the sodden prisoners were edging backwards towards their huts. Every shred of resistance had gone and the wet air was heavy with fine particles of dust. Within a few minutes, the last of them had slipped away.

## 36

As the troops dispersed, he could feel a bad cloud lifting from the entire rotten place. It was so pungent you could almost smell it.

Back in their huts, the ordinary soldiers would be rejoicing. For a week or two, at least, they could rest easy, cleansed of the spies and fanatics. No one from Goltz's poisonous assembly would be coming back, and Christmas would no longer feel like an act of treason.

There'd be repercussions, certainly. Less food, less fuel and their footballs would be confiscated, but on both sides of the fence, dawn would bring relief. No one had been killed and the camp's agitators were being swiftly shipped out. For the thousands who remained, there'd be letters from home, and a few exultant renditions of 'Silent Night'.

Lucky bastards, thought Hartmann.

Their lives would be good – cold, but good. Even the damned rain had stopped falling.

Standing alone by the gate, he gazed out across the curved iron rooftops for the last time. Everyone else – including Rosterg – had vanished and the only sounds were the tanks and troop-carriers returning to their depots. Within a few days, the entire place would be ringed by razor wire, high-powered lights and dog patrols. No one would come close to getting out again.

'You. Here. Now. Nazi scum.'

Hartmann raised his arms and moved towards the main gate, where a large crowd of soldiers was still gathered. He could hear relieved laughter beneath the grey cloud of cigarette smoke and steam that was rising from their wet uniforms. Most of them had shouldered their machine guns. Only a few kept their weapons trained on the solitary German as he walked towards them with his hands clasped over his head.

'Stand over there.'

Any one of them could have spoken. It didn't matter who. The rifle in the small of his back was telling him where to go, and he'd no intention of testing their resolve. One dead Kraut would probably make their night and Hartmann didn't feel ready to be a dead Kraut just yet. Parked along the main road, he could see a fleet of trucks facing into the town. One by one they were filling with paras and leaving. As he walked out through the twin gates of the camp, he could feel the hot breath of their loathing.

'You're going to hell, you bastard.'

There were other comments – outside the range of his vocabulary – but he'd got the message.

At the corner of the barracks, a dismal band of fellow-conspirators was shuffling to keep warm. Under the lights of the departing convoy, Hartmann was shocked by their pitiful condition. Months of idleness had reduced them to a state of hollow-chested feebleness. Only one of them – Bruling – had retained any physical bearing. The rest were strangers to him; and each man was as defiantly indifferent to his presence as the British. No one would be safe here until they were all as far away as possible.

'The others have already been taken. Gone.'

Hartmann didn't respond. If Bruling wanted to get himself killed for talking, that was his business.

'It's as if they knew all along: who to look for, what we were planning.'

The recriminations could wait. Almost all of the trucks had left, and there'd been no fresh arrests. Up and down the wet streets, normality was returning. At a guess, Hartmann put the time at around 8 p.m. The day's ration of coal would be working its magic in the huts. There'd be a song or two, and a steady trade in home-made liquor before the embers died.

Everyone would be talking about the night's events. They'd talk of nothing else for weeks.

After an hour, their transport came, a sludge-green single-decker bus with muted headlights and a sliding door. When it opened, the smell of warm leather flooded out. There were thirteen soldiers for thirteen German troublemakers. Every window was shut tight and each prisoner was squeezed in with an armed guard alongside covering the aisle. No one was taking any chances, and so far no one – not even the square-jawed military policeman at the wheel – had said where they were going.

Another midnight mystery tour, then. Fine. Just so long as he wasn't sick.

Through the circle he cleared in the wet glass, Devizes came and went. At the station, a train had just arrived, discharging men in suits and frisky couples into the dampness of the night. A little further on, soft gaslight fell through the door of a pub on to a party of carousing soldiers heading home with their berets hanging loosely from their epaulettes. Nothing was ever more than a snapshot framed, but he savoured each one, and the expectation of more along the way took his mind away from the stink of the polish. All around him, the prisoners were drifting off, shaken to sleep by the tremors which ran constantly through the ancient bus. When he returned to his window. he thought, for a moment, that he'd seen the doctor's house with its black car under the sombre trees, but when he craned back to be sure, it was gone.

For a long time after that, Hartmann tried to calculate where they were. If he'd been able to see the sky, he'd have known, but the windows were small and impossible to keep clear of condensation. As the men's clothes dried, the inside of the bus had turned into a hothouse. Every now and then, he saw the lights of a village or a small town, but nothing that told him where they were heading.

'We're stopping for a piss.'

The driver had been squirming in his seat for miles.

'This'll be the only stop.'

Everyone stood, relishing the cold thrill of air as the door opened and the driver stumbled out, tearing at his flies. In groups of two, accompanied by their minders, the prisoners stepped gratefully on to the grassy roadside under the broad silvery stain of the Milky Way.

In the weak light falling from the door of the bus, Hartmann waited his turn, smiling at the sighs of relief from the men. Suddenly, he felt desperately hungry, his appetite stirred by the wintry bite of ozone. The others would be starving too, but no one would ask. Food would have to wait. That's what happened on mystery tours. Tilting back his head, it was easy to trace the familiar line to the North Star, hanging alone beyond the left-hand side of their deserted road. Hartmann checked it carefully.

When they settled back on the bus, and the door slid shut, he knew for certain which direction they were moving in. Black Camp 21 might be their ultimate destination – he didn't doubt that – but right now, they were travelling towards London.

For the most part, the roads were clear and the country abed. Even in the built-up areas, Britain looked abandoned, as if its entire population had fled. Only the military were still up, coiling across the landscape in sinister convoys which required the bus to pull off and wait until their way was clear.

Glossy tanks on low-loaders followed by streams of canvas-clad lorries were rumbling purposefully through the night. At times, they would be stuck for an age, counting yet another chain of camouflaged vehicles as it rattled past their stares. And when the bus could move forward again, the prisoners dropped back in silence, utterly indifferent to where they were going.

Hartmann was thinking too hard to sleep. For weeks, he'd pushed his other life to the very edge of his nocturnal reflections. And yet here it was again: the misplaced optimism, the blind faith, and the quiet delusion of invincibility enhanced by every last, miracle escape. Maybe everyone on the bus, even the Tommies, felt same: that every new journey carried a seed of hope, a prospect of change. It might only be a fighting chance, a small chink in the blackness, but every man still standing had one.

Drugged by the exhaust, Hartmann finally drifted off. When he woke up, the sky was light and the bus was crawling into London's suburbs. It had taken them almost twelve hours to cover less than one hundred miles and the city's morning traffic was working itself up into a dignified frenzy.

As the city crush sucked them in, he stared out at the streets. Deadened by prison life, his senses were thrilled by the overflowing pavements and the scarlet buses crammed with people, by the press of a normal world he'd almost forgotten. If the rockets were still falling, he could see no evidence of it, and if the Allies were being slaughtered in an icy Belgian forest, then Britain seemed indifferent to the setback.

In every winter-dead park, the paths were a whirl of bicycles, and the open mouths of the Underground stations were disgorging office workers by the thousand, almost every one of them still clinging dutifully to their gas mask.

A little way ahead of them, he could make out the woody spread of Kensington Gardens, and among the trees, the roofs of the white palaces which ran along its edge. Everything was rushing back to him quickly now, and the bus was turning left beneath an archway of trees into a broad avenue, flanked by ornate buildings set deep behind high stone walls. At the far end of it, they turned sharply on to the ornamental gravel of a circular drive, ringed with evergreens. There was a second empty green bus parked ahead of them, and then he remembered everything.

The Cage. The London Cage. Sleep-deprived nightmares and a ruby brooch.

Events were coming full circle. Soldiers were yanking them off the bus and pushing them in through the huge oak doors to the dazzling nave of the hall. No reception speeches this time; just the tinny echo of their footsteps, followed by the uncompromising formalities of an ice-cold wash and body search.

Along one wall, he could see a heap of filthy prison outfits. The first busload had been processed already. As he stepped shivering from the shower, one guard held his head down while another rammed half a fist up his backside. Hartmann grunted, wondering if Goltz had liked it any better this time. When he straightened up, there were clean clothes and almost-new boots. All around him, naked boys were shivering with suppressed fury. When the last of them was dressed, they moved on silently, deeper into the labyrinth.

Like before, he was quickly disorientated. Whatever it had been, the building was a miracle of improvisation. Beneath ground level, stone vaults built for wine and cold storage had been re-engineered as cells and interrogation rooms. On the higher levels, there were glimpses of chandeliered ballrooms and mirrored walls covered in maps. In its heyday, he assumed, it had been some sort of aristocratic fun house. There were rooms within rooms within rooms. None of them was numbered, and at times even their armed escort seemed uncertain where they were going.

Eventually, they reached a long corridor with tall windows at either end. Through the glass, Hartmann could see the tops of trees. Doors along both sides of the corridor led into plain rooms with views out over the grounds. Although the windows were barred, there was a small sink and a wooden chair in the corner of each room. The beds looked new and the blankets unused. The name of each prisoner was already pinned to thirteen of the doors.

No one was sharing. Hartmann was alone.

For the rest of that day and night, he waited. Occasionally, there were movements beyond the door, but nothing that made any sense. On three occasions, he was brought food, good food. On three others, he was escorted to a single lavatory at the end of the corridor. As the darkness came, he looked out of his window and waited.

Below him, foot patrols were circling in the gardens. Further away, he could see the warm glow of traffic flowing outwards from the city. All day, he'd listened for the fairground music he'd heard before, but there'd been nothing. It was winter and the golden horses would all be swaddled in canvas. When the city fell quiet, he lay on his bed and stared at the cracks in the softly rippled coving.

And then, just before dawn, they came.

Before he realised what was happening, both of them were in and the door had been closed quietly behind them. An older man with leathery skin was leaning against the wall. The young woman – Helen Waters – had taken the chair and pulled it forward until her stockinged legs were right up against the end of the bed. Both of his visitors were in civilian clothes.

'You were asleep.' She smiled. 'That's an improvement on last time.'

'And now you've woken me up. Thanks.'

Hartmann studied the man's wind-beaten face. The last time they'd met he'd been wearing a colonel's uniform. What was his name? Alexander Scotland. Yes. This was his place, his project: Britain's secret experiment with the dark arts, with its own brand of civilised coercion.

'What are you going to do to me this time? Dripping taps? Loud-speakers playing Wagner for days on end?'

'Ah. We hadn't thought of that one. That really would be a trial.' He, too, employed Hartmann's language perfectly. 'In actual fact, you'll be leaving us in a few hours. All of you. We've completed our assessments. We've just come to say goodbye.'

'You haven't assessed me.'

'Not really any need, is there, old boy? Anyway, that's Helen's honour. Not mine.'

'So let me guess, you're giving me a one-way ticket to the mountains?'

'Naturally. What else? We're hardly going to send you all back to a normal camp to stir things up again.' Scotland took a step forward. 'But listen. If you play your cards right, we could make that a return ticket.'

'Nothing happened in Devizes. You stopped it. You knew it was coming. You had information. All of us in this room know that.'

'Yes, we did. But now that in itself is an issue.'

Scotland had moved back against the wall. Something out in the garden had caught his eye.

'Your Goltz chap is obsessing about why it all went belly up. Seems as though he won't rest until he finds out who betrayed him.'

'But you know who it was.'

They were talking in riddles. Hartmann's brain was starting to hurt. Each of them knew the truth was between the words, not in them.

'Yes, we do.'

'And you'll still let that person travel with Goltz, even though he'll probably be killed?'

'We have to, Max. If we pulled him out, it would be too obvious. If we leave him in, we might stop whatever you lunatics try next.' Scotland was patting his pockets. 'I've been rude. Would you like a smoke? Or some morning tea?'

Hartmann reached out a hand for a cigarette. From her small handbag, Helen produced a gold-plated lighter. Soon all three of them were wrapped in their own smoke.

'I'm afraid it's impossible to get any sensible information out of Germany, Max. We tried, but I've not been able to get any news of your wife,' said Helen.

'This isn't turning out to be much of a deal really, is it? Not for me, anyway.'

'I'm not sure what I can say.'

'Don't say anything, then.'

'Is there anything at all we can do for you?'

'Let me go?'

But she was already standing up, brushing the ash from her skirt and crushing the stub in a single elegant movement. With a kind look, she offered Hartmann her hand, which he took, feeling the soft warmth of her fingers on his palm.

'Why do you call this place a cage? They keep animals in cages.'

'You just answered your own question,' said Scotland. 'Some we train. Some we study to see how dangerous they are.'

'And the animals you can't train? What happens to them?'

'Have a nice trip, Max. I hear it's a magnificent journey.'

# BBC Radio Bulletin
## 17 December 1944

*The Germans have mounted a series of counterattacks on the Western Front allowing them to re-cross the borders of Luxembourg and Belgium.*

*On the second day of what now appears to be a full-scale offensive, the Germans are attacking with tanks and aircraft along a 70-mile front guarded by American forces in the Ardennes region.*

*The German Commander-in-Chief in the west, Field Marshal Gerd von Rundstedt, has ordered his troops to give their all in one last effort. He said: 'Soldiers of the Western Front, your greatest hour has struck. Strong attacking armies are advancing today against the Anglo-Americans. I do not need to say any more to you. You all feel it strongly. Everything is at stake.'*

*The United States Army Air Forces claim to have shot down 97 Luftwaffe planes overnight, and 31 of their own aircraft were lost. According to the reports, the Luftwaffe put up 'what was probably its greatest tactical air effort since D-Day'.*

# 37

The daylight was still fresh when they unlocked his door.

Out in the gardens, the birdsong rang clear above the city's returning tide, and the air – even in his quarters – carried a reviving, wintry bite. Along the corridor, and through the floorboards over his head, he could hear the clatter of dislocation. One by one, the rooms were emptying, and from the window he could see the same two green buses, puffing fumes across the drive.

At the front door, they handed him a thick grey coat and a woollen hat. Everyone was being given the same. No one needed to ask why.

After a final look around, he stepped on board. Only one seat was left and the first bus was already moving out. Towards the back he could see Rosterg and Zuhlsdorff, staring emptily at the indifferent streets. On previous journeys, he'd heard defiance and black humour. Today there were no patriotic songs, and the face of every man seemed disconcertingly blank.

By the time they reached the station, Hartmann was feeling sick. For over an hour, the buses had been crawling painfully through the choking traffic. Even the guards looked ill, and when they arrived at King's Cross Station there was a desperate rush to get out.

'They pulled you in too, Rosterg? Why am I not surprised?'

'I knew you'd all miss me. I'm here just for you.'

'And Eschner? What happened to Eschner?'

'He got patched up and sent back to his hut.'

'Do I thank you?'

'Thank the British.'

Both men were bent over the edge of the pavement. A shiny cord of drool was hanging from the older man's mouth and there was fresh vomit in the gutter. As Rosterg straightened up, he looked up at the huge clock on the central tower. It was 8.16 a.m.

'I can't say I'm looking forward to this.'

'The train, or what's at the end of it?'

'I'm afraid your man Goltz is in rather a bad frame of mind.'

'Meaning what?'

'Humiliated? Incandescent? Desperate to find someone to blame?'

'You could have stayed away. You didn't have to be here.'

'Rather sadly, Max, I think I did.'

There wasn't time for more. Londoners were flowing towards the station's two soaring glass-fronted arches. A thick line of black taxis was shunting steadily past them, and their two empty buses were already nudging back into the torrent along the Euston Road. Across the soft brown brick of the façade, Hartmann read *London & North Eastern Railway* in giant white letters.

Beyond the station entrance, he could see ringlets of steam wrapped around handcarts loaded with tea chests and worn leather cases. There were porters and policemen, schoolgirls and sailors, and in his entire life Hartmann doubted whether he'd ever seen so much headwear.

Londoners seemed obsessed with hats. Trilbies and battered caps for the men; purple felt and chinchilla pillboxes for the women; green tin helmets for the detachment of soldiers now steering them out along platform two, beneath the glorious sweep of the station's glass roof.

Outside the station, the POWs had passed largely unnoticed. Here, there were growling looks and crude asides. Up ahead of him Hartmann could see the newly shaven head of Goltz, and wondered what was going on inside it. Just two days before, the man had been planning a march on London. Now he was dodging abuse from its commuters. Rosterg, as always, was probably right. The man was ticking down to an explosion.

At the far end of the platform, they stopped by a slick green locomotive broiling in its own white vapour. Behind the engine were a coal tender, a luggage wagon and six empty first class carriages. Taking a carriage in the middle, the men were divided equally between six cushioned compartments; five men in each and a handful of guards to watch the doors and patrol the corridor.

Taking a seat by a window, Hartmann watched glumly as the space filled around him. Goltz and Zuhlsdorff on one side, Bruling and Mertens on the other.

'Like old times, Max,' whispered Goltz, leaning forward to pat his knee.

An hour later, they were clear of the city and steaming north across endless watery fields. Hartmann was pleased he'd secured a seat by the window. One by one, the others had quickly lost interest and closed their eyes. No one seemed in the mood for conversation, and the whirl of flashing landscape revived him. With his face to the glass, it was easy to forget where they were going, and he was soothed by the vast sky and the grid of briar-black hedges beneath it.

They stopped for the first time at Peterborough where armed soldiers lined the platform while another batch of prisoners – category black, presumably – was dragooned into the empty carriages.

Hartmann did a few quick sums. If all the carriages were filled, by the time they got to Scotland the train would be ferrying the best part of two hundred high-risk captives, each one convinced that Hitler was riding to his rescue.

It didn't bode well, and the heater had packed up. Hartmann sucked himself down into his coat.

During the wait, they'd been allowed supervised visits to the lavatory and refreshments had been relayed along the carriage: sweet tea and cheese sandwiches passed in through a window by an elderly volunteer in a brown pinafore.

'They're only humans like the rest of us,' she'd said to one of their guards. 'Look at the soft buggers. They're just frozen kids.'

Further on, there were more stops and more prisoners – at Doncaster and York – and to Hartmann it seemed they were making quick progress. In fascinating increments, both the weather and the terrain were shifting. Throughout the day, the sun had swung low across the train, but now the clouds were darkening ominously from the east, and the air temperature was falling fast.

On a distant escarpment, he could see a huge white horse hacked into the rock, and on the higher hills beyond, the black edge where the winter's first real snow met the night.

'Does anyone know more than I do? Does this get there tonight? Wherever "there" is?'

Zuhlsdorff's voice echoed in the carriage. No one had spoken for hours. All five of them were bathed in half-darkness.

'It's called Camp Twenty-one. Somewhere north of a place called Stirling. They'll probably keep us there for years.'

Hartmann had forgotten how every word Mertens uttered had the heft of a prophecy. Hunched deep into the corner, he looked like a fallen tree.

'How come you know all this stuff? You're just a sheep-shagger from the country.'

The submariner shifted in his seat. Zuhlsdorff turned sharply away.

Two tungsten lamps in glass shades clicked on beneath the luggage racks.

Somewhere beneath him, the train's wheels skidded angrily across a set of points, rolling the carriage from side to side. When it settled, all the men were awake, snatching greedily at the packs of cigarettes the guards had tossed into every compartment. Only Bruling had declined.

'So what happened back there, Hartmann? What's your explanation?'

'For what?'

'For the fuck-up.'

'Why ask me? You were there.'

'I'm interested. Isn't that enough?'

'We got through the wire and all fucking hell broke loose with guns everywhere and lights coming on. You know what happened.'

'Just a spot of bad luck then, Max?'

'I don't know. Maybe not. You think they knew? Maybe they did. Anyone else feel the same?'

Hartmann's mouth was dry. His fingers were trembling, too. If he sounded as scared as he felt, he was finished. He brought a hand up to his face, and drew furiously on the cigarette. The compartment was blotted with smoke and the men's faces were fuzzy and grey.

'It was the same for us.'

Mertens had opened up from the corner.

'It was just like he said. We were assigned to get the tanks, but the perimeter wire was surrounded. None of us were convinced the tanks were really there. But we never got to find out. Someone had told them we were coming. No other explanation.'

The glass in the window shuddered again as they ran through a deep cutting.

'There's a rat on the train.'

'That can't be right. No one knew the whole plan,' said Hartmann. 'We only knew what we needed to know.'

'You knew enough though, didn't you, Max?'

'Fuck off, Bruling. I was with you, remember. I could have been shot. Why would I do that?'

From the end of the carriage, they could hear a British soldier singing 'Pack Up Your Troubles'. He sounded drunk and happy.

'You're a good talker, Max. Really smooth.' They were the first words Goltz had spoken since London. 'But you've always seemed a bit doubtful, a bit detached.'

'You picked me. I didn't pick myself. Remember that.'

'I let you back in, Max. Was that a mistake?'

'I found the planes, the lorries. It was me who knew the camp. No one else.'

'Yes, and look what fucking good it did us.'

Hartmann's heart was bumping. It couldn't end like this. With a thud, the train slammed into a tunnel, dimming the lights and crushing the air between his ears.

'Maybe he's got a point.' Bruling was yelling to be heard above the roar. 'I think we're looking in the wrong place.'

'It was this fucker. I know it.'

'You're wrong, Zuhlsdorff. What about that fat fuck, Bultmann? He knew everything, didn't he? Our so-called Lagerführer. And so did Rosterg.'

Goltz sprang up straight, as if scalded. Out of nowhere, Hartmann had been tossed a lifeline.

'Fucking Bultmann. A fucking Wehrmacht major. Not in a million years.'

'He's the only one who didn't get rounded up.'

'Except that's not true,' said Mertens.

'What's not true?'

'Bultmann is on the train. They put him on board at Peterborough.'

## 38

By the time they pulled in to Newcastle, it was snowing heavily.

Through the struts of the Tyne railway bridge they had seen flakes spinning in the weak light cast by the train. Along the centre of the track drifts were already building against the sleepers, and a hard wind was blowing in off the sea.

According to the station clock it was 9.09 p.m., and the only life on the platforms was the shivering detachment of replacement guards which swarmed towards the train the moment it stopped.

Sensing an opportunity, the prisoners stood up, stretching out their cramp and sliding open their doors to survey the corridors. The British soldiers were pushing over each other to get in and out. A huge tea urn was being manhandled aboard, together with open crates packed with silver-wrapped cake and cheese.

For a few minutes, no one was counting, and no one was watching. There was still a long way to go, and the weather was deteriorating.

'Find Bultmann,' hissed Goltz.

Zuhlsdorff was already halfway out of the compartment.

'You too, Hartmann. Quickly.' Zuhlsdorff had turned right, so Hartmann moved left into the crush along the narrow corridor. Knotted groups of prisoners were talking excitedly. Obscene greetings were being bellowed along the length of the carriage.

Bultmann would be easy to find. Bultmann would be alone, and the only man in a uniform.

Under the sepia of the station lights, he could see British soldiers lounging on the platform. No one seemed in a hurry. Maybe there was a problem. Hartmann badly hoped that there was. If the train set off now, Goltz would have to call off the search. Bultmann would be safe.

In the half-lit wagon nearest to the engine, he found him, stretched out on a filthy mattress behind ration boxes in the luggage cage.

Warm steam was blowing in through an open door. A rag-eared newspaper was on his lap.

'Someone wants to talk to you. Get yourself up quickly.'

'I give orders, I don't take them. Who wants to talk to me, and about what?' Bultmann was jabbing at the embroidered silver tabs on his shoulders. 'See these? I have rank over every serving officer on this train.'

'You've got rank but no power, and right now we're all in the same boat, Major.' Hartmann smiled. He was trying to make this easy. 'We just need to figure a few things out, get ourselves organised for what might be coming.'

'We do. That's fine. Just a little more respect, please. Lead on.'

As the officer reached down to pick up his cap, the train lurched violently, throwing both of them against the door. A second engine was being joined to the front and a small contingent of men in blue overalls had gathered round to proffer advice. After a short conference, one of them took a lamp and disappeared underneath. Grabbing the major's arm, Hartmann led him back down the train, squeezing between prisoners who stepped aside in silence.

Word had got round fast. Bultmann was doomed.

'I've found him.' Hartmann steered the major into the space left vacant between Mertens and Zuhlsdorff.

'Blinds. Door,' barked Goltz.

Hartmann complied, and sat down next to Bruling and Goltz. Across from them, the major had removed his cap and placed it on his knee. Under the overhead lights, he looked every one of his years.

Everything about him was depleted. The man was short, and his skin was puffy. His hair, like Bruling's, had been stretched weakly from one ear to the other and his presumption of entitlement was melting away before their eyes.

'Good evening, gentlemen. Good evening.'

Bultmann had broken the silence first. It was Goltz who responded.

'We should be heading south, not north. Don't you agree?'

'I do, I do. Complete disaster.'

'And why do you think that was?'

'Your plan, not mine. I haven't a clue. Perhaps we underestimated our enemy. Easy enough to do.'

'Some of us think they knew we were coming.'

'Yes, that's very possible.' The major appeared insensible of the outcome Goltz was leading him towards. 'Secrets are hard to keep in prison, especially valuable ones. People who have nothing are susceptible to temptation. Quite so.'

'But only a tiny number of people were in on the secret.' Goltz took a deep breath. Everyone, except Bultmann, knew what was next. 'And you were one of them.'

There was an instant, ghastly flash of awareness. Bruling had stood up to guard the door.

'That's preposterous.'

'You never liked the idea of a break-out, did you, Major?' Goltz was winding himself up, spitting out his words into Bultmann's ghostly face.

'That's not true. It's simply not true.'

'All you wanted back there was a fat plateful of food three times a day and a fucking cushy life.'

'Everyone in that camp knew something was happening. I promise you all, I'm not your leak.'

'You and all that fucking yellow Wehrmacht scum hanging on to the good life until it's time to go home.'

'Calm down. Think it through.'

'Fuck you.'

'We were there at the gate. We nearly had it down. Not just your men. My men. Everyone.'

'So tell me this, Major. Why weren't you rounded up and hauled down to London? Why weren't you on one of the buses? How come you joined us later?'

'Does it matter? I'm on the train now.' The major's strength was coming back. He'd put his cap on, and there was authority in his voice. 'For the last time, I am not your leak. Now if you're all done . . .'

'You weren't on the buses.'

'I was hiding. They found me after the buses had gone. You're insane.'

It was too much for Zuhlsdorff. Raising his right arm to shoulder height, he twisted and drove the point of his elbow into Bultmann's cheekbone. There was a cry, and the major sprang for the door, holding his face.

Before he could open it, Mertens hauled him down, simultaneously twisting him in the direction of Zuhlsdorff's knotted fist. As it struck, the major moved his head, catching the blow flat on his right ear. For a second time, he lurched towards the door, stumbling across the men's legs with hands snatching at his collar.

'I didn't do this. You're all mad.'

Somehow, he had wriggled on to the floor. When he looked up at Hartmann, his hands were clasped penitentially across his chest and a pink flash of tears and blood was smeared across his forehead. In another second, Zuhlsdorff and Mertens would be into him with their boots.

'Why are you doing this?' Hartmann could scarcely believe his own words. 'He says he didn't do it. What proof do you have that he did? You've already said it could have been any one of us. And that means you, me, anyone with half an inkling. This man is a German officer with an Iron Cross on his neck. You can't treat him like this.'

Later, he would wonder what would have happened if the whistle hadn't blown; if the doors hadn't started to slam shut along the length of the train; if there'd been no warning knock on the window.

Along the length of the platform, the station was clearing. Prisoners were being marshalled back into their correct compartments. Names were being checked off against lists. Bultmann needed to be safely back where they'd found him.

'We'll finish this properly later. It's not over.' The rage had all drained from Goltz. 'Take the fucker back.'

Already the train was gliding out of the station. Beneath its muted lights, the city had been transformed under the still-falling snow. Nothing was moving on the streets, and the hard edges of the roofs had been blunted by a thick white cushion.

Everyone could feel the extra power generated by their second locomotive. Everyone assumed it would be needed for the hills ahead, where the arctic conditions would soon be muffling the sound of their passage, and driving snow into the carriages around every withered seal.

'Do I thank you, Herr Hartmann?' asked the major.

'No. You just give me that newspaper.'

If he was lucky, *The Times* might save him.

According to the front page, their much-derided German army – propelled by SS Panzer divisions – was fighting back in Belgium along an eighty-mile front. For once, even the British press had put a lid on its jingoism.

'What's the date on it?' demanded Goltz. Hartmann's curious outburst appeared entirely forgotten.

'December nineteenth. Yesterday. Or near enough.'

'Read it again. Slowly. Don't miss anything out.'

Everyone on the train soon knew a garbled version of what the report said. From one end to the other, a cheer built until it was picked up by every single prisoner. And as that noise faded, a sustained, steady clap took over, spreading into each steamy compartment, until every man was banging his hands together. Several of them stood on the seats and jeered at the line of anxious guards looking in from the corridor.

*'SS marschiert in Feindesland*
*Und singt ein Teufelslied . . .'*

Someone was singing the SS marching song in a perfect, unbroken castrato.

*'Wo wir sind da geht's immer vorwärts*
*Und der Teufel der lacht nur dazu!*
*Ha, ha, ha, ha, ha!'*

'Tell them what it means,' ordered Goltz. 'Tell them we can teach them the words.'

Hartmann slid open the door. Two rifles were immediately aimed at his belly.

'Don't get excited. I speak English. I just wondered if you'd like a translation.'

'Go and tell him to shut his fucking mouth.'

'It says that the SS marches in enemy land and sings a devil's song. Wherever they go, they always go forward and the devil merely laughs. And then there's the laughing bit. Ha, ha, ha, ha, ha.'

'Hilarious.' One of the guards was looking away, down the corridor. He smirked. 'Let's see if this makes him laugh.'

Out of Hartmann's sight, a door had been rocked back hard. There was a dull thump, and the solitary voice fell silent.

Later, when the engines crashed into the snowdrift, most of the men were sleeping.

Since London, they'd grown accustomed to the random stops. None of them lasted for long, a few hours, at most. Everyone assumed this one would be the same.

With the day's first feeble light, however, that presumption quickly changed. On one side, a wall of thick snow rose steeply above the height of the train, shielding them from the landscape beyond. On the other, every living thing between them and the sea had vanished.

As the temperature inside tumbled, the men quickly came round. Each of them reached for the thick coats and hats on the racks. From the front they could hear melted snow hissing on the boilers. Out of the frosted windows, they could make out guards with shovels and lanterns trudging past them in thigh-deep snow.

'We're stuck,' said Mertens. 'The heating will be off until we get moving again.'

To Hartmann, it seemed as if the dawn couldn't be bothered. Apart from a peculiar grey glow, the morning offered no light. Although the wind had eased, there was no sun and no warmth. No one fed them, or spoke to them, and just a single guard was left in each carriage.

Up front, the rest were busily cursing their way through the blockage. Every sound seemed to be amplified by the stillness and the cold was beyond anything they'd ever experienced. Nothing could keep you warm in this. If the prisoners wanted to escape, that would be fine. No one would give chase. A few minutes in these temperatures and they'd be dead anyway.

By mid-morning, the noises changed. Coal was being tossed into the fireboxes. There was laughter as the digging party tumbled back inside, knocking matted clumps of ice from their greatcoats. Without warning they were jerking backwards, slowly and with a deafening eruption of steam.

After a few minutes they stopped again. Every face was pressed to a window. When the train switched gears, the long limb of metal and wood stiffened until it was inching back towards the drift, so slowly they could hear the snow squeaking under its wheels.

'Jesus. Look at that.'

Everyone on the train had seen it.

It was Bultmann, just a few yards away, in cap and full uniform, sitting upright in a deep fold of snow. His eyes were frozen open, and his right arm was straight, as if it had collapsed in a dying salute.

Just one set of footprints led out to his corpse.

There were none coming back.

From: Lieutenant-Colonel Archibald Wilson, Commandant, Camp 21, Comrie.

To: Alexander Scotland, London Cage.

Date: 18th Dec. 1944

Although I'm fully aware they've nowhere else to go, I think you should know what is happening up here. Very shortly we will have 4,000 of Germany's worst, and the safe management of these brutes is exerting a strain on my staff no one could possibly have anticipated.

Behind the wire, the SS run what is effectively a secret police force, complete with routine beatings and punishments for 'anti-Nazi behaviour'. Any of the sad individuals found 'guilty' are told that their property will be confiscated and their families liquidated, once the war is satisfactorily concluded. It is, in short, a terror state in miniature and recent developments on the continent have merely added to the insufferable swagger of the SS bullies who preside over it.

We must disagree over the imminent arrival of the Polish guards. I fear they may make things significantly worse. However, I have noted your other remarks on the party in transit which includes Herr Goltz. We will do what we can to restrain him, while encouraging the 'softer' elements you described. Maybe the weather will help. Not even Russia can compete with the winter we're expecting this year in the Highlands.

Archie

# 39

It was much calmer on the train after that.

There were no celebrations, and all the ecstasy of the previous night had disappeared. As he had no friends – and his body had been left in the snow – the major was quickly forgotten; another insignificant casualty, nothing more.

Most of the prisoners had been moving constantly since the summer, and they were content to gape blankly at the dull waters of the North Sea, wondering if their journey would ever end.

Few of them expected to get back to the front. Instead their hatred was turning inwards, seeking objects among their own. If Goltz felt satisfied by Bultmann's death, he hadn't said so. Apart from a low grunt of satisfaction, he'd said nothing.

By mid-morning they were switching trains in Edinburgh. By noon, they were crossing the Forth Bridge in scintillating winter light, crowding their faces to the glass to watch the fishing boats under the giant central arch of the span.

On the northern side of the river, the scenery quickly changed. In place of the soft lowland hills, there were mountains from which ice-crusted rivers curled around spurs of Scots pine, and down past turreted Gothic mansions cut from deep red granite. If anything, the winter had bitten even deeper here. Every tree seemed exhausted by its burden of snow, and apart from a few tractors, the roads looked impassable.

In Perth, a plough blade was bolted to their lead train, and along the flat valley bottoms their progress was swift. With no reason to, Hartmann began to feel they were getting close. All around them, the horizons were closing in. Beyond the freshly turned fields and the neat hedges the terrain rose steeply, and the way forward seemed closed by a distant line of rocky peaks.

Before, they'd been riding the main route north. Now they were trundling along a branch line, moving west alongside villages nestled in woodsmoke and whiteness. Never in the last five years had Hartmann seen anywhere so untouched by the war. And then, just as he remembered the train and its cargo of two hundred black hearts, they stopped.

There was a white sign on the platform with the town's name picked out in large black capitals.

COMRIE.

Up front, their two locomotives were cooling noisily, and the pistons were releasing a few dying gasps of steam. In a flurry of boots and commands, the guards were tumbling out into formation, shoulder to shoulder, with every eye focused on the prisoners stepping awkwardly from their six carriages.

Judging by the colour of the sky, Hartmann reckoned they had less than two hours' good daylight left. Wherever they were going, it would have to be near by.

In the thrill of being outside, no one else was thinking that far ahead. Since London, they'd been recycling their own stinking breath, and the Highland air tasted sweet. Among the crowd of tired faces, beneath their ragged assortment of woolly hats and army caps, Hartmann sensed a kind of happiness. When the order came to march, everyone was glad to stretch their legs. They turned left out of the tiny station on to a single street smothered in snow.

On each side, sturdy stone houses and shops ran away towards a church topped by the elegant taper of a grey steeple, and a clock which read five past two. There were multicoloured Christmas lights in the windows and every door was jammed with spectators. Without instruction, the prisoners had straightened their backs and dropped into formation; two abreast, legs kicked high, they strode down the centre of the road.

Alongside them, small gangs of red-faced children ran whooping and shouting in an accent Hartmann couldn't comprehend. Everywhere he turned, the locals seemed curious but unintimidated. Not even the goosestep, or the lusty refrain of the singing, seemed to trouble them. Nothing provoked a reaction more alarming than the occasional snowball. Either they'd seen it before, or they knew where the Germans were heading.

At the church they turned left over a wide river, heading south along a straight road towards a line of low hills. A hook of moon was just visible above the horizon and a bitter breeze was pushing down on to their backs off the northern snowfields. No one was singing now, and every man had his hands thrust deep into his pockets. Just here, the valley plain was wide and featureless, offering no shelter for either the prisoners or the sheep which stared after the near-silent line of intruders.

Since leaving the station, Hartmann had been walking alongside Rosterg. 'You saw what happened to Bultmann?' Icy smoke seemed to hang in the air around Hartmann's mouth as he spoke.

'Of course. He wasn't a stupid man. He would have known what was coming.' There was a terrible droop in the older man's voice. 'Doing it that way must have felt like a better option.'

'Goltz thought he was the rat.'

'Goltz was mistaken.'

'Someone must have told the British.' Hartmann was looking for a clue on Rosterg's face. The only thing there was exhaustion. 'If it wasn't Bultmann, then he's done somebody a big favour.'

'Still so naïve, Max.' Rosterg checked to make sure no one was listening. Two buzzards were tracing giant circles overhead. 'These people are completely mad,' he continued. 'They're being eaten alive by their own paranoia. They've got nothing left to feed on but each other. All the major did was deprive Goltz of a confession. Inside his head, he'll still be wondering. Who was it? Who was it?'

'He'll get bored eventually. There'll be other distractions here. We just have to get through the winter.'

'And then what? The wine cellar? Home? Feels like a very long way away right now. The Russians have probably drunk right through it already.'

'Chin up, Rosterg. The Russians don't like wine.'

'Take care in here, my young friend.' The convoy had slowed and Rosterg's weariness seemed to reach deep down into his boots. 'Watch your back.'

Both of them could see the camp clearly now on their right flank. From a distance, it looked innocent enough; just a few dozen huts, drowsing in the snow, with no sign of life apart from the cloudy smudge of newly lit fires. As they drew nearer, the men could see watchtowers on every corner and a formidable wire fence topped by lights which were already shining brightly.

In this last twitch of daylight, it looked like the end of the world. No one would escape from here, unless they wanted to die of hypothermia. Black woods and mountains were their only company. High over their heads, squabbling rooks were heading back to roost. Even the birds appeared desperate to leave.

At the gate, they were processed quickly. Apart from Bultmann, no one had vanished in transit, and the guards worked smoothly, checking ranks and names before ushering them through a sequence of huts for new prison uniforms, sleeping bags, blankets and a cursory medical inspection.

One by one, they emerged to stand – freshly deloused – under the camp's sodium lights, wearing clean clothes beneath their filthy coats. A light fall of snow was settling on their shoulders. Ahead of them, in the half-dark, lay their new home.

As the prisoners awaited instructions, Hartmann was doing a hurried calculation. There appeared to be four identical compounds, separated by ferocious double fencing, with twelve huts in each. If they were full, that amounted to some four thousand prisoners.

Four thousand.

His mind spun; the numbers were extraordinary. A vast nationwide infrastructure had been willed into existence almost overnight, simply to keep men speaking German apart from men who didn't.

Shaking his head clear, he peered forward.

'Hello. Listen. Everyone. Please. To make this quicker, I've been asked to interpret, so here's what they want me to say.'

Rosterg was standing next to a British officer, scrutinising sheets of information through his golden spectacles.

Alarm fluttered in Hartmann's gut but there was nothing he could do.

'I'm going to read out names, followed by your compound – A, B, C or D – and then a hut number. You'll then be taken to your quarters. I'm afraid there's no food tonight. The next meal will be breakfast at eight a.m. after roll call.'

Everyone was too tired to care where they slept. There seemed no logic behind the selections, and Hartmann wasn't surprised to be heading for Compound B with so many familiar faces. Somewhere back on the road, their destinies had become synchronised. Even Rosterg had joined them, skidding along icy concrete pathways towards the curved metal shelter of Hut 4.

'You didn't waste any time,' said Hartmann. 'Are you sure that was wise?'

'It wasn't intended, Max. I'd been hoping to keep my head down. Unfortunately, that isn't going to be possible.'

'Because?'

'Because as of yesterday, most of the guards here are Polish.'

Inside the hut there were twenty wooden bunks down each side, positioned at right angles to the walls. Along the apex of the rippled iron roof, bare bulbs hung from uneven lengths of flex. One of the bulbs was dead.

Around three pot-bellied stoves, the established occupants were hunched in tight contemplative circles. Excited by the sudden influx, there was an explosion of chatter, a hungry thirsting after gossip. Strangers were embracing, names and stories were pouring out, and every bed but one soon had a body.

Hartmann's was on the top right, four bunks down from the door. Rosterg's was underneath.

'Polish guards. What will that mean?'

'Our compatriots have been torching their country for five years. I dare say we represent an opportunity to level the score.'

Hartmann busied himself with his bedding. There were eighty people in there – a sea of blond-capped faces – and the braying made it sound like an abattoir. Everyone was celebrating the news from Belgium. He didn't doubt it was being twisted beyond recognition.

Along each side of the hut he'd noticed two wooden ledges for

313

the men's personal possessions. From one end to the other there was nothing on either.

'Why did you have to get involved, Rosterg? You're mad.'

'I speak the language. No one else can. You never know. I might be able to stop another war.'

'Back on the train – before they questioned Bultmann – your name got mentioned.'

Rosterg had placed his glasses on the ledge and lain back, hidden in the shadow cast by Hartmann's bunk.

'I'm very many things, Max. Very few of them are particularly noteworthy. But I'm not an informer.'

Hartmann flopped back, too. Since London, he'd not slept, and he had no appetite for an SS party, especially one without cigarettes or schnapps. Soon enough, the coal would run out and after that they'd all be fleeing to bed in their coats.

As he drifted, the last sound he remembered was the rustle of a poker stirring the embers in a grate.

After that, nothing.

# 40

The one empty bed was filled around dawn.

Hartmann watched the door open on the hard silhouette of a man. Around it, the frozen air seemed to be swimming like smoke. As he stepped in, the figure tousled his hair sleepily and waited for his eyes to adjust. It had been a long, cold week in the cell block, and the hut had been less than half full when he last slept there. Now the place was packed, but at least his bed by the door was still free.

With his left foot, he pushed the door shut and stepped towards the first stove, hoping to find some heat. There was none. Down the length of the hut, bodies were turning. Reveille had already been blown, and the newcomer would have to wait for his rest. It didn't matter. He'd got something else on his mind. Once the light was stronger, as he had done every day for six weeks, he'd be searching among the newcomers for a face.

But Hartmann had seen his first.

'I knew you'd be here, you bastard!'

Still wrapped in his sleeping bag, he slithered down on to the concrete floor and opened his arms for an embrace. When Koenig didn't move, he hopped clumsily forward and the two men hugged tightly, feeling the rasp of each other's stubble and the deep, warm breath of relief.

'Talk later? There's no time now. You look knackered.' Koenig had pushed his friend back and was examining the lines on his face.

'That's fine. As soon as we can.'

Until breakfast, there would be no chance of a conversation. In the glacial latrines, no one lingered once they'd squatted and splashed. Anyone who took too long brought down the fury of those standing waiting in the cold.

During roll call – when the men stamped impatiently between

315

the huts – everyone's eyes were on the kitchen. Overnight, the temperature had nose-dived. Spears of ice hung from every window ledge and a ribbon of snow lay balanced on the electric wires which criss-crossed the camp.

Once their names had been checked, they were free to move; a motley stampede of grey coats thundered in through the red wooden door of the canteen, grabbing chairs and mugs of dark tea, followed by oatmeal and bottomless piles of bread and marmalade. During the dreary namecheck, Hartmann had stood behind Koenig, studying his outline. Everyone looked the same in a greatcoat but Koenig seemed horribly thin, and his hair had grown over his collar again in thick, greasy curls.

Across the metal breakfast table, he looked even worse. Around his cheeks the flesh had shrunk, dropping his eyes into dark pits from which deep cracks ran down to the corners of his mouth. What light Hartmann had ever known there was extinguished. The boy's face was dead, and his eyes had turned grey.

'Stop inspecting me, Max. You look like shit too.'

Koenig had finished one bowl of porridge and was casting round greedily for more. 'I've been in solitary for a week. Bread and water. I'm due some decent grub.'

All the tables were full now. Eighty men squeezed thigh to thigh. Most of them had arrived the night before.

'What happened? You're a wreck.' Hartmann slid across his helping of bread. 'I think you need this more than I do.'

Koenig tore into it greedily. 'You'll like it here. It's more like Germany than Germany.'

'We're in Scotland. We're beyond being nowhere. The war might as well be on another planet.'

Koenig stopped eating and scrutinised his friend's face. 'We look older than our grandfathers.'

Both of them laughed. Koenig had a point. War had drained them all. Apart from Rosterg, there was no one in the room over twenty-five.

'So how come you were locked up?'

'You won't like it.'

'Tell me.'

'Nothing serious. Not really. Sometimes we get the odd newcomer who needs to be shown the way things are, that's all.'

'The way things are?'

'People who've forgotten the oaths we took. Not traitors, exactly, but weaklings requiring some degree of realignment.'

'Realignment? You beat people up?'

'I issue reminders.' Koenig laughed. 'Only this time I got caught.'

Prisoners were slowly drifting out, and a polar blast could be felt from the door. Every plate had been scraped and licked until it shone.

'And for what reason did you issue this latest "reminder"?'

'We don't build snowmen, Max. Not here.'

'You gave someone a kicking because they built a snowman?'

'We don't build snowmen who look like Hitler.'

'Do I laugh or do I cry?'

Koenig smiled. 'I said you wouldn't like it.'

For a little while longer, they caught up with each other's news. After their adventures in the doctor's car, Koenig had been questioned and shipped straight to Camp 21, where sketchy rumours of the Devizes plot had been circulating for days, alongside reports of a fresh German offensive and yet more V2 rockets over the Home Counties. Only two recent developments had dampened the mood of patriotic expectation.

The first was the rapid onset of severe winter weather.

The second was the deployment – only twenty-four hours earlier – of the 7th Polish Guard Company.

'What difference will that make?' Hartmann asked.

'I guess we'll find out later.'


As he always did, Hartmann killed the day studying people and the clouds. Neither was markedly more interesting than the other.

A little way beyond the wire, he felt certain he would find the river; the same ice-glazed waters he'd already crossed on his march from the station. Behind that, a broad wood rose steeply to a crest which fanned out in both directions. Pale smoke from the chimneys of the nearby village seemed to have merged with a late afternoon mist, forming a translucent disc which hung over the valley floor.

By Hartmann's calculations it was the shortest day – the winter solstice – and a hard crust was already forming where the men's boots had trodden down the snow. Around noon, the sun had made a token appearance low in the southern sky but there'd been no appreciable lift in temperature.

Between the compound office block and the wire, a group of prisoners had scuffed away a small clearing on the grass, forming goalposts with piles of icy slush. Almost all the day's light had gone and a misshapen football had been produced which the prisoners were kicking half-heartedly and without any discernible skill. As Hartmann watched, the ball was booted randomly until it came to rest at the foot of the perimeter fence between two concrete stanchions.

In one of the guard towers overlooking their compound, a shadow moved; then two shadows, and a furious cry which none of them could understand. For a few moments, the prisoners were too stunned to move. Then one of them started walking deliberately towards the ball.

From the tower, there were more alien shouts and the click-click of a round being pushed into position by the bolt of a rifle. When the prisoner reached the wire, a single shot rang out. Hissing flaps of wet leather seemed to explode in every direction. Chunks of ice rang down on the metal rooftops and suddenly the footballers were skittering back across the packed snow.

Everyone had heard the shot. For the duration of its echo, the entire camp seemed to shrink back in puzzled silence, and then, bedlam. From inside every hut, there was a clattering of furniture as doors were flung open and bleary-faced prisoners ran screaming to the fence, scavenging for missiles to hurl at an enemy they couldn't yet see.

Somewhere near the main gate, Hartmann could hear approaching dogs, and the swirl of men's footsteps. Two lines of armed men in green coats had materialised, between which an entire company of guards was suddenly jogging into the compound, firing wildly into the sky. From the watchtowers, spotlights swung on the prisoners, forcing them to swivel away from the fence and head back to their huts, pursued by a phalanx of Polish guards tugged on by yowling Alsatians.

Everything had been ready for this, thought Hartmann. The football had nothing to do with it.

'I'm thinking maybe we should have stayed out of Poland.'

Hartmann hadn't seen Rosterg all day. Now, like everyone else, he was rushing for the sanctuary of their quarters.

'They were only playing football.'

Out in the darkness beyond their compound, a flare had gone off, illuminating the entire camp in spectral orange light.

'I'm not sure the Poles were causing much trouble in thirty-nine, Max.'

'Well, they're certainly making up for it now.'

To Hartmann's ears, the gunfire was getting worse – as if more troops had entered their compound. Behind the closed doors of their hut, the prisoners were panting in a state of black-eyed expectation. In battle, he'd seen the same look on a thousand faces – ordinary men at the tipping point where adrenaline neutralised fear.

'We could take them if we rushed.' Goltz's voice crackled. His fists were knotted, and his cheeks flushed. 'How many of us are there? Eighty in this hut. Eighty in all the rest? We could take the fuckers. Easily we could.'

Outside, they could hear the dogs scratching on the iron sheets. There were faces at the window – another disjointed spatter of shots – and then the door was kicked open in a volley of orders and abuse. Underneath their green hats, the soldiers appeared heavy-featured and pale, the exact same look Hartmann had seen on the corpses in Russia.

Koenig had always said you couldn't tell one dead Slav from another. Looking at them now – spitting incomprehensible instructions from the thick end of their rifles – the living ones weren't much different.

'What the fuck are they saying?'

Goltz was backing off. A dozen armed guards were pushing the prisoners towards their bunks. Behind them, a second mob of younger soldiers was rifling through the blankets and tossing mattresses to the floor. Unsettled by the rush of air, the wood stoves roared, sending a pulse of heat along the length of the hut. One by one, every bed was being stripped and searched.

'Rosterg. You speak their fucking language. What the fuck is going on?'

In their identical winter coats, it wasn't easy to know who was in charge. But only one of them had removed his headgear and Rosterg turned towards him. For a few minutes, they spoke calmly in Polish. Every bunk had been violated, and the torn bedding was strewn across puddles of melting snow.

'*Nigdy więcej problemów prosimy?*' The Polish captain had pouched his revolver and extended a hand to Rosterg.

'*Nigdy więcej problemów,*' said Rosterg, reciprocating with a formal embrace.

Satisfied, the Pole bowed and gestured towards the door. Along the length of the hut, the guards lowered their rifles and headed for their own barracks. Even to Hartmann, their strut seemed insufferable, stirring a flicker of national humiliation he'd thought long extinguished.

From the open door, the prisoners could smell the mess left by the waiting dogs and the stink stirred their silent anger.

'What were you saying to each other? Tell me,' Goltz demanded.

'He asked me for an assurance that there'd be no more problems, and I gave him one.' Rosterg busied himself hanging a blanket over the hot pipes which ran from the stove along the inside of the roof.

'On whose authority? Not mine. Nor theirs.' Goltz indicated the crush of men packed around to listen. 'You shouldn't have done that. They're our enemy. We're at war with them. Look at me when I'm speaking to you, for fuck's sake.'

Rosterg turned. His voice sounded perfectly calm. Neutral. 'You're right, but they'd have torn this place apart if I hadn't. So forgive me, but I took the liberty of assuming you'd regard that to be a bad thing.'

A stray thought seemed to tug in Rosterg's brain, drawing a smile to his face. 'There were some new house rules too. No coats in bed.

No visits to the toilet block after nine, and regular unscheduled visits along the lines of this one. If anyone is found wearing coats in bed, we all – all – get dragged out in the night for a midnight roll call. Sounds like we're going to get along just fine.'

'You're a fucking arse-licker, Rosterg. Do you know that?'

'They're not my rules. They're his. You remain absolutely free to violate them.'

'Who the fuck are you, anyway?'

'I'm the person who tells you things. I'm the person who warns you about things. I'm the person who can find out what you'll never know. Beyond that I am utterly useless and whether you like me or not is a matter of absolutely no concern to me. Do you understand?'

But Goltz had lost interest. 'You bore me, Rosterg.'

For a half-second, Rosterg stared back, before removing his glasses and polishing them on the little that remained of his monogrammed handkerchief.

'Likewise,' he muttered, and then left.

The next day was December 22nd. Hartmann was almost certain of it. It might even be Christmas Eve, but if it was, no one said so. Back in Devizes, there'd be rousing concerts and home-made decorations. Here, every first conversation was about the war and every second one was about loyalty.

Although not all the inmates of Black Camp 21 were SS – he'd seen fliers and submariners, even a scattering of officers – every one of them wore the black mark, and tinsel would be regarded as a sign of suspect deviancy.

On Christmas Day – if they got that far – '*Deutschland Über Alles*' might be as good as it got.

Overnight, more heavy snow had fallen, driven horizontally by a lacerating northerly. As the prisoners dressed, not even the stoves could turn the cold round.

Choosing not to risk the consequences, most had slept without their coats.

Outside, every footstep across the camp had been filled afresh, and when the men left their huts they found drifts heaped up against their doors. For a few precious minutes, the fuggy heat of the canteen revived them, but once breakfast was done the day yawned out like all the others, distinguished only by the combination of severe weather and boredom.

No one had forgotten the events of the previous night. Over breakfast, the men had talked of nothing else. But as the light strengthened, so did the storm, pinning them deep inside their huts and hiding the tops of the watchtowers in dizzying clouds of snow.

'We've got to go out, Max. I'm going mad.'

Koenig was lying on his bed by the door on the opposite side from Hartmann's bunk. Only his face was visible and a cruel wind was shrieking in the gaps around the window.

'We'll die out there. What the hell for?'

'It's easing off a bit. Seriously. It is.' Koenig twisted to look through panes thick with snow. If anything, it was worse. 'And I've got something I want to show you.'

Outside, nothing but the sky was moving. Even when the snow stopped, the wind didn't, and the two men were soon dangerously cold.

'My teeth hurt. This is fucking insane.'

'The colder we get, the warmer you'll feel when we go back in. Just be glad you're not one of those Polish cunts. They're stuck out in it regardless.'

It was true. Ghostly figures were still out there patrolling the fence.

'They could do themselves a favour; stay inside. No one's going to be causing any trouble in this.' Hartmann held the corners of his collar and pulled them tight across his neck. 'Why are the Poles here anyway?'

'These ones got out of Poland just before we went in. Thousands of them. Smart move by the British. Who better to guard a bunch of SS psychopaths than another bunch of bitter, homeless exiles?' Koenig had stopped behind the corner hut on the northern edge of their compound. 'Apart from the Russians, there can't be many people who hate us more.'

Hartmann peered back into the blizzard. The guards were no longer visible in a whiteout that was devouring their entire world. Nothing was left; no one; just the two of them.

'Why are you stamping your feet?' he asked.

'Because there's a tunnel under here.'

Satisfied that he was at the right spot, Koenig had carefully kicked away the snow around the flap of a large brick coal bunker.

'It was here when I arrived. Finished, but unused. No one seems sure who dug it. Possibly some prisoners who've been moved further north.'

'There are worse places than this? That isn't possible.'

Koenig smiled. Snow had started to tumble again, thicker than before. 'Don't tell me you're not enjoying it here.'

Hartmann had wandered closer to the wire. Out in the field, white eddies of crystals were spinning over the lip of a ditch, settling in hard shapes like breaking waves.

'Have you been inside it?' he shouted back.

'I have. It comes out just short of the river. It's only fifteen yards or so long but it's pitch black all the way through. And very wet. Horrible.'

'So why are you still here?'

'Where would I go? And why would I go?'

'That's not what you said before, back on the hill. Remember?'

'It's different now. We've nearly won, Max. I can feel it.'

'You're wrong. Completely wrong.' Hartmann was screaming to be heard above the tearing wind. 'Too many people hate us. The world fucking hates us. You said it yourself, just now. Do you think these Poles want to be here? They've got homes in Wrocław and Poznań and Prague. They've got families and kids. Just like everyone else we've shat on. No one wants us. No one ever did. We're on our own now. It's finished.'

'You shouldn't be saying any of this, Max.'

'Because what? Because you'll *realign* me if I do?'

'Because people don't – can't – think like that in here.'

'And if I'm right?'

'You can't possibly be right.'

Something colder even than the rising gale seemed to spin in the air. 'Of course. I'd forgotten. What could possibly go wrong?'

'You should be careful,' Koenig hissed.

'Tell me. Will it be you, or someone else who comes to issue my reminder?'

'Listen. Goltz doesn't think it was Bultmann who blew you all out at Devizes.'

The two men had pulled close to one another. Pearls of ice were clinging to their exposed straggles of hair.

'Does he think it was me, Erich? Does he? Is this a warning?'

But Koenig was already walking away, head bent into the storm.

'Why did you show me this? You never said.'

The words seemed to break up on a withering gust before being tossed in pieces across the camp.

As Hartmann caught up with his friend, he could feel the fracture. This time there would be no coming back. For years, he had tried to see the world as Koenig did, knowing his life would be easier, yet always secretly hoping that he would fail. And he had failed. Now, in this place, at least, they both knew who they were.

At the corner of their hut, Koenig swung towards the knot of buildings which included the canteen and the office block. Uncertain what else to do, Hartmann followed. It was nearly lunchtime, and the smell of boiled cabbage was building. In a few minutes, the rush for food would begin.

Walking past the kitchens, the two men reached a smaller brick building, with a raked felt roof. Looking in at the window, they could see Rosterg smoking a cigarette and reading a newspaper. Through the walls, they could feel the power of his fire.

'It's the compound office block,' mumbled Koenig.

Perfunctory. Indifferent.

Hartmann nodded. 'Right.'

Koenig booted the snow away from around the door and led the way in.

Inside, there was a small metal desk, two wooden chairs and a stove. Rosterg had pulled one of the chairs close to the fire. Koenig grabbed the second and sat down next to him. Hartmann stood at the back, uncertain why he was there, content with the forgotten draw of tobacco.

'If you're wondering, Max,' explained Rosterg, 'this is apparently where the compound committee meets. Someone has to tell the people out there what we want. Food orders, medical supplies, Red Cross parcels, coal. That sort of stuff. Anything that needs paperwork. Or a translator.'

'And the cigarettes?' Koenig asked.

He sounded hostile, dangerous. The door was banging impatiently in its frame at musical intervals. Whump. Whump.

Rosterg tugged a crushed blue packet from his breast pocket. Gauloises. 'Help yourself.'

'The sweetest perk of victory,' said Hartmann. 'Remember that?'

'I don't know what you're talking about.' Koenig had stretched his arms until his hands were almost touching the hot metal.

'That's what you called them. Six months ago.'

'They were my price for translating a letter from Polish into English,' Rosterg explained. 'One of our guards has fallen in love with a local.'

Koenig lit a cigarette off the fire, and handed the packet straight back. Hartmann wasn't going to get one. Outside, the sky had blackened again, and the only meaningful light in the cabin was coming from the stove.

'What are you reading?'

'You know what I'm reading. *Die Wochenpost*. We could all be reading it. You merely choose not to.'

'It's British propaganda. It's full of crap and lies.'

'It's a newspaper produced for German prisoners by the British. Of course it's full of crap. But it's words on a page. It's something to read. It's a tiny window out of this place. And I'm old enough to know the difference between crap and the truth, if there is such a thing. But then maybe you're not.' Rosterg folded the paper carefully and passed it over. 'Either way, you should read it before you condemn it.'

Koenig took the newspaper, kicked open the blackened hatch, and bundled it into the fire.

'You do know there's more than one copy?' Brittle flakes of scorched paper were rising towards the patterns on the ceiling. 'There's always more than one copy.'

'Goltz is right. You're fucking weird.'

'A validated man of distinction, then. You have made my day.'

'You shouldn't be here.'

'Well, I can't argue with that.'

Hartmann had listened to the exchange with despair. For months, Rosterg had always seemed two moves ahead, the one prisoner he felt certain would make it home. Perhaps it was the cold – or the weeks of extended isolation – but he finally sounded crushed.

'Come on. Both of you. Lighten up. It's Christmas. Or near enough. If I'm allowed to say it.'

'I'm not sure you are.'

'What will they be doing right now? Your wife and kids.'

'To be honest, I try very hard not to think about that. How about you?'

The watchtowers were already wiping the camp with their lights. The day had scarcely begun and yet to Hartmann it felt over.

'I had a photograph once. Now I'm not even sure she existed.'

Koenig had heard enough. 'I'll have one for later. Correction. I'll have them all. Give them here.'

Rosterg handed over the pack. Through the window, they could see the pathways busy with men sliding towards the canteen. Insipid fragments of blue sky were showing through the last straggling flakes of the storm.

'Be careful with what you eat today,' said Rosterg. The three men had stood. Koenig was halfway out of the door. 'There's been no fresh food here for days.'

As the door slammed, a trail of delicate black motes followed the two prisoners out on to the snow.

## 41

By evening roll call, all the clouds had moved away, bringing a frost which bit deep into the earth.

During the afternoon, the prisoners had been quiet, as if survival precluded all other preoccupations. Outside, there was nothing they could do to stay warm, and their clothing, in these conditions, was pitifully inadequate.

After their food, most of the men had galloped back to their huts, gasping as the cold gnawed on their jawbones, alchemising their breath into frozen dust. Even the guards seemed incapacitated. So far, there'd been no intrusions, and the routine nightly namecheck – in Hartmann's hut, at least – had proceeded without incident. Everyone was still there. No one had the energy for a fight.

'My fingers froze to the roof out there. Look. I've torn the fucking skin.'

Hartmann was wrapped in his bedding. Maybe it was hunger, but something felt as if it was decomposing inside his belly. At the best of times, he wasn't in the mood for small talk with Bruling. And this wasn't the best of times.

'Do you ever wonder where we might be if Devizes had worked, Max?'

'Dead, maybe?'

'We'll be back soon. In London, I mean. I'm certain of it.'

'I'm sure you're right.'

Bruling was the only person, Hartmann realised, who looked healthier than before. Like most of them, his beard was more down than stubble, but his face had fleshed out and his skin glowed like a child's.

'I was thinking I might pick up my mathematics again. One day. In Cambridge. What do you think?'

Hartmann rolled over to face the wall. The man was like a Jehovah's Witness. With luck, he'd soon get bored and knock on someone else's door.

'You don't look too good, Max. Talk later, maybe.'

For as long as he could, he lay still, hoping that his stomach would settle. Apart from the shrunken helpings, nothing about the day's food had seemed odd. The tinned liver hadn't smelled great, but who liked liver? As soon as Bruling had gone, he repositioned himself and surveyed the hut.

Rosterg hadn't been seen for hours, and their quarters felt disquietingly still, without even the comforting clank of the heating. He reached up to feel the pipe which ran above his bunk. It was lukewarm. On the previous two evenings it had been too hot to touch. Forgetting his discomfort, he swung down off his bunk to inspect the nearest stove. Just a handful of cinders was smouldering in the grate, and the coal scuttle alongside was virtually empty.

'There are two hundred stoves in this camp and the fuel is running out.'

Goltz was stretched out, motionless, like the lid of a medieval tomb.

'So who do you think will get the last few lumps of coal, Hartmann? Us or the Poles?'

From deeper down the hut there was a sustained groan, followed by the clatter of an ashen-faced figure rushing past them to the door. Moments later, he was followed by others, thrusting their heads into the block's steel buckets, or stumbling desperately towards salvation with hands clamped across their mouths.

In the chill air, the smell of vomit rose and spread, triggering a fresh chorus of retching, watched in disgust by the handful – which included Goltz – who remained unaffected.

'We've been poisoned, Max,' he whispered. But Max had gone. Back up on his bunk, Hartmann felt certain the pain would pass if he kept still. Halfway along the hut, men were defecating into buckets which were already full. Through the thin metal wall he could hear the traffic of misery, despite which he drifted into a feverish sleep, waking only when he knew for certain the battle against his own bowels was lost.

Below him, Rosterg's bed was still empty and the entire stinking hut seemed to be sleeping. Lights out had been and gone.

It was insane, but there wasn't an alternative.

Standing at the hut door, he wondered what time it was. The whole camp seemed crushed into silence by the sheer weight of stars. Apart from the searchlights playing out across the snow, nothing was moving. No toilet visits after nine. That's what they'd been told. He hoped the guards had been bluffing.

Twenty strides would get him to a wooden seat over a hole in the ground. He took a breath, and tested his foot on the ice which had formed around the entrance. A faint crack was followed by a squeal of crushed snow. He took another step. This time the noise seemed louder, causing him to stop mid-stride, horribly aware of his heart and the surge pressing down on his stomach.

It was no use. There wasn't any time. Pulling his coat around his shoulders, Hartmann half ran, half hobbled to the safety of the wash block. Ten seconds. Maybe less. He was all right. Knackered but alive. No one had seen him. Just as he thought, the Poles had been bluffing. Most likely, they were fighting off the cold like everyone else.

Feeling his way in the black, Hartmann found a lavatory and ripped down his pants. While his bowels voided, sick rose up through his throat; bitter lumps of undigested liver sprayed between his feet. Now, surely, somebody would discover him, bent at the waist with filth hanging from either end.

The back of his shirt was sticky with sweat, but the pain had gone and there was nothing left in his stomach to give. In his weakness, he thought of Sieber choking on a noose in a moonlit latrine. He'd probably never find out how he died. What difference would it make if he did?

He stood up and rinsed his face under a cold tap.

Through the doorway, he could see folds of glorious green light in the northern sky above the sharp edge of the mountains. Down at his feet, he could see his own shadow.

For the first time that night, he felt terrified.

In the stillness, whatever sound he made would be quadrupled. From the direction of the camp gates he could hear music: a gramophone record. Every word was clear, even the crackle of the needle. Maybe the guards were enjoying a Christmas party.

He stepped out, seeing his outline reach across the snow. The music seemed to bump louder, backed by a wave of drunk-sounding laughter. Another step. And then another. He was halfway back to the hut and his boots were struggling for traction on the ice. Three more paces and he'd be there, but the surface was treacherous and his legs felt horribly weak.

Within touching distance he slipped, falling backwards into the deep snow which bordered the path. As the air fled his lungs, he heard his own gasp of shock rising up over the camp. A moment later, the music faltered and he heard a single shot. And then a short pause.

He rolled over and stood up awkwardly. The spotlight was swinging round. As it circled him, the bullets were everywhere, whining past his ears into the fields and digging up plumes of snow around his feet. As quickly as he could, he stepped backwards out of the beam. The firing immediately stopped. Up on the tower, the lamp would be bulky and hard to manoeuvre. All he needed was a few seconds, just enough to reach the door and fall through it. Someone was shouting, and the light was still locked on the place where he'd gone down. Hartmann shuffled sideways until he was concealed from the beam by the rippled flank of the hut.

'Come on. You're safe. Run.'

Someone – Zuhlsdorff – had pushed the hut door open and Hartmann slid quickly inside to a ripple of sarcastic applause.

'Why didn't you just shit on the floor like all the rest of them?' Goltz was lying back on his bunk with his hands clasped behind his head. He sounded calm, but preoccupied – as if a difficult decision had been made which required considered action.

'I didn't know what time it was,' panted Hartmann. 'To be honest, I didn't think they were serious about the curfew.'

'Did you see him anywhere?'

'Who?'

'You know who.' Rosterg's bed was still empty. Untouched. 'Where the fuck is he?'

'I've no idea. What does it matter? He's probably sick somewhere.'

'Is that what you really think? Or are you in this together?'

'In what? I don't know where he is. Fuck. You've just watched me being shot at.'

'I've watched a bunch of Polish guards miss a sitting duck.'

'Not for the first time, Goltz, so fuck off.'

Hartmann climbed back on to his bed and pulled himself deep into his bedclothes. One way or another, it would surely soon be over. Now that the snow had stopped, there would be a fresh delivery of fuel. Without it, there seemed no way any of them could survive in this place for very much longer. In defiance of orders, the men were sleeping in their coats again, and within a day or so, Hartmann felt certain, they'd all be burning their beds to keep warm.

That's if Goltz hadn't killed him first.

Black Camp 21. It was well named.

A few hours later he awoke, suddenly. He'd been dreaming and a weak light was burning unexpectedly in a stove.

While his head spun for focus in the darkness, two things became horribly clear. The first was the wickedness of the cold. The second was the sound of a man pleading without expectation for his life.

# Extract from Witness Statement
# to Military Court
# 12/7/45

*Someone told me I should go to Hut 4 where I saw Rosterg in front of the stove. His face was badly swollen and he was surrounded by the men whose names I have already supplied. Someone was reading out from a piece of paper that had been found either on Rosterg or in his kit. At least that is what I was told.*

*The effect of what was read out was that he had given away bombing targets in France to French patriots. There was also supposedly a list of prisoners involved in the situation at Devizes. However, I did not actually see the paper, either then or subsequently.*

*Rosterg was being accused of treason and told that he had the deaths of many thousands of Germans on his conscience.*

*Around one hundred men were witness to this.*

## 42

Three candle stubs were burning in the open stove. The rest of the hut was in darkness.

As his eyes widened, he could make out the silhouette of a man, and then much more. Rosterg was sitting on a chair in the narrow space between the bunks with his back to the door. As yet, no daylight was showing through the windows, and the hut felt icier than ever.

At a guess, Hartmann put the time at two or three hours past midnight, and in the blackness beyond the puddle of yellow light it was obvious that no one was asleep. There were no coughs or snores, and between the awful whimpers which had woken him, it felt as though eighty men were holding their breath. After a few seconds, he could see why.

Something terrible had happened to Rosterg.

From each of his nostrils, a thin red crust ran down to a mouth he seemed unable to close. Every lungful of air was an effort. Every exhalation was accompanied by a defeated sigh, and his head, which was thrown back, seemed to be rolling from side to side in a futile search for salvation.

When his eyes swung past Hartmann, they registered nothing. Like his boots and his jacket, Rosterg's gold spectacles had vanished, and his hair was a ruin of dirt and blood. Such clothing as remained appeared mud-streaked and wet, as if the wearer had been pulled forcibly through the snow.

'Sit up, man. Sit the fuck up. Stop fucking whining.'

With a horrible sigh, Rosterg's whole body slumped forward.

As quietly as he could, Hartmann eased himself into a better position. Whatever was happening had already been going on for quite some time. Every pair of eyes in the hut was focused on that single chair.

Everything was exactly as it had been for Hartmann on the night Rosterg saved him: the same judge, the same jury. Only the defendant had changed.

On the lower bunk opposite, he could make out Mertens, Bruling and Koenig leaning forwards, elbows on knees. Standing behind the chair, with his hands clamped on Rosterg's shoulders, hauling him upright, was Zuhlsdorff. Another twenty or so prisoners were crammed in on either side of the stove and a small clearing had been left directly in front of the one occupied seat.

The shaven-headed figure of Goltz was prowling around in the space.

'Straighten your fucking back and look at me.'

A weary moan rose from Rosterg's chest. Briefly he looked up, but when his head fell forward again, Zuhlsdorff pulled it back until he could see nothing but Goltz's face. With no protection from the cold, Rosterg's entire body was quivering and the tips of his fingers had gone white.

'You can make all this go away. You just need to talk to us. Where were you tonight?'

Rosterg mumbled a response. There was fresh blood on his lips.

'Speak up. The whole hut wants to hear you.'

'Water first. Then I'll answer your questions.'

Somehow, a full canteen was located and passed to the seated prisoner. After a few awkward swallows, he wiped his mouth, and sat as straight as he could. Over his head, the corrugated iron ceiling seemed to ripple as a gust of wind passed over the hut.

'I've told you this already, but I'll tell you again.'

There were long gaps between the phrases.

'Dozens of people right across the camp have been sick. Very sick. They could have died. You know that's true. You've seen it. All I've been doing is making sure our people – *our* people – got treated well.'

He hesitated again, making eye contact with as many of his accusers as possible.

'When it was clear we were all being looked after, I was allowed to come back. That was when you decided to start beating me up.'

'What made them all sick?'

'I've told you a dozen times. Dodgy tins of liver? Cooks with filthy hands? Medieval plumbing? I don't know. No one knows. You tell me.'

There was a twist in Rosterg's voice, as if his tongue was swollen, but his breathing had steadied, but – after the uncertain start – the words were coming without hesitation.

'It was poison,' Goltz stated flatly.

Hartmann could see Koenig nodding furiously.

'That's a joke. Please tell me that is a joke. Who the fuck poisoned who here? Even the guards have been throwing up.'

'No joke.'

'You've seen the weather. We've had no fresh supplies. We've been eating what was left. You're insane.'

At a nod from Goltz, Zuhlsdorff came round from behind the chair and slashed the back of his right hand hard across Rosterg's face in a single, smooth action, followed by a matching swipe with the left.

After the first blow, Rosterg winced. After the second, he fell heavily to the floor, catching his forehead on the concrete plinth of the stove. When Zuhlsdorff pulled him back, there was a steady drip from a new wound on the right side of his forehead.

'It's funny that you didn't get sick. Why was that?' Goltz's intonation hadn't changed.

'Because I didn't eat the fucking liver.'

'Why didn't you eat the liver?'

'I don't like fucking liver. Lots of people don't like liver. Lots of people weren't sick.'

'But you like the newspaper the British print for us?'

'I read it. I don't like it. I don't really have a view on it.'

The blood had reached Rosterg's collar and was spreading down the arm of his shirt.

'Listen to me. I haven't read a book since I left home. Back home, I have a room full of books. When I see words on a page, I read them. I read posters on a wall, names on a list, destinations on a timetable.

335

I'll read anything. Just because I read their paper doesn't mean I believe what it says. There's stuff in there about new films and new books. You really shouldn't be so frightened of it.'

Hartmann glanced again at Goltz. His cheeks were livid, and he was crouching by the stove with his back to Rosterg, stirring the cold ashes with a poker.

'What does it say about the war? How does it say we are doing?' Still holding the poker, he had moved to within a few feet of Rosterg. 'Tell us all what it says about the war.'

'It says we are losing.'

From the rear of the hut, there was a murmuring of furious discontent and a single anonymous shout: *'Der Verräter. Töte ihn.'*

'Well, traitor? Should we kill you? Do you believe what it says about the war?'

'Do I know what is happening in Belgium? No. Of course not. No more than you do. Or anyone else who claims to.'

'But you believe that we will win the war eventually?'

Somehow, Rosterg had straightened his back, sufficient to angle a bloodshot stare up at his accuser. 'No, I do not.'

Hartmann looked away but could not hide from the sound – the soft thud of the poker as it smashed against Rosterg's cheekbone, and then the terrible yowl of pain which echoed out and up towards the stars.

'I'll ask you again. Who is going to win this war?'

'It's lost already, you fucking imbeciles.'

He was shrieking and the blow had sliced open the flesh, driving his left eye behind an ugly lump of bone.

'Killing me won't make any difference. I've been counting prisoners since I got off the boat in fucking Southampton. Listen to me. There are hundreds of thousands of us here. Here, not there. Here. We haven't got an army. We can't breed a new one fast enough. We can't fight a war without one. That's not treason. That's a fact.'

Koenig had stepped forward and was standing over the bloodied prisoner. 'Give me the poker.'

Goltz handed it across.

Just in time, Rosterg pulled his head down under his arms, feeling the first blow smash through his fingers, and the second cleave a wound across the top of his scalp.

Rosterg squinted down at his shattered hands. Tears were clearing lines through the mess on his face. 'No, I'm not.' His words were horribly slurred and his one working eye could see no more than a few blurred shapes. 'Hitler will be dead within a year. Where will you all go then?'

The bloody poker slipped from Koenig's grasp.

'And now,' Rosterg added, calmly, 'can I have some more water?'

This time, it was Bruling who handed him the flask. 'Come on. Take a drink. You're talking crap.'

They were alike, these two men, the mathematician and the entrepreneur. In another life they could have been members of the same gentlemen's club.

'What did you do back in France? Before we were captured?'

Bruling sounded reasonable. Both Koenig and Goltz had temporarily withdrawn into the shadows.

'I ran the supply lines. I filled out forms,' Rosterg mumbled. 'I kept you all fed. I kept you all in petrol and bullets. And then they ran out. *Heil Hitler*.'

'There were rumours.'

'Such as? What kinds of rumours?'

'That you gave ammunition to the resistance? That you sold our food into French villages? That you gave away our positions to the enemy?'

'Horseshit. I'd have been killed months ago if any of that was true.'

'All lies?'

Rosterg's voice was fading fast. Only Bruling was close enough to hear. 'I bought a few beers once in a bar. Maybe some champagne. Maybe I gave them some food. I can't remember. I can't remember. I can speak French, so it was easy. *Très facile*. We were stealing all their livestock. Fucking their women. Fucky fucky. Maybe I felt bad about that. Seriously, if I did anything, it wasn't much. A gesture. Shit. Would that have been so bad?'

'Not if that's all you ever did.'

Bruling paused to pat his hands around his own prison clothing. 'You'd never betray anyone. That's what you say?'

'I wouldn't. I didn't.'

Bruling had produced a handwritten note. He was holding it out as if it had a bad smell. 'This is a list of names. Do you recognise it?'

Rosterg sniffed, shook his head, and swiped the blood from his mouth with his forearm.

'You don't recognise your own writing?'

'I've been attacked with an iron bar. I wouldn't recognise my own wife.'

'Then let me help. This was found today in your jacket.'

'I'm cold. Really cold. I'd like my jacket back.'

'Koenig. Hartmann. Wunderlich. Zuhlsdorff. Goltz. Klein. Pirau. Mertens.' Bruling swung round to look down the length of the hut. 'I see my own name is on it too.'

'It's a delousing list. Or a hut list. I don't know. Show me it. There are all sorts of lists. The British love lists even more than we do. What's your point?'

It was too much for Goltz. Pushing Bruling aside, he knelt down by the chair. 'Devizes.'

'Yes. What about it? Fine town.'

'Devizes was betrayed.'

'Yes, I agree. It must have been.'

'Everyone on that list was rounded up in Devizes and moved here.'

Up on his bunk, Hartmann stiffened. Lacking the courage to intervene, he felt tortured by shame.

'That proves nothing. Every man named on every list in this camp has come from somewhere else.'

'Did Bultmann betray us?'

'No. I'm certain that he did not.'

'Then why did he go and sit in the fucking snow?'

For a second, Rosterg looked like he was trying to stand. His arms were extended wide, and his head tilted from one broken hand to the other. 'Perhaps he didn't want to end up like this.'

'It was you, then.'

'No.'

'You're a fucking liar. We've got your own list of names here.'

'No. I have never betrayed you. You're wrong.'

'Do you think we will win the war?'

'You know I don't. And neither do you.'

This time, Goltz used his fists, driven with the full weight of his body into Rosterg's face. After a few blows, his victim was unconscious, held upright only by the hands on his shoulders.

'Get the rope.'

A flurry of figures slipped out through the door. Inside, no one moved. The only sound was the scraping of feet, and the terrible breathing of the man in the chair. When the group returned, they were carrying a coil of agricultural hemp.

The cord was no thicker than a man's finger. One end of it had already been knotted into a noose.

'Shut the door.'

Through the window, under the camp lights, Hartmann could see another blizzard building.

'Bind him to the chair. Get the rope round his neck.'

A wider space had been cleared. The prisoners were pressed tight around it. Rosterg's arms were being lashed behind him, and the noose was already knotted into place.

'Wake him up.'

Koenig stepped under the solitary lightbulb and emptied a bucket of icy water over Rosterg's head. Life seemed to jolt back into his body, sucked up through the ragged hole of his mouth. As his right eye swivelled, his shoulders hunched forward, pulling the binding tighter round his wrists.

When he twisted against the knot, he felt the coarse hair of the rope on his chin.

Before he could scream, Zuhlsdorff squeezed his hand around his face. All that escaped was a feeble, despairing sigh. Slowly, he rotated his head until he could make out Goltz among the packed ring of accusers. Goltz glared back.

'I'm listening.'

'What do you want?' They were sounds, not words, like a drunk's. Rosterg's lips were so battered, he could barely move them.

'I want you to confess.'

Rosterg nodded.

'I want it in writing. When it's light, we'll get paper.'

'And then I'll go home?'

'And then it will be over.'

'Can I sleep now?'

'We can all sleep now,' whispered Goltz. 'But you sleep on the chair.'

For another hour, Hartmann waited.

As soon as the candles had been snuffed, the prisoners had returned quickly to their blankets. Each of them was tired and there was nothing to discuss. In the morning, the traitor would be given the opportunity to take his own life. If not, it would be taken forcibly from him. After a few moments, the entire hut appeared to be sleeping.

When it felt safe, Hartmann moved. Prisoners were always going to the buckets during the night. No one would be alarmed by a little movement.

Sliding his legs over the side of his bunk, he eased himself on to the floor. Two short steps and he was down by Rosterg's side. Poor bastard. This close, every breath sounded like a struggle.

In the darkness, Hartmann ran a hand gently over his friend's swollen face, willing the pain to subside. In one of Rosterg's pockets he found what he was looking for.

'You and your bloody handkerchiefs,' he whispered.

Rosterg didn't seem to have heard him.

Quietly, Hartmann rinsed the filthy cloth in a puddle of cold water beneath the chair before stretching it across Rosterg's bruised forehead. 'I'm sorry,' he mouthed.

Rosterg stirred. The touch of the cold fabric had woken him and his head moved slightly towards Hartmann.

A word. A phrase. The faintest release of air. Hartmann moved closer until their two faces were almost touching.

'Max. Listen. You can't save me.' A rasp, like the rustle of dry leaves.

'You saved me.'

'I like you.'

'But you know that I could?'

'You think you could. But you can't.'

'Have you always known?'

'It doesn't matter.'

'I could try.'

'I'm dead. You know it. They destroy what they don't understand. Save yourself.'

'You didn't do anything wrong.'

'No. I didn't. Neither did you.'

Hartmann stepped back.

When the bugle blew at 6.30, only two of the prisoners in Hut 4 were awake. Squinting through the slits that were his eyes, Rosterg had stayed alert, too cold to sleep. On his nearby bunk, Hartmann had spent what remained of the night staring at his wall.

When the horn blew impatiently for a second time, they knew it was over.

Queues of shivering men were soon streaming to and from the latrines, indifferent to the grey-faced captive on the chair. The same old jokes were cracked as the men wrestled with their bowels beneath the icicles. Someone had even found a little coal, supplemented by broken wooden boxes from the kitchen, and a small fire was soon flickering in each of the stoves.

Rosterg was thankful for the heat, feeling it first in his toes – a painful pricking as his circulation revived – and then at the tips of his broken fingers. As much as possible, he kept absolutely still. If he moved his head, he felt the noose. If he moved anything else, he felt certain he would scream or faint, and he was determined to do neither. In the night, he had wanted a bucket but gone without. The humiliating alternative had seemed a wiser option.

As the men returned from their wash, the mood swiftly changed. Rumours had been running around the compound since reveille.

Outside the hut, prisoners from neighbouring blocks were thronging expectantly in the snow, indifferent to the smell of freshly baked bread from the kitchens. Inside it, a crowd was circling the silent figure of Rosterg, and for once no one was thinking about their stomach.

'Stand up.'

Koenig and Goltz were standing side by side in front of their captive. It was Koenig who had given the order.

'You'll have to loosen this first.'

Rosterg's voice sounded old and his face was swollen beyond easy recognition. Where the poker had been driven into his scalp, the wound was black with blood and matted hair. When he tried to get to his feet – no longer able to use his hands – he slumped helplessly on to the floor.

'I'm sorry. I can do this. Just give me time.'

'Fuck time.' Holding the loose end of the rope, Koenig yanked hard until Rosterg felt it tighten around his neck. With an elbow on the back of the chair, he forced himself on to his feet. As he was led out towards the daylight, wild punches poured in from every direction. At the same time, a chorus of grunts seemed to grow up out of the ground, driven by the heavy pulse of the men's feet.

On the threshold, Rosterg hesitated. It was a perfect morning: no wind, just a sweet, frosty air. From somewhere in the valley bottom, he could smell woodsmoke rising from hidden chimneys. Along the hard edge of the mountains, he could sense the glowing return of the sun. From the direction of the town there was a cock crowing, but he couldn't see it. In the day's stillness, every noise would roll on for miles.

There was a sharp tug on his neck. He felt the rope bite into tendons, and he stepped bare-footed out into the snow.

Along with the crowd which had swarmed out of Hut 4, Hartmann surged towards the compound office. Ahead of him he saw Koenig kick open the door and pull Rosterg through after him. Forcing his way up through the mob, Hartmann squeezed forward until he could see clearly what was happening inside. About ten men were packed into the room.

Goltz was sitting behind its solitary desk. Rosterg was drooping in front of him, flanked by Koenig and Zuhlsdorff.

'You agreed to confess.' Goltz slid a pad of paper and a pencil across the metal surface.

There was a slight movement of Rosterg's head. It was no longer possible to tell what – if anything – he was looking at. 'It's a blank piece of paper.'

'Just sign your name.'

'I haven't done anything wrong.'

There was a hand tugging at Rosterg's left arm. When he turned, Zuhlsdorff planted a fist in his face and brought a knee up hard into his groin. As the prisoner doubled over, Koenig hauled in the slack on the rope.

'For God's sake. Please.'

The desk had broken his fall. The pad of paper was under his left cheek. Furiously, Koenig wound him back until he was standing again.

'Just sign your name.'

'No. I'm not a traitor.'

'You're a spy. You don't belong here.'

'Go fuck yourself.'

'We should be in London. We had a fucking plan.'

'You're a lunatic, Goltz. Let me write that.' Somehow he had forced the broken components of his face into a sneer. 'I couldn't even sign if I wanted to.' He dangled his blackened fingers over the table. 'You smashed my hands, you prick. Remember?'

Kicking his chair back behind him, Goltz rose to his feet. 'Is there anything else you want to say?'

'Would some breakfast be out of the question?'

In the furious rush for the door, Koenig – still holding one end of the rope – was the first one out. He gave a single tug, and Rosterg flew out behind him into the snow. Over one hundred men were waiting.

In that sickening moment, Hartmann watched Rosterg drop to his knees, rolling his head in every direction, and hoped he was unaware of the dark human shapes closing in, no longer even conscious of any pain.

343

When he tried to lift himself up, a dozen boots kicked him back down. When he curled tight, the men stamped on his face and his back, lashing out at whichever part of him they could see.

'Out of the fucking way.'

Goltz was barging through the scrum of assailants to where Rosterg was lying motionless on his side, half covered in blood-spattered snow. Taking the loose end of the rope from Koenig, he sat down across Rosterg's chest and squeezed the noose tight until bubbles began to froth around the corners of the dying man's mouth, and a single quavering note, like the squealing of an animal, was trapped in the back of his throat.

Goltz passed the loose end of the rope to Koenig. With the momentary slackening, Rosterg's scream was released and the sound rang out around the bowl of white hills.

None of this is happening, thought Hartmann. This isn't me. This isn't us. This isn't Koenig.

'We can't do it here.'

Mertens had pushed past Hartmann. Bruling and Zuhlsdorff were alongside him. More and more prisoners seemed to be flooding from the adjacent huts, each one hunched inside his thick trench coat. As the mob looked on, the three men grabbed the rope from Koenig and began hauling Rosterg face down in the snow towards the lavatory block. A memory of defiance seemed to stir in their captive. Unable to release the tension in the noose with his fingers, he was kicking into the ice, hopelessly thrashing for purchase with his frozen feet.

After just a few seconds, he stopped.

At the entrance to the block, he was lifted up and taken inside. As the door was narrow, Mertens and Bruling did the carrying while Zuhlsdorff directed them to a metal water pipe which ran along the inside ceiling. When they were directly underneath it, Rosterg was dumped down on the concrete.

Behind them, a steady stream of spectators had filled the space around the sinks. Others were standing on the wooden seats for a better view. No one could see any life in the twisted figure lying alone in a pool of melted ice.

To Hartmann, it seemed as if everything had been rehearsed. Beneath the rusted pipe, Rosterg's killers were moving with the righteous efficiency of surgeons, and the foul concrete block was quieter than a bombed chapel. From where he was standing – with his back crushed to a wall – he could see only Rosterg's legs. One of them was bent out from the knee at a grotesque angle but neither was moving, and there were no longer any groans of protest. With a bit of luck, he was already dead.

Together, Goltz and Zuhlsdorff had run the rope over and round the pipe. With the loose end wrapped around his wrists, the enormous figure of Mertens was now struggling to haul Rosterg up off the floor.

'Fat bastard. I need someone to hold him up.' His body had become stuck in the sitting position. His eyes were closed and his head was lolling on his left shoulder. The noose had been pulled so tight round his neck, the rope had almost disappeared. Taking one arm each, Zuhlsdorff and Bruling shouldered the man's weight while Mertens reeled in the slack.

Above them, the pipe was sagging and flakes of ancient black paint floated down on Rosterg's face.

For the last time, he was upright again.

'That's it. That's it. Now tie this off.'

The face of Mertens was scarlet with effort. Koenig reached forward for the end of the rope, passing it back to Goltz who knotted it tight around a tap. And then let go.

There were six inches between Rosterg's feet and the ground.

Although he was still moving, it was nothing more than the gentle sway of a pendulum finding its own centre.

The only sound was the angry chirrup of the rope rubbing down through the old paint until the metal hidden beneath it was shining again.

# 43

The prisoners were eating breakfast when the siren went off.

From the canteen windows, they could see the camp suddenly erupt with men and dogs. One frowning guard and two British medics were jogging purposefully alongside a solitary civilian policeman in a helmet.

Fifteen minutes later they were back, walking slowly towards the gatehouse with Rosterg's body laid out between them on a stretcher hidden by a grey blanket. When the compound was locked behind them, almost every Polish guard was still on the inside.

Throughout the rest of that morning, they ripped the place apart. Every building was cleared and searched. Mattresses and bedding were hauled out under the sun; chairs and clothing and the men's feeble ragbags of personal belongings were tossed on piles in the snow.

For the first time in weeks, the air temperature had pulled itself above freezing, and as the men stood to attention outside their huts the snow softened and slid from the roofs in shapeless clumps.

Without Rosterg to translate, the Poles got on with their work in silence. By the middle of the morning, the bloody poker had been taken away from Hut 4 along with the charred remains of Rosterg's army tunic, pulled from the innards of a stove. By lunchtime, the last of the soldiers had backed out of the compound, carrying with him a bloodied length of rope.

Hartmann had kept himself out of sight. Between the huts and the perimeter fence – looking out across the fields to the town's church spire – there were places where he could lean back and enjoy the rare warmth on his face, trying fruitlessly to erase the night's memories. When the siren finally stopped, he made his way to the latrine block and entered the narrow door through which Rosterg's body had been dragged just a few hours before.

Inside, the place was still freezing. Bare metal was showing where the noose had worn through the paint on the pipe, but the pools of blood had been hosed away, leaving only the nose-curling tang of bleach.

'He had to die, Max. All the rotten apples are gone now.'

He hadn't heard Bruling come in. He'd felt certain everyone would be eating.

'You didn't know him the way I did.'

They were standing side by side, looking down on the same blotted patch of concrete.

'You don't think he was a traitor?'

'He was cleverer than that.'

'Well, as I say, he's gone now anyway.'

'And that's it? We all get on with the war?'

Bruling turned, pulling a grimy cap down tight over his forehead. 'I'm hungry. We should go before it's all gone.'

'You can have mine. I'll give it a miss.'

'You should have a little faith.'

'You should enjoy your lunch. You've earned it.' He doubted whether Bruling would have noticed the sarcasm.

In the afternoon, the search parties came back: a show of strength, a provocation. Everyone knew there was nothing to find – no one had been hauled in for questioning – and by sunset the prisoners' ebullience had revived.

One murdered German; one thousand possible suspects; almost all of them bearded, blue-eyed and blond. Even if the guards cared – which they didn't – no one was ever going to find out what had happened.

Whatever passed for normality in Camp 21 had returned, and as the floodlights flicked back on sporadic shouts of abuse from one side were again met by random spurts of gunfire from the other. Inside every hut there was a hum of hopeful, boyish chatter, as if Rosterg's death had made them strong once more, and victory was – yet again – just a breath or two away.

From his bunk, Hartmann listened, and felt the empty space beneath him like a terrible secret.

Rosterg had vanished – written out of the men's conversations, and his bed occupied by a new arrival. Like Bultmann, no one had really known him. That was how you got through the war. Minimise friendships; friends were always a complication. Without ceremony, his body would be buried nearby. Very soon, it would be as though he'd never lived. For the first time, the camp seemed to float on a wave of optimism. By day, a light wind blew in over the southern hills, bringing warmer air under bubbling blue skies. After nightfall, the Northern Lights danced and the glassy traces of the men's footprints froze hard on the footpaths.

With the kinder weather came fresh supplies. Trucks were moving again on the road up from the town. Dusty coal bunkers were refilled, and the kitchens creaked under the weight of new rations. For a handful, there were even letters – old news posted months ago by people who might no longer be alive. Only seven prisoners inside Hut 4 received one. The rest feigned indifference, as if contact with home – like Christmas – was a weakness.

There had been nothing for Hartmann. He wasn't surprised.

Despite themselves, however, the men briefly succumbed to the season. There were no presents or decorations, but on Christmas Eve there was singing and a double supply of coal. For Christmas Day lunch, there was cold sausage, mince pies and extra mutton in the stew, along with five cigarettes for every prisoner. Within an hour most of them had been smoked, and the men – heads spinning with tobacco – tumbled out of their canteens to chase a limp football around in the slush.

Even Hartmann had surrendered, enjoying the mindless exuberance and the alien burn in his lungs. Just for a few happy minutes, they could have been kids in a school playground. Mertens had stationed himself in goal, and no one could get the ball past him. When Hartmann had been about to take a shot, Bruling tripped him from behind, and the two had rolled away, half laughing, through the snow.

Since the murder, he had spoken to scarcely anyone.

Koenig turned away whenever he saw him. And for two days, Goltz had done nothing but fester on his bunk. No one was fooled by a kickabout in the snow. Beneath the surface nothing had really changed, and as the daylight drained out of Christmas Day, so did the camp's high spirits. Irrational elation surrendered to private despair.

Alone in his sleeping bag – listening to the snow melting through the cracks in the roof – even the hardest captive knew the drill.

No one was marching to free them. This was as good as it would get.

On Boxing Day, the wind swung back round, bringing blizzards down from the mountains.

Two days later, in the neighbouring compound, a nineteen-year-old prisoner visiting the toilets after curfew was shot through the neck. Abandoned overnight, he'd bled out and died and fury stirred again through the huts.

Hartmann knew what would follow. In the loneliness which had engulfed him after Rosterg's murder, everything had become clearer. Men like Goltz alchemised outrage into power, and the humiliation felt by his defeated comrades could only be assuaged by violence.

Everywhere he went now, Hartmann could sense the sideward glances. When the time was right – when another scapegoat was required – it would be his head in the noose. Koenig's cold shoulder wasn't shame or discomfort; it was a kind of warning.

In the bitter days which followed Christmas, Hartmann's certainty grew. All over the site, tension was rising, inflamed by the shooting of the teenager. With no let-up in the weather, the prisoners hunkered inside. Once again, fuel supplies were dwindling. By the morning of New Year's Eve, in Hut 4, they'd scarcely enough to keep one stove going all day and boredom twisted in the damp air like spindrift.

Whenever he could, Hartmann took himself outside. For almost five days, no one had spoken to him, and he'd grown to love the company of the distant pines. Just as he had in Devizes, he'd plotted and mapped every single feature he could see. He'd looked on as a hooded crow pecked the eyes from a dead sheep. He'd watched as a fox crept under the wire, rooting out the peelings from the dustbins. When the clouds split, it felt like the whole world had been washed and hung out to dry. Wherever he turned, you could see for ever.

Every colour and every shape was rendered perfectly, like the two black cars moving quickly towards the camp, turning right against the entrance where the white swing gate lifted and the sentry studied their documentation.

As Hartmann watched, he heard the engines die, a shudder of pistons and then silence.

Two people were slowly getting out from the back of each vehicle.

Three were wearing long black coats and identical city hats.

Hartmann shuffled closer, shivering as the powder filled his boots.

The fourth was wearing brown and standing slightly apart from the others.

A door was opening in a low concrete admin block, and a British officer was beckoning the four strangers towards it. Oddly, the head-lights on both cars were still shining.

The figure turned, carefully taking in the camp and the men in the towers.

It was her. He was absolutely certain of it.

The interrogations started shortly afterwards.

Hartmann had returned to his hut. Breakfast was over, and a silent group had gathered around the stove. Zuhlsdorff was jabbing at the coals with a charred stick, probing for life. Damp blankets had once again been draped hopefully over the pipes and apart from three men playing cards, the prisoners had reoccupied their beds. No one heard the detachment of six Polish armed guards walking briskly behind their own shadows.

When the hut door cracked open, Zuhlsdorff spun from the stove to face them holding his makeshift poker. As he stood, his chair fell backwards, and a soldier stepped forward to swipe the stick from his hand.

A ribbon of sunlight had rolled out between the two rows of bunks, into which the prisoners now stepped, shading their eyes to see what was happening.

'Bruling, Mertens and Dahl, please. Here. Now. With me.'

There was a moment's confusion. The guard's German had been under-rehearsed. Goltz had rolled off his bunk, and was looking round for the three named men.

'Bruling, Mertens, Dahl. Now, please.'

The guards were fanning out in a half-circle with their rifles aimed into the belly of the hut. Bruling was the first to step forward.

'It's all right. It's fine. We're coming. Anything to liven up the day.'

An hour later, they were back. As three more prisoners were led away, Goltz pounced on Bruling. 'What the fuck's happening? Tell me.'

'Three prisoners at a time. Three separate rooms. One in each. They're asking about Rosterg.'

'He killed himself. That's what we say.'

'Yes. We do.' Bruling looked down at his feet. 'However, I think it's pretty obvious they know that didn't happen.'

'Who's *they*? What the fuck did you tell them?'

'They're from London. I only recognised one of them. I told them nothing.'

Up on his bunk, Hartmann was listening. Eighty people in the hut, minus Rosterg. It could take all day, and Goltz had sounded rattled.

It was the middle of the afternoon before his name was called.

'Goltz, Zuhlsdorff, Hartmann. With us, please.'

Together. He hadn't expected that. There was no turning back now. He'd been on this course for too long.

In single file, the three men were marched from the hut. Hartmann was in the middle.

'I know what you are, Max. I always have.'

Hartmann turned into the snarling face of Zuhlsdorff. 'Two words.'

'What?'

'Blood transfusion.'

Ahead of them, on the other side of the main fence, he could see the cluster of barracks and buildings reserved for their keepers. Inside, the electric lights were already on – dusk was fading quickly – and as the gates swung open they were guided in through a black-painted metal door. Goltz's skin was paler than he'd ever seen it.

'You'll tell them nothing.'

It was someone else's turn to be terrified. Hartmann met his eyes. 'Trust me. Don't worry. I'll be absolutely fine.'

There were three interview rooms off a damp corridor. At the

351

edge of the middle door, he felt certain he could smell perfume, and headed for that one.

This would be for Rosterg and Wirz.

When they were marched back an hour later, the sky was stretched across the mountains like a bruise. Goltz seemed pleased.

'Piss easy. Thick as pigshit. They know absolutely nothing.'

Hartmann clambered up on to his bunk. He knew what was coming. He didn't need to see it. Behind them, their escort had lined up, three on either side of the entrance.

There were no more names being called, and the door had been left open. Out in the gloom, four figures were moving towards it.

There was a healthy crackle in the wood-burner and Goltz had pulled up a chair to rub his hands in its glow.

'Piss easy,' he repeated for anyone who was listening. 'We're all safe.'

The four figures entered the hut. Three men in black and the woman in brown.

It was Helen who spoke. Hartmann was glad about that.

'Joachim Goltz. Kurt Zuhlsdorff. Erich Koenig. Josef Mertens. Heinz Bruling. Please make yourselves known.' She looked up into the silence. Everyone in the hut was gaping back. 'We are arresting you for the murder of Wolfgang Rosterg.'

She had more to say, but it was lost in the thunderclap of protest, in the melee of guards pushing past and penning prisoners back on their bunks. Goltz and Bruling were being dragged away and strong arms had locked tight around Mertens. Only Zuhlsdorff had mustered any resistance, lashing out with his boots before collapsing under a barrage of fists.

As the four men were removed, the uproar died instantly.

Four men. Just four.

In the doorway, Hartmann could see the party from London anxiously surveying the hut. He was thinking the same thing.

Koenig. Where the hell was Koenig?

# 44

It wasn't easy to find in the dark.

Patchy cloud had pushed in, concealing the moon, and the coal bunker was hidden from the camp's ring of artificial light. Back in his hut, the pieces would be falling into place. Even without Goltz to prompt them, the prisoners would quickly work things out.

As soon as the official search for Koenig had spread out over the entire camp, Hartmann had slipped away, and his absence was all the proof they'd need.

Zuhlsdorff had been right, they'd say. But Zuhlsdorff was gone.

Whatever happened now, Hartmann could never go back.

He studied the bunker, feeling the shape of it with his hands. Down at ground level, the snow had been scraped away around a square hatch. He knelt down and reached his arms inside. There was no coal in it. There'd been no coal in it for weeks. A cold draught was blowing from the opening, and as his fingers inched forward he felt the edge first, and then the nothingness of the hole. As if bitten, he pulled his arms back sharply.

Koenig had come this way. He knew it.

For a second, he squatted, trying to make out the trees along the edge of the river. Somewhere near the water, that's where he'd said it emerged. As he hesitated, the light from a watchtower spun out across the field, catching the gorse-choked dip where the bank fell away into the brook. Above the ground, it looked a long way to the exit. Below ground, it didn't bear too much lengthy contemplation.

I don't have to do this, he thought. Either Koenig would die out there, or they'd catch him. In the end, it would come to the same thing. No point thinking otherwise.

From a long time before, he recalled a cognac-fuelled drive through the French night in an open-topped staff car. There'd been a stupefied boar watching at a crossroads as they sped past, and when they'd parted at dawn, he'd told Koenig about Alize and the child. Maybe that was when he'd started falling. No. Koenig had always been falling.

He crawled forward and disappeared into the bunker. They were all probably doomed, but Koenig had no one else. It had to be Hartmann.

Within a few heartbeats, he was in absolute darkness.

There was a square opening in the ground. Leaning into it, he could feel the four sides of a vertical timber-lined shaft. A rich, black smell filled his nostrils, and the wood felt rotten with damp. He reached deeper, stretching down with his arms until he could touch the bottom, before sliding his body down over the edge into the cavity below. Loose grains of dirt came slithering down the shaft alongside him, but there was room to turn round, and he could soon feel the way forward in the ghastly nothingness where his flapping hands met no resistance.

Under his knees, the ground felt sticky with mud. Everything else appeared comfortingly solid. The walls and ceiling had been panelled and the flow of good air was unexpectedly reassuring. Ahead of him, he imagined a straight crawl towards the riverbank. No junctions or choices. To the touch, although he could see nothing of it, the tunnel seemed well constructed.

From somewhere far ahead, he heard stones cascading on wood. Either Koenig was still in there too, or it wasn't as well built as he'd hoped.

He put a hand up against his nose – perplexed by the sensation of total blindness – and then wriggled forward into the draught.

After a minute, he was breathing heavily, and his back was coated with sweat. To make progress required him to crawl on his knees and elbows, while twisting his head to avoid collisions with the ceiling. Since there was nowhere to turn round, he had to keep going. And the further he went, the more concerned he became.

In some places, invisible streams of icy water seemed to have sprung from the roof. In others, he could feel splintered wood where the earth had bulged against the shoring. Fearing that he would be crushed if he rested, Hartmann pressed on until his eyes burned with dirt and salt, and his tongue tasted the blood running down from his battered scalp. Above him he imagined a field full of cold, clean snow, and the thought drove him harder.

Time and space had disintegrated. All that remained was blackness and scraping and the hollow wheeze of his lungs.

What if there was no end? What if the end was sealed, or unfinished – a coffin? Pressure was building behind his forehead. He could feel a deep pounding between his ears. Panic. He had to keep going. He had to keep going. But the draught had suddenly stopped and the air smelled rank. He licked the back of his hand, spat out the grit, and held his arm forward. No. The air current was still there. He felt the wet patch cool and then dry, and shuffled forward. Then he stopped sharply. A noise. Not his own hard breathing but something else – or someone else – a little further ahead.

Again, a clatter of rocks; and then, definitely, the low background trill of water. Now he didn't care. Now he followed the smell of damp ferns to the ragged tear of pale light which grew bigger with every agonising contortion of his body. In front of him, he could see the shapes of his arms again, and the spot where the tunnel turned sharply up towards the sky.

He was almost through. Sitting back against the passage wall, he studied the square of night framed by the exit above his head. Torn fragments of night-cloud were moving over the gap and a few stars were showing. Now that he was no longer moving, he felt a sudden piercing of cold. With a shudder, he stood up cautiously until his head was clear of the hole.

A rusty lid of metal had been dragged to one side, and there were fresh footprints in the snow. He'd guessed right.

Looking back across the field, he could see the lights of the camp. They'd be searching for two people now. Hopefully, he'd get to the other one first.

With an awkward hop, he was out, running low towards the curved bank of the river. At the edge, he slid on to a dry bed of shingle, and crouched down in the shadow of the trees. In a few months' time, the water would be unfordable, but tonight it was winter-low, and a silver wafer of ice had formed wherever the current was slack. In the weak moonlight, he could see a way across using the large smooth rocks which broke up the flow. As his eyes picked out the route, he saw a figure move up and out on to the far bank.

'Erich. Koenig. Is that you?'

Hartman's question was lost under the hissing of the water. Any louder, and he risked being heard elsewhere. He picked up a stone and threw it, hearing the splash as it fell short of the far bank. He tried again, striking the mossy trunk of a tree, and the figure opposite tensed under the thick overhead canopy of pine.

'I know it's you. Listen. It's me, Max. We have to talk. I want to explain.' He had stepped into the river. An icy whirlpool of water was dragging at his legs. 'There's nowhere to go out here. Nothing. We should go back – together.'

Koenig stepped from under the tree. His hands were thrust deep into his pockets. Out in the middle of the flow, Hartmann was struggling to keep his feet. From the edge, it hadn't looked so deep – or so swift – and the cold was rapidly sapping the power from his arms and legs.

'Look at yourself, Max. Pathetic. You're no soldier. You never were.'

Somehow, he had to get across, but every step put him at risk of falling and he had seen what exposure could do. If he got a soaking in these temperatures, he'd be a jabbering imbecile in minutes. Shuffling from rock to rock was slow, but there was no other way. By the time he staggered out on to the opposite bank all the feeling in his fingers had gone. And so had Koenig.

Panting into his cupped hands, Hartmann took in his new surroundings. Under the trees, where he stood, the snow was thin. A few yards back from the river, he could see the narrow band of a track, and beyond it, the forest which sheltered the cultivated fields from the mountains.

Under the night's peculiar lunar glow the landscape seemed grey, not white, and everywhere he looked, the snow had been perforated by the meandering toes of wild animals. To his left, the track wound back towards the camp. To the right, he saw another set of prints: human ones, deep and crisp and even.

He set off, half jogging to beat away the cold, stopping only where the snow was too thin to make out Koenig's tracks. It was much easier than he'd expected. Whenever the moon broke clear, visibility was perfect, and in the windless night he could hear Koenig up ahead, panting hard and moving quickly away from the camp.

For around an hour, Hartmann maintained his pursuit.

At times, he could make Koenig out, a black outline, easily followed. Mostly, however, he relied on the boot prints. Or the distant crunch of snow. But the gap never closed, and, although their pace was slow, neither man showed any sign of stopping.

After a mile, Koenig veered left along the northern edge of a young plantation, and now – whenever there was a choice – he took the path that gained the most elevation. Looking back across the valley, Hartmann could make out the squat grid of the town, and the looping reflection of the river threading through it.

Down on the road from the camp there was a line of vehicles moving – military trucks, probably – but apart from a single farm they'd seen no buildings, and, as the treeline approached, the tracks were narrowing, no longer wide enough for vehicles and peppered with frozen sheep droppings.

Both men were exhausted.

Ahead of them was a broad mountain spur broken by a series of low crags. Koenig was already traversing its lower edge, making towards a cleft which ran steeply back up towards a rolling line of summits. Now they were wading through deep drifts of snow, and the effort had slowed Koenig to a heavy trudge. Behind him, walking in the broken trail, Hartmann was making better progress, and the gap between the two had narrowed to shouting distance.

'Wait. Stop. There's no point in any of this.' He had pulled up for breath, leaning back on a stone wall which marked the boundary between the trees and the unwooded shoulder of the hill. In the stillness of the night, Koenig's labours were the only sound, rolling back to him clearly across the glassy sheen of the snowfield.

'For fuck's sake, let's just talk.'

There was no reaction from Koenig, just the same mechanical upward plod.

From somewhere below, Hartmann thought he heard the chug of a petrol engine, but when he turned to locate it, it was gone. 'We're both going to die up here. Is that what you want?'

The words seemed to hang and echo, but still no response. Hartmann was suddenly aware of his own heart, and the shocking deadness in his feet.

'Fuck you. Fuck you,' he cursed, stepping back into the trail.

Above Hartmann, Koenig had entered a narrow ravine along the bank of a frozen stream. At last, he was clear of the drifts, but where the bone-hard plate of older ice had been exposed, the going was treacherous.

After a few hundred yards, he turned hard right, following the easier line of a steep, rocky gulley running directly down from the summit. Here, he could use his hands, heaving himself up by the rocky outcrops, wedging his feet against the trunks of the few plucky rowan trees which had driven roots into the scree.

When he finally looked down, he could sense Hartmann drawing closer – a human shape, edged in silver. For the first time, he felt scared. Not of his friend, but of where he was. Incrementally, the gulley had given way to a steep wall of hard-packed snow broken by wide patches of pale blue ice. Without extra grip, he was finished.

Kicking around on his stance he loosened two hand-sized rocks. When he felt ready to resume, he drove each one into the snow like an axe before digging his boots in for whatever grip he could find.

Every step was an ordeal and his legs were quivering, but his progress was good. From what he could tell, he was nearly at the top. The gradient was easing and a bitter summit wind was blowing down his neck off the ridge, showering him with hard pellets of old snow. Another few nightmare steps and he'd be out of danger. Sensing an end, he dropped his weight on to his left leg and stretched forward.

He was falling before he knew it, a tangled ball of limbs tumbling at sickening speed across the rocks and the snow.

Hartmann had heard nothing. As Koenig rocked backwards, the impact had driven the air from his lungs. The only sounds were the skittering of disturbed powder, and the dull thump of his body as it crashed off the mountain.

When he struck Hartmann, neither man knew what had happened.

Somehow, they were sliding together, locked in a twisted embrace, but where the snow deepened again the pair bounced apart, spinning horribly until their bodies came to a halt close to the silent remnant of a frozen stream.

Hartmann surfaced first, uninjured but floundering for balance and spitting the snow from his mouth. A few yards away, he could see Koenig lying face down and motionless where his fall had been broken by a huge slab of rock.

'Erich. What happened? Are you all right?'

Two clumsy steps and he was at his side. Gently, he rotated his friend's head until he could see the damage. There was a low gurgle of disquiet, and blood was bubbling out between ashen lips, but Koenig's eyes were open and his breathing was steady.

'It's my leg.' It was a pained whisper, no more.

Hartmann carefully brushed away the snow.

'Jesus. Go easy.'

Hartmann winced. So did Koenig. His right leg had snapped at the shin, driving the bone out through the fabric of his trousers. There was bleeding, but not much, and the cold seemed to have momentarily frozen the pain.

'It's a mess. Do you think you can sit up?' Wrapping his arm around Koenig's shoulder, Hartmann eased him over and back until both men were able to lean against the rock.

'I couldn't hang on up there. It was like glass.'

'You're going to need help to get down. I'll wait with you till dawn and then fetch someone.'

'I don't want to go down.'

Somewhere nearby, water could be heard threading its way downhill under the ice covering the stream. After the tumult of the fall, the noise was soothing and the men were in no hurry to talk. It was Koenig who broke the silence.

'Why did you come after me, Max?'

'You shouldn't have killed Rosterg.'

'He had it coming. You heard what he said.'

'What you did to him. That wasn't you. I don't believe it was you.'

'It was me. Accept it. You always had a soft spot for him.' Koenig had scooped up a fistful of snow and was drinking the liquid as it melted through his fingers.

'I did. But listen: it wasn't just that.'

'What then? He was a fucking rat. What else is there?'

'It wasn't Rosterg.'

'I don't understand what you're saying.'

'It wasn't Bultmann either.' Hartmann looked down at his hands. 'You killed the wrong man, Erich.'

'No.'

'It was me at Devizes. It was me here. I told them about the plot. I did. I told them who murdered Rosterg. Everything.'

With a pained scream, Koenig wrenched himself sideways, catching Hartmann's head in a weak armlock.

'I'll fucking kill you now. Why did you do that? Why?'

Hartmann rolled forward to break the grip. Too weak to resist, Koenig's hands slipped down until they were feebly clutching his friend's ankles. With a sigh, he threw himself back against the rock, just as Hartmann twisted, driving his left fist hard into Koenig's jaw.

'Go on then. You want to. So do it. Do it.'

There were two more horrible blows, spraying dark spots of blood across the ice.

Hartmann let go, straightened himself and took a breath. He was panting hard and felt dizzy. Koenig had slid sideways across the large rock and was spitting something out on to the snow.

'Why?' he mumbled.

There was blood on Hartmann's fists. Something in his right hand felt broken. He kneeled down at Koenig's side and eased the boy up until his back was straight and then sat down beside him.

'I'm sorry. You all right?'

'Never better. Did you enjoy it?'

'Yes. I did.'

There was a pause.

'Why, Max?'

'Lots of reasons. Different reasons. The reasons kept changing.'

'I don't believe you.'

'In the beginning it was Alize, or mainly Alize.'

'This started before her. You know it.'

'Maybe. I'm not sure. But they promised me they'd find her if I helped, when we were in London. And so I helped.'

'And that's it?'

'I wasn't even sure I'd told them anything to begin with. I was so fucked up, so fucking tired, but then that woman – Helen – came back to see me again.'

'Helen? Fucking hell.'

'By that time, you and I had been on our travels in the doctor's car, and the breakout had gone from being a lunatic fantasy to something that might happen.'

'*You* thought it was a fantasy. No one else did.'

'It was make-believe. We'd have been massacred.'

'We found the lorries. We found the planes. We saw them.'

'There were no tanks though, no guns. It was all lies.'

'And then you watched Bultmann kill himself before we beat the living crap out of your pal. You're really some kind of hero, Max.'

'You'd have killed Rosterg anyway.'

'You don't know that.'

'He knew that. He was different. You people don't like different.'

'You're dead, Max. They'll tear you apart.'

'I used to think that if I could make myself more like you, all this would be piss easy. But what you did back there, that's not me.'

'Fuck you, Max.'

They were quiet then, and the night's cold burrowed deep into their bruised limbs. Koenig was the first to speak again.

'Cigarette?'

'Very funny. I always wanted your sense of humour, too.'

'I mean it.' Koenig tunnelled into his pockets, pulling out four battered Gauloises.

'I kept them from Rosterg's. Matches from Christmas, too. British matches. Much better than ours.'

'They'll never light.'

'You're probably right.' Koenig grated a match hard against the granite. 'Magic. Works every time.'

He lit the two longest tabs quickly and slid one across to Hartmann who placed it thankfully between his lips.

'Why did you run, Erich?' he asked. 'You stopped me escaping once. Remember?'

'Maybe we should have gone together. I'd go now.'

In unison, the two men drew deeply and held onto the breath. For almost a minute, Hartmann locked the smoke in his lungs before spewing out the fumes in a single, calming gasp. Seconds later, Koenig followed suit.

'Like old times. I was always better at this than you.'

'You were better at most things. Why did you run?'

'They'll hang me, Max. Like that kid.'

'That isn't going to happen.'

'I don't want to hang.'

'I don't suppose Rosterg was terribly keen either.'

There was one last, long silence.

'We'll get back home eventually,' whispered Koenig. 'Don't you think?'

A half-mile or so below them, there were loud voices and a line of torches bobbing across the snow.

As they watched, a yellow flare rose and fell in a glorious arc, followed by two more, and then the sound of frantic dogs closing in on where they sat.

# April 1945

*On the occasion of the 56th birthday of our Führer we send you with our birthday regards a donation of RM 327,230 in the name of all the German soldiers of Camp 21 in Scotland as a sign of our unbroken loyalty to our Führer and our nation and as a birthday present for our beloved leader.*

*We think about our brave German homeland, and we are sure that we shall gain a heroic victory in spite of a very great misfortune.*

*Although our hands are bound, our hearts believe in you, our Führer.*

*Long live the Führer.*

*Long live Greater Germany.*

*Heil Hitler.*

# Afterword
## 17 October 1945
## Camp 83, Malton, North Yorkshire

He loved the new place.

Through the spring into glorious summer, he'd watched the green shoots reaching up out of the clay until the valley floor creaked under the weight of its dusty grain.

There was a wire fence – and there were guards – but as the winter receded, almost every prisoner had been summoned to help on the land: strolling to work between neatly trimmed hedgerows; turning the wet earth until their hands bled while checking the sky for the first swallows.

Slowly, it seemed, the land became their own. By night, they rubbed lamp oil into their calluses and fashioned scarecrows out of old rags and sticks. By day, they worked with shovel and scythe, proudly watching as the barley and the corn took hold.

Even when the war was over, no one ever tried to escape.

At the end of every day, guards and prisoners ambled back together, a single warm mass of men. And then months later, when the harvest was in, they shared bottles of brown ale between the hayricks and rubbed pollen from their dripping noses. That August, there'd even been a few local girls, spilling away from the victory celebrations to plant kisses on eager mouths, and sometimes much more. Everywhere, the dividing lines were melting, and with them were going the lunacy and the hate. No one talked about the war much. Mostly, all they talked about was home.

But of them all, Hartmann said the least.

He'd left Camp 21 the same day.

After a few hours shivering in a cell, he'd been smuggled south; just him and two silent guards, switching from train to train, until the snow gradually gave way to the joyless moors of northern England.

Before he left, they'd offered him a new name, but he'd said no. Max Hartmann was who he was. Hartmann would do just fine. If people asked him what he'd done, he would tell them.

But when the last train finally stopped he was no longer a black. By some act of bureaucratic magic, he'd been reclassified. Now he was a 'friend of peace' — a zero-risk prisoner — and the few companions he found asked him nothing and volunteered less.

All of them, he guessed, were carrying secrets of one size or another.

As summer approached, the fields bounced with new-born lambs and every morning began with birdsong. Horse-drawn wagons dragged mountains of wet meadow grass along lanes buzzing with insects, and wild poppies taller than a man blazed defiantly among the golden stalks.

Every night — still exultant after their labours — the men played games until dusk: learning cricket with the guards when it was fine, rehearsing plays and musical cabaret when it was not. For the most part, Hartmann was content merely to watch. Whenever possible — as he always had done — he preferred his own company to that of others. It was a relief for him not to have his solitude questioned; and, when he could find it, the silence of his new life was a perpetual joy.

On a whim, he had taken up painting, finding a talent which the prison staff was happy to encourage, and by early spring his pictures ringed the inside of the prisoners' canteen.

Whenever he was asked for a portrait, Hartmann declined.

Around the camp, he painted only the flowers which the men cultivated in beds thick with night stocks and lupin. Away from it — sketching quickly while the others ate their lunch — he filled his pages with clouds. Portraits required eye contact, and, for reasons he fully understood, no one seemed to look at each other for too long any more.

In August, he allowed his birthday to pass unnoticed.

In September, there were fires on the moorland which rose to the north in a wide purple band. Every day for a week, the men were bussed up to the heather, armed with brushes to beat down the snaking lines of flame. Stretched out across the blackened fell, prisoners and farmers had stood shoulder to shoulder, struggling on until the last flicker was extinguished.

When it was over, they'd all shaken hands and embraced, chalky grins in sooty faces.

Then one day in late October, he was told not to report for work the next day. There was a visitor coming. They'd need some time together alone. Without even asking, he knew who it was.


'You look well,' she said.

It was a warm morning – an unexpected summer encore – and they'd chosen to sit on a wooden bench looking out across the stubbled fields.

'Is everything all right?'

Alongside her, Hartmann felt filthy. He looked at his hands. The palms were scored with dirt.

'I love it here. Thank you. I paint now.'

'Yes, I heard. No problems? No questions?'

He knew what she meant. 'The war's finished. No one talks about that any more.'

A breeze stirred, dislodging the first weakened leaves of the season.

'Listen. I've come with some news.'

Hartmann felt himself freeze.

'They were hanged. Yesterday morning.'

'Koenig?'

'All five of them.'

Somewhere out of sight, a wagon loaded with squealing pigs was heading to the weekly market.

'You should have been here a few months ago,' he said. 'The flowers were amazing.'

'It wasn't your fault. We'd have found them without you.'

For the first time, Hartmann looked at her properly. 'And Sieber?'

'Nothing. No one ever admitted to anything.'

Soon they would be needing wood for the stoves, Hartmann thought. For weeks, the prisoners had been stacking it undercover, seasoned and ready for the winter.

'Are you staying nearby? Is this the last time we meet?'

'No to the first question. Train back to London this evening.'

'And the second question?'

'Yes. This is the last time.'

Of course. He knew that. She had only ever been doing her job.

'Koenig asked me to pass on a message.'

'Really?'

'He said he was sorry.'

Hartmann might think about that later. But not now. And maybe not ever. 'Did they find your boyfriend?'

'No news, sadly. I don't suppose there will be now.'

'I'm sorry.'

'I was happy for you, though.'

Hartmann smiled, and she leaned sideways to kiss him on the cheek.

'At last.' He laughed. 'The ice melts.'

'You really do look well. More like your age at last.'

'They sent me a photograph. Would you like to see it?'

'I'd love to.'

He reached into the inside pocket of his tunic.

With luck he'd be home by Christmas.

The three of them. Together at last.

# Author's Note

A few years ago, the newspapers – and the television – got wind of a magical story.

A former member of the 12th SS Panzer Division had left £430,000 to the Scottish village of Comrie where he was imprisoned during, and after, the war. His name was Heinrich Steinmeyer. He'd been a self-confessed Nazi fanatic, and five years of his life had been spent behind the wires of Black Camp 21.

Steinmeyer had been lucky. Steinmeyer had got home, albeit a different person, softened by his time amid the Perthshire hills.

Sadly Wolfgang Rosterg never did. His remains were taken to the Cannock Chase German Military Cemetery, together with 2,797 other POWs, airmen and submariners whose lives ended on or around these shores during the last war.

He can be found there still, surrounded by whispering birch trees in Plot 4, Row 15, sharing his final resting place with Willy Thormann, a forty-three-year-old Oberleutnant whose body was found hanging from a tree outside Camp 21 just a few weeks before the events in this book transpired.

The whereabouts of Goltz, Bruling, Mertens, Zuhlsdorff and Koenig, however, are much less certain.

After a military trial lasting several months, they were executed on the same day at Pentonville Prison in October 1945 by the state executioner Albert Pierrepoint, thereby entering the record books as the largest number of men ever put to death in England for the same crime. Their bodies were interred within the grounds of the prison and to the best of my knowledge, they were never repatriated.

Many things intrigued me about their story and led to the writing of this book. To begin with, very few people are aware of the scale of the German POW presence in Britain between 1944 and 1947.

Nor are people aware of the tensions – and recurring violence – that erupted in so many of the 600 ad hoc camps thrown up to accommodate such an overwhelming flood of men. Sadly, given the paucity of oral testimony, it is likely much of this history has been lost for ever.

Most of the camps themselves disappeared as quickly as they had first arrived. In September 1946, there were still over 400,000 German prisoners stuck in Britain. But just two years later, the only ones who remained were the dead ones – or the ones who'd fallen in love with local girls. Nissen huts not reclaimed as barns or pigsties were quickly flattened by the weather or by bulldozers. Virtually all the fascinating graffiti, murals and hidden tunnels which the German prisoners had created were gone.

However, the Devizes plot and the murder at Camp 21 achieved a sufficient degree of notoriety for a few records to be kept. Highly censored accounts of the men's trial, together with the official investigations into the so-called 'March on London' mean that we have names, dates and horrific first-hand testimony. There have also been two non-fiction accounts of these events.

The first – *The March on London* by Charles Whiting – is best forgotten. The second – *For Führer and Fatherland* by Roderick de Normann – is a far more sober account which draws on those public records which are available, together with detailed witness testimony from the few who were sought out at the time to give their stories.

Common to both books are the holes and gaps which can never be filled. For obvious reasons, almost every aspect of the case was shrouded in official secrecy and no merit whatsoever was seen in publicising the glaring weaknesses in camp security which led to these incidents . . . and many others. Such information as did get out was carefully managed and doctored to minimise public anxiety.

However, the key scaffolding of my story is grounded in absolute and unchallenged fact. During late 1944, a large group of SS prisoners attempted to break out of Devizes POW camp using stolen munitions, in the vague expectation of making some headway towards London. Details of the plot were leaked, and the conspirators – who had indeed checked out local airfields and munitions stores – achieved little more than a very boisterous riot which was silenced (as in this book) by paras wielding machine guns.

Within a few hours of that episode, the ringleaders were sent for interrogation in London and from there to Comrie in Scotland, the setting for what became known as Black Camp 21. Tragically their number included one Wolfgang Rosterg, an intriguing polyglot whose presence in Scotland remains a matter of no little mystery.

What we can be sure of is that he was much older than the undisputed conspirators; that he took (at best) a doubtful view of Hitler's war, and (at worst) an openly sceptical one which would certainly have contributed to his unpopularity; and that his skill in languages granted him privileged access to senior German and British officers in both Devizes and Comrie.

Whether he was an active mole will forever remain unknown. What is certain, however, is that his professional experience would have made him an attractive recruit, and that British military intelligence were actively engaged in the 'turning' of German prisoners whenever, and wherever, they could.

The London Cage was central to this tactic, and the character of Colonel Alexander Scotland was central to its operations throughout the period in question. For insights into what went on there, I am especially thankful for Ian Cobain's book *Cruel Britannia* as Scotland's own post-war memoir was so massively censored that we will never know the full extent (or legality) of the interrogation techniques used in what is now part of the Russian Embassy.

So who had betrayed the Devizes plot?

The absolute truth is, we will never know. And quite possibly, it was not one single person. The cabal of SS hardliners behind it was so riven with self-seeking fantasists that the information could have seeped out anywhere, and (according to de Normann's book) American intelligence had caught wind of the Devizes planning long before it happened. However, in the accounts of Rosterg's murder hearing, I was intrigued to see that seven men had been charged initially and that the cases against two of them quickly faded. Were they informants? What deal had been struck to save them from

371

the noose? Or was the evidence against them simply not persuasive enough?

Using fiction to explore this story seemed to me to offer a real and exciting way of plumbing the holes behind all these questions. For one thing, I could start the narrative back in the chaos that followed the D-Day landings in June 1944, enabling me to trace the very real trajectories of thousands of Germans after their capture that summer. For another, I could ascribe character and motive to real people who, because they died so young, can only ever exist now in just one dimension. And since I was keen to write a book about the nature of friendship, the story seemed horribly well suited.

But please note: this is *fiction*, and scrupulous readers may well take issue with the liberties that have been taken. The italicised letters and memoranda, for instance, are based on actual contemporary documents and interviews, but are, in most cases, composite representations and *not* word-for-word originals. If there are factual errors in here (although obviously I hope there are none) I apologise. Great pains have been taken to ensure authenticity throughout, but military historians with a fine-tooth comb may think otherwise.

Hartmann, of course, is my single biggest invention, although the trajectory of his life is real in every detail. From Vienna to Yorkshire via Normandy and the Russian front is the exact same journey undertaken by many thousands of young German men.

Far and away the biggest license has been taken with the five men who went to the scaffold. What little information is known about Rosterg's killers would scarcely cover the back of an envelope, and, initially, this dearth of fact made me hesitate before telling this story in a fictional form. My only clue to their characters – and it was a substantial one – lay in the violence they brought to bear on the tragic, helpless figure of Rosterg. Whoever they were – and they were all scarily young – they were deemed to have been sufficiently dangerous by the British authorities to be sent north to Camp 21. Misguided they may have been, but innocent they were not, and although we can never know, I sincerely hope that my unflinching portrayal of them is a fair one.

In any case, it is Rosterg who exerts the biggest pull on our curiosity and although more is known about him than the others, he still floats through the facts in a tantalising and ambiguous way.

According to some reports, he was a deserter and a collaborator. However, neither of those things is likely to be true. Rosterg was significantly older than his fellow-prisoners; he was well travelled; and his job – which de Normann claims linked him to the manufacturers of Zyklon B – marked him as an outsider. When you factor in an air of cosmopolitan self-importance, it suddenly becomes easy to imagine him being dangerously vulnerable to the paranoia of his fellow-prisoners.

However, no speculation is required about the circumstances of his death. For sheer horror, the official account of his murder has few parallels in prison history, and there is something about his resting place that craves our empathy. If readers find the descriptions in this book upsetting, then they should steer clear of the official accounts. Rosterg's death was an act of sustained savagery which led to a relentless search for the perpetrators. Camp *omerta* ensured that it would be several weeks before the culprits' names were leaked and the early arrests triggered in my book by Hartmann's disclosures are this writer's act of necessary licence.

I have drawn wisdom from a number of excellent books which deal with this period in our history. Some I have already mentioned. *D-Day: The Battle for Normandy* by Antony Beevor is a masterpiece, as is his *Stalingrad*. Several books have looked at POW camps in Britain, in particular *Prisoner of War Camps in Britain During the Second World War* by Jon and Diane Sutherland; *Churchill's Unexpected Guests: Prisoners of War in Britain in World War II* by Sophie Jackson; and *Camp 165 Watten: Scotland's Most Secretive Prisoner of War Camp* by Valerie Campbell. *Soldaten: On Fighting, Killing and Dying* is another truly extraordinary book which draws together transcripts of interviews secretly recorded during interrogation at the London Cage and elsewhere. Compiled by Sonke Neitzel and Harald Welzer, it provides the authentic voice of the German soldier, and it helped me in my bid to understand how they talked to each other . . . and how they talked to their British captors.

A few other key people have helped me to complete this book. My agent Mark Stanton who (wisely) sent me back to the drawing board so often, I lost count. Alison Rae, the managing editor at Polygon, who, bizarrely, turned out to have a family connection to the village of Comrie. Nancy Webber, whose enthusiasm for the manuscript as a reader was followed by the painstaking diligence she showed in her copy-edit of the final text. And at the camp itself, Fiona Davidson, who was kind enough to take me around the site on two memorable occasions. Finally – and they'll know why I'm thanking them – honourable mentions for Freddy Markham, Margot Jones, Brian Dorling, Martin Plant, Fay Markham, along with my sons Sam and Alex – every one of whom will be glad if I never mention this story again.

Last of all, I wonder sometimes if this was a story I was destined to write.

Camp 21 is still uniquely intact – sitting serene in its bowl of hills, a sea of rusty orange roofs, almost exactly as it was when Rosterg was killed there.

In early June 1968, as a fourteen-year-old schoolboy, I spent a week at the place when it was still open for cadet groups from all over the country. To us (and thousands of others like me) it was known simply as Cultybraggan Camp, and during the long spring evenings we would gather around a transistor radio to listen to the new Rolling Stones record 'Jumping Jack Flash', and it is for this reason that I can date it so precisely.

We slept in bunks in one of the Nissen huts, although not the one where Rosterg was killed, as that had been knocked down some years before. No one shared with us the story of what had happened there. But we all still felt the ghosts, and when the week was up, none of us was sorry to leave.

Now I know why.